AS THE SUN BREAKS THROUGH

by

Ellie Dean

Magna Large Print Books
Gargrave, North Yorkshire,
BD23 3SE, England.

British Library Cataloguing in Publication Data.

A catalogue record of this book is
available from the British Library

ISBN   978-0-7505-4750-5

First published in Great Britain by Arrow Books in 2018

Published in Large Print 2019 by arrangement with
Random House Group

Magna Large Print is an imprint of Library Magna Books Ltd.

Printed and bound in Great Britain by
T.J. (International) Ltd., Cornwall, PL28 8RW

Acknowledgements

As I began to write the Cliffehaven series, I soon realised that I would need to do a great deal of research if I was going to get my facts right, and I fully acknowledge that I've made a few blunders along the way.

I would like to thank Paul Nash – my favourite anorak – who is so knowledgeable about all things related to the aircraft which fought during the Second World War and the battles and the viewpoints of both sides. His patience in answering my often daft questions and researching into particular areas of the war has been very much appreciated, along with his ability to find interesting incidents that are not commonly known but which have enhanced my stories and given my imagination wings.

Thank you, too, to Jean Relf, who lent me her father's diaries and letters which have given me such a terrific insight into what it was really like in Burma with the Chindits.

I would also like to thank my dear husband, Oliver, for never begrudging the hours I spend in my office, for providing coffee and encouragement, and for reminding me that it's been eight hours since I started writing that day and it's now time to stop and eat. His skills at 'cooking' salad have become legendary in our house!

A Map of Cliffehaven

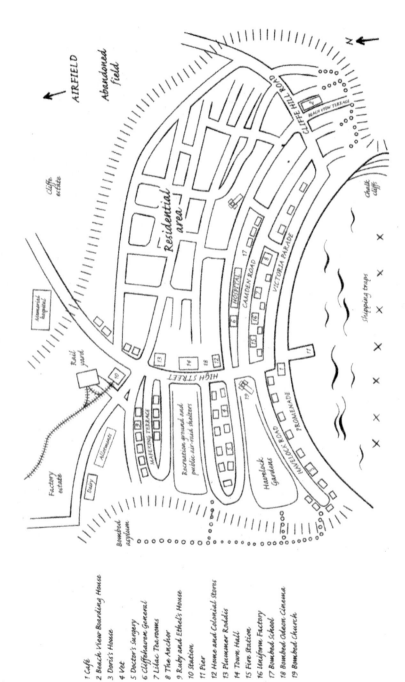

AIRFIELD

Abandoned field

Cliffe estate

Residential area

Memorial hospital

Rail yard

Factory estate

Dairy

Allotments

Bombed asylum

MAFEKING TERRACE

Recreation grounds and public air-raid shelters

HIGH STREET

HOSPITAL

CAMDEN ROAD

VICTORIA PARADE

Havelock Gardens

HAVELOCK ROAD

PROMENADE

CLIFFE HILL ROAD

BEACH VIEW TERRACE

Chalk cliffs

Shipping traps

1 Café
2 Beach View Boarding House
3 Doris's House
4 Vet
5 Doctor's surgery
6 Cliffehaven General
7 Lilac Tea-rooms
8 The Anchor
9 Ruby and Ethel's House
10 Station
11 Pier
12 Home and Colonial Stores
13 Plummer Roddis
14 Town Hall
15 Fire Station
16 Uniform Factory
17 Bombed school
18 Bombed Odeon Cinema
19 Bombed Church

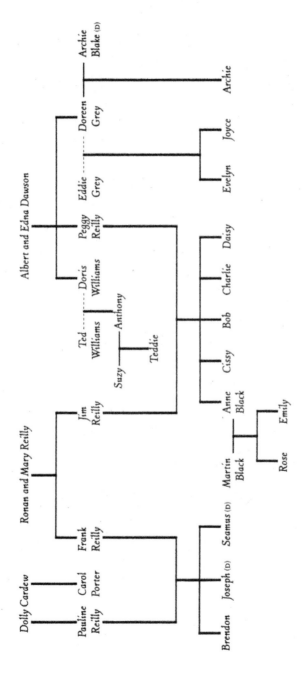

The Cliffehaven Family Tree

1

Cliffehaven June 1944

All was still in the rooms above the Anchor as Cliffehaven slept beneath a veil of sea mist and Harvey lay on the hearthrug, basking in the glow from the fire. Rosie's sitting room was a haven of warmth and comfort in the soft light, but an icy chill had begun to creep through Ron.

Harvey lifted his head and looked enquiringly at Ron as the mantel clock chimed three. Ron stirred uneasily in his chair. All hope that Rosie would return slowly died along with the flames in the hearth, to be replaced by a terrible dread. Something must have happened to her – or had she simply changed her mind about coming home and stayed with Major Radwell? The thought of them being together whilst he waited here made his stomach churn. He couldn't lose her – not without talking to her face-to-face, and not without a fight. Yet who could he fight? Certainly not a one-armed war hero.

He gave a deep sigh, knowing there was nothing he could do until Rosie came home and they had the chance to try and pick up the pieces.

The slam of the side door to the Anchor snapped him from his thoughts and hope reignited at the sound of Monty's paws scrabbling on the stairs, and a familiar voice calling up to him.

'Ron? Is that you?'

'Aye,' he called back, leaping to his feet, his heart joyful as the dogs greeted one another and Rosie emerged at the top of the stairs laden with a suitcase and several large brown paper parcels tied up with string.

A quick glance over her shoulder told him she was alone and he rushed to relieve her of the luggage before he gathered her into his arms 'I was so afraid you weren't coming back,' he breathed against her soft cheek.

She leaned into him and briefly rested her head on his shoulder before looking up at him with a wan smile. 'Silly man,' she chided softly. 'Of course I was coming home.'

Ron wanted to kiss the very breath from her, to hold her to his heart and sweep her off to the bedroom to finally make her his own, but he could feel the tension in her body as she didn't encourage a more intimate kiss but began to slowly pull from his embrace. This was clearly not the moment to declare himself, let alone take it for granted that she'd want to be ravished.

He swallowed his disappointment, noting the shadows beneath her blue eyes and the signs of strain around her lovely mouth. 'It's very late, and you must be exhausted,' he murmured.

'The whole episode has been a nightmare,' she replied, taking off her hat and gloves and shedding her overcoat. 'Compounded by the fact the journey home seemed to go on forever. The trains were full and horribly slow, and when I thought that at last we were making headway, we were held up for hours outside Dartford because a V-1 had blown

14

up the tracks.' She kicked off her shoes, then made a fuss of Harvey and checked there was food and water for Monty.

Ron watched this flurry of activity, noting how she avoided looking at him. He felt awkward and suddenly unsure of what to do or say, for it was clear she wasn't that delighted to see him, and he suspected by her use of words that she hadn't travelled alone. But he didn't ask the questions that were clamouring in his head, for he was afraid of what she might tell him. 'To be sure, 'tis thankful I am that you're home and safe,' he managed gruffly.

'So am I,' she replied, looking at him finally with a warm smile. 'Thank you for looking after things whilst I was away, and for waiting up for me, Ron. I do appreciate it, but if I don't wash and get to bed, I'll keel over.'

'I made sandwiches in case you were hungry,' he said, 'and even managed to get hold of a lemon for your gin and tonic.' He looked at her hopefully even though he knew he was being selfish in wanting to keep her with him for a few moments more.

Rosie's expression was rueful as she regarded his suit and tie, the roses on the mantel and the carefully arranged refreshments on the sideboard. She touched his face with light fingers. 'I can see you've made a huge effort to welcome me back, Ron, but I can barely think straight after the day I've had, let alone eat anything.' She feathered her lips over his cheek. 'I'm sorry.'

Ron's spirits flagged. He'd hoped for too much from this homecoming. All his plans for a loving reconciliation had been shattered by the lateness of the hour and Rosie's exhaustion. 'I could scrub your back and keep you warm between those sheets,' he offered, desperately trying to rekindle the spark that had always been between them before tonight.

Rosie shook her head, her eyes dull with weariness. 'That's not a good idea, Ron,' she said. 'I'm sorry, but I need to be alone tonight.'

A wave of hope washed through him that there would come a night when they could be together, and he tentatively reached for her hand. 'I love you, Rosie,' he said, 'and am willing to wait for as long as you need. I'm sorry you had to deal with everything on your own, but–'

'We'll talk tomorrow,' she replied softly before glancing at the clock and shooting him a wry smile, for it was already a new day.

'Everything *is* all right between us, isn't it, Rosie?' He could hear the plaintiveness in his voice and despised it, for it made him sound weak.

Rosie squeezed his fingers. 'Later, Ron. We'll sort it all out later.' She picked up her case and turned towards her bedroom. 'Goodnight, Ron. Drop the latch on your way out, will you?'

Rosie left the room without a backward glance, and Ron felt as if he'd been cast adrift. He took a shuddering breath and reached for his army greatcoat. 'Come on, Harvey. We're not wanted here.'

Harvey disentangled himself from his pup Monty, and climbed off the couch to nudge his nose against Ron's hand in sympathy.

Ron stroked his brindled head and then clumped down the stairs. This ignominious departure was not how he'd imagined things

16

going tonight, and as he closed the side door behind him, he was engulfed by a sense of helplessness, and a terrible suspicion that Rosie was hiding something from him.

He took a deep breath of the cool, salty air and looked up at the sky. The sea mist had cleared to reveal the first few streaks of pearly dawn light and the promise of another fine June day – but what would this day bring, and how would he cope if it turned out Rosie no longer loved him?

The Town Hall clock struck the half-hour as yet another squadron of RAF bombers took off from Cliffe aerodrome, accompanied as always by their night fighters. The war and the rest of the world were carrying on oblivious of the turmoil in his heart, and although he knew that his troubles were nothing compared to what was happening in the world, it didn't lessen his anguish.

'Come, Harvey,' he said softly to the lurcher sitting at his feet. 'There'll not be much sleep to be had now. Let's go to the seafront.'

Harvey yawned and shook himself before reluctantly following him down the hill and away from the comforts of Beach View to the promenade. Cliffehaven was still asleep except for those working the night shift on the factory estate and the soldiers manning the big guns along the shore, but the skies over France glowed with a false red dawn, and the sounds of the distant booms and crumps of bombs were carried across the water in the stillness.

Ron moved within the darker shadows cast by the remaining buildings that lined the coast road where the tram used to run day trippers back and forth. There was no curfew and he wasn't using a torch, so he was perfectly within his rights to be out here, but his old pal, Sergeant Bert Williams, was known to prowl the town at all hours, and Ron wasn't in the mood to talk to anyone.

He sat on a stone bench set within the sturdy Victorian shelter which had survived a bomb blast and bullets with only a few scars to show for it. Reaching into his greatcoat pocket, he pulled out his pipe and spent some minutes filling and lighting it whilst a disgruntled Harvey sprawled beneath the bench with a stoic sigh.

Ron tried to rein in his turbulent emotions as he looked gloomily beyond the coils of barbed wire and heavily mined shingle to the concrete tank traps which were strung in an ugly line across the bay. Despite the continuous roar of the RAF planes and the distant sounds of warfare, the sea was calm, the early light turning it into a sheet of molten silver which gently undulated and broke with a soft hiss against the shore. The old pier was a sorry sight; cut off from the beach to prevent enemy landings, its skeleton stark against the lightening sky, the bones of what had once been the ballroom and amusement arcade now embracing the rusting carcass of a German fighter plane.

He regarded his surroundings through the pipe smoke, remembering how he and Rosie had gone swimming in the sea in those halcyon days between the wars. They'd danced in the pier ballroom, and enjoyed picnics on the beach with his sons, Jim and Frank, and their wives, Peggy and Pauline, and all the children. He could almost hear the happy laughter of those children as they'd played in the sand, and the music that had drifted to them from the bandstand, and thought he could catch the merest hint of toffee apples and candy floss mingling sweetly with the salty air.

In his despondent mood, the happy memories were overshadowed by darker thoughts. How very different they all now were from those carefree people. Jim was fighting the Japs in Burma; Peggy was working for Solly Goldman at his uniform factory whilst caring for her lodgers at Beach View; and Frank and Pauline were not only mourning the loss of two of their precious sons, but praying that their surviving boy would come home unscathed from the Allied invasion into France.

Ron shivered, although his greatcoat was thick enough to ward off the cold. Peggy's daughter, Anne, now had children of her own and was waiting anxiously in Somerset for news of her fighter pilot husband who was a POW. Young Cissy was a WAAF and stationed at nearby Cliffe, where she'd had to witness the horrors of planes crash-landing and the endless lists of the missing as she too waited to hear from her American pilot who was also a POW. Peggy's two younger boys were with Anne and maturing fast – especially Bob, who was rapidly approaching call-up age. Beach View Boarding House still rang with the laughter of their evacuees, but with the family scattered and only little Daisy to watch over, the laughter often sounded hollow to Ron.

He bit down on the stem of his pipe as his thoughts turned inevitably to the previous war. By some miracle, he and his two sons had survived

19

what the politicians had called the 'war to end all wars', and they'd firmly believed that after the horrors of the Somme and the death of a generation of young men the future would hold new purpose and opportunity. And yet the bitter reality was that war had come again and another generation of youngsters was being called upon to make the ultimate sacrifice for the sake of peace.

He shifted on the bench and grimaced as he felt the familiar sharp twinge in his back. The splinter of shrapnel had embedded itself there when the Huns bombarded no-man's-land as he'd been carrying a wounded comrade back to the British trenches. He'd managed to drag them both to safety, only to learn that he'd been carrying a dead man.

The shrapnel was a constant reminder of that friend and their war, and although his family had urged him to see a doctor about it, he'd come to think of it as an intrinsic part of who he was – a memorial to all the pals he'd lost and who would never grow old as he was growing old. He'd come to the decision long ago that it was his penance for surviving and that he'd carry it with him until the end.

Determined to ignore the pain and not dwell on those dark days, he turned his mind back to the town which had been his home for almost fifty years.

Some of the grander hotels along the seafront had been blown to smithereens; the small fishing fleet his father had bequeathed him was no longer moored beneath the towering white cliffs at the far end of the beach; and to the north of the town where there had once been grazing land and farm buildings, there now stood an ugly sprawl of factories. The High Street was scarred by rubble-filled bomb sites, and the slums beyond the badly damaged station had been wiped out with fire-bombs.

Ron grimaced. At least the war had done some good by clearing those rat-infested hovels, and once peace was restored, it would hopefully force the council to build proper housing for the displaced families.

He puffed on his pipe, his thoughts rambling and disjointed as he tried not to focus on the coming day. Yet it was impossible. He knew Rosie too well, and her evasiveness increased his suspicion that she was hiding something from him. Had the events surrounding her husband's death made her turn to Radwell for comfort, or was she having second thoughts about spending the rest of her life with a man who could offer her very little but his heart? Radwell's absence was a good sign, but that didn't mean he wasn't still in the picture.

He felt a chill run through him as the sun started to rise above the sea, its golden orb stained by the blood-red of the fires over France. He had to believe Rosie had stayed true, and that it was just the aftermath of a rotten journey that had made her short with him. Once she was fully rested they would talk, and then, if the spark had been rekindled... He dipped his hand into his coat pocket and touched the small jewellery box. Then he would propose.

Ron suddenly became aware of Harvey, who was whining and shivering, and felt a mortifying wave of guilt. 'Poor old boy,' he murmured, stroking his head as he emerged from beneath the bench to lay his muzzle on Ron's knee. 'It's not fair of me to keep you sitting about in this cold.'

Harvey's eyes were liquid and beseeching as he looked back at him.

Ron stood up. 'Come on then, ye heathen beast. Let's be off home to see what we can filch from Peggy's larder for breakfast. I don't know about you, but I'm going to need a full stomach to get through today.'

Despite her exhaustion, Rosie was finding it almost impossible to relax, for her thoughts and emotions were all over the place. She'd defied government restrictions by filling the bathtub almost to the top and adding scented crystals, but now she climbed out of the cooling water, and wrapped herself in her warm dressing gown.

Wiping away the steam from the bathroom mirror and catching sight of her reflection, she winced. Her face was drawn, her complexion wan, the blue of her eyes dulled by weariness and the experiences of the past few weeks. Turning her back on this unedifying sight, she padded barefoot into the sitting room to pour a stiff drink in the hope it might help her to sleep.

Monty was sprawled in front of the dying fire, his brindled coat and sleek lines enhanced by the faint glow. Smaller than his sire, he possessed the delicate build of his mother – a pedigree whippet Harvey had slyly deflowered to the fury of her owner. He opened an eye and frowned at being disturbed before dropping back to sleep with a soft grunt of contentment.

Rosie sipped the gin and tonic and leaned back in the fireside chair, wishing that she too could relax and sleep with a clear conscience. It was lovely to be home finally – to be amongst all that was familiar and comforting after the dramas and confrontations she'd had to put up with during her time away – but she could have done without Ron being here. She'd been too overwrought and disorientated to really appreciate his welcome, yet she'd seen the hurt and bewilderment in his eyes when she'd turned away from his loving overtures, and as she replayed the scene in her mind she felt an awful twist of regret. She hadn't meant to be so distant with him, and now he was probably worrying and wondering why.

Rosie moved restlessly in the chair. She was aching for sleep, but her mind refused to be still, running amok with images of the day; what she'd gone through over the past few weeks – and what still lay ahead of her. Refusing to contemplate the undoubted dramas yet to come, she deliberately turned her thoughts to the ghastly events that had followed her husband's death.

Her husband James's sudden passing had been traumatic enough, even though it had been expected several times over the long years of his incarceration in that mental asylum; but it had widened the rift between her and his family, and rather than offering sympathy and help with all the paperwork and arrangements, they'd coldly isolated and thwarted her at every turn. Rosie had never needed Ron more, and could only thank her lucky stars that Henry Radwell had been there to counter the hostility with tact and an air of quiet command to ensure that James's last wishes were carried out – and to offer solace when it all had become too much for her.

Snapping out of these uncomfortable memories, Rosie swallowed a slug of gin and looked around the room, at the beautiful flowers on the mantel, the polished furniture, the supper dish, and warm fire. Ron was such a dear man and he had obviously gone to a great deal of trouble – even to the point of wearing a suit and getting a haircut. She felt shame heat her face, for he'd deserved much better than her almost dismissive reaction to his loving welcome.

She'd known full well how anxious he would have been as the time of her arrival had come and gone, and then stretched into the early hours. He'd probably fretted that she'd had an accident – or worse – that she'd fallen for Henry Radwell and wasn't coming back at all. She knew too that her sudden departure with Henry and rather terse letter would have done nothing to allay his fears over their silly falling-out and he'd have been anxious to make amends.

Rosie ran her fingers through her platinum curls and then rubbed her hands over her face. She had a lot of explaining to do, and wasn't looking forward to it. But it wasn't fair on Ron to keep him in the dark. Fences had to be mended and things put back on a more even keel so they could take stock, think things through and come to a fully reasoned decision together. It would bring heartache, but it was the only way to allow them to wipe the slate clean and move on with their lives.

She bit her lip and tried to keep the tears at bay, but they came anyway, and she was too physically and mentally exhausted to do anything about them.

Eventually, she realised that the fire had gone out and that it was almost six o'clock. The night was over, and within just a few hours she would have to be ready to serve behind the bar. But perhaps that would be better than sitting about feeling sorry for herself.

She dried her tears, then carried the glass and the plate of uneaten sandwiches into the kitchen before setting the guard in front of the fire and turning out the lights. Sliding between the sheets, her feet touched the stone water bottle Ron must have placed there earlier, and his thoughtfulness and undoubted love brought fresh tears.

It had been so lovely to be in his arms again, and to feel his strength and the security in his embrace that she'd missed whilst she'd been away. Yet there were things she needed to say to him – things he would find hurtful, and just the thought of how he would react made her want to curl up and hide from the world.

Rosie kicked away the cold bottle, heard it thud onto the floor and buried her face in her pillow. Moments later Monty climbed onto the bed and snuggled down beside her, instinctively knowing she needed his warmth and consoling presence.

2

Peggy was still suffering from the shock of that V-1 exploding in Havelock Road three days ago, and knew that everyone who'd been there that day was similarly affected – except for two-year-old Daisy, who was thankfully too young to understand how very close they'd all come to being killed.

It was the images of those poor dead soldiers that came to haunt Peggy at unexpected moments, bringing back the awful, gut-wrenching fear, as well as the heat of those ravenous flames and the terror of cowering against the initial blast which had uprooted trees and flung lethal debris for hundreds of feet – and the explosions that had followed soon after when Doris's illicit store of petrol cans had caught alight.

She shuddered as she revisited the horrific scene in her mind. John Hicks and his fire crew had been incredibly brave as they'd tried to fight the raging inferno, but there had been nothing they could do to save those unfortunate women trapped in Doris's house. Peggy could only pray they'd died instantly, for the alternative was just too appalling to contemplate.

As for her sister, Peggy had been so relieved and thankful that Doris had been away when the V-1 had hit she'd immediately brought her home without giving a thought to the consequences. Three days later it was proving to be a big mistake, for her sister had taken full advantage of Peggy's loving kindness by demanding she had the best bedroom and ordering the others about as if she owned the place.

Peggy's low spirits sank further. With the whole world in turmoil, she'd come to see the tranquillity and harmony of Beach View as her sanctuary, but if Doris didn't mend her ways there would be trouble, and it would be up to her to defuse it.

'Mumma. I got duck. Play with duck.'

Peggy dragged herself back to the present and forced a smile at Daisy as they shared the bath. She took the plastic duck, made it squeak and then drew her little daughter into her arms, revelling in the weight and scent of her – in her aliveness.

Slippery as an eel, Daisy squirmed and kicked the rapidly cooling few inches of water before crawling away to float the duck amid the soap bubbles Peggy had added as a treat.

Peggy got out of the bath shakily and, with trembling hands, hurriedly dried herself and got dressed. She was all fingers and thumbs and it took longer than usual to do up the buttons on her dress and fasten the belt. Annoyed with herself for being so feeble, she took a deep breath and glared defiantly at her reflection in the mirror as she brushed her hair.

She hadn't been hurt and her loved ones were safe, so there was no earthly reason why she couldn't pull herself together and get on.

Strapping on her watch, she noted the time with some alarm. It was almost seven, the girls were probably waiting to use the bathroom, and within a few hours she had to be at work. Clearly life had to go on despite Hitler's demonic new weapon, and it did no good to dwell on all the 'what ifs' when other things had to be seen to. And in a way these day-to-day responsibilities were helping her to cope, for without them she'd have had too much time to think. And that wouldn't do any good at all.

Having wrestled a protesting Daisy out of the bath, she wrapped her firmly in a towel and quickly dried and dressed her. Once that was achieved she cleaned the bath and then peeked in on Cordelia. The elderly lady had lived at Beach View for years and was now an intrinsic and very important part of Peggy's family. Poor Cordelia had caught a nasty chill after hiding from the V-1's blast in that water-filled ditch, and Peggy fretted that it could turn to something nasty if not kept an eye on.

'How are you feeling this morning?' she asked, alarmed by the high colour in Cordelia's cheeks and the way her breath was rattling as she fiddled with her hearing aid.

'Not very chipper,' she confessed. 'This blessed chill has gone to my chest, and I'm finding it a bit hard to breathe.'

Peggy saw what an effort it took for her to smile at Daisy, who was chattering away and trying to climb onto the bed. She lifted Daisy away and told her to go downstairs – which elicited a pout and the stamp of a small foot. 'Do as I say,' she said sternly. 'Gan Gan's tired and can't get any rest with you climbing all over her.'

As Daisy stomped out of the room and slowly

slid feet first down the stairs on her stomach, Peggy turned back to Cordelia. 'I'll get you a fresh hot-water bottle, a cup of tea and then call the doctor.'

'Please don't fuss, dear,' she wheezed. 'I shall be fine after a couple more days in bed, and the poor doctor has enough to do without being dragged out on a house call.'

Peggy didn't agree, but said nothing as she plumped the pillows, adjusted the blankets and fished out the cold bottle from the bottom of the bed. Cordelia would be eighty in a matter of months, and although she'd always been a bird-like little woman, she'd never looked this frail before, and it worried her deeply.

'Do you need the bathroom before I go downstairs?'

'If I do, then I'm perfectly capable of going on my own,' Cordelia replied tetchily. 'Do stop fussing and go and see to Daisy. She shouldn't be alone down there.'

Torn between the needs of Cordelia and the safety of her child, Peggy knew she really had no choice. With a promise to return soon, she hurried out of the room, thoughts of kettles and fires uppermost in her mind, and ran downstairs to the kitchen to find Daisy sitting on the floor next to Queenie the cat, pretending to read her a story from a picture book.

Peggy breathed a sigh of relief and put the kettle on the hob before returning to the hall. She dialled the doctor's number and within a few minutes had his promise to call in after morning surgery. Bustling back into the kitchen, she fed the demanding cat which was winding itself round her legs and threatening to trip her up, filled the hot-water bottle, wrapped it in a knitted cover and poured a cup of tea.

A glance at the clock told her there was some time to go before the news came on the wireless, and she began to get anxious that there was no sign of Sarah, who was in danger of being late for work – or of Ron and Harvey, who were usually up and about much earlier than this.

Settling Daisy safely at the table with a slice of toast and a cup of milk, she hurried back upstairs to Cordelia, smiling at the thought that Ron must have struck lucky with Rosie and stayed the night at the Anchor. The idea warmed her and she was still smiling as she placed the tea on the bedside table and tucked the hot-water bottle into the bed by Cordelia's little feet.

'I take it from that silly smirk that the old rogue didn't come home last night,' said Cordelia with a raised eyebrow. At Peggy's nod she clucked her tongue. 'Good luck to them. But I hope Rosie knows what she's letting herself in for by taking him back.'

'I'm sure she does,' said Peggy, opening the blackout curtains to the bright June day. She studied Cordelia, who was having a coughing fit, then hurried into the bathroom to fetch her some cough linctus, a glass of water and a couple of aspirin. It was always worrying when Cordelia was unwell, for at her age one never knew…

She helped her to a spoonful of linctus and waited for her to swallow the aspirin. 'You rest and enjoy that tea. I'll be up later with some porridge.'

'Dearest Peggy,' croaked Cordelia. 'What would I do without you?'

Peggy kissed her cheek and was alarmed at how hot she felt. 'If you need anything, bang on the floor with your stick,' she said, unearthing the walking stick from beneath a pile of clothes and placing it on the bed. 'I'll leave your door open so I can keep an eye on you if that's all right.'

Cordelia sipped her tea and then wearily sank back into the pillows. 'I think I'll sleep for a bit. Didn't get much last night,' she murmured, closing her eyes.

Peggy bit her lip, torn between wanting to stay and the knowledge that Daisy was downstairs with a pot of hot tea sitting on the draining board. She reluctantly left the room, jamming the door open with a chair before hurrying back to the kitchen to discover that Daisy now had company.

'Hello, Ron. I didn't expect to see you this morning now Rosie's back,' she said brightly. 'I thought you'd be all tucked up billing and cooing until at least lunchtime,' she teased. Her smile faded at his dour expression. 'She did come home last night, didn't she?'

'Oh aye, that she did. But it was very late and the poor wee girl was exhausted, so I left her to sleep.' He signalled the end of the conversation by reaching over to turn on the wireless which stood in a large wooden cabinet in the corner.

Peggy's disappointment was sharp, but she made no comment. Poor Ron had set such store in Rosie's return, and it was clear things hadn't gone to plan, but with Rosie back in Cliffehaven, she was sure they'd find some way of healing the

31

breach between them.

She surreptitiously watched him whilst she prepared the breakfast porridge, noting that he'd shaved and was wearing decent clothes for a change. He'd certainly made a tremendous effort to turn over a new leaf these past weeks, for his bedroom had stayed neat and sweeter smelling, and he'd taken more care in his appearance – even going so far as getting Fran to cut his hair and trim his eyebrows. Peggy mentally crossed her fingers that all this change would continue, and that he and Rosie would be all right.

'Where's that sister of yours?' Ron asked gruffly.

'She must still be in bed. She's in terrible shock, you know, and I think it's affecting her nerves.' Peggy could see by his expression what he was about to say and forestalled him. 'I know she rubs you up the wrong way, but Doris has lost everything, and because she'd arranged that lunch party, she blames herself for the deaths of those women. Try and show some sympathy for her, Ron.'

'I'd be nicer to her if she didn't order you about like a skivvy,' he replied. 'You haven't stopped pandering to her from the moment she stepped through the door.'

Peggy slopped some thin porridge into the bowls and set them on the table. 'I thought I'd lost her,' she said firmly, 'and she needs a bit of pampering after what she's been through.'

'That doesn't mean she can ride roughshod over everyone,' he muttered. 'I don't see why she couldn't have had the double room at the top of the house instead of evicting Rita and Ivy from theirs. The view's the same and the size is almost identical – and to be sure, it's not as if she's got a lot of stuff to put in it,' he added grumpily.

'Ron, please don't keep on. The girls were happy enough to go up there, and Doris will find it easier without so many stairs to negotiate.'

'Hmph. There's nothing wrong with her legs, going by the way she strides about issuing orders. It seems to me she just likes to cause as much fuss as she can.'

Peggy took a deep breath before sitting down to pour out the tea and help Daisy with her porridge. Ron and Doris had never seen eye to eye, and Peggy knew how difficult her sister could be. She was so thankful Doris was alive, she was willing to put up with a lot of things – and yet Ron had a point. Doris was a fit and healthy woman in her early fifties and could quite easily have moved into the room at the top of the house – especially as Rita had a cast on her leg after her motorbike accident. And Doris didn't need to be quite so bossy. Everyone understood how awful it must be to lose absolutely everything and they were all doing their best to make her feel welcome, even though none of them liked her.

Peggy stirred a few grains of sugar into her tea as she mulled over what to do for the best. Her patience was wearing thin after only three days, and if things weren't resolved soon there would be an almighty row, which had to be avoided at all costs. Perhaps, once Doris had recovered from the worst of the shock, she would have another quiet word with her about her attitude. It would be tricky, for her elder sister was bound to take it the wrong way again, but Peggy could see that if things went on as they were the happy atmosphere of Beach View would be destroyed.

'Is there no sign of that husband of hers?' said Ron over the atmospherics coming from the wireless as it warmed up.

'Ted's still away,' she replied, 'and no one knows where he is so he can't be contacted.' Peggy regarded him over the rim of her teacup. 'Besides, they're no longer married, so he's not responsible for her.'

'Well, I'm thinking he should be, husband or not.'

Peggy folded her arms and regarded him evenly. 'And just what do you expect him to do, Ron? He lives in a one-bedroom apartment above the Home and Colonial, and has a lovely new lady friend. The last person he needs is Doris moving in and playing gooseberry.'

'He's got money enough to find her a flat somewhere,' he replied grumpily.

'Why should he? Doris is my responsibility now, and this is her home for as long as she wants it.'

'I was afraid you'd say that,' he grumbled, fiddling with the knobs on the wireless until he got a clear reception for the BBC. 'Perhaps you should write to Anthony and tell him his mother needs a roof over her head. To be sure, he has a fine house with plenty of room.'

Peggy shook her head. 'Anthony might see it as his duty, he's a good son, but he and Suzy have the baby now, and it's not fair to expect them to take Doris on. Especially as Doris and Suzy get on each other's nerves.'

'It strikes me that woman gets on everyone's nerves,' Ron muttered sourly. ''Tis a pity it's us that's lumbered with her.'

Peggy agreed with him whole-heartedly but was in no mood to continue the argument at this time of the morning, so she finished her breakfast in silence. Lending half an ear to the news, she tried not to worry over Cordelia, the strained atmosphere Doris was already causing and the uncharacteristic absence of Sarah, who was usually an early riser.

The newscaster's plummy voice filled the silence. The Allied troops had secured the beachheads and were still making progress into France despite some resistance. The RAF was continuing their nightly bombing raids over Dunkirk, Boulogne and the Ruhr, and the Americans were now raiding during the day. The Allied losses were reported to be light, with only five planes brought down, but there was, Peggy noted, little mention of the casualties that must have been inflicted amongst the invading troops. The news at home was of a V-1 attack in London which had tragically killed twenty people.

Peggy's hand trembled as she clattered the spoons into the empty bowls and carried them to the sink. There had been so much excitement when news of the invasion had broken, but Hitler's latest terrifying weapon served to remind them all that victory was far from being assured, and after five long years of struggle and deprivation this war was wearing down even the hardiest of souls.

She blinked away the thought, determined to remain positive, and glanced up at the clock.

'Where on earth has Sarah got to?' she muttered. 'She'll be late for work at this rate, and it's a long walk to the Cliffe estate.'

Without waiting for a reply from Ron, who was engrossed in the war report, she dashed upstairs and peeked into Cordelia's room to check she was still asleep, then hurried along the landing to the bedroom Sarah shared with Fran.

She tapped lightly on the door, feeling guilty that she might wake Fran, who'd just come off night duty at the hospital and was having a precious day off. Getting no reply, she eased the door open and in the light coming through from the hall, found both girls fast asleep. She tiptoed across the room to the single bed beneath the window.

'Sarah,' she whispered, giving her shoulder a gentle shake. 'It's after seven. You have to get up.'

Sarah, who was usually so lively in the mornings, mumbled something and rolled over, pulling the bedclothes with her until she was buried within them.

Peggy gave her a more determined shake. 'Wake up, Sarah,' she hissed. 'It's late, and you won't have time for breakfast if you leave it much longer.'

Reluctantly, Sarah drew back the bedclothes and sat up, her fair hair tousled, her blue eyes heavy-lidded and dull. 'Sorry, Aunt Peg,' she said through a vast yawn. 'I didn't get much rest last night. I kept having the most horrible dreams.'

Peggy wondered fleetingly if her nightmares had more to do with her heart-wrenching dilemma over her fiancé Philip and her sweetheart Delaney than the V-1 explosion. She put a loving hand on her slim shoulder as Fran mumbled and moved

36

about restlessly in the other bed. 'I know, dear,' she whispered, 'and you're not alone. Now get dressed and you can tell me all about them whilst you're having breakfast. They won't seem so frightening in the daylight.'

Sarah rubbed her eyes then reached for her wash-bag. 'I wish that was true,' she sighed.

Peggy squeezed her shoulder in sympathy then hurried out of the room before Fran was disturbed any further. She decided that whilst she was here she'd go and check on the two girls at the top of the house, for she couldn't hear them moving about up there. They were both reluctant to leave their beds in the morning, and she'd always had trouble digging them out so they weren't late for work.

Ivy was due to start her shift at the armaments factory in an hour, and although Rita was still hampered by the plaster cast on her leg and couldn't play much part in her work at the fire station, she still needed to keep proper hours and do something useful with her day.

She was a bit out of breath by the time she reached the second-floor landing, but on opening the bedroom door was pleasantly surprised to see that Ivy was already dressed in her dungarees and sturdy boots, and Rita was dragging on a skirt over her heavily plastered leg.

'I just thought I'd make sure you were up,' said Peggy. She cast a despairing look at the discarded clothes and dirty crockery scattered about the room. 'I'd appreciate it if you could tidy up before you leave the house. This place looks like a bomb's hit it.'

Ivy, who'd now survived two bomb attacks, shuddered. 'No, it doesn't, Aunty Peg. A bomb makes much more mess.'

'And we firefighters make it worse by chucking gallons of water over everything,' said Rita airily. She shot Peggy an impish grin. 'So, all in all, it's quite tidy really.'

'Just get on and do it,' Peggy replied, trying not to smile at her cheek. She closed the door and hurried back to the first-floor landing. They were a couple of little imps, cheeky with it, and too sharp for their own good. But oh how she wished they'd at least make some effort to keep that room straight.

She listened at Doris's door, but hearing nothing, went along to peek in at Cordelia again. Her breathing was still rasping, but the aspirin seemed to have lowered her temperature, which was a relief. Realising that the cup of tea had gone cold on the bedside table, she decided to make a fresh one when Cordelia awoke.

Peggy's bedroom was off the hall, and as the girls bustled about upstairs with their usual chatter to get ready for their day, she checked her watch and calculated she just had time to sort out some more clothes for Doris. Not that she had a lot, but she was sure there was enough to tide Doris over until she got her compensation through and felt like going out to the shops.

She pushed the door open and froze at the sight of Doris in Peggy's old dressing gown and hairnet, rifling through her chest of drawers, pulling out clothes and tossing them onto the unmade bed. 'What on *earth* do you think you're doing?'

'I'm looking for something respectable to wear,' said Doris, not at all fazed by being caught red-handed. 'I must say, Margaret, most of your clothes are fit only to be used as cleaning rags – especially your underwear.' She held up a frayed petticoat that had seen better days.

In rising fury, Peggy strode in, snatched up the petticoat and slammed the drawer shut, narrowly missing Doris's fingers. 'You could at least have had the decency to ask first,' she said tersely. 'Not creep in here on the sly when my back's turned.'

Doris folded her arms and glared at her. 'I'm not being sly. As your sister, I didn't think I had to ask permission.'

'Sister or not, it would have been the polite thing to do,' Peggy retorted. She took a steadying breath in an attempt to keep her temper. 'Just because you live here doesn't give you the right to go through my private things,' she said, noting the open wardrobe doors, the empty hangers and shelves and the pile of clothing on the bed.

'But they're not yours, are they?' said Doris, plucking the lovely blue woollen overcoat, the tweed skirt and pale lilac twinset from the pile as if to demonstrate the point. 'I bought these and as an act of charity let you use them when I'd finished with them because you clearly needed something proper to wear.'

'I didn't realise I was a charity case, or that they were on loan,' said Peggy through gritted teeth. 'It still doesn't alter the fact that you should have asked before coming in here.'

'I had hoped you'd return the favour without making a fuss,' said Doris, tightening the belt on

Peggy's old dressing gown. 'After all, I've lost everything but for what I was wearing that day, and am now forced to avail myself of your cast-offs.'

'They are *not* cast-offs,' Peggy hissed, stung by the insult. 'That dressing gown and nightdress are perfectly adequate.'

Doris sniffed. 'I'm not used to adequate,' she said flatly, eyeing up the thick dressing gown which was hanging from a hook on the back of the door. 'Why didn't you give me that instead? It looks almost new and is of far better quality.'

Peggy snatched the dressing gown out of her reach and held it to her chest. 'This is Jim's and it's staying here with me.'

'Jim's not here and my need is greater,' said Doris. 'Don't be a dog in the manger about it, Margaret. Sentimentality is all very well, but it butters no parsnips.'

'You're not having it,' said Peggy, stuffing it into a drawer and standing guard over it. 'And I'm not being dog in the manger about anything. If you'd had the decency to wait until I had the time to sort through all *your* cast-offs, you'd have had the lot back anyway.'

'Then I've saved you the bother,' said Doris unrepentantly. She eyed the denuded cupboard. 'Where's the mink wrap I brought over at Christmas?'

'In the box on top of the wardrobe,' said Peggy crossly. 'Like the overcoat, I never got the chance to wear it – so they're as good as when you *lent* them to me.'

'That's hardly surprising,' said Doris, reaching

for the box. 'You don't exactly have the sort of social life that warrants such things, and I don't really know what I was thinking of to pass them on to you in the first place.'

Peggy folded her arms tightly about her waist and bunched her fists. 'Neither do I,' she said, cold with fury. 'I might not gad about with the snobs in posh furs and expensive overcoats, but I do have a sense of what's right, and I'd never dream of ransacking your room or being so nasty.'

'Oh, for goodness' sake, Margaret, stop dramatising everything,' Doris said impatiently. 'You want to thank your lucky stars it wasn't your home that was blown to bits.' Her lip curled as she regarded the shabby room. 'Though it has to be said, it might be an improvement,' she added.

Peggy saw red, and before she knew it she'd dealt a ringing slap to Doris's cheek. 'You bitch,' she spat. 'Take that back – or I'll slap the other one to match.'

Doris cupped her rapidly reddening cheek with her hand. 'How *dare* you strike me!' she gasped.

Peggy's dander was well and truly up. She gave Doris a shove that sent her stumbling against the bed. 'And how dare you denigrate me and my home! You're the rudest, most ungrateful person I've had the misfortune to know, and if you don't mend your ways quick smart, I'll do more than smack your smug face.'

There was sudden fear in Doris's eyes as she backed away. 'Now, Margaret, there's no need...'

'And stop calling me Margaret!' Peggy yelled.

'But–'

'I'm not listening to you any more,' Peggy

stormed. 'This is my home, and I will *not* have you ordering people about or taking it for granted you can come in here and help yourself to things – even if they are yours Your attitude is rotten, Doris – and I've had enough of it.'

'Yours is hardly pleasant,' shouted Doris. 'And I'm mortified that I'm forced to put up with it.'

'No one's forcing you to do anything,' Peggy shot back. 'If you don't like it here, then you can sling your blooming hook and be done with it.'

'Hear, hear,' said Ron.

Peggy whipped round to see Ron, Harvey and the four girls standing wide-eyed in the doorway. 'Clear off. This is a private row,' she said furiously, slamming the door in their faces before turning back to Doris. 'Not that it will stay private now they've all witnessed that,' she snapped.

Doris had gone a dark red, the mark of Peggy's fingers visible on her hot cheek. 'You've made it intolerable for me to stay here,' she said, clearly struggling to regain her dignity in the shame of having witnesses to their angry exchange.

'No,' said Peggy firmly. 'It's you who's been in-tolerable. Bossing everyone about like Lady Muck; demanding things as if this is a blooming hotel and turning up your nose at everything. It's got to stop.' The fire went out of her suddenly and she sank wearily onto the bed amongst the scattered clothes. 'I'm not proud of losing my temper like that, but if you hadn't been so high-handed and sneering we wouldn't have had this set-to in the first place.'

Doris's face worked as she tried to rein in her emotions and come up with a face-saving reply.

'You really should learn to control your temper, Mar... Peggy,' she said, gingerly touching her cheek. 'It's not ladylike, and violence solves nothing.'

'That slap has been a long time coming,' Peggy replied evenly, 'and you deserved it. Don't expect me to apologise, either, because hell will freeze over before I do.'

They glared at one another in silence until Peggy broke eye contact and began to gather up the clothing. The row had shaken her to the core, but she was damned if she'd let her sister know that. All she wanted now was an end to it. She grabbed the clothes into a rough bundle and thrust them into her sister's arms.

'You've got what you came for,' she said, adding the box containing the fur wrap to the pile. 'I suggest you have a long, hard think about things before I have to face you again today.'

Peggy didn't offer to help as Doris wrestled with the unwieldy bundle and tried to turn the door-knob without dropping anything. When the door opened to reveal that the others were still earwigging, she saw Doris turn an even deeper puce and determinedly refused to feel sorry for her.

Ron and the girls couldn't hide their glee at Doris's humiliation. They refused to budge, thereby forcing her to push her way through them, and there were smothered giggles as she fled up the stairs.

'The show's over,' Peggy said tightly. 'And I'll thank you all to keep what you heard to yourselves.'

Closing the bedroom door on them, she sank

back onto the bed and tried to regain her equilibrium. The unpleasant scene, coming so soon after the shock and horror of the bomb attack, had shaken her already unsteady nerves, and Doris's arrogance and disdain for all she held dear had been the last straw. She'd never lost her temper like that before – and the power of it frightened her. And yet, as her pulse steadied and the anger subsided, she realised the set-to had been inevitable from the moment Doris had moved in.

She regarded the shabby bedroom with its worn linoleum, battered furniture and peeling paintwork. It might not be up to much, but it was her refuge, and if Jim was here, he too would have told Doris to sling her hook. She gave a deep sigh and began to tidy the mess.

As she folded her few remaining clothes and closed the wardrobe door on the empty hangers, she wished circumstances were different, and that Doris *could* move out. But with the war on, and so many people made homeless, accommodation wasn't that easy to find, and she couldn't bear the thought of her sister being forced to share a room in a hostel, or having to bed down in a church hall.

Feeling dispirited, she went to stand by the heavily taped window to watch another squadron of American fighters and bombers head for France. The vibration caused by their powerful engines rattled the rotting window frames and shuddered through the old walls, bringing yet another drift of plaster from the ceiling to settle on the floor.

Peggy bit her lip in consternation. The war still dragged on despite the Allied invasion and the liberation of Rome, and it seemed they still had more of it to contend with. The knowledge that she was stuck with Doris until peace was declared made her even more depressed.

'I just hope she comes to realise how lucky she is to have a roof over her head,' she muttered. 'It might not be as grand as she's used to, but it's better than some.'

The rap of the door knocker brought her out of her gloomy thoughts and she hurried into the hall to find old Doctor Sayer greeting Ron and Harvey and looking more like Father Christmas than ever now he'd put on weight and let his silky white beard grow even bushier.

'My boy Michael is taking morning surgery,' he explained in his deep baritone voice, 'and I thought that as Cordelia is getting on a bit, I'd pop in early. Chills can be nasty things for elderly ladies.'

Peggy's smile was wry, for Dr Sayer was a year older than Cordelia, but thanks to the war, he'd had to come back from retirement. 'Thank you for taking such trouble,' she said, leading the way upstairs. 'I don't like calling you out when you're so busy, but I am worried about her.'

Dr Sayer proved to be very sprightly for a man fast approaching his eighty-first year, and he reached the landing without pausing for breath. 'In here?' he asked, waving at the open door, and sweeping in before she could reply.

He placed his black bag on the bed and plonked down next to it, making the mattress dip so alarmingly that Cordelia had to grip the blankets to stay on board. 'Now then, Cordelia,' he

45

boomed, 'what's all this I hear about you not feeling the full ticket?'

'There's no need to shout, Herbert Sayer,' said Cordelia, fiddling with her hearing aid. 'I don't want the entire neighbourhood knowing my business.'

He chuckled and dug a stethoscope out of his bag. Waiting for Cordelia to get over her coughing fit, he then listened carefully to her chest, felt the glands in her neck and took her temperature. 'Hmm. It's a bit high, old thing,' he rumbled, putting the thermometer back in its case. 'What have you been up to?'

'Standing about in water-filled ditches trying to avoid Hitler's V-1,' she rasped.

'Good Lord,' he breathed. 'Were you caught up in that?'

Cordelia had another coughing fit and could only nod.

Herbert Sayer dug about in his bag and brought out a bottle of pills and a prescription pad. He scrawled something on the pad, tore off the page and handed it to Peggy. 'She's to take one of those pills every four hours, and the Friars' Balsam will help ease her chest. You know the drill, Peggy. Big bowl, lots of very hot water to infuse the Balsam and a towel placed over the head whilst she inhales the steam.'

'I am here, you know,' said Cordelia crossly. 'And quite capable of following orders.'

He patted her hand. 'I'll be back this evening to check on you, but should you want me, day or night, just get Peggy to telephone the surgery and one of us will come.'

'Is it very serious?' asked a fretful Peggy.

'Not yet. I think we've caught it in time before it turns to something more complex, but she will need a close eye kept on her for a day or two.' He smiled at Cordelia. 'Now you rest, take in plenty of fluids, and we'll soon have you up and about causing mischief again.'

There was a gleam in Cordelia's eyes which bore no relation to her high temperature. 'It's not me who causes mischief, Herbert Sayer. I heard all about you and the widow at the golf club.'

He twirled his waxed moustache and wriggled his fine white eyebrows, grinning broadly. 'Your chap Bertie's too sharp for his own good,' he said, rising from the bed. 'You really shouldn't believe *everything* he tells you.' He winked at Peggy. 'I'll see you both later.'

Peggy was most intrigued to hear about the doctor's dalliance, for the old man had been on his own for many years since his wife died. Cordelia obviously knew more than she was letting on, so once she was feeling brighter, Peggy decided she'd try to find out more.

After she'd shown the doctor out, she told the others what he'd said and then ran back upstairs with a jug of water. She waited for Cordelia to swallow the pill and then dashed back to the kitchen to make her fresh tea and warm the porridge. It was barely past eight o'clock. *At this rate*, she thought wryly, *I'll be worn out by the time I have to leave for work.*

'Right,' said Ron as she returned once more to the kitchen and dropped thankfully into a chair to relax with a cigarette and cup of tea. 'You're to stay there until you have to leave for work. Young Fran's gone back to bed for a couple of hours and Sarah's left for Cliffe estate, but we'll manage. I'll keep Daisy amused for now, get the prescription from the chemist the minute it's open, and do the shopping if you've got a list.'

'It's on the table,' said Peggy, 'but with Cordelia so poorly I think it might be best if I telephoned Solly and warned him I can't come in today.'

'You'll do no such thing,' said Ron sternly. 'Rita and I will keep an eye out for her until lunchtime, and Fran has promised to take over this afternoon.'

'But that's not fair,' Peggy protested. 'It's her one day off, and I'm sure she's made plans to meet up with Robert later.'

'She's 'appy to do it, Aunty Peg,' said Ivy through a mouthful of toast. 'Grandma Cordy needs us to rally around, and I'm sure Robert won't mind coming 'ere for his tea.' She gulped down the last of her hurried breakfast. 'Talking of which, me and Rita are in charge of cooking tonight, so there's no need to get into a flap if you're late back from visiting Danuta.'

Peggy looked at her askance, knowing only too well that Ivy could burn water.

Ivy giggled. 'It's vegetable stew, Aunty Peg, and even I can manage not to ruin that.'

'I'll keep an eye on it, so don't worry, Aunt Peg,' said Rita. 'I reckon you've had enough drama for one day.'

'You're beginning to sound like your Australian,' Peggy teased, warmed by their loving kindness.

Rita turned pink. 'Peter Ryan is not *my* Australian. He's just a friend.'

'Yeah, tell that to the marines,' retorted Ivy, dragging on her coat and grabbing her gas mask. 'I seen the way you eyes 'im when you thinks no one's looking.' She dodged Rita's swiping hand and giggled. 'I'll see you all after me shift.'

Rita busied herself at the sink. It had only been a year since her lovely young Matthew Champion had been shot down and killed on a raid over Germany, and although her loss was still clear in unguarded moments, she'd begun to slowly blossom and enjoy life again now she'd met Peter Ryan. Peggy had fretted that this new attraction of Rita's was on the rebound, and that the very likeable Australian might prove too good to be true, and end up hurting her. But these past weeks had proved her wrong, and she was glad of it.

'So, what are we going to do about Doris?' asked Ron, busy helping Daisy with a jigsaw puzzle he'd made for her the previous Christmas.

'*We* are doing nothing,' said Peggy firmly. 'What was said was in the heat of the moment, and of course I'm not about to throw her out.'

'Then she needs to pull her silk stockings up and behave,' said Ron. 'I'll not be having her upset you like that again.'

Peggy patted his hand whilst Rita clattered dishes in the sink. 'Thanks, Ron, but I'll deal with Doris. You concentrate on making things right with Rosie.'

3

Harvey was already on guard duty at the side of Cordelia's bed, having refused to budge when it became apparent she was not coming downstairs today. He looked up as Ron carried in the large bowl of steaming water and set it carefully on the bedside table, then with a snort, rested his nose back on his paws, his eyebrows twitching as he watched Rita fussing with pillows

'Is there anything else I can do?' Ron asked, feeling rather awkward amongst Cordelia's clutter of clothes, delicate furniture and china ornaments.

Rita finished plumping the pillows and smiled back at him. 'Thanks, Grandpa Ron, but Grandma Cordy and I can manage from now on.'

'I expect he's in a lather to get back to Rosie,' said Cordelia.

'Aye, well, I thought I'd see if she needed a hand before opening time,' he muttered. He looked down at Harvey. 'Out you come,' he ordered.

Harvey closed his eyes and ignored him.

'Leave him be,' said Rita. 'He's doing no harm.'

Ron made his escape and stomped down the stars, wincing at the pain shooting up his back. Determined not to let it hamper him, he strode into the kitchen to fetch his jacket, hat and gas-mask box. He checked there was enough fuel in the kitchener range to keep it going so the water was heated and they could cook, and then went down the concrete steps to the basement.

Closing the back door behind him, he stepped out into the garden where Queenie was sunning herself on the herbs he'd seeded into the turfs he'd laid over the Anderson shelter. Reluctant to shoo her off in case she took it into her head to follow him, he left her to sleep, hoping the delicate little plants wouldn't suffer too much.

He squinted against the sun to watch the American bombers go over with their escort of Hurricanes and Typhoons, and then settled his fedora to a rakish angle over his brow. It was actually Jim's hat, but as he was in Burma and it was only gathering dust, Ron had decided to make use of it. The dark blue fedora was much smarter than his greasy old cap, and it certainly lent him an air of sophistication which had been sorely lacking until recently.

Smothering a vast yawn, he stood for a moment to enjoy the day's warmth, wishing he wasn't quite so tired. He'd managed to snatch an hour of sleep on his return this morning, and with all the hoo-ha over Cordelia and Doris, and dashing about shopping and collecting prescriptions, he felt drained. He pulled his pipe out of his jacket pocket and went to lean against the flint wall as he filled it with tobacco and got it alight.

As he puffed sweet-scented smoke into the still, warm air, he mulled over the scene with Doris and gave a chuckle. Peggy had certainly shown her mettle this morning and no mistake, and he'd been amazed to discover that beneath that gentle exterior lay a veritable tiger – in fact it had quite shocked the girls, who'd never seen that side of

Peggy before. Yet none of them blamed her for losing her temper, for Doris had fully deserved that slap, and if it had been up to them, she'd have been booted out there and then.

Ron bit down on the stem of his pipe. It was not in Peggy's nature to be unkind, and he suspected she was already bitterly regretting that row. Doris was a trial, and not the most welcome guest, but Peggy's loyalty to her sister meant she would ask her to stay. He gave a sigh, took one last puff of his pipe and pushed through the gate. He could only hope that Doris kept her mouth shut and her head down, for there was trouble enough in the world without bringing it into the heart of Beach View.

He strolled along the alleyway, noting the potholes that needed filling with ashes from the range, and the trails of bramble and ivy eating into the flint walls of the gardens which, like his, had been turned into vegetable plots. Tarpaulins had been stretched over damaged roofs; bullets had scarred walls; shattered chimney stacks had been taken down, and far too many windows had been boarded over. All in all, it was a gloomy scene, and did nothing to lift his flagging spirits.

Yet, as he crossed the road coming up from the seafront and began to amble down Camden Road, Ron became aware that he was being watched. The queues of gossiping women outside the shops looked at him admiringly – in fact a few were openly flirtatious – and passing them by, he heard their whispering and tittering. His spirits rose, for they'd clearly noticed this new and very smart Ron, and going by some of their comments, it seemed they approved.

He lifted his chin a little higher, squared his shoulders and stuck out his chest, tipping his hat at their greetings and grinning at the more daring who called out cheeky remarks. If Rosie was half as impressed by this new and improved Ron, then he had a fighting chance of persuading her to accept his proposal.

The Town Hall clock struggled to be heard above the racket of the American planes as it struck eleven forty-five and Ron reached the Anchor's side door. He thought it wise to knock, rather than just go in, for he needed to mind his manners and not upset Rosie from the outset by taking liberties.

The heavy oak door creaked open, and Rosie stood there looking magnificent in her white frilly blouse, tight black skirt, dark stockings and high-heeled shoes. There was no sign of the previous night's exhaustion, for her platinum hair shone in the sunlight and her smile was warm as she regarded him with sparkling blue eyes.

'My goodness, you do look smart,' she said, holding fast to Monty's collar to stop him climbing all over Ron. 'It's most impressive, but why the sudden transformation?'

'I've turned over a new leaf,' he said, positively preening in her admiration. He stepped into the narrow hallway and patted Monty's head. 'To be sure, the effort was worth that lovely smile, Rosie.' He reached for her hand, his heart thudding. 'Would it also be worthy of a wee kiss?'

Rosie giggled. 'Just a small one. I've got a pub to open.'

He shed the hat and gas-mask box to gather her tenderly into his arms, feeling her softness mould against him as her familiar perfume heightened his senses and their lips met. His heart sang as she put her arms round his neck and returned his kiss, her breasts rising and falling against his chest as her pulse quickened.

All too suddenly she was pulling away from him and looking flustered. 'Gosh,' she breathed, tugging at her blouse which had come loose from her skirt. 'Now you've got me all of a dither.'

'Then let me kiss you again before the feeling wears off,' he said, reaching for her once more.

She shook her head and stepped away. 'That's really not a good idea, Ron. It's almost opening time and I need to keep my wits about me.'

'Brenda can manage perfectly well on her own,' he persisted. 'Come on, Rosie,' he pleaded. 'We've been apart for weeks and I want to show you how much I've missed you and how sorry I am that I upset you.'

She still looked flustered, but kept her distance as Monty got bored and sloped off into the bar. 'I've missed you too, and of course I know how sorry you are – I feel the same. But Brenda isn't coming in today, and I just don't have the time for canoodling' – she shot him an almost shy smile – 'regardless of how very pleasant it is.'

Ron was crestfallen. 'I was hoping we could have time to talk quietly about things,' he said.

She cupped his freshly shaven chin and brushed her lips against his cheek. 'And we will, Ron, I promise. But now there's a pub to run.' She smiled up at him. 'D'you fancy helping out?'

It was an olive branch of sorts, and although his disappointment was raw, he accepted it. 'To be sure, I've nothing better to do,' he said nonchalantly.

'Thanks, Ron, you're a star.' She turned away and made for the bar.

Ron was thoughtful as he hung his hat, jacket and gas-mask box on the hall stand. He was confused. Her welcoming kiss had said one thing, her demeanour another – and he wasn't at all sure where he stood with her. And yet it seemed she'd forgiven him his drunken behaviour that fateful night before she'd left, and still wanted his company – even if it was only to help behind the bar – so there was a glimmer of hope that all was not lost.

He recalled his years of soldiering and decided he needed a new strategy. Every mission called for a carefully laid plan, and if he was to win Rosie, then it was vital he go about it with military precision. He would hold back, gauge the lie of the land for any hidden stumbling blocks – like Major Radwell – and then assess the best way to advance.

Feeling rather more confident, he rolled up his shirt-sleeves and strode purposefully into the bar.

Peggy enjoyed her work at the uniform factory, for it gave her a chance to do something useful, provided interesting new social contact, a very welcome wage, and respite from all the responsibilities at Beach View. Now she was on her lunch break, and as it was such a lovely day, she and her friend Gracie had decided to sit on the wall outside the factory to eat their sandwiches and catch up on their news.

'It's a shame that lot are making such a racket,' said Gracie, looking up at the bombers and fighters. 'I'm sure the birds must be singing, but I'm blowed if anyone can hear them above that.'

'I'd rather that than the drone of a V-1,' said Peggy. 'I'll never get over the way it got louder and louder and then went silent as it dropped from the sky and blew Havelock Road to smithereens.'

'It must have been terrifying,' agreed Gracie with a shudder. 'We all heard the explosions and rushed out to see if there was anything we could do. I was so frightened for you when I saw where it had landed, and so thankful when I realised you and the others were all right.'

'I'm just glad you were working that day, otherwise you and little Chloe would have been at the picnic and got caught up in it too.'

Peggy twisted round to watch the children from the factory crèche scrambling about in the small playground, their laughter and chatter bringing a lightening to her spirits. She waved at Daisy, but her daughter was too busy playing chase with Gracie's Chloe to take any notice, so she turned back to finish her sandwich.

'I can tell you're still shaken up, Peg. Are you sure you should have come back to work so soon?'

Peggy's smile was rueful. 'I need the money, Gracie – and besides, now we've got Doris living with us, I'm glad to escape the house.' She told her friend about the row that morning. 'I'm not proud of what I did,' she finished, 'but I have to admit, I do feel better at letting it all out.'

'I'm not surprised,' said Gracie, squeezing her

hand in sympathy. 'From the sound of it, Doris has been a complete pain for years and it was time to let her know how you felt.' She giggled. 'I can't imagine you going for her like that. You come across as so warm and cuddly. It must have been quite a shock to Doris.'

Peggy chuckled. 'It certainly shocked me. But the worm has finally turned, Gracie, and Doris had better watch her step from now on.'

Despite making light of it, Peggy still felt ashamed, and not wishing to dwell upon that unpleasant exchange, she pulled the thermos out of her string bag and poured them both a cup of tea. 'Changing the subject, have you heard from your Clive?'

Gracie bit her lip and shook her head. 'It's been nearly a week since his last letter, and although I know he must be horribly busy with all the raids the RAF is on now, I'm a bit miffed he couldn't find the time to send me a couple of lines.'

She grimaced. 'Still, he's probably exhausted, poor darling. These endless sorties are bound to be telling on all the air crews, and I'm being selfish wanting him to write letters when he needs to sleep.'

'It's not at all selfish, Gracie,' Peggy soothed. 'We women wait in hope for a letter or card, and when it doesn't come we fret that they've forgotten us because they're so taken up with their war duties. The mail from India isn't always reliable, and it can be delayed by weeks. And when I do hear from Jim, it's usually an indecipherable scrawl on a grubby page torn out of a notebook.' She gave a sigh. 'It's all rather disheartening.'

'Is it as bad as they say over there?' asked Gracie, offering her packet of Lucky Strike cigarettes to Peggy.

Peggy raised an eyebrow but didn't ask where she'd got them as she took one and lit up, plucking a thread of tobacco from her lip. 'He tells me nothing, really – but that's not a bad thing. What I hear on the news is enough to get my imagination going, and I don't really want to know what he's having to face over there.'

'At least as long as there's no telegram we know they're still alive,' sighed Gracie. 'To be honest, I dread the knock on the door.'

'We all do.' Peggy smoked the American cigarette which tasted so different from her usual Park Drive, and tried not to think about telegrams.

Sarah Fuller was also on her lunch break at the Cliffe estate. Once she'd finished her meal in the noisy canteen with the other girls of the Women's Timber Corps, she went into the manor house gardens to read her letters in peace and quiet.

It was a warm day, and she wished she was wearing a cotton frock and sandals instead of the WTC uniform of heavy jodhpurs, thick shirt, sweater and stout boots. However, if the rumours were correct, and the Timber Corps was moving to another site, she'd soon be in a civilian office job and swapping her uniform for something more appropriate for the weather.

Heading for her favourite spot, which was sheltered from the busy pathway by a rose arbour and huge rhododendron bushes, she stripped off her sweater and sat down on the lichen-stained stone bench. Lighting a cigarette, she shuffled the three letters, returning repeatedly to the one bearing the American Forces franking, and the familiar handwriting. She hadn't expected to hear from Delaney after that heart-breaking letter she'd had to write to call things off between them, and although she was intrigued to know what he'd said, she was also fearful of his undoubted hurt and anger at being rejected so swiftly – and unexpectedly – after his loving proposal.

She had met Lieutenant Colonel Delaney Hammond at Cliffe when the American regiment had been billeted here. Despite the fact he'd told her he was married, and that she was engaged to Philip, who was now in the hands of the Japanese, their friendship had blossomed into something far deeper than either of them had expected – or indeed, wanted.

Sarah had tried hard to resist, hoping that by some miracle Philip was still alive and would come home to her. But the feelings for Delaney proved too strong, and when he'd confessed he'd foolishly lied about having a wife and family, and asked her to marry him, she'd allowed herself to believe they had a future together.

Then a letter had come from her mother containing a copy of the recently arrived note her father Jock had managed to smuggle out of Changi Prison two and a half years ago. At the bottom of the note Philip had begged Sarah to cherish his engagement ring and the promises they'd made to one another, for the love they shared would see him through whatever lay ahead. That note had been written within weeks of the fall of Singapore, and anything could have happened to them since – but it had forced Sarah to realise that she'd betrayed Philip by falling for Delaney, and had no choice but to honour her promise to Philip.

She set Delaney's letter to one side, not ready to read it yet, and opened the pale blue airmail letter from her mother instead. Tucked between the folded sheets of thin paper, she found several small black and white photographs, and with a soft gasp of pleasure, she examined the snapshots of little James, the brother who'd been born during the final, terrifying days of Singapore's fall into Japanese hands, and who she and her sister Jane had yet to meet.

She smiled at the chubby, laughing little boy as he sat on a sandy Australian beach lined with palm trees, or played with a puppy on the lawn at the back of her grandparents' house. He was clearly thriving – as was her mother, Sylvia, who looked cool and elegant in a pale summer frock and broad-brimmed hat, standing on the veranda between her parents.

Sarah had never been to Australia, but from the photographs her mother had previously sent, the countryside around Cairns looked very similar to Malaya, with its rainforests, pristine beaches, cane fields and large white single-storey wooden houses that were built on stilts to deter the termites and avoid the flooding during the rainy season.

She studied this latest batch with longing. It had been almost three years since she'd seen her mother, and many years before that when her grandparents had travelled from their vast sugar cane and banana plantation outside Cairns to visit them in Malaya. Her grandfather looked much the same as she remembered: a tall, wiry man with a strong-featured, weathered face and a shock of sun-bleached, almost white, hair. Her grandmother was rounder and smaller, but her fine bone structure meant she still retained some of the youthful beauty she'd passed on to her daughter.

Sliding the photographs back into the envelope, she began to read her mother's letter, smiling at her vivid descriptions of the social clubs she'd joined and the wide variety of rather eccentric people she'd met there. It seemed there were a lot of expats living in Cairns, and there was a hectic social whirl of tennis parties, cocktails, barbecues and dances, so it must have felt quite like home to Sylvia, who'd lived in the tropics all her married life.

Sylvia was positively brimming over with enthusiasm at her future plans, her pen flowing so swiftly over the pages that at times her writing was difficult to decipher. However, as she read on, Sarah's smile faded, and a sense of foreboding made her frown.

Now the news is more cheerful, with the Allied invasion into France and the liberation of Rome, one can at last dare to look forward. It will be so wonderful to see you both when this beastly war is over, and you and Jane must come immediately peace is declared, so we can be ready to welcome Jock and Philip home.

I have informed the authorities of my address here, as I'm sure that when they're released, Australia will be the best place for them to come as it's much nearer than England, the weather is more predictable, and there's no shortage of good fruit, meat and vegetables, which will help them recover from what must be a ghastly ordeal.

Mummy and Daddy have drawn up plans to build another Queenslander homestead on the property, and it would be perfect for you and Philip to have the space to settle down to married life and raise lots of lovely babies. I've already spoken to our local vicar, who's very willing to do the service, although he's warned me there will be positively <u>acres</u> of paperwork to fill in as neither of you are Australian citizens – but don't worry about that, it will be easily sorted once I get your grandfather on the case.

The timing of the wedding would, of course, depend entirely on the season they are released; but I thought we could have the reception in the garden, which looks particularly lovely in the spring. The flowers here are quite spectacular, and will be perfect for your bouquet and the table decorations. Jock will, of course, give you away and be the proud father, and I'm sure Jane will jump at the chance to be your bridesmaid.

I doubt very much if you'll find anything suitable to wear for your special day in England, what with the rationing and everything – so dreary – so I've started ordering pattern books from Sydney and catalogues from Myers, which is a large department store that stocks just about everything, and is almost as good as Harrods in London where I bought my wedding dress all those years ago. I would have passed it on to you, but sadly it was one of the many precious things I had to leave behind when we fled Singapore.

Mummy says I'm rather getting ahead of myself, and should stop and think about how things might actually *turn out. I know she means well, but I daren't let myself contemplate anything so horrifying, for it will simply crush me. So I'm making plans and looking forward to having you all home and safe so we can be a real family again.*

Sarah took a quavering breath and closed her eyes. Her mother's determination to believe that everything would turn out all right was admirable, but Grandma's cautionary advice was far more sensible in the light of the fact that the Japanese refused to publish any data concerning their prisoners – alive or dead – and barred the Red Cross observers from entering their camps.

Sarah could only hope her mother came back down to earth and listened to that advice, for if she didn't, and all her hopes turned to dust, the fallout would be catastrophic, and Sarah dreaded to think what that would do to her.

She scanned the rest of the letter, which continued in much the same vein, and then tucked it back with the photographs before staring gloomily into space, feeling trapped and utterly helpless. It was as if Sylvia still thought of her and Jane as children – not young women in their twenties with minds of their own – for she'd mapped out their future in the finest of detail without a thought for what they might actually want to do once the war was over.

Sarah smoked her cigarette and glanced down at her sister's letter lying on the bench. Jane was twenty years old and a thoroughly modern young woman who was immersed in an important job for the MOD, and living an independent life far from Beach View. What her plans were for the future, Sarah had no idea, but she doubted they gelled with Sylvia's.

She noted the postal date, surprised it had arrived within twenty-four hours, for the mail was never usually that reliable. Opening the letter, she found a single, closely typewritten page, signed with Jane's usual flourish. The forthright tone of the letter made her smile, for it showed just how far Jane had come since leaving Singapore.

Dear Sarah,

I'm guessing you've received the latest missive from Mummy, and I have to say I found it positively alarming. It's clear she has no intention of coming to England after the war and simply assumes we'll drop everything and go over there, no matter how inconvenient it might be. Of course it would be lovely to see her and the grandparents again, and to get to know little James, but I have no ambition to spend the rest of my life in the middle of nowhere – and I suspect you feel the same.

As for the wedding plans, they are quite awful, and my heart goes out to you, knowing how trapped they must have made you feel. Apart from the fact you've admitted you're in love with someone else and only marrying Philip through some misguided sense of loyalty, none of us know if he and Pops are even still alive. It would be miraculous if they were, and of course one must continue to hope – but we're both wise enough to realise it's most unlikely. I very much fear that Mother has been affected by living in the tropics for too long, and that her latest letter was written whilst she was having some sort of brain-fever. I do hope Grandma can talk some sense into her before it goes any further, otherwise goodness only knows what she'll come up with next.

By the time you read this, I shall have written back telling her that my life here is busy and fulfilling, and although I will of course go to Australia for a holiday after the war, I will not be settling there. I've met a chap, you see, and we're rather keen on one another. But more of that in my next letter, for now I have work to do and must dash.

Stay firm, Sarah, and don't let Mummy bully you – and please, please, think long and hard about Delaney. It would be too awful to think of you spending the rest of your life in regret, and in this time of terrible uncertainty, we must grab every chance of happiness that comes our way.

Please give my love to Peggy, Ron and all the others at Beach View. I do miss you all.

TTFN, Jane. Xx

Sarah put the letter away and crushed the butt of her cigarette beneath her boot. Dearest Jane, how very much she'd evolved from that childlike girl who'd left Singapore almost three years ago, reliant on Sarah and lacking self-confidence. Her letter spoke volumes about her character, her energy and enthusiasm, and it gladdened Sarah's heart to know she was well, happy and perhaps in love for the first time. It was also good to know that her sister's opinion of their mother's plans mirrored her own and that she felt just as strongly about it all. However, her advice on Delaney could not be heeded, for it was too late.

She felt the prick of tears and impatiently

blinked them away as she reached for Delaney's letter and held it to her heart. She had made her choice, now she must live with it regardless of whether Philip survived or not. And even if he had, he might not want to marry her. They both must have been changed by this war – Philip especially after being taken prisoner by the Japs – and she was certainly not the naïve girl he'd proposed to back in Singapore.

Sarah thought back to that protected, privileged life they'd led. They'd both been too young, unprepared for what the outside world was about to throw at them, and in consequence they'd been made to mature very quickly. And now Philip was in the hands of the Japanese and she had broken her vow to love him always by giving her heart to Delaney.

Her gaze fell on Delaney's letter and she ached at the knowledge that she'd lost him. But she had meant what she'd said to Peggy that awful night she'd let her read her mother's devastating letter. If Philip was still alive when this war was over, and wanted to marry her, then she would learn to love him again and be the very best wife she could be.

And yet she knew that despite the sacrifice and good intentions to atone for breaking her promise to Philip, a piece of her heart would always be Delaney's – a very secret part which she would keep locked away except for those quiet, still moments she knew would come when the need to remember was too powerful to resist.

Sarah's fingers trembled as she opened his letter. It was only a few lines long, but it broke her heart.

My dearest girl,

I sadly accept your reasons for ending it between us, but love and admire you even more for the strength you're showing in doing what you feel is right. My heart will always be yours, my sweet English rose, and should fate be kind enough to see me through this war, I will return home to America and continue to hope that one day you might need me.
Delaney

Sarah folded the letter away, buried her face in her hands and wept.

4

Ron bolted the Anchor door after the last customer. The lunchtime session was over, and it would be four hours before the pub was opened again – so the afternoon stretched before him, the confusion over where he stood with Rosie still unresolved.

They'd had little time to talk during the busy two hours, but he had managed to tell her about her letter going astray, and how he'd spent most of the three weeks worrying over where she'd gone with Major Radwell – and if she was planning to return.

Rosie had been horrified to learn that Ethel had kept the letter out of spite, and that her own swift departure with Radwell had caused him such anguish. But on hearing that Ethel and her cohort, the odious Olive Grayson, were now in prison for stealing food from the Red Cross distribution centre to sell on the black market, she'd perked up no end.

Ron had been a bit miffed that she'd treated his concerns over Radwell so lightly, but as there hadn't been time to question her further, he'd had to put his feelings aside and get on with serving the customers. Now the pub was closed, he had no idea what Rosie's plans were for the afternoon, and sensing he shouldn't push his luck by asking her out to lunch or assuming she'd even want his company, he began to clean the tables, empty ashtrays and tidy up.

'It looks as if it's a lovely day out there,' she said, glancing through the window. 'Why don't we take those sandwiches you made yesterday to the old ruins, and let Monty get some exercise? You could fetch Harvey on the way.'

Ron's heart missed a beat at this unexpected invitation. 'To be sure, those sandwiches will be curling and dry by now. Why don't I treat you to some fish and chips – or lunch at the Officers' Club?'

She smiled at him and shook her head. 'The sandwiches have been wrapped in a damp tea towel and kept in the fridge, so they're fine – and the dogs have been indoors all day and need some exercise.' She eased off her high heels and headed for the stairs. 'I'll just get changed into something more comfortable and dig out the picnic blanket and hamper. Grab a few bottled beers, will you? That climb will be thirsty work.'

Ron looked down at his polished brogues and carefully pressed twill trousers and gave a sigh. He could get changed, he supposed, but other than his suit, he possessed only his scruffy old corduroys which had to be held up by thick string – not at all suitable to impress a lady. He fished six bottles of beer from under the counter and went to collect his hat and tweed jacket from the hall, deciding he'd just change his shoes and hope Peggy could get any grass stains out of his trousers.

Rosie came downstairs in flat shoes, high-waisted cream linen trousers and a blue twinset. She'd tied a matching blue silk scarf in her hair, freshened her red lipstick, and was carrying the picnic basket and rug. 'Let's get out of here,' she said cheerfully, handing over the rug and basket, and clipping the lead to an excited Monty's collar.

Ron's heart swelled at how lovely she looked, and having placed the beer bottles inside the basket, he opened the side door with a flourish to let her pass. 'It's not like you to want to walk the hills,' he teased as they headed down Camden Road.

'I know, but I've spent the last three weeks cooped up in various dark and dingy places dealing with unpleasant people and solicitors, and I need to get out, breathe fresh air and stretch my legs.'

They walked in companionable silence until they reached Beach View. All was quiet but for the soft murmur of voices coming from Cordelia's room, so Ron could only assume everything was all right. Not wanting to get involved in any more domestic chores, he swiftly changed into his walking boots and closed the kitchen door on the cat to stop her from following them. Minutes later he and Rosie were traipsing up the hill with both dogs galloping ahead of them in gay abandon.

Rosie was not a natural hill walker, preferring to potter around the shops in high heels, and certainly didn't have the breath to talk as she heroically tried to keep pace with him.

Ron slowed and waited patiently when she had to stop to catch her breath and ease her leg muscles. He kept his thoughts and hopes to himself as they reached the brow and began to tramp across the gentler undulating clifftops. Rosie seemed to be in a good mood; she hadn't given him the cold shoulder and it was a beautiful day despite the racket the planes were making overhead. He'd let her guide the conversation, and not badger her with all the questions that were clamouring in his head – then perhaps he'd know better where he stood.

Passing the track that led down to Tamarisk Bay where his son Frank lived with Pauline, they headed across the wind-flattened grass to the ruined farmhouse. Whilst the dogs hurtled about exploring every blade of grass and thicket of gorse, Ron spread the blanket in a sheltered, sunny corner and placed the basket by his feet.

Rosie plumped down beside him, stripped off her cardigan and tried to get her breath back. 'I always forget how steep that hill is,' she panted. 'But my goodness, the view's worth it, isn't it?'

'Aye,' he agreed. ''Tis a grand sight, so it is.'

In the brief respite between the bombers and

fighter planes taking off and landing, they could hear the skylarks, and they admired the shimmering water in the Channel, the sweep of blue sky and the startling white of the hovering gulls. Choosing to ignore the distant sounds of warfare drifting over from France and the ugly gun emplacements that were dotted along the cliffs, they regarded instead the green hills which swept away from the craggy chalk cliffs, down to the dark woodlands of the Cliffe estate, the fields of ripening wheat and the sprawl of the Cliffe aerodrome which swam in the haze of heat.

Rosie let him light her cigarette and, whilst Ron filled his pipe, idly watched the two dogs haring about. 'You'd hardly know there was a war on up here, would you?' she murmured a while later, her eyes closed, her face lifted to the sun. 'It's so still and peaceful.'

As if on cue a squadron of Tornados screamed overhead, and she broke into a chuckle. 'I obviously spoke too soon,' she shouted above the noise. 'Let's eat. I'm starving.'

Ron opened the basket and discovered not only sandwiches, but a packet of biscuits, a flask of tea, a dog's bowl and a large bottle of water. He set the bowl on a flat bit of ground and poured some water for the dogs, then offered Rosie a beer and a sandwich.

She stubbed out her cigarette and, between bites of the sandwich, sipped on the beer as the planes continued to thunder overhead, making conversation almost impossible.

Harvey and Monty saw the sandwiches and came charging back to drink noisily from the bowl and beg for something to eat.

Ron had slipped a few dog biscuits into his pocket before leaving the house and he gave them a couple in the forlorn hope they would suffice. They didn't, of course, and when they began to snuffle about in the basket, he slammed down the lid and shooed them away.

They sloped off in high dudgeon until a rabbit caught their attention and they went charging off in pursuit. Ron sipped his beer and puffed on his pipe, content simply to be with Rosie in his favourite place. But he did wish she'd give him some clue as to what was on her mind.

'Thanks for telling me about Ethel and my letter,' she said as soon as there was a brief lull between flights. 'I'm not surprised she's been thrown into prison with that awful Olive, but I do feel for poor Stan. How's he coping?'

Stan had been Ron's pal since they were boys, and they'd survived the horrors of the Somme together and come home to pick up the threads of their lives again. 'He's getting over it and running the station as usual,' Ron replied. 'He was knocked for six over it all, but Ethel's young Ruby is standing by him, as is his niece, April.' He took the pipe from his mouth and studied the burning tobacco. 'Stan's made of stern stuff, Rosie. With all the love and support he has, he'll pull through.'

Rosie nodded. 'I'll make a point of going to see him tomorrow. I've always liked Stan, but he should never have married that cow in the first place. We all knew what she was like, but–'

'I know,' said Ron. 'Love is blind and makes fools of us all.'

She raised an eyebrow and changed the subject. 'There was a lot of talk in the pub today about that V-1 attack in London,' she said. 'It came as a terrible shock to learn you and Peggy had suffered the same thing in Havelock Road. Thank goodness you all came out of it unscathed.' She grasped Ron's hand and gave it a squeeze. 'It would have been awful if I'd lost you,' she said unsteadily.

Ron's heartbeat stuttered, and he returned the pressure on her fingers. 'It'll take more than a V-1 to get rid of the Reilly clan,' he said gruffly before ramming his pipe stem between his teeth. 'The problem is that most of Havelock Road is now a pile of rubble and we've been lumbered with Doris.'

'Oh, no, poor Peggy,' Rosie breathed. 'How is she coping?'

Ron told her about the row that morning. 'To be sure, she'll not let that woman boss her about any more,' he concluded. 'I'm thinking Doris knows she's overstepped the mark and will behave herself from now on.'

'Families are a pain, aren't they?' she sighed, freeing her hand from his grasp and reaching for another beer. 'I could certainly have done without James's lot.'

Ron's attention sharpened. 'Was it very bad up there?'

Rosie nodded and the light in her eyes dimmed at the memory. 'By the time I got there, they'd already tried to sign the papers at the asylum so James's body would be released to them for burial.'

She bit her lip. 'His sister actually told them I'd

given them permission as I didn't want to be bothered about it,' she said bitterly. 'They didn't know that upon receiving that telegram, I'd immediately telephoned the head administrator and warned him this might happen, and that under no circumstances were they to have access to him.'

Ron stayed silent as he absorbed this and felt a stab of guilt that he hadn't been by her side at the time.

'The biggest shock came when I arrived at the funeral parlour only to be asked who I was and what relationship I had with the deceased. It turned out his sister and parents were already in the back office, and after the undertaker had been to talk to them, he returned to me looking very shamefaced. It seems they'd said they were the only family, and denied vehemently that I had any rights to organise his funeral.'

She lit another cigarette, and Ron felt his heart clench as he noticed that her hands were trembling. Yet he made no move towards her and kept silent, realising she needed to let out all the anguish she'd clearly been holding back.

'I had to show him my marriage certificate, my power of attorney and the papers I'd signed at the asylum before he would allow me into that damned office.' She took a sharp drag on her cigarette. 'You can have no idea of how furious I was, but I tell you straight, Ron, if I'd had a gun I'd've shot the blooming lot of them.'

'And I wouldn't have blamed you,' Ron muttered.

Rosie shot him a fleeting smile. 'The atmosphere in that office could have been cut with a knife,' she continued. 'The poor undertaker realised there would be a blazing row and fled. It was all horribly embarrassing, but I wasn't about to cave in to them.'

Ron grinned. Rosie had always been feisty, so he wasn't at all surprised.

Rosie didn't return his smile. 'I told them what I thought of them, and they didn't hold back either. They went on about my relationship with you, the shame I'd brought on the family by owning a pub, and the way I'd had James committed to that asylum when I should have been a proper wife to him and nursed him at home.'

She gave a snort of derision. 'As if that had ever been a possibility. He was way beyond my care and far too violent a risk to himself as well as everyone else. But they chose to ignore that fact, of course.'

She took a breath and stubbed out the cigarette with unnecessary vigour. 'To top all that, they then accused me of forcing him to give me power of attorney over his estate so I could cut them out of the will.'

'Where there's a will, there's always a greedy relative,' said Ron.

Rosie nodded. 'You can say that again. The estate came to a sizeable amount despite the years of hospital fees that had come out of it – and to be honest, I'd always felt awkward about being the sole beneficiary. But James was quite sane when he wrote that will and organised the power of attorney before he went off to war in 1914, and adamant that I should inherit it all.'

'He probably suspected his family were grasping and wanted to protect you.' Ron regarded her sharply from beneath his brows. 'I hope you didn't give them anything after the disgusting way they behaved.'

'If they'd actually mourned his passing and been kinder to me, I would probably have given them something,' she admitted. 'As it was, I decided to give a chunk to charity and keep the rest of the investments to see me through once I retire from the Anchor.'

'I'm sorry you had to go through all that,' Ron murmured. 'No wonder you were so exhausted when you got back. But what of the Major? Where was he when all this was going on?'

'Henry was at my side throughout, thank goodness. I couldn't have got through it without him.'

Ron put his pipe in his jacket pocket and tried to quell the sudden dart of jealousy as he watched her gaze drift beyond the ruined flint walls to the sea and sky.

'He was marvellous,' she murmured. 'James's sister and mother were like two spitting cats, and believe me, Ron, I was in the mood to give as good as I got until Henry stepped in and defused the situation.'

'And how did he do that?' asked Ron, the jealousy stabbing again.

'He quietly and firmly took command, which silenced those grasping, vicious harpies, and then spoke directly to James's father – who was clearly uncomfortable about the whole situation, but not man enough to stand up to his wife and daughter. Henry reminded him that it was time for mourning a lost son, not for airing old grievances, throwing accusations about or haggling over his son's will.'

Rosie's mouth twisted in disgust. 'James's father has always been spineless, but he actually had the decency to look ashamed when Henry went on to say that the memory of James and how he'd once been was being tarnished by this tasteless and unedifying fracas. Henry also pointed out that James's final wish to be cremated had been entrusted to me, and as his widow, it was my duty to see it through despite their objections.'

Ron grudgingly admired the man for standing up to them, but it didn't lessen his mistrust of his motives for doing so. 'And how did they take that?'

'Not too well at first,' she admitted. 'They didn't like the idea of cremation at all – which actually I could understand, it being a bit out of the ordinary – and wanted to bury James in their local church-yard. But Henry's measured tone and undoubted air of command silenced them in the end,' she continued, her admiration for the Major clear in her expression. 'James's wishes were carried out and I brought his ashes home to be scattered on the beach.'

She closed her eyes, hugged her knees, and took a tremulous breath. 'The years of James's war brought torment to his mind and soul, keep-ing him as much a prisoner as those asylum walls. In one of his rare lucid moments early on in his sickness, he told me he wanted the wind and the sea to carry him to freedom – not to spend eternity in darkness beneath the ground.'

Ron thought about his time in the trenches where horror upon horror had come thick and fast in unrelenting waves. Some men, like Rosie's

James, were broken by it, others were made stronger, but for all of them who'd survived, that nightmare still came to haunt them in unexpected moments, and Ron had often wondered if the dead had been the lucky ones.

He shook off those dark memories. 'I can understand why he wanted to be free,' he murmured, cautiously putting his arm round her shoulders and drawing her to his side. 'He's finally at peace, Rosie. The torment he suffered is at an end, and he would want you to remember him the way he was before he went to war.'

She nodded against his shoulder. 'It's how I always think of him – handsome, young, full of vigour, waving excitedly from that damned train that was going to take him to hell.'

He held her closer as she sobbed. 'To be sure, we were all changed by that war,' he murmured, the unwanted memories rolling back in. He determinedly banished them and concentrated on Rosie, who was very much alive and in need of his consolation.

'I wish I could have been with you to shield you from all the spite and hurt you've had to go through these past weeks,' he said softly into her hair. 'But 'tis grateful I am to the Major for standing by you.'

She slowly eased from his embrace, dried her eyes and made a concerted effort to keep further tears at bay. 'I know you don't want to hear this, Ron, but he was a great comfort,' she said eventually. 'I was seething and ready to do battle, but he was calm and reasonable, countering every argument with logic, wearing them down until they saw they had no case to answer.'

'I would have been the same,' he said.

She shot him a wan smile. 'I'm sure you would once you'd punched a nose or two. But you weren't there.'

'I would have been if you'd told me,' he protested.

'I couldn't get hold of you, which is why I wrote you that letter.' She looked at him with some exasperation. 'Don't tell me you're still sore about Henry going with me?'

'Not at all,' he lied.

'Oh, Ron, do get a grip. Henry's a lovely man and an attractive one too. I admit I was drawn to him. But for all his lovely manners and sharp suits, he's not you – will never be you.'

Ron's heart missed a beat. 'Drawn to him?' he rasped.

She looked at him evenly. 'It was a mutual attraction, Ron, born from spending hours together during what turned out to be a harrowing time. He comforted me and bolstered my spirits, made sure I ate properly and even walked Monty. He was an attentive companion, and did all he could to make things easier for me.'

The blasted man was a positive saint, Ron thought bitterly, his hackles rising. 'And what sort of comfort did he offer, Rosie?'

Rosie held his gaze. 'He held me when I cried. He listened when I needed to talk and was there when I couldn't stand being alone.'

'How very noble of him,' Ron said sourly.

Rosie lifted her chin. 'Yes, he was noble – and you've no cause to be so bitter about it,' she said

79

tightly. 'He's a good, honourable man and...' She faltered and her gaze drifted away. 'It was entirely my fault things went a bit haywire,' she said in a rush.

Ron went cold and he stared at her. 'What do you mean, haywire?'

She avoided his gaze. 'Not what you're thinking,' she said hurriedly. 'It was just a kiss.'

'You *kissed* him?'

'It meant nothing, really it didn't,' she gabbled, finally looking at him. 'I was tired and feeling emotional and one minute I was sobbing in his arms, the next we were kissing. It lasted mere seconds, Ron, I swear. I suddenly realised what I was doing and immediately broke away.'

Ron's insides clenched, and he felt sick.

Rosie's hands fluttered helplessly. 'It was all frightfully awkward after that, for I realised he was smitten and had been hoping I felt the same way.' She dropped her chin and plucked at the fabric of her trousers. 'He'd taken my relief and gratitude for something more, you see – which led to him going down on one knee and proposing.'

Acid burned in his throat, every nerve and tendon as taut as wire. 'He did *what?*'

Rosie's gaze slid away. 'You heard.'

'Well, I hope you told him where to get off behaving like that when he knew how vulnerable you were,' stormed Ron.

'There's no need to shout at me, Ron. Of course I turned him down,' Rosie snapped.

'I'm glad to hear it,' he replied, barely mollified and still as tense as steel.

'He got carried away in the moment, Ron, and

I felt an utter heel at rejecting him. It was awful to see him so hurt after all he'd done for me.'

Ron's emotions were going helter-skelter with relief, pain and shock at Rosie's revelation, and it took a long moment before he could respond. 'I hope you aren't regretting that decision,' he managed finally.

'Not for one minute,' she replied solemnly. 'He's a fine man and will make some woman a wonderful, caring husband. But he's not the one for me.'

Ron still burned with jealousy as he looked into her lovely eyes. 'To be sure, Rosie girl, you know how to tear at a man's heart,' he said brokenly.

She reached out to touch his face, her eyes once more bright with tears. 'Oh, Ron, I didn't want to hurt you. I'm not proud of what I did, and there's really no excuse for it, but I wanted there to be no secrets between us. Not if we're to have any sort of future together.'

Hope battled with suspicion, anguish and jealousy, but she'd hurt him deeply and he remained cautious. 'So, you've told me everything that went on between you?' At her nod, he continued, 'Where is the Major now? Do you plan to see him again?'

'No, Ron,' she said evenly. 'He's rented a house in Fulham and is planning to write a book. If he's successful at getting it published, he's promised to send me a copy. He now understands how I feel about you, and has apologised for any hurt his actions might have caused, so that's an end to it.'

Ron knew her well enough to see she was truly sorry, and if he was ever to call this wonderful, desirable woman his own he had to rein in all jealousy and mistrust and grab the moment. He reached for her hand. 'Does this mean we can go back to how we were?' he asked tentatively.

She smiled. 'Together yes – but not as we were,' she said.

He looked at her in bewilderment. 'But I thought–'

'I've had a long time to mull over things and have come to a decision,' she said evenly. 'You'll need to shape up, Ron. And I don't just mean sharpening up your appearance, although it's already a vast improvement on the old rags you used to wear, but by paying me more attention and not taking me or my feelings for granted.'

'I've never taken you for granted,' he gasped.

'Yes, you have,' she retorted. 'You come and go as you please, sometimes disappearing for days without letting me know where you are or what you're up to. You've always assumed I'll forgive you when you've been up to some mischief or other and come crawling back full of Irish charm and far too much whiskey, expecting me to fall into your arms without a murmur.'

She took a breath and hurried on over his protest. 'In the normal course of events, I've been willing to put up with it all because I love you. But hearing about you and Gloria Stevens sparking in the Crown when you knew how I felt about you going in there was the last straw. This merry-go-round ride we've been on is at an end, Ron,' she said firmly. 'Go near her or her pub again, and that will be the end of you and me.'

Ron firmly damped down on the thought that this was a bit rich coming from a woman who'd confessed to kissing another man, and held back on a bitter retort. 'We only went in there because she has a snug where we could talk privately,' he replied. 'It wasn't my fault the ferrets got loose and caused mayhem.'

'Nothing's ever your fault, is it?' she said, folding her arms at her waist and eyeing him with some amusement. 'Think about it, Ron. Going into a pub, any pub, with ferrets in your pockets is simply asking for trouble – doing it in the Crown and showing yourself up with Gloria is bordering on madness.'

He had no answer to this so remained silent.

There was a sparkle in her eyes as she regarded him. 'As for trying to serenade me with that terrible voice of yours...' She giggled. 'I'd rather you didn't do that again.'

'Then how can I persuade you I've turned over a new leaf and will never do any of those things again? Would a promise suffice, or...' He fumbled in his jacket pocket and pulled out the little jewellery box. 'Perhaps if I asked you to marry me, would that convince you?'

She looked down at the sparkling ruby and diamond ring and gently closed the box before handing it back. 'Perhaps one day, Ron, but not now.'

His spirits plummeted. 'But why, Rosie? We're both free, and this is what we've planned and waited for, for years.'

'It's too soon, and I'm not ready,' she replied.

'Then what *do* you want, Rosie?' he asked in despair.

'I want to be taken dancing and to the pictures. I want to share picnics with you and snuggle up on the couch after closing time to listen to the wireless without you badgering me to sleep with you.' She regarded him evenly. 'I'm not ready for that either, not so soon after losing James. It wouldn't feel right.'

'Then I don't understand,' he muttered in bewilderment.

'I want to be wooed.'

'Wooed?' he breathed.

She nodded solemnly. 'Wooed. Which means being treated like a lady, being confided in and cherished with flowers and the occasional treat – being noticed and cared for whatever mood I'm in, and never taken for granted.'

Ron was perplexed and couldn't think of anything to say, for he'd always thought he'd regarded Rosie as a lady to be cherished and spoilt.

She saw his frown and broke into a broad smile. 'If all that is acceptable, you can make a start by giving me a kiss.'

Ron's bewilderment fled, and without a thought of how on earth he was going to comply with this new regimen, he joyfully gathered her into his arms and kissed the very breath from her.

5

Peggy emerged from the factory after her seven-hour shift and went to the crèche to pick up Daisy. She could see Fred the Fish and his Cockney wife Lil at the kerb in the delivery van, and not wanting to keep them waiting, hurried over with Daisy slung across her hip.

'Hello, ducks,' said Lil, reaching for Daisy and giving her a kiss and cuddle. 'My word, this one's growing a mile a minute!' she exclaimed. She put her free arm around Peggy's waist. 'And how's you today, Peg? You looks a bit tired, if yer don't mind me saying. Are you still in shock from that blooming bomb?'

'It's been a long day, but I'm fine,' Peggy assured her. 'Are you sure it's not too much bother having Daisy as well as those boys to look after?'

'Lawks almighty, none of them ain't no trouble,' said Lil with a dismissive wave of her plump hand. 'Them boys is as good as gold now they've settled down wiv us, and it's lovely to have a little girl to play with again now our two are all grown up.'

She climbed in beside Fred, with Daisy on her lap, and Peggy squashed in for the ride up to the Memorial Hospital to visit Danuta, the little Polish refugee who'd once been Peggy's evacuee and who was now recovering from the terrible injuries inflicted by the Gestapo. Fred and Lil had no idea of the part Danuta had played behind enemy lines after she'd left Beach View, and thought she'd fallen victim to a London bombing raid, but as she was someone Peggy cared for, they were happy to help out.

Fred turned the ignition and the rather smelly old delivery van wheezed and groaned out of Camden Road and up the High Street. Fred was an old pal of Ron's, and well into his sixties. He and Lil ran the local fish shop in Camden Road and lived three streets away from Peggy. They had raised their two girls and seen them fly the nest a long while ago. There were no grandchildren yet, much to their disappointment, but when they saw the plight of the four little brothers who'd lived next door to them, they took them in in their kind-hearted way and formally adopted them.

The children had already lost their father in the first battle of El Alamein when their mother was killed during an air raid on the factory estate. Bewildered and afraid, those little boys had blossomed in their care, and were now a tremendous source of pride to both of them.

'How are the boys?' asked Peggy as the old van struggled over the humped bridge by the station and on up the steep hill into the countryside.

'Doing ever so well,' said Lil with a beaming smile. 'Johnnie's just sat his exams for the grammar school, and 'is teacher reckons 'e'll pass with flying colours. Graham's top of 'is class in English and arithmetic; Ian's doing really well at sport, and little Billy will go up into the secondary school next term.'

She jiggled Daisy on her lap and made her giggle. 'It's a bit of a bind getting them all to school 'cos of course we has to go out of town now for the older ones, but it'll get easier when Billy joins them.'

'How will you cope with the grammar school?' asked Peggy, knowing it was almost eight miles away.

'We'll manage,' said Fred firmly. 'The boy's bright, and travel restrictions and petrol rationing won't stop us getting him there. If push comes to shove, then he'll have to go and board with my

86

nephew who lives nearby. He'll be all right there, although we'll miss not having him around. We'll probably bring him home at the weekends.'

Fred pulled up in the driveway of the Memorial Hospital. 'I'll be back for you in an hour as usual,' he said. 'And don't worry about Daisy. We'll feed her, and Lil will drop her off at Beach View to put her to bed.'

'Thank you both,' Peggy said earnestly. 'I don't know how I'd have managed without you giving me a lift every night.'

'Glad to do it, Peg,' said Lil. 'And from what you've said, it won't be long before that girl is well enough for you to bring her home.' She grimaced. 'Bloody Hitler and his bloody bombs. I tell you straight, Peg, I've just about had enough of it all.'

'Language, Lil,' Frank reproved with a frown and a glance at a wide-eyed Daisy who was taking it all in.

Peggy chuckled, kissed Daisy and climbed out. 'See you in an hour.'

Fred tooted the horn and drove off, and Peggy stood for a moment gazing at the burgeoning flower beds and the sturdy walls of the old manor house, needing to catch her breath before she went to see Danuta. The day had felt endless, and she had yet to face Doris and try to make peace with her, but in the tranquillity of this lush garden it was easy to shed the stresses and strains and find calm again.

There was no sign of Matron Billings, who could only be described as a tartar, and a bad-tempered one at that. Peggy hurried along the corridors, hearing the rattle of food trolleys and the squeak of rubber-soled shoes as the nurses bustled about and patients prepared for their evening meal.

The usual hospital smells of boiled cabbage and disinfectant accompanied her as she nodded greetings to the nurses she'd come to know during the course of her visits, first with Kitty Pargeter, and now with Danuta.

Kitty had been brought here after she'd crashed a plane she'd been delivering for the ATA. She'd lost most of one leg, but her will to carry on regardless proved to be strong, and she'd learnt to manage the prosthesis during her stay at Beach View and had ended up marrying Wing Commander Roger Makepeace and returning to flying. Now she was expecting her first baby and waiting in hope to hear from Roger, who was a POW in the same camp as her brother, Freddy, Peggy's son-in-law, Martin, and young Cissy's American flier Randolph Stevens.

Peggy made a mental note to try and ring Cissy at the aerodrome tonight. She hadn't seen her since before her twenty-second birthday the previous month, or even heard from her for a while, and she needed to be reassured that her girl was coping now the activity up there was reaching fever-pitch. Cissy was right on the front line of the action and probably witnessing too many aircraft crashing or blowing up as they came in torn to bits by enemy gunfire and tried to land – and of course she'd have seen the long lists of those who had not returned, and felt the gnawing anxiety every time the squadron left on another sortie.

Peggy turned the corner and headed down yet another long corridor. Due to the injuries she'd suffered, and the questions they might elicit from the other patients, Danuta was still in the private room that overlooked the sweep of lawn and colourful flower beds at the back of the manor house. She'd been at the Memorial for several months since escaping from the Gestapo, and it had been touch and go as to whether she would survive – but Danuta's spirit was strong and determined and it seemed that at last she was on the road to recovery.

As the door was ajar, Peggy went in without knocking only to come to an abrupt halt.

Danuta was not in bed as usual, covered with sheets and blankets, but struggling to stand un-aided on her tortured feet as the nurse divested her of her nightdress to replace it with a fresh one.

Peggy saw how thin she was, her ribs, hips and backbone jutting through papery flesh that was scarred by beatings and numerous burns. Her legs were similarly marked, and around her ankles were the unmistakable scars left by tight shackles. Peggy gave an involuntary gasp and the nurse looked up angrily.

'You shouldn't be in here,' she snapped. 'Wait outside until I've finished.'

'No,' said Danuta. 'She can see. I am not ashamed.'

Peggy was in a daze as she stepped into the room and closed the door behind her, for Danuta was twenty-seven, but now resembled a very thin, fragile thirteen. She had pushed away the fresh nightdress and stood before her naked, the evidence of what the Gestapo had done to her all too clear. Peggy bit hard on the inside of her cheek to stop herself from crying, but the pitiful sight made her tremble inside.

'Is not pretty, I think, but they did not win.' Danuta ran her bandaged hands through the jagged tufts of her hair and looked at her defiantly. 'The burns are fading and my nails and hair have already started to grow again. Please not cry, Peggy.'

'How can I not?' she said, the tears falling despite her sterling effort to keep them at bay. 'Oh, Danuta, my sweet girl. What did they do to you?'

Danuta took the nightdress from the nurse and almost nonchalantly pulled it over her head until it covered her from neck to ankle. She looked at Peggy and grinned. 'They made me angry and more determined than ever to survive. I think, as you say, they are laughing on the other side of their faces now we are closing in on them.'

Peggy was astounded that the girl could even smile, let alone make a joke about it, and she was lost for words.

Danuta sank onto the bed as the nurse began to tidy up. 'Come, sit beside me, Mama Peggy, and tell me how you are.'

'I'm fine,' she stuttered, perching awkwardly on the edge of the bed, her handbag clutched in her lap whilst the nurse bustled about and finally left the room with a backward glare of disapproval.

'You are being brave too, I think,' Danuta replied. 'I can see you are tired and troubled. It is a long way to come to visit me after you have been working, and you are still shocked by what happened in the park.'

'Yes, I'm still shaken up, but it'll pass,' said

Peggy, unwilling to talk about the row with her sister and the unexpected moments of sheer terror that caught her out every time she heard the buzz of an engine in the sky. Danuta had witnessed and suffered far worse things – the scars on her body only the outward sign of what had been done to her – the rest hidden inside and in her mind. If Danuta could smile and make light of them, then so would she.

Danuta regarded her steadily and then smiled. 'You will not have to worry about coming to see me very soon, for the doctor is saying that if I keep improving, I can come home to Beach View next week.'

'Really?' Peggy breathed. 'Oh, Danuta, that would be wonderful. But are you sure you'll be ready? You've had a big operation and–'

Danuta placed her bandaged hand on Peggy's shoulder. 'I am strong like you. A bit shaken up, but it will pass and I'll be fine,' she teased.

Peggy chuckled. 'Now you're being cheeky.'

'Ah, yes, but it has made you smile. And that is a good thing, I think. Yes?'

'Yes,' said Peggy, taking her cautiously into her arms and holding her to her heart. 'And from now on, Danuta, you will know only good things. I promise.'

Fred dropped Peggy off at the end of the alleyway, and with a couple of toots from his horn, set off for his home three streets away. Peggy hurried along the rutted path, hungry for her evening meal and elated by Danuta's news, but nervous about facing Doris. She didn't want any more ructions today, for there had been enough drama already, and she could only hope that her sister was in a conciliatory mood.

Peggy opened the scullery door and listened to the bright chatter coming from the kitchen. Her chicks were home by the sound of it, along with Ron and young Fran's Robert. Her heart lightened and she went up the concrete steps, taking off her scarf and jacket along the way.

It was still light enough to keep the curtains open, and the glow of the fire in the range chased away the slight chill that still came when the sun began to sink towards the western hills. She took one look at the bright faces round her table and knew something was up. 'What is it?' she asked. 'What are you all grinning about?'

Fran got up from the table and went to stand by Robert, who was looking positively full of himself as he placed a protective arm about her waist. Her lovely face was radiant as she swept back her Titian curls so that the diamond on her finger sparked fire in the last rays of the sun.

Peggy squeaked in delight. 'You've done it at last,' she breathed. 'Oh, Fran, Robert, I'm so happy for you both.' She rushed across the room and threw her arms about them. 'When's the wedding? Are you having an engagement party?' she babbled, examining the beautiful ring through happy tears.

Everyone laughed at this, for Peggy's enthusiasm for romance was well known. Robert, who'd always been painfully shy, went a deeper scarlet as he chuckled. 'One thing at a time, Aunt Peggy. I've yet to write and ask her father's permission.'

Peggy's delight was tempered by the knowledge that there could be ructions ahead, for Fran's family were staunch Catholics, and Robert was a Protestant. 'I'm sure he'll be delighted to have such a handsome, clever son-in-law,' she said, stoutly refusing to let the thought mar the occasion. 'It's utterly silly to let religion get in the way of anything – especially as we're fighting a war to get rid of such prejudices.'

'Easier said than done, Aunt Peg,' said Fran with a lightness that belied the cloud of worry that dimmed her green eyes. 'To be sure, you've not met my father.'

'I'll be writing to him,' said Ron from his chair by the wireless. 'He'll see sense if I have anything to do with it.'

Robert pushed his fingers through his brutally short dark hair as he eyed Ron warily. 'Thanks, Ron. I appreciate your support, but if anyone has to persuade Fran's father it will have to be me.'

'It'll be terribly difficult to do that while travel to and from Ireland is banned,' fretted Peggy. 'Will you have to wait until the war's over before you can get married?'

Fran glanced up at Robert and then shot them all a beaming smile which chased away the doubts and lit up her eyes. 'We might just have to go ahead anyway. Da will blow a fuse, but hopefully, once this war is over and he's met Robert, he'll have calmed down.'

Peggy wasn't sure this would be a wise course of action, for if Fran's father was a dyed-in-the-wool traditionalist who was against mixed marriages, he could very well shun his oldest daughter and refuse to let the rest of the family have anything to do with her. She caught Fran's eye and knew then that beneath the defiant, bright smile was a worried girl.

Robert broke into her thoughts. 'I managed to telephone my mother this afternoon, and she's thrilled, so there are no worries there,' he said, hugging Fran to his side. 'I suspect that once the travel ban is lifted, she'll be down from Warwick to find out for herself why I love this girl so very much.'

Peggy smiled at him with great fondness. He and Doris's son, Anthony, had become best pals when they'd worked together at the Fort for the MOD, and it was through Anthony's persuading him to join the local orchestra that he'd met Fran. Robert played the saxophone, and Fran had borrowed Doris's violin, and together they made the most beautiful music. Impatient with her soppy thoughts, she poured a cup of tea.

'I wish I had something stronger to celebrate with,' she said. 'But I'm afraid tea, or a rather cheap sherry, is all I have.'

'The sherry's all gone, but I'll see if Rosie has a bottle of something before I have to leave for fire-watch duty,' said Ron, slipping on his coat.

Peggy looked at him in hopeful delight. 'Does that mean you two have made it up?' she asked.

'Aye, to be sure, the air is cleared.' He gave her a stern look from beneath his brows. 'But don't be getting ahead of yourself, Peggy, girl. There's to be no wedding yet.'

'But I thought–'

'Aye, well, I have to prove meself first before

she'll take me on,' he muttered, pulling on his old cap. 'She wants to be wooed.'

Peggy was unable to smother her giggles. 'Wooed?' she spluttered.

'Yes,' he replied, his expression determined as he shot a glare at the chortling girls. 'Though to be sure I've not a clue what that's supposed to mean.'

'Then I suggest you have a word with my Robert,' said Fran, kissing his cheek. 'He knows how to woo a girl.'

'Ach, 'tis not funny,' grumbled Ron. 'I don't know where you women get your daft ideas.'

'Before you go, Ron, I have some good news too,' said Peggy, 'Danuta will be coming home next week.' She was gratified to see the delight in his smile, but hurried on before he could say anything. 'You'll have to mend that window in Cissy's room – it still gets stuck – and sort out the lino. It's so worn I can see the wooden floor in places. And that bed leg needs tightening up. I don't want it collapsing on her.'

Ron made a great show of being put upon, but as no one was taken in by it, he grinned. 'Of course. I'll see to it all tomorrow,' he said before making his escape down the steps and out of the back door with Harvey at his heels.

Peggy was warmed by all the good news, but she still had Doris to sort out – and as there was no sign of her in the kitchen, she could only assume she was in her room. Not wanting to spoil the mood, she sipped her tea and lit a cigarette. 'I do so love weddings,' she said to no one in particular, 'even though I cry all the way through them and positively ruin my make-up.'

'You and Cordelia are completely hopeless,' teased Rita. 'I've never seen anyone get through quite so many handkerchiefs as you both did when Kitty married Roger.'

Peggy grinned and gently patted her face. 'You wait, young lady. When you get to my age and see a beloved girl walking down the aisle, you'll turn on the waterworks too.'

Rita grinned. 'If you say so, Aunty Peg. But I've decided that if I ever get married it will be at the registry office with as little fuss as possible.'

'Over my dead body,' said Peggy. 'When you get married, you'll have the whole works, or I'm not Peggy Reilly.' She shot a look at Fran and the other girls. 'And that goes for all of my chicks.'

She saw the stricken look on Sarah's face and felt a pang of remorse for not thinking before speaking. 'How's Cordelia?' she asked the room in general, hastily changing the subject.

'The Friars' Balsam is really helping and the doctor's very pleased with her,' said Fran. 'Her temperature is down and she's breathing much more easily.' She shot a loving look at Robert. 'We went up to tell her our news and she was all for coming downstairs.' She giggled. 'We had the devil's own job of persuading her it wouldn't be wise, and had to promise we'd take her up a glass of sherry to help her celebrate.'

'It was a big glass, an' all,' said Ivy, frowning. 'She knocked it back and was asleep within seconds. I don't reckon it went too well with them pills she's on.'

'She's fine,' soothed Fran. 'And sleeping like a baby. She probably won't wake until morning now, and feel all the better for it.'

Sarah took the plate out of the warming oven and placed it on the table. 'I checked Daisy just before you got home, and she's fast asleep too. So you sit down, Aunt Peg, and eat. You must be hungry after your long day.'

'Bless you, dear, yes, I am.' She sat down at the table and regarded the stew, which looked quite appetising, even though Ivy had been in charge of the cooking. She was about to tuck in when she suddenly remembered Doris. 'Oh, lawks,' she breathed. 'Where's my sister?'

'She's been banging about upstairs most of the day,' said Rita, 'and I only saw her when she came down to fetch her plate of supper.'

'Banging about?' Peggy was bewildered.

'I don't know what she was up to,' said Fran, 'but she did ask Robert to help her with something earlier. In all the excitement, I forgot to ask him what she'd wanted him to do.'

As Robert had gone upstairs to the bathroom, Peggy was unable to question him. 'What sort of mood was she in?' she asked warily.

Ivy shrugged. 'Hard to tell. She didn't say nothing to me, just swanned in, took her portion of stew and swanned out again, nose in the air like she could smell something 'orrid.'

Peggy groaned. 'That doesn't bode well.'

'Leave her to get on with it, I say,' Ivy retorted. 'You eat your tea and don't let her upset you. It were time she were taken down a peg or two.' She nudged Peggy and gave a cackle of laughter. 'A peg or two! Get it? A Peg certainly sorted her out this morning, and no mistake.'

Peggy's smile was polite as the others tittered. She hadn't found Ivy's joke at all funny, and could only hope that when she went upstairs to see Doris there wouldn't be a repeat of the earlier unpleasantness.

Robert came back into the room just as Ron returned with a bottle of gin and a crate of beer, which he deposited on the table. 'Rosie said congratulations, and there's a drink for you both behind the bar the next time you drop in.' He shot Robert a wink before heading off for fire-watch duty with Harvey.

Peggy decided she'd find out for herself what Doris had been up to. Once she'd finished the stew, she went to check on Daisy, who was indeed fast asleep and cuddling the knitted toy Lil had given her some time ago. With a longing look at the telephone, she slowly went upstairs, promising herself she'd ring Cissy as soon as she'd dealt with Doris.

Cordelia was asleep and breathing much easier, her silver hair glistening like frost in the light from the bedside lamp, her little face slightly flushed with the remains of her fever. Peggy carefully placed her library book and glasses on the table and softly kissed her forehead before switching off the light. Leaving the door open so they could hear if she called out, Peggy made her way along to the large front bedroom which had provided a brief home and respite to so many of her chicks during these past five war-torn years.

She tapped on the door.

'What do you want?'

'It's me,' said Peggy. She heard footsteps cross

the room and the key turn in the lock before the door was opened.

'I'm in no mood for an argument,' said Doris.

'Neither am I.' Peggy noted she was wearing the tweed skirt and twinset she'd taken back that morning, and which had been her favourite outfit for when she'd gone out to somewhere special. 'Can I come in?'

'I don't really have a say in the matter, do I?' Doris said tartly. 'You made it very plain this morning that this is your house, and you therefore have a right to come and go as you please.'

Refusing to rise to the bait, Peggy stepped in and closed the door behind her, fully intending to be pleasant. However, a swift glance round the room showed her exactly what Doris had been doing all day, and it set her seething.

The furniture had been shifted and added to from other parts of the house with little thought of how inconvenient that might be to everyone else. The heavy brocade curtains from the dining room had replaced the sprigged cotton ones over the bay window; the stool and kidney-shaped dressing table had been brought from Cissy's room; and one of the armchairs from the dining room was now placed by the gas fire, above which hung a large mirror, also from the dining room. The standard lamp from Ivy and Rita's room now stood in a corner; the rug from Fran and Sarah's room lay before the hearth; Peggy's linen cupboard had been raided of embroidered tablecloths which now covered the bedside tables; and Cordelia's spare eiderdown and lace-edged linen pillowcases and sheets adorned Doris's double bed.

To cap it all, Jim's dressing gown was hanging on the back of the door and the lovely, expensive nightdress he'd bought her the last Christmas he'd been home was draped over the foot of the bed.

She regarded her sister coldly. 'I came up to try and mend things between us – to actually apologise for what I said this morning and ask you to stay. But seeing what you've done has changed all that.'

She snatched the dressing gown from the door and gathered up the precious nightdress she'd been saving for Jim's homecoming. 'Your arrogance is unbelievable, Doris, and I'm lost for words.'

Doris had the grace to look uncomfortable. 'I didn't think you'd really mind,' she muttered.

'Which part of "you're not having this" didn't you understand, Doris?' Peggy hissed, clutching the nightwear to her chest. 'And what right have you to help yourself to other people's things without bothering to even ask?'

'You never use the dining room, and those curtains cut out the draught much better than those thin cotton things. I assumed the bedding and tablecloths were going spare. As for the bedroom furniture, Cissy hasn't lived here for at least two years, so she's hardly going to miss it, is she?'

Whilst Peggy stood dumbfounded, Doris lit a cigarette. 'I'd appreciate it if Ron would remove that ugly old dressing table. It's too heavy for me to shift.'

Peggy was trembling with rage. 'I tell you what, Doris. Ron will come tomorrow morning and take back Cissy's things as well as the standard lamp and rug. You can keep the damn chair and the bedclothes unless Cordelia needs them – they are hers, you know, not mine.'

'I wondered where you'd got the money to buy such good quality bedding,' said Doris. 'Look, Mar– Peggy, I know you're cross, but–'

'Cross?' snapped Peggy. 'Oh, I'm way beyond blooming cross! I'm bloody furious.'

Doris grimaced. 'I don't know what all the fuss is about, but language like that is most unbecoming – especially from a woman.'

Peggy clutched the nightwear in an attempt to cool down and resist hitting her sister again. 'Danuta is coming home next week and will go into Cissy's room, so that furniture is needed. And if you go into my room again and take things which you know damned well you shouldn't have, I really will show you the bloody door.'

Before Doris could say anything, she'd turned on her heel, stomped along the landing and run down the stairs, blinded with tears.

Reaching the sanctuary of her room, she quietly closed the door so she wouldn't wake Daisy, and then slumped onto the bed, the dressing gown held to her face so she could breathe in the essence of Jim which still lingered in the fabric.

'I'll kill her if she stays much longer,' she muttered to his photograph. 'Honestly, Jim, that woman is driving me demented.'

The light tap on the door roused her from her dark thoughts and she swiped back her tears as she went to answer it, hoping it wasn't Doris come to torment her again.

But it wasn't Doris. Peggy gasped in delight as

Cissy gathered her into her arms.

'Cissy? Oh, darling,' Peggy sighed tremulously. 'What a wonderful surprise! I was going to call you tonight.'

'What's the matter, Mum? Are you still in shock after that V-1?'

'How did you hear about that?' Peggy asked in dismay.

'It was hardly a secret, Mum, which is why I managed to persuade the Chief WAAF to let me come and visit.'

'I'm fine, really. Still a bit shaken, but it'll pass.'

Peggy looked at her beautiful daughter, with her radiant skin and worried expression. At twenty-two, Cissy had turned into a sophisticated young woman who looked quite wonderful in her WAAF uniform, her fair hair curled back in victory rolls beneath the perky little cap, her make-up flawless.

'Are you sure, Mum? Only I can tell you've been crying.'

'It's just Doris,' she said lightly. 'You know how we're always falling out.' She hugged Cissy to her, breathing in the scent of her, delighted to see her after so long.

'Doris has always been a cow,' said Cissy with feeling. 'I'd tell her straight what I think of her if it didn't upset you – but it's Ted who should step up and sort her out really. He must know of somewhere she could go.'

Peggy dredged up a smile and closed the door on the noise coming from the celebrations in the kitchen. 'Don't let's waste this precious time we have talking about Doris,' she said, keeping tight hold of her daughter's hand as she sat on the bed.

'How are you? Are you coping with things? Have you heard from Randolph – and how long have I got you for?'

Cissy sat down beside her on the bed. She watched Daisy sleeping for a moment, then turned back to her mother. 'It's pretty hair-raising, many ops going on day and night,' she murmured. 'But the sheer force of our air power seems to be having an effect. There are fewer Jerry planes going up and our losses are at last slowing down.'

She stroked the dressing gown. 'This is Dad's, isn't it?' At Peggy's nod she rubbed her cheek against the fabric and gave a little sigh. 'I wish I had something of Randy's, but all his stuff went into storage on the American base when he was taken prisoner.' She held the dressing gown to her cheek for a moment more whilst she gazed at her father's photograph, and then set it tenderly aside.

'I've got two hours before I have to be back, but at least I won't have to walk. The Chief WAAF let me borrow a car from the pool.'

Peggy saw how she bit her lip and knotted her hands in her lap. 'What is it, Cissy?' she asked fearfully.

'I got a notification from the American airbase this morning,' she said. 'The Red Cross have reported that Randy's been moved to another Stalag, which I've since learnt is near the Polish border. Why he's been moved, I have no idea, and I did wonder if Martin, Roger and Freddy had been moved with him. But I phoned Kitty earlier and she's heard nothing. Has Anne called you about Martin?'

'No, darling, I'm sorry. But I'm sure if she had

any news she'd tell us straight away.'

Cissy nodded. 'That's what I thought.' She took a tremulous breath. 'I wonder why he was singled out. Was it because he's an American, do you think?'

'I have no idea,' said Peggy, aching for her daughter's dilemma. 'But at least you know where he is. That's German efficiency for you – which is more than one can say about the Japs. Poor Sarah still doesn't know what's happened to her father and Philip.'

A burst of laughter from the kitchen brought a wan smile to Cissy's face and she made a concerted effort to dismiss her worries and appear cheerful. 'The celebrations seem to be going well. It's lovely those two have finally got engaged – lovely too that Danuta's at last coming home, and Grandpa has made it up with Rosie. Shall we join them?'

Peggy didn't really want to share her with everyone else, but it seemed churlish to refuse. 'Why not?' she said. 'I could certainly do with a large gin after dealing with Doris.'

'Then let's hope they've left us some,' said Cissy. 'But if they haven't,' she added with an impish grin, 'I've got another bottle from the mess that I managed to smuggle out courtesy of a rather smitten rear gunner.'

'Cissy Reilly, you are a naughty girl,' teased Peggy, giving her a nudge towards the door. 'You're as bad as your dad and granddad.'

'They taught me everything I know,' she replied with a giggle.

The crate of beers had been raided and the first bottle of gin was almost empty, so there were shouts of glee as Cissy produced the second bottle and poured drinks all round. The noise level rose; the cat beat a hasty retreat and the girls started dancing as Fran struck up a jig on the violin.

Peggy wondered momentarily what Doris must be thinking to hear her expensive violin being played so exuberantly, and then dismissed all thoughts of her selfish and utterly maddening sister, and joined in the fun.

As the level in the gin bottle went down and the noise level rose, Peggy had little fear of either Daisy or Cordelia being disturbed, for Cordelia's hearing aid had been taken out, and Daisy could sleep through countless numbers of fighters and bombers roaring overhead. As for Doris, she could stew.

Peggy watched her daughter's every move throughout what was left of their precious two hours together. She had evolved into a lovely young woman, far removed from the young girl who'd had ambitions to be a star of stage and screen despite her lowly job as a sales girl in Woolworths. She'd found love with Randy Stevens, and had witnessed things no girl should ever witness, but her posting at Cliffe aerodrome had given her strength of purpose and a maturity she might not have had if it hadn't been for this blasted war.

Cissy finally had to leave, and Peggy followed her out to the front step. She enfolded her in her arms and held her tight, knowing that every day she was on that airfield she was in danger of coming under enemy fire. 'Be careful,' she whispered against her cheek. 'And try to ring when you can. I do worry about you.'

'I worry about you too,' Cissy replied, hugging her back. 'And if Doris winds you up like a clock, just walk away from her. She's not worth it, Mum. Really she's not.'

'I know. But she's still my sister, and I feel responsible for her.'

Cissy chuckled. 'You're too soft, that's your trouble, Mum. But none of us would have it any other way.' She hitched the strap of her service issue handbag over her shoulder. 'If you hear anything from the others about their men, you will let me know, won't you?'

'Of course I will, but I'm sure if Kitty gets anything through she'll be able to wangle her way into the aerodrome to tell you.'

Cissy hugged and kissed her one last time then ran down the steps and climbed into the car. 'I love you, Mum,' she called through the open window.

'I love you too,' Peggy called back. But her endearment was lost in the roar of the car's powerful engine and the screech of tyres as Cissy shot out of the cul-de-sac, up the hill and out of sight.

Peggy folded her arms tightly about her waist, took a shaky breath and looked up at the starlit sky. There was a golden ring hazed around the moon, and she could only pray that it augured well.

6

Ron had planned to surprise Rosie this morning by taking her warm fresh bread straight from the bakery and an egg from his hens to make her breakfast before he walked the dogs. However, as he stepped into the kitchen to make the early morning tea and stoke the fire, he found Peggy bright-eyed and far too bushy-tailed for a woman who'd helped sink two bottles of gin the previous night. He eyed her warily as she placed a long list on the table.

'I realise it's a bit early, but this can't wait,' she said. 'These are the things I want removed from Doris's room and put back where they belong. And while you're at it, you can go up into the attic and look for those old velvet curtains I used to have in the dining room.' Her mouth formed a thin line. 'Doris has commandeered the heavy brocade ones, so they'll need to be taken back down and replaced with the velvets, seeing as how my cotton curtains are deemed far too inferior.'

Ron frowned as he read down the list. 'What's all this doing in her room in the first place?'

'She decided to refurnish,' said Peggy tightly. She placed a large pot of tea on the table with a dull thud.

'I have plans for this morning,' he said. 'I'll do it later.'

'Ron, please don't be trying,' she replied, sitting

107

at the table and cutting Daisy's toast into fingers. 'Those things are to be put back before you go anywhere. Doris has gone too far this time, and I won't stand for it.'

Ron poured out the tea whilst Peggy reeled off the catalogue of Doris's wrongdoings, and when she'd finally paused for breath, he grinned. 'To be sure, I'll do it the minute I've had this tea but first, I'm nipping out to the bakery.'

Peggy smiled as he told her his plans. 'You see, you do know how to woo a woman,' she teased. 'It's a lovely idea. I'll keep the bread warm in the slow oven whilst you sort out that furniture. The other jobs can wait until later today.'

Ron drank down his tea, eyeing the gathering clouds outside, and decided this was not the sort of day to be jaunting about in his jacket and fedora. He rammed on his old cap, snatched up a couple of sheets of yesterday's newspaper and stuffed them into his poacher's coat pocket, then hurried off to Camden Road, his heart light.

It was still very early and the street was almost deserted, but despite the strong wind coming off the sea and the scudding clouds that promised rain, he could smell the heavenly aroma of baking bread waft towards him.

Changing his mind about picking up the bread now, he nipped down the side alley towards the back of the bakery and ordered Harvey to sit and stay, then stepped straight into the large, warm kitchen where the new owner was just drawing the loaves and – miracle of miracles – white rolls, out of the huge brick oven.

'Hello, Horace,' Ron said cheerfully. 'I was

wondering if you could do me a favour.'

Horace was a short, tubby little man with a bristling moustache and an air of self-importance that made him look more like an officious bank manager than a baker. He eyed Ron warily, having been caught out doing him favours before. 'Depends what it is,' he muttered.

'Could you hold back a cottage loaf and some of those lovely bread rolls for me and keep them warm for about an hour?'

'The rolls are a special order,' said Horace, continuing to draw the large trays from the hot oven and setting them on the battered wooden table. 'And I don't do cottage any more, just wholemeal tins.'

Ron swallowed his disappointment. 'I only want two bread rolls,' he said, looking longingly at the beautiful golden crusty treats on the tray. He hadn't seen such things for ages, and they were making his mouth water.

As Horace thought about this, his expression became speculative. 'If you don't want them straight away, I suppose I could do a few extra. But they'll cost you, Ron – and I'll need paying in advance. And you'll have to take six, or it won't be worth my while making more dough.'

He's a wily old fox, thought Ron, who'd hoped he'd just give him two as there were so many. 'To be sure, six will be fine,' he replied, rubbing his hands together and dismissing all thoughts of how much this might cost him.

'Can I take four from this tray now? It will be such a treat for Peggy,' he added slyly, knowing Horace had a bit of a crush on Peggy and often slipped her an extra half-loaf when no one was looking.

'I don't see why not,' said Horace, going a bit pink as he selected the four most perfect rolls and wrapped them in the newspaper Ron had brought. 'The order isn't due to be picked up until eleven, so I've got time to do a fresh batch before I open the shop.'

Ron took the warm parcel and held it to his chest before tucking it away in an inside pocket. The smell was making him feel quite light-headed. 'Someone's got a bob or two to order that many,' he said, eyeing the two full trays and flinching as he handed over what seemed to be an inordinate amount of money.

'It's the memorial service for those women who were killed in Havelock Road,' said Horace, his expression suitably mournful. 'Lord Chumley's holding a reception afterwards up at that posh house of his, and wholemeal bread isn't good enough for the likes of those attending such a grand do. Lucky for me they've got more money than sense.' He brushed his moustache with a floury finger. 'I had to order in that white flour especially and it didn't come cheap.'

It certainly didn't if the price of those rolls was anything to go by. But Horace's revelation made Ron wonder if Doris knew about the service. She hadn't said anything – not that she'd said much to him at all since invading his home and his life.

'Thanks for these, Horace,' he said. 'I'll be back for the bread.' His gaze drifted to the gorgeous white loaves Horace was now placing on the table. 'I don't suppose...?'

'No, Ron. Those are for the reception sandwiches,' said Horace firmly.

Ron shrugged and then shot him a grin. 'Oh well, it was worth a try.'

He hurried back to Beach View, having to resist picking bits off the rolls along the way. Running up the concrete steps into the kitchen, he discovered everyone was up, including Doris, who was sitting on her own at the end of the table and rather pointedly being ignored.

'Look at what I've got,' he said, unfolding the paper to reveal the rolls like a magician. There were oohs and aahs, and everyone started talking at once. 'You've got half each,' he added, 'and I suggest you eat them while they're still hot.'

'I'll take Cordelia's up,' said Peggy, swiftly cutting into the crisp, golden crust and through the fluffy white bread, breathing in the delicious aroma. 'But as there are nine of us, Ron, you'll have to share my half.'

'To be sure, there's no need for you to go short, wee girl,' he said. 'I've ordered more for me and Rosie and will pick them up after I've moved the furniture from Doris's room.'

'It's not convenient this morning,' said Doris, greedily slathering margarine and jam on her roll. 'I have to get ready for the memorial service, and I certainly don't want you in and out whilst I'm trying to compose myself.'

Peggy scuttled out of the kitchen with Cordelia's breakfast as Ron eyed Doris from beneath his brows. 'Ach, it's barely eight o'clock and the service isn't until midday. Even *you* can't take that long to get dressed.'

111

'They were my dearest friends,' said Doris dramatically, dabbing her dry eyes with a scrap of lace-edged handkerchief, 'and some of the most influential and important women in the town – if not in the county. I blame myself entirely for their demise, and it's my duty to honour them by being calm and dignified at the service.'

'To be sure, I can understand that,' said Ron, fully suspecting that Doris was already planning to take over Lady Chumley's position as head witch of all the societies and charities in the town – and probably plotting to snare Lord Chumley and his title whilst she was at it. 'But I'll do it now, whilst you have breakfast, so you won't be discombobulated.'

'I am *never* discombobulated,' she said icily.

'You were yesterday morning,' he retorted and made a hasty exit as she turned scarlet at the reminder of that slap.

Ron took the stairs two at a time until he reached the first floor. Passing Cordelia's open door, he gave her a wave, pleased to see her sitting up in bed and chatting to Peggy as she tucked into her breakfast. She looked a good deal better, but Harvey had again decided he'd keep her company whilst Ron was busy elsewhere – although it was probably the siren call of food that had really attracted him.

Ron didn't stop to chat, for the morning was already racing away from him. Entering Doris's bedroom, he grimaced, fully understanding now why Peggy had been so incandescent.

It took almost an hour to shift everything back to where it belonged, and dig out the old velvet curtains from the loft. Having given them a good shake out of the window and exchanged them, he then went back downstairs with Harvey, to rehang the brocades in the dining room. They were a bit dusty too, but a good few bashes with a cane carpet beater saw to the worst of it.

Feeling grubby and a bit out of sorts, he discovered someone was in the bathroom, so he hurried down to the scullery to have a wash, comb his hair and brush down his twill trousers, which were flecked with dust and lint.

He returned to the kitchen to find that Peggy was alone with Daisy and listening to the war report on the wireless. 'Anything new?' he asked, shrugging his poacher's coat over his smart jacket.

'The Americans won the battle in the seas off the Philippines after just two days,' said Peggy, her face radiant with relief and hope. 'The Japs lost three carriers, two oil tankers and over six hundred planes.' She took a breath, her eyes shining with happy tears. 'But the very best news of all is that the battle of Kohima and the siege of Imphal is over.'

'That is grand news, so it is,' he agreed, giving her a hug. 'But how did they manage that? I thought they were stuck there for the long haul.'

Peggy grinned. 'The Second British Division linked up with the Fifth Indian Division at Milestone 107 on the Imphal to Kohima Road – whatever that is – and simply overpowered the Japs.' She hugged herself in delight. 'Oh, Ron,' she breathed. 'If it goes on like this, our Jim will soon be on his way home.'

'Don't get your hopes too high, Peggy, girl.

There's a long way to go yet before all the Japs are sent packing out of that part of the world. And we still have Hitler to deal with.'

'I know,' she sighed. 'But at least we seem to be making headway at last.'

He kissed her cheek and winked. 'If only the battles at home were easier to win, eh?' he teased.

'I wish,' she sighed and rolled her eyes. 'Doris is in the bathroom – probably using all the hot water again, which means Cordelia will have to wait for the tank to fill and heat up before she can have her bath. I dread to think what the electricity bills will be with her using the immersion heater so often.'

Ron placed a tender hand on her shoulder. 'Don't fret yourself, wee girl. I'll make sure she pays her share of the bills and find some way of getting her out from under your feet – though it may take a bit of clever manoeuvring, and calling in favours.'

'Bless you, Ron,' she sighed. 'If anyone can do it, it's you. I have to admit that after that trick she pulled yesterday, I've had enough of her. I'm seriously thinking of getting a lock put on my door.'

Ron hoped it wouldn't come to that, but didn't want to waste time talking about Doris and her nefarious ways. 'I'll see if I can get hold of Ted later on. I'm sure he'll know how to deal with her.'

He patted his coat pocket to check he had his pipe and some paper to wrap the bread in, before placing the fedora at just the right angle over his brow and picking up the box of eggs. 'I'll be off to Rosie's now. The other jobs will get done before Danuta comes home, I promise.' He kissed her cheek. 'Try and have a good day, Peggy.'

'You too,' she replied affectionately. 'And, Ron – don't rush things with Rosie. Let her be the one to set the pace.'

He grinned and tapped the side of his nose. 'To be sure, I know that.'

He stepped outside with Harvey to be met by a blustery wind and the first heavy drops of rain. Determined not to let the weather dampen his spirits, he pulled up his coat collar, and with Harvey trotting miserably beside him, strode down Camden Road again – a silly smile on his face at the thought of waking Rosie with the delights of fresh white bread rolls and a loving kiss.

He'd almost reached the bakery when he caught sight of his old pal, Sergeant Albert Williams, walking along the other pavement. Knowing how Bert loved to talk his ear off, and not having the time for it today, Ron ducked quickly into the shop, hoping his friend hadn't seen him.

He emerged back onto the pavement some minutes later, his pockets loaded with bread, eggs, rolls and a bag of crumbs which he planned to mix in with the chicken's feed later.

'Good morning, Ron.'

His heart sank as he came face-to-face with the police sergeant. 'Morning, Bert. Can't stop, sorry,' he said, trying to dodge round him.

Bert was a big man and he blocked Ron's escape. 'I was just on the way to Beach View as it happens,' he said. 'But meeting like this is much better, because there's something I need to tell you.'

Ron silently groaned. 'Get on with it, Bert. The

bread's getting cold and Rosie's surprise will be spoilt.'

Bert raised a greying eyebrow at this, but his expression boded ill. 'This is far more important than surprises for Rosie,' he said.

'Nothing's more important than that,' said Ron. 'To be sure, Bert, will you spit it out and let me be on me way?'

Bert held up a brown envelope and Ron froze, his impatience dashed by icy dread as he stared at the telegram. 'Holy Mary and all the saints,' he breathed. 'Please tell me it's not my Jim.'

Bert's meaty hand squeezed Ron's shoulder. 'You'd better read it, old pal.'

Ron's hands were shaking and his heart was pounding, and he found that he had to read it twice, for he simply couldn't focus on those few stark words. When he'd finally absorbed the terrible news, he looked back at Bert and took a trembling breath. 'To be sure, you were right to collar me, Bert. This isn't something any woman should hear without someone at her side.'

Bert nodded. 'It's my duty to tell her, Ron. But I'd be glad of your company whilst I do. I'm never easy with this sort of thing.'

'Of course I'll go with you.' Ron was shaken, but still managed to think quickly and clearly. 'Just give me five minutes to tell Rosie where I am, and then I'm all yours.'

Ron's heart was pounding as he let himself into the Anchor through the side door and went upstairs to place the bread and eggs on the kitchen drainer. All was quiet, so he walked down the passage to Rosie's bedroom. She was asleep still, looking lovely and rather vulnerable in that big bed, with Monty curled at her feet, and he didn't have the heart to wake her.

The dog raised his head and wagged his tail, so Ron quickly closed the door to stop him from following him. The news he had was not the sort to be woken to, so he scrabbled in the kitchen drawer for paper and pencil and hastily wrote a note explaining everything. Propping the note next to the kettle so she couldn't fail to find it, he hurried back to where Bert was waiting for him on the pavement.

The two old friends exchanged mournful looks, and without a word, tucked their chins into their coat collars and reluctantly headed very slowly through the rain for Beach View.

Peggy was washing up the breakfast things whilst Daisy was chasing Queenie about the kitchen with her wheeled horse. The noise of the squeaking wheels and Daisy's yelling was beginning to get on her nerves, so Peggy opened the kitchen door to let the poor cat escape through the flap in the back door. The rain was coming down like stair rods now, but Queenie always managed to find the most sheltered spots, so Peggy accepted she'd be all right out there for a bit.

Daisy started wailing and throwing her wooden bricks about in a tantrum at being thwarted in her game. Peggy calmly ignored her and went back to the sink, knowing it wouldn't last long if she didn't make anything of it.

'You really should control that child,' said Doris. 'Letting her get away with such behaviour

117

is making a rod for your own back and teaching her a very bad lesson.'

Peggy turned from the sink ready with a retort and then realised it would fall on deaf ears anyway, so she shouldn't waste her breath. She picked up Daisy instead and sat her down rather firmly at the table with her colouring book and crayons. 'Behave,' she said sternly, 'or you won't go to play with Chloe later.'

Daisy pursed her lips and eyed her belligerently, but thought better of continuing the tantrum and began to vent her spleen by forcefully colouring in a picture.

Doris sat down by the fire, still in Peggy's old dressing gown, but with her face made up and her nails freshly painted. 'Before you accuse me of anything,' she said flatly, 'Fran lent me the nail polish. Luckily I had my Coty make-up in my handbag, so at least I wasn't forced to borrow her cheap Woolworths powder and lipstick.'

'That was lucky,' muttered Peggy with more than a hint of sarcasm.

'Look, Mar– I mean Peggy. I realise I went a bit too far yesterday, but you have to understand I'm really not myself. It's all been such a terrible shock I can barely think straight, let alone sleep. And now I've got this awful day to get through.' She twisted the diamond ring on her finger. 'I'm dreading having to face those poor bereaved husbands and families knowing that if I hadn't insisted upon holding that meeting at my place, they'd all still be alive.'

'If that was some sort of apology, then I accept it,' said Peggy coolly.

'Thank you,' Doris replied with a gracious dip of her chin.

'And it wasn't your fault those women were killed. No one could have foreseen that happening. It was just bad luck and rotten timing.' Peggy lit a cigarette and sat opposite her sister. 'We've all been on a knife-edge ever since the war started, never knowing from one breath to the next if it will be our last. Now we have this new weapon of Hitler's which has already killed over a hundred people – some of whom were attending a church service at Wellington Barracks. It seems to me that regardless of who you are, or what you are, if your name's on it, then your number's up – and there's not a thing anyone of us can do about it.'

Doris studied her freshly painted nails. 'I don't suppose you have any scent I could borrow? I don't feel dressed without a dab of Guerlain's Vol de Nuit on my neck and wrists.'

'Have you even been listening to me?' asked Peggy crossly.

'They're just words,' said Doris dismissively. 'Nothing can ease the pain I'm going through.' She regarded Peggy evenly. 'Well, do you have any scent, or not?'

Peggy had seen that Guerlain perfume advertised in the well-thumbed glossy magazines Solly's wife, Rachel, had left in the staff canteen at the factory, and knew the name meant Night Flight in honour of the brave pioneer aviators who'd opened up a mail service across Africa. It was a pretty bottle, but after browsing the perfumery counter in Plummer's she'd discovered that the price was way beyond her purse. Fortunately, the

119

woman behind the counter had taken pity on her and dabbed a tiny drop on her wrist. It had lasted for hours and smelled glorious.

'I've got some 4711 eau de cologne,' she said. 'But please be sparing with it. There isn't much left, and it's impossible to get hold of now.'

Doris's lip curled 'I'm not surprised. It's German and even the most unpatriotic woman wouldn't dream of using it.'

'Well, it's been around long before Germany kept declaring war on everybody,' said Peggy with some asperity. 'Jim gave me that bottle over five years ago, and as it's all I have, you'll just have to either lump it or leave it.'

'I'd rather go without,' said Doris with a sniff.

Rita came in from the hall and shed her jacket. 'It's horrid out there now there's wind and rain,' she said, dumping the jacket and her crutches on a nearby chair as she sat down at the table and shook the damp from her dark curls. 'It's bad enough this war's dragging on, but we could have done with some decent weather for a change after such a foul winter and spring.'

Peggy poured her a cup of tea. 'Warm up by the fire, dear. I'm sure the weather will improve soon.'

Rita sipped the tea and studiously ignored Doris, who was looking askance at her leather jacket and shabby old skirt and jumper. 'By the way, Aunty Peggy, I thought Ron was planning to be with Rosie this morning?'

Peggy frowned. 'He said he was – why?'

'I've just seen him and Bert Williams go into the back alley on the way here. Both of them were looking very serious.' She looked nervously at Peggy. 'You don't think something's happened, do you?'

'Rosie's probably sent Ron off with a flea in his ear for waking her so early, and Bert's more than likely just coming in for a cuppa to avoid going home to his awful wife,' said Peggy, going across to lean over the sink and look out of the rain-streaked window.

But what she saw didn't look like a social visit, for despite the appalling weather, both men were standing by the gate, deep in conversation, their expressions grim. Her heart missed a beat then began to thud, and she found she could barely breathe as all her fears rose to smother her. There was a stoic purpose in their steps as they approached the scullery door – and it could only spell trouble – serious, terrible trouble.

'Please, please don't bring us bad news,' she whispered, grabbing hold of the back of a chair and almost falling into, it as her legs gave out on her.

'What's happening, Peggy?' asked Doris in alarm. 'Why have you suddenly gone so white?'

Peggy couldn't answer, and sat there dumb with dread as Ron and Bert came stony-faced up the steps into the kitchen. She felt Doris's hand on her shoulder and Rita trembling at her side, but couldn't tear her eyes away from the two men standing before her.

'It's not Jim,' said Ron immediately. 'And its not your dad either, Rita.'

Peggy let out the breath she'd been holding as Rita burst into relieved tears and Doris started to protest at the fright they'd given them all.

Bert stepped further into the room and cut off Doris's protest. 'I'm sorry, Mrs Williams, but this arrived at the police station this morning.'

Doris took the brown envelope with trembling fingers and fumbled to draw out the telegram. She scanned the few words on the slip of paper and then let it flutter to the floor as she sank slowly into a chair. 'No,' she breathed. 'It can't be right. They've made a mistake.'

'I'm sorry, Mrs Williams,' said Bert, 'but there's no mistake, I'm afraid. I telephoned the London police station when I received this, and got confirmation that Mr Edward Williams's body was formally identified late last night.'

He shuffled his feet, his face pale with anguish as Doris stared at him. 'He was one of over twenty victims to be killed in a series of V-1 attacks on London almost a week ago, which is why it's taken so long to identify some of the victims and inform the next of kin.'

Doris regarded him in bewilderment. 'But what was he doing in London? How could he possibly have got there with all the travel restrictions in place?' Her face was bleached of colour beneath the carefully applied make-up, her eyes huge and dark with shock and disbelief as she shook her head. 'You've got it wrong, Sergeant. It couldn't have been Edward.'

Bert cleared his throat and studiously kept his gaze fixed to his size twelve boots. 'I can't rightly say how he got there or what he was doing in London,' he rumbled. 'There was speculation that he might have been staying in the hotel that took the direct hit – or he could simply have been

122

passing by, or eating in a nearby restaurant or pub. It was a busy street, you see, and the V-1 obliterated everything in the explosion.'

Doris shuddered, and twisted her handkerchief in her lap. 'Was he alone?'

'Don't torture yourself by asking such questions,' urged Peggy, putting her arm about Doris's shoulder. 'How could anyone know that if ... if it took so long to identify the victims, and the damage was so complete?' Her words faded into silence.

'I need to know,' Doris replied, shrugging off Peggy's hand and fixing her gaze on the policeman. 'Sergeant, I have a *right* to know. Was he alone when he was found?'

Bert looked to Ron for guidance, but received only an encouraging nod. He took a deep breath and met Doris's glare. 'It's impossible to say,' he said miserably. 'It was a scene of carnage according to my London colleague, and I'm sorry, Mrs Williams, but not all of the bodies could be identified because ... because there wasn't much left of them after the blast and following firestorm.'

'Come on, Doris,' urged Peggy. 'You've seen what that V-1 did to Havelock Road, and you know they only managed to identify your women friends because you told the firemen who was in the house at the time.' She hugged her to her side, feeling her resist and stiffen. 'Ted's gone, Doris. It's time to mourn. Not to ask questions.'

Doris wrenched away and stood up. 'Tell me, Sergeant, was there any other victim amongst those identified who came from outside London?' She took a steadying breath as she saw him hesitate. 'To put it more clearly, Sergeant, was Edward the only victim from Cliffehaven?'

'No,' he said reluctantly, his gaze directed everywhere but on Doris. 'That's not to say they were together, though,' he added hurriedly.

'It was Martha Holbrook, wasn't it?' rasped Doris.

Bert gasped. 'How did...?'

'So it was her,' she snapped.

He dipped his chin and went scarlet. 'I'm afraid so, yes,' he muttered. 'But that doesn't mean–'

'It certainly *does* mean *exactly* what I've suspected for months,' said Doris, tightening the belt on the borrowed dressing gown whilst making a concerted effort to remain calm. 'Thank you for coming to tell me, Sergeant,' she said stiffly. 'Now if you will excuse me, I have to prepare for my friends' memorial service. Good day to you.' She brushed past Peggy and walked quite steadily out of the room, her head held high.

Peggy dithered, not knowing what to do. 'Should I go to her, Ron?'

He shook his head. 'She hasn't really taken it in yet, I don't think. Besides, I suspect she's more upset that he was with Martha when he died, than over his actual passing. There was little love lost between her and Ted, and they had been divorced for a while.'

'She's a cool one, I'll give her that,' said Rita with a shudder.

'I'd better get over to the other family,' said Bert, clearly uncomfortable with the situation as he buttoned up his heavy raincoat.

'Have a cuppa before you go, Bert,' said Ron.

'It'll steady your nerves and keep you warm on that long walk to the Holbrooks' place.'

'Thanks, old chum,' he replied. 'I could certainly do with one before I have to face Martha's parents.' He sank into a kitchen chair and unfastened his coat again. 'Goodness knows how they'll take the news. They're old and getting frail and depended on Martha for everything.'

Peggy was only vaguely aware of the conversation going on around her, for she was listening to her sister's steady footsteps on the stairs and suspecting that her cool façade was for show. Doris was all about keeping up appearances and would never reveal her true feelings in front of others. She'd keep it locked inside her until the news had sunk in, and that would be the time for Peggy to offer consolation and comfort.

'What about Ted's son, Anthony?' she asked Bert. 'He'll have to be told.'

'I sent a telegram before I came here. Hopefully the local bobby will deliver it personally as I instructed. Suzy will no doubt be at home alone with the baby, and I just hope the bobby stays with her until Anthony can get there.'

Peggy nodded, glanced at the clock and then scooped up Daisy. 'I have to go to work,' she said fretfully. 'Are you sure you can manage on your own with Cordelia, Rita?'

'I'll tell Cordelia,' said Ron. 'She hardly knew Ted, so she shouldn't take it too hard, and if she's feeling well enough, I'll bring her downstairs where it'll be easier for Rita to keep an eye on her whilst I'm out.'

'Peter and I have had a brilliant idea about how

we can make life easier for Grandma Cordy,' said Rita, her eyes now shining with delight and not tears.

'I'd love to hear all about it, dear,' said Peggy, 'but if I don't get a move on I shall be late and have my wages docked.' She wrestled Daisy into her coat and hat before donning her own raincoat and headscarf and kissing Rita's cheek. 'You can tell me this evening.'

'It's probably best you stay here tonight to keep an eye on Doris,' said Ron. 'I'll see Danuta this afternoon and explain the situation.'

'Thanks, Ron. I think you're right.' Peggy hurried down to the scullery to get Daisy in the pushchair and the rain covers clipped on. She could hear the wind moaning outside, and the splatters of rain on the back window and, like Rita, bemoaned the lack of a decent spring and summer which they so needed after the five long, dreary years of war.

As she walked towards the clothing factory, her thoughts were filled with Ted – dear, kind, patient Ted, who'd put up with all sorts of nonsense from Doris over the years. He'd found the courage to leave her; to make his home above the Home and Colonial store he managed and live his life without being nagged. He'd been generous to a fault, providing Doris with evidence for the divorce, and giving her a large settlement as well as a monthly allowance so she could stay in the house and continue the same standard of living.

Peggy couldn't help but feel terribly sad for her sister, even though she was the most irritating, impossible woman to live with. Doris had ideas above her station and was constantly aiming for a higher social standing. She thought she was better than the rest of the family because she had a big house and posh clothes – and was bossy and overbearing to boot.

But for all her money and lofty ambitions, she'd lost sight of the really important things. Her beloved son Anthony had married and moved as far away as possible to avoid her meddling in his marriage, which meant she had little contact with her grandson. She'd discovered that the stalwart Ted, who she'd barely had time for, had been having an affair for years – and refused to return home when it had ended. The separation and divorce had been bitter as it had caused scandal and derision within the spiteful coterie of women that Doris had aspired to join.

Peggy's shoulders slumped as she wheeled the pushchair down the road. Doris had weathered it all, but now those women were dead and dear, sweet Ted would never come home again. As for their own relationship, Peggy just couldn't see a way for them to ever be close – or even friends – and the knowledge saddened her. They were chalk and cheese, and although Peggy felt deeply sorry for her, it was becoming increasingly difficult to put up with her rude and grasping behaviour.

And yet Peggy also realised she would go on trying with Doris, for she was homeless – and now friendless – and Peggy suspected her sister had cared more for Ted than she'd let on. When the news of his passing had sunk in, Doris would need an enormous amount of support, for the manner of his death and the knowledge he'd been with Martha at the time would create emotional turmoil, leaving a terrible void in her life which she would find very hard to fill.

Peggy's footsteps faltered at the shocking thought she'd never see Ted or his bright smile again; never chat to him over the cheese counter, or share a pot of tea at her kitchen table. His loss was a hammer blow, and it would reverberate right through Cliffehaven, for Ted had been a popular man and an intrinsic part of the fabric of the town.

She reached the factory gates and came to a brief halt. Perhaps she should go back to be with Doris after all, for surely she wasn't really meaning to go to that memorial service today? The thought of her sister mourning alone tugged at her heart. What was the loss of seven hours' pay compared to the loss of a husband even if he had been estranged?

'Mamma, wanna see Chloe. Come on!'

Peggy resisted her daughter's urging and peered through the rain to the far end of Camden Road, torn between wanting to be there for Doris and her duty to Solly, who'd been good enough to give her this machinist's job when she'd hardly known how to thread a needle.

And then just at that moment she saw Doris's gleaming car coming towards her. She stared at her sister, who looked perfectly calm and relaxed in her mink coat and smart little hat as she turned the car into the High Street.

'Well, if that doesn't take the biscuit, nothing will,' muttered Peggy, no longer resisting her daughter's demands. If Doris could be that cool so soon after losing her husband, then there was no point in missing out on a day's wages. As for Danuta, she would definitely be getting a visit from Peggy tonight.

Doris had seen Peggy outside the factory gates, noted her stricken expression and chosen to ignore her. She was hurting so much she could barely concentrate on the road, let alone face her sister's undoubtedly genuine sympathy. Peggy's loving kindness would be her undoing, and she was determined to get her emotions under control before she had to face the others at the memorial service.

She drove along the High Street and headed up the steep hill to the east of the town, half-blinded by the tears she refused to let fall. Yet her hands were trembling and great waves of anguish threatened to swamp her, and she suddenly realised that if she didn't stop, she'd crash the car.

Pulling into a lay-by on the brow of the hill that overlooked Cliffehaven, she switched off the engine and slumped in the leather seat. She felt cold to the core despite the mink coat, and when she tried to light a cigarette she fumbled so badly it took several attempts.

Doris battled the tears as the rain hammered on the car roof and the windscreen misted over. She would not cry. Would not allow herself to weep and wail for a man who'd betrayed her so cruelly. She'd heard the whispers about him and Martha Holbrook, and although she and Ted had been divorced for over a year, it had come as a bitter blow to realise that what they'd once shared was well and truly over, for Edward had fallen hard for

Martha, and was rumoured to be on the point of proposing to her. Perhaps he'd done just that, and they'd gone to London to celebrate?

She shivered and sank deeper into the fur as she opened the quarter-light window to let fresh air in and the smoke out. Her heart clenched in pain as memories flooded back to haunt her. She should have been kinder to Ted and told him how she'd grown to love and admire him so very much over the years; forgiven him for straying and taken him back whilst he was still willing to make another go at their marriage.

In the cold light of this grey, dismal day, Doris realised that it was only now that he was truly gone from her life that she could see she'd been too proud to admit she'd played a big part in the breakdown of their relationship; too hurt to forgive, and far too self-possessed to consider his feelings.

The pain and anguish finally overwhelmed her and she buried her face in her hands and wept for all that she'd lost.

7

Burma

The mood in the jungle camp was electric, and Jim joined in with the massive cheer that went up at the news of the British and Indian Brigades' victory at Imphal. 'To be sure, Ernie,' he shouted above the noise, 'it's true what they say about good things coming in threes.'

'You're right there, Jim,' the smaller man replied, his face red and perspiring in the debilitating heat. 'D-Day has come, we've got the Japs on the run, and to top it all we saw Vera Lynn.' He took a slug of beer from the bottle and wiped his mouth on his arm. 'The wife will be ever so jealous – she loves our Vera.'

Jim grinned and concentrated on rolling a cigarette, which wasn't an easy task when your fingers were sweaty and the cigarette paper tissue-thin. The night of Vera's jungle concert had been an eye-opener, for he'd always considered her songs to be too soppy, which was why Peggy, Cordelia and the girls back home loved them. But seeing that tall, fair young lass on that makeshift stage singing her heart out to the accompaniment of a badly tuned piano and the joyous roars of the hundreds of servicemen had filled him with a deep sense of pride.

Vera had braved a dangerous journey to be here in Burma, and it couldn't have been easy for a young woman to cope with such adulation in the intense heat and humidity and with the lack of decent facilities. She must have been warned there were still pockets of Japs all around, and yet she'd turned up looking as fresh as a daisy and seemingly without a care in the world to sing for over an hour in that insect-infested jungle clearing, the men refusing to let her leave by shouting and whistling and begging for more.

Jim lit his cigarette, the memory of that wonderful night three weeks before, still very vivid.

The British stiff upper lip had melted under the spell Vera had cast, and Jim had been moved, not only by the songs which reminded him of Peggy and linked him with home and family, but by the way barriers had come down, and there was no shame amongst these battle-weary, hardened men as they shed a tear and clapped until their hands were stinging.

He'd managed to hold onto his emotions until she'd begun to sing 'Yours', a beautiful, heart-breaking love song he'd danced to with Peggy on his last leave. After that he'd been a complete wreck, saved only by her follow-up of 'If I had My Way', which was a light-hearted and rather saucy piece that had the men cheering again.

Jim had seen other concerts when he'd first been posted to India. They were jolly affairs put on by ENSA – or, as it was more fondly known; 'Every Night Something Awful' – and usually in-volved a bad comedian, some over-the-hill dancers and a glamorous singer or two. But Vera was different. She wasn't a pin-up girl like some he'd seen, with lots of leg and cleavage showing, but the well-brought-up girl next door – the girl you could take home to Mum. And that made her very special, for she'd reminded him of his darling Peggy and his beautiful daughters, and somehow brought them a little closer.

There was no doubt that General Slim, who was in charge of operations in Burma, under-stood that the men serving under him needed emotional and spiritual nourishment as well as bully beef, bullets and beer. He'd realised his men were in danger of being the forgotten army, for the focus back home was on the invasion into Europe, and no other entertainers had dared to come into such a hostile environment. Jim suspected he was as surprised as everyone else that Vera hadn't hesitated to accept the invitation.

Morale was intangible, but Jim's experiences here and in India had proved to him that it could stir a man into giving his last ounce of strength to achieve something without counting the cost to himself. It was a force which made each man feel a part of something far greater than anything he'd encountered before, and therefore instilled in him the courage and energy to do his best and make his mark.

Big Bert came and sat down next to Jim on the fallen tree. 'We'll be off any minute,' he warned. He took out an oily old rag and began to clean his gun and check the firing mechanism. 'The CO's just got a message through from HQ. The Japs are retreating from the Imphal to Kohima Road, and it's suspected they'll be making for a large camp to the north-east of us. Reports have come in that they've got a hospital, ammunition dumps, truck parks and the whole kit and caboodle there, so whilst they're being held up by Vinegar Joe Stilwell's brigade, we're going in the back way to cause havoc.' He grinned with relish at the idea of blowing things up.

'How far is this place?' asked Ernie.

Big Bert shrugged. 'Who knows? But we'll have to get a move on. Can't let Stilwell have all the fun.'

Jim quickly stripped off his sodden shirt and used his scrap of towel to rub himself dry of salty sweat. He took the shirt to the nearby stream, rinsed it out and then filled his hat several times to douse his head with the cold, clean water. Feeling much better, he dabbed antiseptic cream on the wounds in his cheek and ear, stuck on a fresh plaster and slipped on the wet shirt. It felt cool and refreshing against his sun-darkened skin, and he didn't mind at all that it was soaking through his shorts into his underpants. It would dry within minutes and then soak through with sweat again before the hour was over, but for now he felt ready to face anything.

They were called to attention to be told by their commanding officer that they needed to move fast if they were to reach their rendezvous with the 2nd Brigade in time.

Jim and the others set off across the plain and marched on through marshes and reed beds, past bamboo and reed houses on stilts, to a cluster of deserted villages where they were joined by the other brigade as planned. A large airdrop took place that night, and after a swim in a nearby stream, they ate and slept.

Dawn saw them on the move again. It was a stinking hot day, and they were faced with a long and very steep climb. It seemed they were heading for an unpronounceable village which was marked on the map as being halfway down an easterly ridge which eventually sloped off into a series of valleys.

Jim and the others trudged on at a fast pace, heads down, regulating their breathing as their shirts blackened with sweat and their broad-brimmed hats became even more salt-stained.

'Let's hope this place we're heading for is still there, and not buried in the jungle,' Jim muttered. 'You know what these people are like. They use up the goodness in the soil around their village and move on, sometimes miles away. Then they burn a few more acres of jungle, plant their crops, build new homes and call the damned thing by the same name. Ten years later they do it all again, and we end up chasing our tails looking for them.'

'We'll soon find out,' said Big Bert. 'We can only hope the CO and his pathfinders can read co-ordinates on a flaming map and don't get us lost.'

Just before nightfall they were called to a halt. The men, horses and mules were swaying with exhaustion and thirst, and Jim cast a glance at those around him, seeing his own doubts reflected in their eyes. Had the CO taken a wrong turning? Were they lost? One bit of jungle looked the same as the next, and the markings on the maps couldn't be relied upon. There was no sign of the village they should have reached by now. To cap it all, there was no fresh water, just a steep, rocky track running through dense scrub and tall jungle.

The order came down the line to rest easy. It seemed the CO was sending out scouts to try and find the village.

'I knew it,' said an exasperated Ernie, dumping his backpack on the ground. 'He's got us flaming lost.'

'To be sure, it looks that way,' Jim replied mournfully. He eased off his heavy backpack. 'I wonder if we'll have time for a brew-up and a bit of nosh?'

'We will if the scouts don't find anything,' said

Ernie, lighting a cigarette. 'And I doubt they will now. It'll be dark before you know it.'

'Ever the optimist, eh, Ernie?' teased Jim, rolling a smoke.

A mutter went through the lines like wind through a dry wheat field, but before anyone could catch their breath, men further up the line were getting back to their feet as mules and horses were released from their hobbles and reloaded. The word reached them that the original village had been found, and they were to proceed with utmost caution and absolute silence.

Jim heaved the backpack over his shoulders, stuffed his unlit cigarette in his mouth, and gathered up his carbine and spare ammunition belts. Wedging his hat brim low over his eyes to counter the last blinding rays of the low sun, he got into line. He was gagging for a cuppa and something to eat, but he'd learnt long ago that this army didn't march on its stomach, but on sheer determination and bloody-mindedness to get to their destination.

They passed the remains of three villages that were all overgrown and barely discernible in the regrowth of the surrounding jungle. Then the long column was brought to a halt again. The small reconnaissance group was sent out, guards were posted and everyone waited stoically for the next order.

They soon heard that the fourth village of the same name had been sighted two miles away in a shallow river valley, and that people were living in it. No Japs had been reported, but that wasn't proof there weren't any, so Jim and the others quietly moved into the valley and made camp out of sight of the village around the bend in the river.

There could be no cooking fires, no smoking and no noise, so they washed in the river, drank the water and ate cold rations, armed and alert for any sounds coming out of the jungle that might be a native, or a prowling Japanese patrol.

There was a good deal of muttering which petered out as the familiar nightly routine swung into action. Guards were posted, the animals watered, canisters replenished with water and salt tablets – and a day's worth of K-rations dumped in a metal eating can to be stirred into a glutinous mess and gobbled down at a rate of knots before they fell asleep over it.

Too tired to even think straight, Jim eased off his boots, stuffed his socks inside them and plonked his hat on top, the chinstrap tethered firmly beneath the boots so it didn't blow away. It was unlikely that it would, for the air was breathlessly still, the heat of the day continuing to hum in the ground as the chirrups and buzzing of the insects slowly faded away, leaving the jungle silent.

Jim undid the top button of his flies, loosened his belt and propped his loaded carbine between his knees, barrel down, safety catch on. There wasn't enough light to see to read or write, so he rested his head on his backpack, pulled the strip of blanket over him and was asleep within seconds.

He was startled awake by someone digging him none too gently in the ribs with a boot, and automatically reached for his gun.

Big Bert grinned down at him, his teeth gleaming in the moon's glow. 'Your turn for watch,' he whispered.

Jim dragged himself to his feet and went to his guard post, which was a tree some two hundred yards away at the top of the slope. He settled on his belly, checked the sights on his gun and tried to shake off the strange dream he'd been having when Bert had so rudely woken him. He'd dreamt that Peggy and Vera Lynn were sitting at his kitchen table at Beach View whilst Cordelia sang out of tune and Harvey – resplendent in a bow tie, top hat and fancy waistcoat – played the piano. He shook his head and gave a wry smile. He'd clearly been in the jungle for too long.

It was an hour before dawn when he noticed that there was a quiet conflab going on amongst the column commanders, and he guessed they were probably discussing what to do next. He watched them for a while, but as he couldn't hear what they were saying, he grew bored, his concentration flitting between the view into the valley from his guard post, his full bladder and rumbling stomach.

Jim came off guard duty half an hour later, and noted that the conference was still going on. He dipped into the jungle to relieve his aching bladder, and returned to his backpack and blanket, hoping to get some food and kip before the day's orders came through. He was about to reach for his rations when he saw his brigade commander approach, noted the look in his eye and felt his spirits tumble. He just knew he was about to be volunteered for something.

'The CO's going in to recce a decent place for

the next airdrop and HQ block,' he said just above a whisper as he squatted in front of Jim. 'And he's taking six men with him: you, me, three Gurkha riflemen to cover our backs and translate if we come across the natives – and Flight Lieutenant Simms, who'll check if the place has a decent landing site.'

'Why me?' Jim asked, getting to his feet.

'Because you're an engineer and I recommended you,' the man replied flatly. He leaned towards Jim. 'This is a covert op and must not attract attention. You'll take no papers, no marked maps or notes and only light arms. Is that understood, Warrant Officer Reilly?'

'Sir, yes, sir,' he said, smartly standing to attention and saluting.

'Good chap. Be ready in five, get the shirt off and put this longyi on.' He handed Jim a length of filthy green checked cloth and then walked away to speak to the Gurkhas.

'Bloody hell, Jim,' breathed Ernie. 'What's with the fancy dress?'

'Perhaps the CO thinks the Burmans will take me for one of them, though I don't see how,' he muttered, stripping off his shirt and tying the ragged, filthy piece of cloth at his waist so it fell in folds over his shorts to his boots. 'In reality, it's just another layer to make me even hotter, and I really can't see the point of it because I don't look a bit like a native.'

Ernie grinned. 'I reckon you do, mate,' he said, eyeing him up and down. 'You're certainly brown enough, and with that black hair...'

Jim swiped him playfully with his hat. 'You're

only jealous of my tan because you burn, peel and go back to being pink,' he retorted.

'Orders is orders, even if you do look daft,' muttered Big Bert, who was clearly not happy at being left out of the party. 'By the looks of it the CO and the other officers are going along with the charade – even though they're keeping on their shirts. But why on earth he's got the Gurkhas to change into those filthy torn uniforms I don't know.'

'They're officers, Bert,' said Jim, picking up his carbine and settling his hat firmly on his head. 'They don't think like normal humans.' He looked down at his two mates. 'If I don't come back, will you be after sending a letter to Peggy telling her how fearless and handsome I looked the last time you saw me?' he asked lightly to cover the sudden rush of nerves.

His joke fell flat, and both men merely grunted. 'Piss off and get on with it,' muttered Ernie. 'It's too bloody hot to be sitting about waiting for you to play the hero.'

Jim just grinned, for he knew they cared about him really. He turned away, and went to join the CO and the rest of the small gathering down by the river.

The sky was pearly grey, the night mist dwindling away from the forest floor as they began to climb out of the steep-sided valley. Bird calls rang through the jungle and, aware that it could be the Japs signalling to one another, all seven men remained alert, their fingers poised on their triggers.

As the light strengthened they encountered a long-abandoned village and had to struggle

140

through dense thorny undergrowth, lantana, bamboo, weeds and crops that had run wild. Upon reaching the summit of the hill and entering the jungle again, they all breathed a sigh of relief, to be back in the relative shade.

Jim kept tripping over the blasted skirt, and in the end, he tucked the hem into the pockets of his shorts, promising the commanding officer he'd be properly attired when the time came. They'd left the camp an hour ago, and were now moving along the ridge towards what the CO was calling the railway valley, the site of the Japanese enclave they would be targeting.

Jim and the Gurkhas followed closely behind the officers, their eyes constantly moving for any sight of the enemy, their fingers still poised by their triggers as they carefully descended the ridge to the full-flowing river that ran between low cliffs. Always on the alert, the small party waded through the deep water for about a mile before climbing out and up into yet another band of high ridges and steep hills.

They came to a halt and the CO ordered Jim and the Gurkhas to remain on guard whilst he crouched down and surveyed the area through his binoculars. Jim was near enough to the officers to be able to catch what they were saying, and form his own opinion.

'The flanking hills are too close to the north,' the CO murmured, 'but the water's good and plentiful as well as being clean. The perimeter length is about right, but protection against artillery fire is only just adequate.' He swung the binoculars over the valley and neighbouring hills.

'Observation is good,' he murmured. 'Fields of fire are fair in most directions.'

'The aerial photographs haven't shown anything better in this area,' said Jim's brigade CO. 'We could hold this place well against attack. Once we've got the C-47 field sorted, we'll have our heavy artillery and really chew up any enemy within five miles, north or south.'

Jim could see the railway line and station from his vantage point, and the scatter of native buildings he now knew to be, not part of a Burmese village, but the Japanese hospital, ammunition dumps, stores, mess huts, garages and sleeping accommodation. All looked quiet down there, but that was probably because the main body of men were still being kept busy by Stilwell, and the few Japs there were probably only moved about after dark to escape the attention of the Allied Air Forces which patrolled this area regularly.

He listened to the senior officers and wondered why they didn't just get on and destroy the place whilst it was still vulnerable, for once the C-47s and gliders came with more men and machinery, they'd be alerted to what was going on and react swiftly. Still, he mused, he wasn't in charge, and no doubt the officers knew what they were doing-even if it didn't seem to make much sense to him.

Jim got to his feet and followed the officers as they turned away from the railway valley and headed across the ridge. The sun was high, and he was sweating profusely as his eyes darted back and forth searching for any enemy patrol which could be hiding in any one of the rocky defiles. He could only hope that the aerial photographs proved to be right and there was somewhere nearby to build an airfield big enough to take a C-47 – or they would be clambering about in these damned hills for days.

They came to a halt again and then began to descend into another valley, most of which was taken up by an enormous paddy field. Hunkering down in the shade of the trees and scrub on the edge of the paddy, they were glad of the brief respite from the blazing sun. There was a cluster of bamboo huts on stilts in the trees and a few Burmese working in the field, but nothing else moved, and all was silent.

'Right, Warrant Officer Reilly,' whispered the CO. 'Now it's your turn. Take off the hat and wind this cloth round your head like the natives do. You and Flight Lieutenant Simms are going to walk right down the middle of that paddy to measure it and see if it's long enough for an airstrip. Your job will be to gauge what machinery we'll need and the number of men it will take to clear it. As you walk, you must both look as if you're going somewhere, but not be in a hurry. Understood?'

The airman muttered confirmation, and Jim just nodded and copied the way the other man was wrapping the black cloth over his hair.

'Stick your carbines down your longyis like this,' said the CO shoving his gun down his shorts and adjusting the native cloth over the handle so it couldn't be seen. He waited for both men to comply, looked them up and down and nodded. 'You'll do. Off you go.'

With the others poised in the scrub to give covering fire, Jim and the RAF man cautiously stepped out into the brilliant morning sunshine and began the slow, heart-stopping walk across the paddy field under the very noses of the Burmese workers and any Japanese who happened to be hiding in those bamboo huts or surrounding trees.

Jim's heart was hammering, his hand sweating on the stock of his gun as he counted each step. The Burmese watched them from beneath their conical reed hats, but mercifully soon returned to their work. With the sun directly overhead, he and the other man cast no shadows, but the water was seeping into his boots and making squelching noises he was certain could be heard by those natives, and recognised as unusual, for they worked bare-footed.

They'd gone four hundred yards by Jim's reckoning when they reached a steep decline in the land that hadn't been visible before. They both squatted down like natives and surveyed the stretch of paddy still to cross, and the ominous dark line of jungle and scrub that lay on three sides of the paddy.

Jim could feel the sweat sheen his skin and run in rivulets over his torso. They were horribly exposed out here – sitting ducks for any Japanese patrol – or a Burman who decided to question their presence, for this disguise would fool no one on close inspection.

He slid his finger down the stock of his carbine, releasing the safety catch, and narrowing his eyes against the glare of the sun on the water in the field to try and spot any suspicious glint of metal or movement in the distant jungle. From this position he could actually make out the roofs of the Japanese HQ through the shimmering heat haze. This was utter, bloody madness, and every minute they stayed here was a minute too long.

The RAF man leaned towards Jim and whispered, 'You carry on, Reilly. I'll stay here and cover you. Keep counting every step, and then make your way back to the others.'

Jim was only too pleased to be on the move again. He waited for the other man to discreetly draw his carbine from his clothing and click off the safety catch. At his nod, Jim slowly got to his feet and eased his way down the steep five-foot drop to the continuation of the vast paddy field. He took a deep breath and began to stroll across the second paddy, his fingers gripping the stock of his carbine, ready to fire if anything came out of the jungle.

This second half of the paddy turned out to be around another four hundred yards. Jim sighed with relief as he drifted into the long grass at the edge of the field and melted into the dense shadows of the jungle. He squatted down and waited for his heart rate to slow, all the time watching and listening for any sound or glimpse of movement.

His eyes were stinging with his sweat, and he used the dirty longyi to scrub his face dry as he watched the RAF man strolling back the way they'd come as if he was on a Sunday walk in the park. And then, keeping in the shadows of the trees and long grass, Jim began his own cautious journey back through the surrounding jungle.

'Well?' asked the CO as soon as Jim arrived. 'Is it long enough?'

Jim slaked his thirst with a long drink from his canister before answering. 'By my reckoning it's about eight hundred yards long, and will be fine,' he said, pausing to drain the last of the water. 'The steep drop in the middle poses a bit of a problem. But a few bulldozers and two hundred sappers to do the groundwork should flatten it out and drain it within a couple of days. I would suggest we burn back some of that jungle. It's too close to the wires we'll be putting up to defend the airfield, and perfect for ambush as it stands.'

The commanding officer nodded curtly and then looked at the RAF man. 'Is the flying approach good enough?' At the man's nod, the CO looked thoughtful as he surveyed the field and the high escarpment behind him. 'It'll be difficult to defend, but with enough men we should be able to dominate the area. I'll order in another brigade and some heavy artillery along with the bulldozers. Let's get back to camp and report in to HQ.'

'What about the Japs and the railway, sir?' Jim dared to ask.

'We'll deal with them tonight,' he replied tersely.

An hour before dusk the CO faced the fact they would soon be mired in a big battle, so ordered the majority of the horses and mules to be evacuated under guard of a small patrol to the distant American base at Mokso Kasan. There would be no room for them in the new block, and the effect of heavy gunfire and mortars would send them berserk, making them impossible to control. As this was happening, Ernie and the mixed brigades were marching back to the appointed block that would be their HQ and airdrop site, to set up communications, dig in, and make a start on the runway.

Jim and Big Bert left the riverside camp with a group of thirty marauders which included sappers, Gurkhas and Indian Riflemen. As the light faded they were wading through the river and up the steep hill to the viewpoint where they could see the layout of their night's objective – the railway station and Japanese camp.

At their senior officer's signal they silently moved as one down the steep decline and, upon reaching the clearing, went their separate ways. All was still, and apart from the occasional glimmer of light coming from around the edges of the carelessly blacked-out windows of the mess, there was little sign of life.

Jim and some of the other sappers split from the main group and began to lay charges round the ammunition dump, communications hut and garage workshops, whilst the rest turned their attention to the station signal box and railway lines. Moving like shadows in the darkness, the others reconnoitred the area and checked all the buildings.

Jim raced back to join Big Bert, who'd taken up a post near what they guessed was the mess hall, for they could hear music and voices and the clatter of metal plates. He fixed the wires to the detonator and awaited the signal. 'What's the conclusion, Bert?' he whispered.

'Everywhere's deserted but for the mess,' he whispered back. 'One guard on the northern perimeter, another to the south; both dealt with.'

Jim nodded with some relief. He hadn't liked the thought of killing wounded or sick men in the hospital – even if they were the enemy.

The signal from the leading officer came at last, and Jim pushed the plunger down to detonate the charges they'd laid. And held his breath.

There was an awful moment of silence, and then the night exploded into a series of blinding flashes and deafening booms that lit the compound as bright as day. The blast of heat rolled over the clearing, and the earth rocked beneath the marauders with the aftershocks.

Jim and the others lay flat to withstand the blasts, deafened by the noise and rocked by the shock waves. The ammunition dump went up in a series of great booming roars, spewing flames and sending bullets zipping and whizzing in all directions as mortars thundered and the nearby trucks, jeeps and cars were blown to smithereens.

The storehouse blew, turning sacks of rice to atoms, and tin cans into missiles. And as the fuel dump went with it, there was a massive explosion and a belch of black smoke and orange flames which were fed by the petrol fumes. Burning fuel cans spun in the air, some landing on the roofs of the thatched huts or in the dry grass at the edge of the jungle, setting it all ablaze. Birds rose in panic from the trees to swirl amid the pall of black smoke that was now rising into the night sky.

This cacophony of destruction was swiftly followed by the railway signal box, the warehouses, and about three hundred yards of rail being thrown several hundred feet into the air as if they

148

weighed nothing.

Jim exchanged delighted grins with Big Bert as they hugged the ground and waited for the explosions to die down. This was better than any Bonfire Night.

As the explosions stuttered to a halt and the mess hall began to burn, the Japanese poured out into the glare of the many fires. The marauders made short work of them, and after searching through the other buildings for anyone that might have escaped, they set fire to them and left them to burn. There would be reprisals, no doubt, for the conflagration could probably be seen from miles away and any Japanese in the area would soon be on their way.

By Jim's reckoning, they had about forty-eight hours to get the paddy flattened into an airfield so the C-47s could bring in the heavy machinery, artillery and fresh men. If it took longer, then they'd be trapped and have to fight their way out.

8

Doris had powdered her nose and repaired her lipstick before setting off again, but it had still taken an enormous effort of will to climb out of the car and follow the last few stragglers into the private chapel on the Chumleys' estate.

The heavy door creaked horribly as she closed it behind her, and she became all too aware of the turning heads and glaring eyes as she quickly slid into a rear pew. This was really the last place she wanted to be today. She'd hoped for some sort of welcoming smile from the women she'd worked alongside for so many years, but it seemed the occasion was too solemn for smiles, and her late arrival had not eased the chilly mood. She sat through the interminable service, listening to the fulsome eulogies for the women who'd been killed on that awful day – the guilt at having survived becoming harder to bear by the minute.

And then it was over at last, and as the chief mourners came down the aisle, she tried to catch their eyes to convey her sympathy, but they were too wrapped up in their own misery to notice. Doris followed them outside to discover they were already huddled beneath umbrellas and hurrying towards the manor house. 'Such a shame the weather is so awful,' she said to the woman standing next to her as she unfurled her own umbrella.

Cold blue eyes regarded her, and without a word the other woman strode away.

Doris frowned, for she'd always considered Lucinda Franklin to be a friend. Perhaps it was her own frail state that was making her feel uncomfortable, and she'd just imagined the hostility?

The manor house was warm and welcoming after the walk through the dreary rain and wind, and Doris quickly stowed her umbrella, tidied her hair and went into the vast drawing room where drinks were being served. The mood had lightened amongst the mourners, but as she approached one little group after another, she found their backs turned to her and heard sly comments and sniggers. It seemed she was being shunned – that her presence here was far from welcome – and she struggled to understand why.

'I must say,' said a plummy voice nearby, 'some people have a frightful nerve, haven't they? I mean, it isn't as if she's one of us, is she?' Grey eyes slid to Doris momentarily.

'Ghastly woman,' came the reply. 'And when I think of how much Lady Chumley did for her over the years...' There was a ripple of agreement from the circle of women, and sharp, hostile gazes darted over Doris before moving away. 'Still,' said another, 'she can be quite useful when it comes to running about for us, but turning up here today is really beyond the pale. One would have thought she'd have known she wouldn't be welcome.'

Doris stood isolated in that room full of chattering, catty women feeling horribly vulnerable as she listened to their scorn and felt their enmity. She wondered why on earth she'd ever believed she could be a part of this vicious circle who seemed to delight in denigrating those they saw as beneath them.

To her distress, she discovered her hand was shaking as she put the glass of sherry on a nearby table and tried to muster up the courage to walk through the gathering with dignity and leave them to it. She'd taken a few steps towards the door when Lord Chumley stepped into her path and took her hand.

'Thank you very much for coming today, Mrs Williams,' he said with a warm smile. 'How are you coping at Beach View? Not too much of a wrench after losing your own home, I hope?'

Doris was so grateful to him for talking to her

151

that her pent-up emotions were unleashed in a great rush of noisy tears. Unable to reply to him, she took flight, pushing her way through the crush to retrieve her umbrella and fur coat and find sanctuary in her car.

She had no idea of how long she sat there watching the rain come down and the sky darken, but eventually she dried her tears, and took a long, hard look at what today had taught her. What Lord Chumley must have thought of her running off like that, she didn't know or really care any more – and as for all those painted, bejewelled and scented cats, how they must be sniggering into their furs. And well they might, for she'd certainly given them enough fuel to stoke their gossip today.

To her surprise, Doris found she didn't actually care. She decided to put the whole humiliating episode firmly to the back of her mind, and concentrate on what really mattered to her. She would go and see her solicitor to inform him about Ted's death, and ask his advice about what to do with regards to a burial service.

It was five in the afternoon when Doris parked the car outside Beach View, switched off the engine and tried to come to terms with what had turned out to be the worst day of her life.

Through the drizzling rain, she regarded the rubble at the end of the cul-de-sac and the shabby Victorian villas that had survived the gas explosion, but not the Luftwaffe's bullets. Many of the windows had been boarded over, the paint was peeling on the doors and window frames and there hadn't been a brush of whitewash on the front steps since war had been declared. Like her mood, it was all desperately depressing, and she found she couldn't summon up the energy to get out of the car.

Not yet ready to face the inevitable questions from whoever might be at home, Doris lit a cigarette and tried to instil some sort of optimism into her dispirited and weary self – but it was no good.

The afternoon had finally opened her eyes and made her see with shaming clarity that Peggy had been right all along. She didn't fit in with that crowd, had never really been a part of that well-to-do, smug circle which had kept her at arm's length for years and laughed about her behind her back. She'd tried so hard to be part of that clique, willing to do the tasks they found distasteful and, like a fool, running about after them in the hope that one day they would accept her.

Doris took a tremulous breath. She should have listened to Peggy and learnt the lessons of the past, for this afternoon had been utterly humiliating. And to compound it all, she'd been faced with shocking revelations which had come out of the blue and rocked her to the very core. She eyed the papers on the passenger seat and shivered. Looking determinedly away, she regarded Beach View with a fondness that surprised her. Shabby and run-down it might be, but it was the house where she and her two sisters had been born and raised by loving parents who'd probably had their own dreams, but who'd had to work long, hard hours for everything they'd achieved.

This was the home she'd left for a job in London and her own dreams of becoming someone she realised now she was never meant to be. What a fool she'd been to believe she was any better than her sisters – and what harsh lessons she'd had to learn along the way – for here she was, back where she'd started. Only now, she barely had more than the clothes on her back, and was staring into a very bleak future. The terror of what might happen to her was a living thing squirming inside her and she felt quite sick. The cushion of hope that her situation was merely temporary had been swept away, and for the first time in her life she felt vulnerable and horribly afraid.

Doris looked down at the papers and a wave of anger consumed her. She wouldn't give in to this awful fear – she was strong and capable and this latest blow would not defeat her. She gathered the papers and stuffed them in her leather handbag. She would say nothing of what had happened today until she could be alone with Peggy. Dear, sweet Peggy who'd had to put up with so much from her over the years, and yet never seemed to bear a grudge. She would understand and be there to help her through the next few months, she was certain.

Doris gave a wry smile as she touched her cheek, which was still quite tender from that slap. Peggy could certainly pack a wallop when roused – and Doris acknowledged that she'd had a perfect right to do so after her appalling behaviour. What sort of woman had she become? And what on earth had possessed her to be so high-handed and mean after Peggy had been so generous and loving – so grateful she hadn't been killed?

Doris let out a long breath before climbing out

of the car. This day was thankfully almost over, but from now on she would do her utmost to make things up to Peggy and learn to be satisfied with her lot. After all, she reasoned, she had her health, her mink and her diamond ring as well as a fairly healthy chunk of the divorce settlement, and she was still young enough to seek useful employment and join in the war effort – though not on a factory floor. She'd rather go without than bear that humiliation.

Doris locked the car, gave the roof an affectionate pat and went up the steps to the front door. She would ask Ron to help her find somewhere to store it for the duration now she could no longer afford to run it.

Fred dropped Peggy off by the twitten as usual and she hurried through the greyness of early evening to the back door. Stepping into the scullery, she shook the damp from her headscarf and raincoat, smiling at the sound of happy voices up in the kitchen.

She climbed the steps and entered the lovely warmth of the heart of her home, delighted to see Cordelia ensconced in her usual fireside chair, her tangled knitting abandoned in her lap as Sarah handed her a cup of tea.

'Hello, Cordy,' said Peggy, giving her an affectionate kiss on the cheek. 'How lovely to see you downstairs again – and looking so much better too.'

'I'm feeling almost the full ticket now, dear. Another day and I shall be able to go out for some fresh air.'

'Well, we'll see how you are tomorrow,' murmured Peggy, nodding her thanks to Sarah for the welcome cup of tea. 'You don't want to rush things and make yourself ill again.'

Cordelia clucked her tongue. 'Bertie promised to take me out to lunch at the Officers' Club on Saturday, and I'm not missing out on that,' she said firmly. She sipped her tea and then looked at Peggy over her half-moon glasses, her blue eyes twinkling. 'We've all got lots to tell you, Peggy.'

Peggy grinned, relieved that Cordelia was almost her old self again. 'I'm all ears,' she replied. 'But I'll have my supper whilst I listen, if you don't mind.'

Cordelia nodded to Sarah. 'You first.'

Sarah placed Peggy's plate of supper on the table and sat down beside her. 'I've just finished my last day with the WTC,' she said. 'Everyone is moving out tomorrow for Scotland, and the manor house and WTC buildings will be taken over by the Red Cross to treat some of the wounded that are coming back from France. The local hospitals can't cope, you see, but the walking wounded can recuperate in comfort there.'

'Are you sad to be leaving?' asked Peggy.

'In a way,' Sarah replied. 'I made some lovely friends there, and I shall miss not seeing them every day.' She smiled. 'But at least I won't have to wear that bulky uniform again – or walk all that way twice a day.'

'I have a friend who works at the Town Hall who might know of a job going,' said Peggy. 'I could telephone her, if it would help.'

'Thank you, Aunt Peggy, but there's no need.

I've already been down to the labour exchange and landed a secretarial post in the Council offices.' She grinned in delight. 'I start tomorrow.'

'Good for you,' breathed Peggy, giving her a hug. 'My goodness. You don't let the grass grow under your feet, do you?'

Sarah giggled. 'Not if I can help it.'

Peggy was tempted to ask how she was coping with her decision to end things with Delaney and wait for Philip to come home – and managed to stop herself. The girl seemed quite happy, and she didn't want to spoil her mood by asking too many questions.

'Where's Doris?' she asked, finishing her supper.

'Upstairs,' said Rita. 'She was acting very strangely when she got back,' she added with a frown.

Peggy's attention sharpened. 'Really? In what way?'

'In a nice way, and with a smile that looked genuine enough,' said Rita, still frowning. 'She actually asked me how I was coping with my leg in plaster, and if I'd heard from Dad.'

'She sat and talked to me too,' said Cordelia, not to be outdone, 'and offered to make us both a cup of tea.' She pursed her lips. 'She's either a very good actress or she's had some sort of miraculous change of attitude. Either way, it's most unsettling.'

'She's had the most awful day, Cordelia,' said Peggy. 'I suspect she just wanted a bit of company to take her mind off things.'

'Then why isn't she down here with us instead

of shut away up there?' retorted Cordelia.

'She's just lost Ted,' Peggy reminded her, 'and has had to attend the service for her dead friends. She's probably exhausted by it all. I know I would be.' Before Cordelia could make her opinion of Doris any clearer, Peggy forestalled her by turning to Rita. 'You were going to tell me about this idea you and Peter had to make Cordelia's life easier.'

'I was telling Grandma Cordy about it this afternoon,' said Rita, drawing several sheets of butcher's white paper from the table. 'Me and Pete are both good with mechanical things, and he remembered an American pal telling him about something that might be really useful in helping Grandma Cordy up and down the stairs. So I went to the library to do a bit of research and we came up with this.'

Peggy regarded the rough drawing of a simple chair and footrest sitting on a sturdy sort of platform which was fixed to four metal rollers that slotted into two lengths of metal. These metal shafts were fixed firmly to a solid metal bar which was pinned to the bannisters. Next to the seat of this contraption was a handle, which seemed to be attached to a small motor beneath it.

'Good heavens,' breathed Peggy. 'Is it quite safe? What if it goes too fast and throws Cordelia out?'

'The motor would be a small one, so it won't be able to go too fast, and of course there's a brake on the handle, like the ones you get in lifts. All Grandma Cordy would have to do is pull on it to stop it.'

'I'm not sure,' said Peggy. 'It's all a bit new-fangled and dangerous-looking.'

Rita smiled and placed a large book in front of her. 'Actually, it's not a new invention at all,' she said, selecting a page with a similar diagram on it. 'This was invented by Mr Crispen in America in the 1920s.' She turned another page. 'And this article here discusses the likelihood that the servants used a series of pulleys on a chair to haul Henry the Eighth to the upper floor of his palace when he was too fat to walk,' she added triumphantly.

Peggy eyed the precarious collection of ropes and pulleys and turned back to the more modern version of what Crispen had called his 'Inclinator'. 'Goodness, are you sure you and Peter are capable of building such a thing? Wouldn't it be better to club together and try and buy one?'

Rita laughed and shook her head, making her dark curls bounce on her shoulders. 'It would cost the earth and have to be brought over from America. Peter and I have been tinkering with motors and suchlike since we were both kids, so of course we can build it, although it could take a bit of time now he's so involved in the invasion.'

Peggy eyed the drawing and then the photograph in the library book. 'Well, if you're sure,' she murmured, still not totally convinced. 'Will it make a horrid mess of my stairs, though?'

Rita shook her head. 'We're going to build it in a corner of the fire station and test it on the stairs to the office before we set it up here. Any mess we make, we'll clear up, I promise.'

'Now that I would like to see,' teased Peggy. 'I

can't remember the last time you tidied anything, let alone your room.'

Rita threw her arms round Peggy's neck and hugged her. 'I do love you, Aunty Peg, but you really are the worst worrier. Our stair climber will work, you'll see.'

Peggy hugged her back and then reluctantly got to her feet. 'Where are the other two?' she asked. 'They should have been home by now.'

'Fran's out with Robert for her tea, and Ivy's gone to the Crown with Andy to have tea with his Aunt Gloria,' said Rita. She shot Peggy a mischievous grin. 'I still find it hard to think of Gloria Stevens being anyone's aunt – she's too ... too...'

'Loud and brassy,' piped up Cordelia, who wasn't afraid of calling a spade a shovel.

'I'm going up to see if Doris needs anything,' said Peggy, unwilling to get caught up in a discussion about Gloria's many failings, for despite being brassy and loud, she had a good heart and would give her last shilling to anyone who needed it, and Peggy rather liked her.

She left the kitchen, peeked in to make sure Daisy was sleeping soundly, and then went up to the first floor. She hesitated outside the door, preparing herself to face whatever Doris might throw at her next, and then knocked and entered as Doris called her to come in.

Doris was sitting in the armchair by the gas fire, wrapped in Peggy's old dressing gown, with her feet propped on the dressing stool and her face clean of make-up. 'Hello, Peggy,' she said, rising to her feet and shooting her a hesitant smile. 'I was hoping you'd come to see me.'

Peggy warily closed the door behind her, noting with a glance that the room was back to how it had been before and that it was as neat as a pin. 'You're obviously tired and ready for bed,' she said, 'but I thought I'd just pop in to see how you were and if you needed anything.'

Doris quickly perched on the stool, indicating that Peggy should take the chair. 'It's been a long and very difficult day,' she admitted, 'and although I'm not yet really ready to face the others downstairs, I'd appreciate it if you would keep me company for a little while.'

Peggy could see the shadows of sorrow and weariness beneath her sister's reddened eyes, and because she looked so down, decided to stay. 'It was the most awful news to get, especially today of all days,' she said, offering her packet of Park Drive. 'I honestly don't know how you coped with the service, and everything.'

'I didn't cope at all,' Doris confessed, lighting their cigarettes with her gold lighter and then turning to stare into the sputtering flames of the gas fire. 'I'm finding it very hard to believe I'll never see Edward again. That he won't suddenly come through that door or telephone me, or turn up with my week's groceries.'

Her voice broke and Peggy could see she was making a stoic effort to steady herself and not break down. 'I can only imagine how you must be feeling,' Peggy said, 'so I won't upset you further by spouting the usual platitudes. I know that if it had been my Jim I'd have wanted to shut myself away from the world too.'

Doris continued to stare into the flames as she

161

smoked her cigarette. 'I knew I'd really lost him when he started seeing Martha,' she said after a moment. 'But to lose him so utterly and so suddenly like that is very hard to take.' She turned her gaze to Peggy. 'I did love him, you know,' she murmured, 'and if I hadn't been so proud and full of myself, he'd still be here, alive and with me – and we could have weathered this awful upheaval together.'

Peggy remained silent, for she understood Doris's pain at losing Ted. She'd felt the same way when her darling Jim had been posted to India. It had been like a death to see him leave – and as the months and years had rolled on she'd come to realise how deeply she adored him and how so much of her life was bound up with him. But Doris had realised too late what Ted had meant to her, and that was the most tragic thing of all.

Doris stubbed out the cigarette in an ashtray and folded her hands in her lap. 'I realised something today, Peggy,' she said quietly, 'and I want to apologise. My behaviour towards you over the years has been unforgivable, and I'd like you to know how very much I care for you, and appreciate all you've done for me.'

'Oh, Doris,' sighed Peggy. 'You don't have to apologise.'

'Indeed I do. I've run roughshod over your feelings, disparaged your family, your home and your work at the factory. I've been mean with my time and mean with my words, and I wouldn't at all blame you if you threw me out.'

'I'd never do that,' gasped Peggy. 'I know I threatened it, but it was only because you wound me up like a clock and I bust a spring.' She realised what she'd said and giggled. 'You know what I mean.'

Doris's returning smile was wan. 'You have a forgiving heart and a generous soul, Peggy,' she said. 'There's been many a time when I've wished I could be more like you.'

Peggy regarded her in some confusion. This was not the Doris she'd fallen out with ever since she could remember – not the cold, sneering woman who'd bossed her about and flaunted her wealth at every turn – but a softer, gentler, repentant Doris who seemed so very eager to put things right between them.

Had she experienced an epiphany? Had the shock of the V-1 and the loss of Ted made her realise how tenuous life was, and this was her way of trying to make amends before it was too late? Peggy didn't know the answer, but, like Cordelia, she was wary, for Doris had made such overtures before and then reverted to being a cow at the first opportunity to take umbrage.

Doris straightened her back and took a deep breath. 'I realise you must be wondering why I'm talking to you like this, and I don't blame you for doubting my sincerity. After all, this is hardly the first time we've tried to heal the breach between us, and I've always been the one to spoil it.'

Peggy regarded her sister evenly, not yet prepared to be taken in by this new Doris. 'This isn't all about losing Ted, is it?' she said finally. 'What else happened today?'

Peggy listened as Doris told her about the humiliation she'd suffered at the memorial service and reception, and felt quite ill at the thought of how awful it must have been for Doris to have abandoned a lifetime of control to rush off like that. Peggy had always thought of Wally Chumley as a jumped-up barrow boy with too much money and an over-developed sense of self-importance, but at least he'd had the grace to talk to Doris, and for that she was grateful.

'Oh, my dear,' she sighed, reaching for her hand. 'I'm so sorry.'

Doris actually smiled. 'Don't be sorry, Peggy. It was a revelation, and I wish I'd listened to your advice to avoid them years ago. You see, I've finally realised you were right. I don't belong with them, no longer want to or ever will after today.'

'You've said that before,' Peggy reminded her gently.

'I know. But now I've seen them for what they really are, and quite honestly want nothing more to do with them.'

Peggy didn't really believe that, and suspected that the minute one of them telephoned asking her to do something she'd be over there like a shot. But she said nothing. Only time would tell if this improved and determined Doris could keep up her good intentions.

'Something else far more important happened today, Peggy,' said Doris, 'and after learning about Edward and through that ghastly charade this lunchtime, it came as a real hammer blow.' She delved into her handbag and pulled out the wad of paper.

Peggy frowned. 'What's that?'

Doris smoothed the papers with her hand and

left them in her lap. 'After leaving the reception I decided to go and see our solicitor to inform him of Edward's death and to find out what I should do about a funeral, or at least some sort of service.' She licked her lips and reached for her cigarettes. Having lit one for each of them, she abandoned the papers and nervously began to pace back and forth.

'Edward and Martha were married at the registry office on the Thursday morning before they left for London on their honeymoon the following Saturday,' she said flatly. 'How they got travel permits, I don't know, but that's neither here nor there,' she continued with an impatient wave of her hand. 'Anyway, it turns out he'd made a new will, leaving some money to Anthony, the house to me, and the rest of his estate to Martha, who'd also left a will leaving everything to her elderly parents.'

Peggy could see by Doris's expression that this wasn't going to end well, but said nothing as it was clear her sister needed to release all the pent-up feelings she'd been harbouring throughout the day.

'As you know,' Doris continued, 'Edward has always played the stock market, and until recently had been very successful at it – which was why he could afford to buy the house, give me a generous settlement on our divorce and a healthy monthly allowance.' She took a shallow, quavering breath. 'But playing the stock market is merely a polite way of saying he was a gambler, and he got over-confident and began to take risks.'

She puffed furiously on her cigarette and then

mashed it out in the ashtray. 'The losses began to mount up, and the bigger they got, the more high-risk stocks he bought to try and recoup.' She folded her arms tightly about her waist. 'It's all gone, Peggy,' she managed, her voice breaking. 'Every last penny.'

Peggy stared at her in horrified disbelief. 'But what about your settlement and the house? I thought he'd turned the deeds over to you after the divorce?'

'The settlement's safe, thank goodness, I've barely touched it. As for the house, he never got round to it,' she said bitterly, 'and as I trusted him, I didn't think it was something I needed to worry about. But it seems he used it as collateral two months ago, and took out a huge mortgage on it to cover his debts to his broker and make further investments.'

Her mouth twisted in disgust. 'He might have left me the house in his will, but it wasn't his to pass on. The bank owns it, and all the government compensation I was hoping for will go straight there – and of course my monthly allowance will stop.'

Peggy was reeling from the shock of learning how devious Ted had been, and took her hand. 'Oh, Doris, you poor love. How awful for you. I can't imagine what Ted was thinking of to write a will like that when he must have known he had nothing to leave.'

'He wasn't expecting to be killed and probably thought he had the time to make enough to pay back the bank loan without me ever knowing what he'd done.' Doris gave a tremulous sigh. 'It just goes to show that you never really know a person, even if you've been married to them for over thirty years,' she said sadly. 'But even now, after all he's done, I do mourn him, Peggy, and so wish we'd been able to sort things out between us. Perhaps then he might have been more cautious in his dealings.'

Peggy doubted that, for once a gambler, always a gambler, and Ted had proved to be devious in the extreme. She folded her arms around her sister and felt her trembling as she held her close. 'You'll always have a home here, Doris,' she murmured.

Doris hugged her back and then gently eased away. 'Thank you, Peggy. I promise that from now on I will do my very best not to make you regret your loving generosity. But I will not be a burden to you. I shall pay you for my board and keep from the settlement, and find a job.'

Peggy stared at her in undisguised shock. 'A job? You?' she managed.

Doris shot her a wan smile. 'There's no need to look so shocked,' she said. 'I'm quite capable of doing accounts and seeing to office administration – even though I might be a bit rusty – and don't forget I was trained as a secretary and have been doing Lady Chumley's charity accounts for years.'

'Well, good for you,' breathed Peggy, stunned at her sister's stoicism in the face of such upheaval. 'I have a friend who works in the Town Hall,' she offered for the second time that evening. 'They're always looking for good secretaries now most of the young women have joined up in the services, and I'm sure if I spoke to her she'd put in a good

167

word for you. At least it would save you the humiliation of having to go to the labour exchange.'

Doris blinked back her tears. 'There's no end to your kindness, is there?' she managed. 'Oh, Peggy, I've been such a cow. Can you *ever* forgive me?'

'Of course I can,' she replied, giving her another hug. 'Just don't wind me up by pinching my Jim's dressing gown again and we'll get along just fine.'

9

Peggy had confided in Ron and the others about Doris's plight the previous evening, and although Doris had upset each of them in the past, they seemed genuinely sorry that she'd received such a life-changing blow, and promised to be extra nice to her. But when Peggy had told them Doris would be looking for work, none of them believed anyone would dare take her on, and if they did, that she'd put everyone's back up and last less than a day. Determined to prove them all wrong, Peggy fretted over the problem through the night.

Rising early, she quickly went through her usual morning routine and then telephoned her friend Claire, who was in charge of the typing pool at the Mayor's office in the Town Hall. Claire was a war widow in her mid-forties and lived alone now her two children had been evacuated to Dorset. She and Peggy had known one another since they'd been in the same class at junior school, and although they didn't get much chance of meeting up, when they did it was as if no time had passed at all.

'Hello, Peggy,' Claire said in delighted surprise. 'My goodness, you're an early bird. I've only just got into my office.'

Peggy sat on the hall chair and they settled in for a bit of a gossip, catching up on things as they hadn't seen one another for some months.

'It's lovely to chat, Peg, but I really do have to get on,' said Claire some minutes later. 'The Mayor's got an important council meeting later this morning.'

'I won't keep you then,' said Peggy. 'Only I was wondering if you had any secretarial jobs going?'

'We always have vacancies with so many young ones joining up, but I thought you were happy at Solly's factory?'

'It's not for me,' Peggy said hurriedly. 'I can't type for toffee.'

'Who is it, then? One of your chicks?' Claire asked with warm amusement.

Peggy gripped the receiver. 'Actually, it's for my sister Doris,' she confessed.

There was a long silence, and Peggy wondered if they'd been cut off, but as she was about to speak again, Claire came back on. 'I'm sorry, Peggy. I'm afraid I can't help.'

'But I thought you said you had vacancies, and Doris is a fully qualified secretary – in fact she once worked as private secretary to the chairman of the board of a large bank in London.' Peggy realised she was gabbling, and shut up.

'I'm sure she's most efficient,' said Claire rather

169

coolly, 'but as much as I'd love to help you, Peggy, I simply can't take your sister on.'

'But why?'

Claire gave a short sigh. 'There have been issues in the past between her and at least three women in my typing pool,' she said reluctantly. 'If I brought Doris in I'd have a mutiny on my hands.'

'I don't understand,' said a perplexed Peggy. 'How could Doris have upset women in a typing pool?'

'They volunteer for the WVS at weekends and evenings,' said Claire. 'I'm so sorry, Peggy, but I simply can't afford to rock the boat as we're so short-staffed already.'

'Oh, dear,' sighed Peggy. 'This isn't going to be as easy as I thought, is it?'

'Doris is her own worst enemy, Peggy, and although there is some sympathy for her losing her home like that, she's too stuck up and overbearing for most people, and, I'm sorry to say, not well liked.'

'Thanks for being so frank with me,' said Peggy sadly. 'I'm sorry, but I had to ask. I don't suppose you know of anywhere else she might find something?'

'Not offhand, but if I do hear of anything, I'll let you know.'

Peggy thanked her again, disconnected the call and then asked her one-time evacuee April, who was working on the telephone exchange, to put her through to the local bank where she knew the manager. That was no-go either and five similarly distressing calls later, Peggy realised that her sister's snooty, bossy reputation had spiked any chance of her being taken on, even as an office junior typist at the billeting office – which Peggy suspected she'd turn down flat anyway. Doris might be willing to work and might have changed her way of thinking, but Peggy knew her well enough to realise she still had some pride.

Peggy lit a cigarette and sat deep in troubled thought for a while and then reluctantly asked April to put her through to the labour exchange. Her friend there probably wouldn't take Doris on either after they'd fallen out over poor Ivy, who'd been made utterly miserable by Doris in Havelock Road – but she might know of an office job elsewhere in the town.

Peggy was proved right, for Betty Miller swiftly rejected any idea of Doris working at the labour exchange, but something had come in late last night which might suit her, as she would be working alone with the administrator of the factory estate. The fact that the man was a retired colonel was all to the good, for it would appeal to Doris's sense of self-importance.

'Now you're just being catty,' muttered Peggy.

'Sorry, Peg, but she winds me up with her snooty ways,' Betty replied. 'I'll arrange an appointment for her anyway. It's the best I can offer her.'

Peggy thanked her, replaced the receiver and stubbed out her cigarette. 'It's a start, I suppose, but, oh, Doris, you really don't make life any easier, do you?' she sighed.

The letters clattered into the wire basket and she hurried across the hall to see who'd written. It was quite a bonanza this morning, with three for Fran, an airmail for Sarah as well as two for

Ivy, one for Doris, two for Cordelia, and one for Rita. And joy of joys, there were letters for her and Ron from Jim. She shoved hers into her apron pocket and took the rest into the kitchen where she dumped them on the table.

With cries of delight, Cordelia, Ivy, Sarah and Fran grabbed them and silence fell as they all became engrossed in news from their loved ones.

'To be sure, that's a fine collection this morning,' said Ron, who was trying to clean Daisy's face of jam and margarine and not having much success as the toddler was wriggling so much.

'We've got two each from Jim,' said Peggy. 'But I'll read mine later. I need to make sure Doris is up.'

'Ach, leave her be, wee girl. After what you told us last night, she needs a lie-in, so she does.'

Peggy shook her head. 'Betty at the labour exchange is arranging a job interview with a Colonel White up at the factory estate at eleven this morning. If she doesn't get a move on, she'll be late, and that won't go down too well with a military man, I'm sure.'

'Oh aye?' Ron's eyebrows shot up. 'I've met the Colonel – good sort of man, so he is – helped poor old Stan out of a very sticky situation when Ethel got arrested for stealing from the Red Cross. Very fair he was with Stan.'

'Then let's hope he and Doris get on,' said Peggy. 'I'm rapidly running out of ideas of where to try next.' She quickly left the kitchen and ran upstairs, meeting Rita slowly making her way down from the top floor on her crutches. 'There's a letter from your dad in the kitchen,' she said, 'but don't rush. I don't want you going headlong down these stairs.'

Rita grinned back at her and swung along the landing before bumping down the stairs on her bottom like a two-year-old. Peggy rolled her eyes and tutted before knocking on Doris's door.

'Good morning,' said Doris who was already dressed for the day in a tweed skirt and plain white blouse. 'It looks like it's going to be nice weather for once,' she added, glancing out of the window.

'I spoke to my friend at the council offices, but she couldn't help,' said Peggy, cutting to the chase. 'But Betty at the labour exchange is arranging an interview at eleven for you up at the factory estate.'

Doris sniffed with disdain. 'I'm not working up there,' she said firmly. 'I might be in a bind, but I'm not that desperate.'

'It's in an office, not a factory,' said Peggy evenly, and went on to explain about the Colonel needing a personal secretary to help him with all the paperwork involved in administering the estate and its security.

Doris broke into a smile. 'Then I'd better polish my shoes and make sure I get there on time.' She clasped Peggy's hand. 'Thank you for arranging it, Peggy.'

'It was no bother,' she fibbed quickly. 'Breakfast is ready, by the way. It'll do you no good going to an interview on an empty stomach.' She hurried out of the bedroom and back downstairs. The time was racing by, and she wanted to make sure Sarah was given a proper send-off on her first day in her new job.

Sarah had finished reading her mother's letter and Peggy noticed that she was looking a little pale. 'You're not nervous about this new job, are you?' she asked.

Sarah shook her head and put on a brave smile. 'It's just Mother's letters I'm finding hard to take,' she admitted. 'She keeps going on about my wedding to Philip and all the plans she has for my future as well as Jane's – and to be frank, Aunt Peggy, it's all getting a bit much. She seems to have completely lost sight of the fact that we're grown up and might have other ideas.'

'Oh dear,' sighed Peggy. 'But it's good that she's looking on the bright side of things, don't you think?'

Sarah shook her head. 'Jane and I are worried about her. She's being too positive – too set on believing Pops and Philip will come through un-scathed and ready to carry on as if nothing had happened. And if they don't, there's no telling how it will affect her.'

'It will affect all of you,' said Peggy, laying a gentle hand on her arm. 'One way or another, it will be you who has to make a terrible sacrifice,' she murmured beneath the other girls' chatter.

'Delaney understands why I'm doing it,' Sarah replied quietly and firmly. 'And my mind is made up, Aunt Peg.' She tucked the letters into her handbag. 'By the way,' she said with a forced brightness, 'Jane has an admirer, and I think she's in love.'

'Oh, how lovely,' breathed Peggy. 'Who is he? Where did they meet? What does he do?'

Sarah's laugh was genuine. 'You are an incorrigible romantic, Peggy. They met at work, so I have no idea what he does as Jane is so secretive about everything. His mother's French and his father's English, and his name is Jeremy Curtis. Jane's being quite coy about him, so there's no more I can tell you.'

She looked at the mantel clock and gathered up her things. 'I'd better get going. Don't want to be late on my first day.'

Peggy admired the sprigged cotton frock, white sandals, pale pink cardigan and matching ribbon in her fair hair. 'You look lovely, dear,' she said, giving her a hug. 'Good luck.'

Ivy was the next to leave, shouldering her bag and gas-mask box and hitching up her oversized dungarees as she kissed Peggy and Cordelia good-bye and plodded out in her heavy boots. Rita rushed off after her on her crutches, eager to do some welding at the fire station, and Fran followed shortly afterwards, looking very purposeful and neat in her nurse's uniform.

Peggy gave a happy sigh. Love was all around her, glowing in Fran, bright in Ivy's eyes and warm in the convivial atmosphere of her kitchen. She poured a second cup of tea, the images of weddings drifting through her thoughts.

'Well, I'll be off to walk the dogs and exercise me ferrets,' said Ron, stuffing his pipe into his mouth and his greasy old cap on his head. 'And then Rosie's taking me shopping.'

Peggy and Cordelia looked at him in disbelief. 'Shopping? You?' they chorused.

'Aye. She seems to think I need smartening up.'

'And she'd be right,' said Cordelia, eyeing the

old corduroy trousers held up by garden twine, and the battered poacher's coat. 'You look like a tramp most of the time.'

'Ach, to be sure, Cordelia, I'm trying me best, but 'tis awful difficult when I've got animals to tend and things to do about the house,' he said gloomily before turning to Peggy. 'Would you be after knowing where me clothing coupons are, wee girl? I seem to have mislaid them.'

'That's hardly surprising as you've barely used any since the war started,' said Peggy, hunting them out of the dresser drawer and handing them over. 'There's a whole year's worth there, and don't forget your wallet. Clothes don't come cheap – even with coupons,' she warned.

'Aye,' he said, his brows drooping. 'I was afraid of that.' He stomped off with Harvey at his heels, and Peggy was only just in time to slam the kitchen door before the cat followed him. 'I don't think Rosie would appreciate him having the cat in his pocket in the middle of Plummer's,' she said to Cordelia with a chuckle.

Cordelia laughed. 'As long as he remembers to drop the ferrets off and get changed before he goes shopping, he should survive the day.'

'It's good to see you back to your old self,' said Peggy warmly. 'But I want you to promise not to overdo things whilst we're all out.'

'If it's nice I'll sit in the garden,' Cordelia re-assured her. 'If not, I'll read my library book or get on with my knitting by the fire.'

'You could always telephone Bertie and ask him to come and keep you company,' said Peggy as she rounded up Daisy and wrestled to get her coat and hat on.

'He's probably playing golf,' Cordelia said dismissively. 'And I'm quite happy with my own company.' She reached out to Daisy, who immediately flew into her arms for a hug. 'Be a good girl for Gan Gan,' she said, 'and you can tell me all about what you and Chloe have been up to when you come home.'

Daisy gave her a kiss and a hug and submitted quite calmly to having her bonnet tied under her chin.

'Where on earth is Doris?' said Peggy impatiently.

'I'm here,' said Doris, stepping into the kitchen looking very smart and efficient, her hair and make-up immaculate, her low-heeled shoes shining.

'You look marvellous,' said Peggy, reaching for her coat and gas-mask box. 'I'm sorry I can't hang about, but I wanted to take Daisy to the park for a bit before work.'

She carefully gave Doris a hug, fearful of crushing the crisp white blouse. 'Good luck, Doris – although I'm sure you won't need it. The Colonel sounds a very nice man.' She wanted to tell her not to get snooty, or put on that silly false voice – but she was probably nervous enough already without being given unwanted advice.

With a wave of her hand, she left the kitchen, almost tripping over Queenie, who darted between her feet to get outside and jump up onto the back garden wall, where she sat mewing piteously for Ron and Harvey. Peggy could only hope they were too far away to hear her, for one answering bark from Harvey and she'd be off after them.

Doris had deliberately taken her time to come downstairs, aware that Peggy had told everyone of her straitened circumstances and reluctant to have to face them all. She loathed the thought of Ivy and Rita smirking at her misfortune, and of Ron making tactless remarks about her going for a job interview.

She realised she had a tough time ahead of her if she was to convince these people she really had turned over a new leaf, but despite all her good intentions, she still felt horribly awkward in their presence. They were united, having lived together for so long and shared so much, and if she was to become part of this household, then she'd have to put all her prejudices aside and really work at it.

She endured Cordelia's withering glances and long silences as she ate some toast for breakfast and smoked a cigarette with her cup of tea whilst she read the letter from Anthony, which had been written before he'd learnt of his father's death. Her son was such a dear boy, so caring and kind, and quite distraught about the situation she'd found herself in. But they'd had a long, reassuring chat on the telephone the previous night, and she'd gone to bed later and slept right through for the first time since the V-1 destroyed her home.

Now she was feeling horribly nervous, and wishing she'd been nicer to Cordelia in the past, for she could have done with some light conversation to take her mind off the coming interview. When it became clear that Cordelia had turned off her hearing aid and was fully engrossed in the newspaper crossword, Doris left her to it and went upstairs.

She eyed her reflection in the mirror, making sure she looked the part, and then sat down to practise her shorthand on some scrap paper. She was a bit rusty, for it had been years since she'd taken dictation, and she could only hope the Colonel wasn't an impatient man like her previous boss, who'd marched back and forth as he dictated and then suddenly leant over her shoulder and jabbed at an outline demanding what it meant, which she'd found most unnerving.

When the time came for her to leave for the long walk to the factory estate, she put on her hat, powdered her nose and nodded to her reflection. Her eyes looked tired and there were lines around her mouth she could have sworn hadn't been there a week ago, but she was as ready as she'd ever be, fully determined to make the very best of this new phase in her life.

She went downstairs and out of the front door. The sun was shining, the sky was blue, and apart from the noise of the planes thundering overhead, it was a pleasant morning. She set off with purpose, determined to quell the butterflies in her stomach and do the best she could to secure this job, for it sounded ideal.

It felt rather strange to be walking up the High Street, for she usually drove everywhere, and by the time she'd crossed the railway bridge and was tackling the steep hill that led to the dairy and the factory estate, she was perspiring and out of breath. Knowing it wouldn't do at all to appear flustered, she paused by the high wire fence surrounding the huge estate, checked her appearance again in her compact mirror and waited until she'd caught her breath.

Approaching the young man on guard duty, she explained who she was and why she'd come. She showed him her identity card and he opened the gate, giving her a cheeky wink, which made her both cross and rather flattered. She hadn't been winked at since she was a girl, but he had a bit of a cheek doing it to someone who was probably old enough to be his mother.

She kept his instructions in her head as she walked through the vast collection of corrugated iron buildings which were buzzing and clanking with machinery, the sound of music coming from multiple wirelesses. She'd never been up here before, and had never planned to either, but it was interesting to see what Ivy and her evacuees had talked about when she'd been forced to take them in and put up with their common chatter.

That was all behind her now, though, she sternly reminded herself. Her future had been shaped by outside influences over which she'd had no control, and it was time to face this new beginning with fortitude and determination whilst hopefully remembering the lessons from her past.

She took a deep breath as she saw the Red Cross distribution centre ahead of her, and hoped she didn't bump into Peggy's sister-in-law, Pauline Reilly, who'd once been a volunteer for the WVS and was now working there. Doris didn't have a high opinion of Pauline – she was inclined to go off into hysterics at the slightest thing – and suspected the feeling was mutual.

She paused at the bottom of the wooden flight of steps which led up to the offices, took a breath of the freshening wind for courage and went up before her nerve failed her. Holding onto her hat, she turned the knob on the door and stepped inside to be greeted by a whirlwind of paper and a tall, silver-haired man who was clearly at the end of his tether.

'Shut the door,' he barked grabbing bits of paper and trying to keep them on the desk.

Doris quickly closed the door, grabbed the stray pieces of paper from around her feet and laid them on the untidy desk. 'I'm sorry,' she said. 'I didn't realise the wind was quite that fierce.'

He gave a deep sigh and smoothed back his hair. 'It's always windier at the top of those steps for some reason, and although I've asked maintenance to do something about it, I'm still waiting.' He regarded her with a rueful smile. 'Sorry for shouting at you like that.'

'That's all right,' said Doris, mollified by his smile and the educated tone of his voice. 'It looks like you could do with some help,' she added, pointing to the mess on the single desk and the numerous files and folders littering the tops of the metal cabinets.

'I'm snowed under with paper and bumf,' he said, 'and if you're Mrs Williams from the labour exchange, you're very welcome.'

'Indeed I am,' she replied.

His smile lit up his face and his handshake was firm and warm. 'Welcome to the madhouse, Mrs Williams. If you can sort this lot out, then you've got the job.'

Doris smiled. 'Don't you want to know if I can type or take shorthand?'

He waved away the suggestion. 'Just get me out of this mess and we'll sort all that out later,' he said. 'But where to start, that's the crux of the thing.'

Doris took off her hat and hung it on the coat-stand along with her handbag. 'Why don't you go and find yourself a nice cup of tea, and leave me to it?' she suggested hopefully. 'I'm sure you could do with one.'

'Indeed I could,' he said. 'But I have a meeting with the security staff in half an hour, so I'll be gone for a while. Will you be all right on your own?'

'I shall be fine,' said Doris, thankful she'd be left to get on without him being in the way.

'Well, if you're sure,' he said, dithering in the doorway.

Doris nodded and purposefully held down the papers on the desk as he opened the door and slammed it behind him. She let out a breath, eyed the task ahead of her and eagerly began to trawl her way through everything so she had a proper sense of what went where and how it should be filed. If this was what the job entailed, then it would be a piece of cake – but she must remember to ask him on his return what salary she was to be paid, and the hours he expected her to do.

She worked through the morning, and by the time Colonel White returned with a thick white mug of tea, the office was as neat as a pin, the desk cleared, the folders correctly filed away, and the box-files neatly stowed on shelves in alphabetical order. She'd polished the desk, unearthed the typewriter from a dusty corner and found notebooks and pencils, which she'd sharpened, in the desk drawers. The small kitchenette which led off the main room gleamed from a good scrubbing with Vim, the kettle and hot-plate now free of grime.

'My goodness, what a transformation,' he said in admiration. 'I can't believe you've brought order to my chaos so quickly.'

Doris positively glowed from his praise, but as he was about to place the hot mug on her freshly polished desk, she whipped a beer mat she'd found in a drawer underneath it. 'You have several letters that need answering today,' she said, grabbing a notebook and pencil. 'And I shall need a chair and a desk of my own.'

'Of course, of course,' he murmured, plonking down in the one chair. 'I'll ring through to supplies and get you those immediately.' His smile was almost shy. 'I'm still not used to being on Civvy Street. The army provided everything and there was always someone to do the fetching and carrying.'

'How long is it since you left?' Doris asked with genuine interest.

'It's been eighteen months since I retired, and I still can't get used to it.' He eyed her quizzically. 'And what about you, Mrs Williams?'

'I trained as a secretary in London more years ago than I care to remember, and then I got married and had my son. I've been doing voluntary work for the WVS, but I'm widowed now and need a paying job,' she finished with a defiant note.

'You must think I'm frightfully disorganised, Mrs Williams, and I do apologise for not dealing with such things earlier. I've been told I can pay you three guineas for a forty-hour week, with a bonus of one pound ten shillings if you're willing to work on a Saturday morning.'

It was much more than Doris expected, and it was quite hard to hide her surprise and delight. 'Thank you, Colonel. That would suit me very well, and I'm willing to work on Saturday if the need arises.'

'Splendid,' he replied, rubbing his hands together whilst admiring the neat office. 'Well, I have to say you've got everything marvellously shipshape in here. It's a pleasure to have someone who knows what they're doing. The last girl hadn't a clue, and left me high and dry without even giving notice.'

'I wouldn't do that,' she assured him.

He smiled at her and picked up one of the letters from the in-tray. 'Let's get on with the mail and see how your shorthand is.'

'I need a chair,' she reminded him gently.

'Goodness me, of course you do,' he said, jumping to his feet and reaching for the telephone. 'Why don't you sit here and enjoy that tea whilst I round up some suitable furniture for you?'

Doris sat in the deep leather chair and watched him make the call as she drank the rather stewed and cooling tea. Colonel White was a handsome man in his mid to late fifties, and beautifully turned out in a tweed suit and crisp shirt, with a gold watch and chain threaded through his matching waistcoat. His voice was educated and had a pleasing timbre, and his silver hair was thick and lustrous, enhancing the blue of his eyes. He clearly found it difficult to keep track of all his responsibilities, but with her talent for keeping things in order, she'd soon become indispensable to him.

Doris smothered a smile. She had the feeling she was going to enjoy working here.

Ron was feeling even grumpier than usual as he stood in the curtained-off cubicle of the menswear department in Plummer's in his less than pristine underpants and socks. He'd exercised the dogs and the ferrets, managed to pop in to see Danuta at the Memorial for a mere five minutes, and then had to dash back to get changed into something smarter for the shopping trip – but he hadn't thought to change the socks with the holes in them, or the underpants with sagging elastic, and realised he looked less than salubrious.

He glowered at his reflection in the long mirror as the elderly sales assistant measured him from head to toe and then got on his knees to measure his inside leg.

'Which side do you dress, sir?' the man asked, tape measure in hand, face aligned with the sagging elastic of Ron's pants.

'On the right,' Ron growled. 'Is all this really necessary?'

The elderly man got to his feet and noted down the measurements in a large book before replying. 'The lady was most insistent, sir,' he replied, mournfully eyeing the socks and underwear before shooting Ron an understanding smile. 'And I've discovered over the years that it is always wise to follow a lady's wishes if one is to have a quiet life.'

'Aye, but 'tis a terrible burden, so it is.'

'I think you'll find, sir, that you will look and feel very much better once we have you suitably attired,' the older man said before backing through the curtain.

Left to his own devices, Ron flexed his muscles, sucked in his stomach and eyed his reflection sourly, for although he was fit for a man of his age with well-toned muscles, he didn't exactly cut a dashing figure at the moment. He was tempted to light his pipe, and then realised it probably wasn't the thing to do in Plummer's, which was Cliffehaven's poshest shop.

Hitching up his baggy pants and eyeing the hole in his sock, he wondered how long he was supposed to hang about, and what Rosie was up to on the other side of the curtain. She'd sent him in here with a cheeky grin and made herself comfortable on a couch, plied with a free glass of sherry and a pile of magazines to keep her amused whilst he was going through all kinds of humiliation in his underwear. It seemed to him that Rosie's idea of being wooed was going a bit far, and if the man didn't come back soon, he'd get dressed and leave.

'Here we are, sir,' said the older man, laden with jackets, shirts and trousers. 'I have brought a selection for you to try on.' He slotted the hangers onto a rail, selected a pair of twill trousers and held them out. 'The lady would like to see each outfit so she can make her choice,' he murmured.

'So I go through all this and don't even have a say in the matter?' growled Ron.

'I'm afraid not, sir,' he replied, before leaving again.

Ron eyed the twill trousers and pulled them on. They fitted very well and felt good against his legs, the turn-ups nestling perfectly over the tops of his shoes. He eyed the shirts and selected a dark green one which buttoned neatly over his chest and flat waist, the collar proving loose enough not to strangle him. Looking over the jackets, he discarded the bilious brown and green, as well as the blue, and plumped for the earthy tones of a fine tweed. Selecting a plain brown tie, he knotted it loosely and then turned to look at himself in the mirror.

'Well, 'tis a fine figure of a man ye are,' he breathed, turning this way and that in delight. 'But what you need now is a hat to finish it off.'

'Are you decent yet?' asked Rosie from the other side of the curtain.

'As decent as I'll ever be,' he replied, sweeping back the curtain to give her the full benefit of his splendour.

Rosie cocked her head and eyed him from head to foot. 'You'll need brown shoes to go with that, and some decent socks,' she said. She looked at him, her blue eyes shining. 'You certainly scrub up well, Ron,' she murmured.

'Aye, it all fits well enough,' he said, trying to be modest. 'But I'll need a hat. The blue fedora won't go with this.'

'Talking of blue,' said Rosie with a naughty

gleam in her eyes. 'I thought the blue jacket would go very well with the pale grey flannels and white shirt.'

'Ach, I'm happy with this,' he said.

'You might be, but you need more than one set of smart clothes if you want me to be seen on your arm, Ronan Reilly.' She gave him a rather firm nudge towards the changing room. 'Now get a move on. I have to open the pub in just over an hour, and I thought we could have morning coffee at the Officers' Club first.'

Ron swallowed a retort and grumpily returned to the changing room. Rosie was getting a bit above herself, but he supposed it was all in a good cause – and he did have to admit the clothes made him look and feel good. He emerged minutes later in the grey flannels, blue jacket and white shirt. 'I look daft,' he rumbled.

'You look wonderful,' sighed Rosie. 'The blue makes your eyes even brighter and that jacket fits as if it's been made for you.' She eyed his black shoes. 'They'll do for now, but you'll need some new ones before the year's out,' she declared.

'There's no need for all this, Rosie,' he complained. 'To be sure, we never go anywhere to warrant such finery, and I have a passable suit.'

'Things are about to change,' she said, a steely glint in her eyes. 'And you'll get a great deal of use out of all of it, I assure you.'

Ron swallowed and smiled nervously at her as the elderly salesman approached.

'We'll take this outfit, the brown tweed, twill trousers and green shirt,' said Rosie. 'I'll hunt out a couple of different ties – and he'll need some brown shoes.'

'And a tweed hat,' said Ron, determined to get his way over something, and yet utterly defeated by the knowledge that this was going to cost him every clothing coupon he had as well as the contents of his wallet.

'He will also need some dark socks and new underwear,' said Rosie, shooting Ron a look he couldn't interpret.

'What was that all about?' he asked as the man collected the clothes from the changing room and went off to pack them up.

Rosie giggled. 'The curtains didn't quite fit together and I saw you in all your glory,' she spluttered.

Ron felt the blush heat his face and couldn't look her in the eye. 'I'm going to change back into my own stuff,' he rumbled.

'No, you're not. You'll wear what you've got on for the Officers' Club and change later,' she said firmly. To forestall any argument, she turned from him and bustled off to look at ties and underwear.

He stood in the middle of the menswear department and admired the way her hips moved beneath that pencil-slim skirt, and how good her legs looked in those high-heeled shoes. Rosie always looked marvellous and he could see heads turning to watch her progress through the department. If he was going to persuade her to marry him, then this expensive torture would be worth it.

He gave a chuckle before gathering up his old jacket, shirt and trousers and taking them to the counter to be wrapped up with the rest. If this was what Rosie wanted, then he would play along

– and although he'd been morose about it, he'd found it fun, and privately admitted that he did look extremely smart in this get-up, even if it did make him feel as if he was one of those snobs who attended garden parties and lounged about on yachts.

Ron found a tweed hat he liked, and a pair of brogues the rich colour of conkers that fitted like a glove and would see him through at least a decade.

Rosie came back from her trawl of the department and met him at the counter armed with socks, handkerchiefs and ties. She cast an approving look over the hat and shoes, and then held up a broad strip of blue and white silk. 'I thought a cravat would finish that outfit off perfectly,' she said purposefully.

'Over my dead body,' he growled, eyeing the object with disgust.

'But–'

'I'll not be wearing that,' he said firmly, taking the cravat and putting it out of her reach. 'Enough is enough, Rosie.'

She regarded him for a moment and then nodded. 'I suppose it is a step too far,' she murmured, 'and as you've been so good about everything else, I'll let it pass.'

Ron eyed the neatly written bill and had to quickly mask his horror. He reluctantly handed over the money and coupons.

Rosie hooked her arm through his as he took charge of the packages. 'I know it was a bit steep,' she murmured as they headed for the door, 'but you'll thank me in the end.'

Ron wasn't at all sure about that, but as he held the door open for her and she sashayed onto the High Street pavement, he noticed their reflection in the heavily taped shop window and realised they made a handsome couple. Feeling slightly mollified, he escorted her along the High Street to the Officers' Club, his mind working furiously on how much he had left in his wallet and what morning coffee would cost him.

Doris pulled on her blue overcoat and tethered her hat with a pin before gathering up the post and slipping it into her handbag. She stood for a moment admiring the office, which she'd re-organised with the help of the maintenance men who'd brought up the second desk and chair. The Colonel's desk was now under the single window, and her own smaller desk had been set up against the wall opposite. Everything was neat and tidy, and she'd elicited a firm promise from the men that they would come tomorrow to build a covered porch over the door so that the wind didn't rush straight in every time the door was opened. Should the men go back on their promise, then they'd soon discover that Doris Williams was no pushover, and that her demands were to be met promptly.

She looked at her watch, checking she had time to catch the evening post, and then used the key the Colonel had given her to lock up. Stepping outside, she was surprised to discover how light and bright it was, and how swiftly the day had flown. With a lightness of heart she hadn't felt for years, she ran down the wooden staircase and hurried towards the gate.

'How'd it go, then?'

Startled, Doris looked down at Ivy, who'd appeared from nowhere, it seemed, and was walking beside her. 'Very well, thank you,' she replied, her smile a little stiff.

'That's good then,' said Ivy. 'The Colonel's nice, ain't 'e? And not a bad looker for a bloke 'is age.'

'I can't say that I noticed,' Doris fibbed.

Ivy gave her a light nudge with her elbow. 'You could be in there if yer play yer cards right.'

Doris bristled and only just remembered she had to be nice to this common girl if her standing at Beach View was to improve. 'I have no idea what you mean by that,' she said coolly. 'But I certainly found him to be a most pleasant man to work for.'

Ivy grinned. 'We 'ad bets on you wouldn't get a job at all,' she said tactlessly, 'but I'm glad you proved us wrong, so good on yer. I knows things ain't been easy for yer lately, but 'aving something proper to do will perk you up no end.'

'I'm sure it will,' said Doris, trying not to show how astonished she was by the girl's bare-faced cheek and over-familiarity.

'This is nice, ain't it?' Ivy carried on with a devilish glint in her eye. 'Who'd'a thought we'd be walking 'ome from work together, eh? If me shifts work out like this, we could be doing it every day, all friendly like. What you say?'

'I might have to come in early or leave late,' said Doris hurriedly. 'The Colonel doesn't keep regular hours.'

Ivy chuckled, hitched up her dungarees and ran

off to join some of the other girls who were pouring through the gate.

Doris slowed her pace to keep well behind them. It was bad enough having to once again share a house with her one-time evacuee, but she wasn't about to encourage any sort of intimacy. After all Ivy had left Havelock Road for Beach View without a by-your-leave and caused her endless trouble with the billeting people because of it. And if she thought she could now take liberties, then she was sorely mistaken.

Doris reached the gate and watched Ivy and the other girls race each other down the hill, their heavy boots clattering on the pavement, their shrieks of laughter echoing through the streets. She took a steadying breath and slowly headed after them. Their short exchange had somewhat blunted her spirits, but the thought that she would back in the neat, quiet office again tomorrow brought back the spring in her step, and she couldn't wait to tell Peggy all about her busy and fulfilling day.

10

Burma

Jim was stripped to the waist, sweating and straining alongside two hundred other men beneath a merciless sun, rifles slung across their backs, and hounded by swarms of mosquitoes as they dug away at the paddy field and tried to even out the five-foot drop in the middle. The natives had disappeared into the jungle as if realising this would soon become a battleground, but so far, nothing had been heard from the Japanese.

As he dug, Jim watched his CO pace the perimeter of the block with his battalion commanders, arranging junction points, and the exact siting of reserves, headquarters and mortar positions. He ordered several strong detachments into the surrounding dense jungle to hunt for Japs, and had set up his HQ on the ridge where he had an overall view of the whole block and the railway valley.

'This is nothing less than slave labour,' moaned Ernie as they finally got to rest in the shade of a craggy rock and drink copious amounts of water to replace what they'd sweated. 'They should pay us better.'

Jim dredged up a wry smile. 'To be sure, Ernie, you do like a good moan, don't you?' he teased, rolling a smoke. 'And what would we spend all that extra money on, eh? It's not as if we've got dancing girls, cinemas and bars here.' He lit the cigarette and eyed the flattened paddy, which still had a five-foot drop in the middle that had proved impossible to fill by hand, and the seemingly deserted jungle looming all round them.

'It's the principle of the thing,' Ernie persisted, stirring his entire day's K-rations into a glutinous mess and stuffing it down. 'A fair day's pay for a rotten job.'

Jim could have given him an argument, but was too tired. It was certainly a rotten job, but it was what they'd both been trained for. And if this war was to end, it was up to men like him, Ernie and Big Bert to strain every muscle and sinew to get the job done – regardless of the lousy pay and conditions.

'Stand by your beds,' muttered Big Bert. 'I can hear the first glider coming in.'

It came in short and too high, and Jim's stomach lurched as its tail suddenly flicked and the glider nose-dived straight into the ground with an almighty crash that reverberated across the entire block and into the hills behind them. It was doubtful anyone could have survived that, he thought sadly, and he was to discover later that indeed all three men had been killed – not by enemy bullets, but most likely a mechanical fault.

The RAF officer was on the wireless shouting orders which appeared to be heard and understood by the pilots already circling overhead, for the next four gliders landed safely on the makeshift runway.

For Jim, Ernie and Big Bert, their all-too-short respite was over, and, as dusk turned to darkness, they were sent as part of the large team to push the gliders to the end of the strip and then unload them. They were already exhausted, but time was of the essence, for they could hear the stutter and pop of small-arms fire coming from somewhere close to the demolished Jap HQ and railway station and the answering rattle of their own guns.

Every man worked at a hectic pace throughout the night and into the next day, using the small bulldozers and graders the gliders had brought in to level the five-foot drop into a gentle enough slope for a heavily loaded C-47 to take at fifty or sixty mph in the middle of its landing run. Employing the remaining mules, working parties carried the wire, ammunition, medical supplies, fresh rations and tools into the block. Others dug trenches, laid cables, wired up lighting on the perimeter, ranged mortars and set up fields of fire on the outskirts of the paddy and along the steep ridge behind it.

Just before nightfall on that second day an enemy shell whooshed across the block and exploded in the river valley behind them. This was swiftly followed by two more, which thankfully fell harmlessly into the jungle. 'The Japs have discovered what we're doing and are trying to find their range,' muttered Jim.

'Bad timing, considering the C-47s are due in tonight,' replied Big Bert, checking his carbine. 'And by the sound of it, they're already here.'

The thinly spaced lights around the airfield were switched on as the drone of the plane grew louder, and they all looked up to see the leader circling above the valley, headlights piercing the black jungle.

'He's coming in too high,' gasped Jim in alarm.

The C-47 seemed to drop out of the sky. It landed abruptly, bounced over the slope in the runway, swung out of control and then roared off into the jungle where it burst into flames.

Jim and the others were too far away to be of any help, but in the flickering light of those flames they could see men jumping out of the plane door and others rushing to help put out the flames and rescue the injured.

The fire had been extinguished by the time the second plane landed without a hitch, but the third got its undercarriage ripped away as it slid on its nose into the bushes. Everyone survived, and the fourth C-47 landed safely.

To the distant sound of enemy rifle fire, Jim and his squad of sappers hurried to the end of the runway to help unload explosives and other desperately needed engineering tools and stores.

As they were hoisting boxes of explosives out of the plane and loading them onto the backs of the few mules they still had, a grenade was thrown out from the jungle and exploded beneath the wing of the C-47 that had lost its belly, setting it on fire. A patrol immediately charged into the jungle, machine guns rattling, in search of the perpetrator.

The already damaged plane was now burning furiously, and as it lay over the wire linking the airfield lights, it short-circuited the entire system and the lights went out.

Chaos descended within seconds. The plane that was about to land opened up its engines and roared off again; the crew of another that had already landed heard the grenade, saw the flames and slammed the door shut as the pilot sent the plane roaring down the strip in the darkness. But before it could reach take-off speed, its wing caught on the C-47 that had landed safely, which made it skew and skid to a halt. Men poured out through the door, and unloading parties swarmed all over it to get the supplies out quickly before it too could catch fire – which thankfully it didn't.

'That's two C-47s written off – and two damaged,' muttered Jim to no one in particular as he fumbled in the pitch black to tie a box of explosives onto the shifting mule's back. 'I hope it was worth it.'

The CO had clearly decided they couldn't afford to lose any more men and planes, and ordered the rest of the incoming C-47s to abort the op and return to base, for there were no more arrivals that night.

With the stores carefully stowed away and the runway lights repaired, the men were stood down. The fresh batch of men who had arrived that night were sent to guard the perimeter of the block and keep watch-from the ridge, whilst a group of Gurkhas had been sent out on patrol to see what the Japs were actually up to, where they were, and how many.

Jim was completely drained of energy, too tired almost to be able to sleep. He settled into a slit-trench halfway up the rocky hill and close to the HQ, and tried to get comfortable, but then lay awake in the darkness listening to the desultory firing of guns to the north. There seemed to be some sort of half-hearted battle going on down on the far side of the ridge where the brigade of Gurkhas must have made contact with the Japs.

The gunfire eventually petered out at about two in the morning, and Jim's eyelids flickered. The Japs were probing, searching for the strongpoints in the British defence and where their machine-gun posts were, but the British Tommy was smarter than any Jap, for they'd returned fire with only Brens, rifles and mortars – the all-important batteries of machine guns had remained silent.

Jim's eyelids grew heavy. Despite the knowledge that the Japs would make a serious assault on the same sector the next night, he was too exhausted to care, and in the moment before he drifted into sleep he thought of Peggy and home, and imagined he was there, holding her in his arms, safe and warm.

The shelling began again an hour before dawn, but this time the Japs were more accurate, and as Jim was about to tuck into a lump of bully beef a great boom sent him diving back into the nearest rocky defile, where he lay, his breakfast in one hand, his rifle in the other as he was showered with debris from the blast.

Shells continued to shriek and explode all around him with growing intensity, and it seemed to go on forever. Jim was beginning to wonder how much longer he could bear the noise, and if his number might be up, when it abruptly came to a halt.

The ensuing silence was deafening. Cautiously, Jim lifted his head, the lump of bully beef between his teeth, his finger on the trigger of his rifle.

Ernie emerged from a nearby slit-trench, a trickle of blood running down his cheek where a sliver of shrapnel had grazed it. Big Bert appeared to be unscathed, but one look at the artillery major who'd only arrived on a C-47 the night before to take command of the field gunners was enough to show that he was dead. A large shell splinter was buried deep in his head. Jim spat out the bully beef, he'd suddenly lost his appetite.

The siting of the Japanese artillery had become

apparent during the bombardment, so the CO quickly shifted his headquarters and the dressing station to a more sheltered spot away from the line of their fire so the injured and dead could be dealt with. The bombardment had lasted two hours, but the more experienced soldiers amongst them warned Jim and Ernie that what they'd experienced was nothing compared to what would surely come.

Jim had a sudden premonition that he might not see the day out, and as it was the first time he'd experienced such a feeling, he decided to use his short time of stand-down to write to Peggy. He settled into a slit-trench, found his notebook, rested it on his knees, and licked the blunted lead of his pencil.

My darling girl,

I love the bones of you, and miss you so much it's an ache inside me that never goes away. I wish I could see you, hold you, and kiss the very breath from you. If anything should happen to me I want you to know that my last thought will be of you.

You have made my life complete, given me love and understanding when I've not deserved it, and above all, given me joy in the precious gifts of our children. I long to see you all again, to hold you to my heart and reacquaint myself with little Daisy and the boys and get to know our granddaughters, but if it's not to be, then perhaps you can keep my memory alive for them by telling them about the daft things me and Da used to get up to.

Those were such happy days. Da is my hero, for I saw him in action during the first shout, and know the price he paid for the courage he showed then. And yet, for all his stories, he's a modest man who never revealed the true depths of his bravery, and the honour that was bestowed on him. He's never failed in his duty as loving father and grandfather, and Frank and I know how blessed we are to have him. I love the scrapes he gets into, and the stories he can tell with that marvellous twinkle in his eyes – and I hope he can forgive my previous waywardness and be proud of who I am and what I've become during these past few years.

Amid the sounds of battle, and in the darkest hours of the night, the love and warmth of home keeps me going, Peggy, and I pray that I will soon know it again, for I'm sick of war and noise; of death and destruction and the endless struggle to remain strong and brave and not let my comrades down.

I'm sealing this letter with kisses, and a prayer that we shall be together again one day very soon,
Jim. Xx

He read it through, saw how soppy it was and was tempted to tear it up. But it had come from the heart, and Peggy deserved to know the depths of his feelings for her and the rest of his family. Before he could change his mind again, he placed it in the envelope, addressed it and took it straight to the communications post. With any luck it would go with one of the C-47s due to fly in tonight with more men and equipment.

Sporadic fire continued throughout the day, and just before dusk, the shelling began again – closer now – and on both sides of the block. Jim and some of his battalion had been posted in a defensive spot close to the wire that surrounded the airfield. He was sweating although it was now dark, for the monsoon was building again, the sky seldom clear and the damp heat oozing into every pore. The fighter planes were occupied in covering a battle further to the north and weren't coming over as regularly, and it seemed the Japs were taking advantage of the situation.

The first assault group of Japs came out of the jungle with blood-curdling screams and yells, the Very lights shining on bared teeth, pot helmets and long bayonets. Jim and his men returned fire, but then the lights fizzled out, and in the sudden, blinding darkness the clatter of bullets rang out as the shelling continued.

In the midst of this mayhem the C-47s came in, and every available man not involved in defending the block was sent swiftly to unload so the planes could take off again.

The stock of Jim's gun was red-hot, his sweating fingers slippery on the trigger as the Japanese assaults continued and their artillery grew increasingly bold, with what seemed an endless supply of ammunition – which could only mean they had a hidden ammunition dump outside the village which hadn't been spotted by air reconnaissance. Sweat stung his eyes as he tried to pierce the darkness, for the Japanese were closer now, and were more than likely dug in twenty yards from the wire, with snipers hiding in the trees.

'Stay low and tight,' came the message down the line from the brigade CO. 'The snipers in the trees might think they've got one over on us, but our snipers have got them in their sights.'

Jim hugged the ground, looking through the

long grass, finger poised to shoot anything that came out of the jungle yelling and screaming. The shelling continued; the snipers picked off anyone who moved, and were themselves picked off by snipers from the King's Own. It was a terrifying and uncomfortable place to be, and although Jim wished the CO would call for mortar fire and back-up from the air to blast the Japs out of the jungle, he knew he'd think long and hard before doing it, for it would be suicidal. The enemy was dug in too close – almost leaning on the perimeter wire and any bombardment from the air or the mortars would kill countless numbers of his own men.

By some miracle, Jim had survived the assaults which had gone on continuously for seven heart-stopping hours before they petered out at two in the morning. Given the order to retreat from the front line, he backed away on his belly from the wire, still poised for any sudden movement in the jungle, and then scuttled to the relative safety of a deep trench at the bottom of the high, craggy ridge.

Ernie swore softly as he slumped down beside him. 'That was too flaming close,' he breathed.

'And it's far from over,' said Big Bert, engrossed in stuffing down his rations and emptying his water canister in three great gulps. 'They've trapped us in this valley and have us in their sights. They'll be back twice as hard, sooner rather than later.'

'Thanks, Bert. That's just what we needed to hear,' said Jim through a vast yawn. 'Let's hope we're allowed a bit of kip before we have to go through that again. I'm dead on me feet, so I am.'

But it was not to be, and Jim's platoon was ordered to help stow away the supplies and equipment that had come in throughout the night. As the sun rose the sky became thick and thunderous, the sweltering heat increasing by the minute. The monsoon was gathering itself to break, and every man in the block prayed it would be soon.

The work was painfully slow, for everyone was exhausted, and because huge numbers of men had been posted in clusters all around the block, and there simply weren't enough hands to do the job quickly.

The heavy artillery had come in with the bulldozers to help shift it, and the men to fire it. Tons of stores, hundreds of Bren guns, machine guns, and thousands of grenades and boxes of arms and ammunition had to be carried from the strip. Miles of wire had to be laid and positions dug deeper or repaired. The injured had been flown out, but the dead had to be buried, and patrols sent into the jungle to protect the airstrip, and in the middle of it all, the CO decided to move all the three-inch mortars into one place to use them as a single battery. Which meant laying more cable.

The Japanese continued to harass them all through the day with small-arms fire and the CO ordered the entire perimeter of the block to be stripped down to one section per platoon, with no battalion reserves, but a good cover of mortars and machine guns. The main core of the block, which was now known as Blighty, would be heavily defended by a full-strength brigade and a rifle company.

Jim and the men understood why he'd done this, for the Japs had curiously left the airfield alone and were definitely concentrating on Blighty – and going by past experience, they would probably continue to do so – but it was a risk, and they could only hope he was proved right.

And he was. Four nights in a row the Japanese attacked Blighty, and furious battles raged from dusk until an hour or so before dawn, fought at ten yards' range with Brens, grenades, rifles, tommy guns, two- and three-inch mortars and machine guns. Three hundred yards to one side of the attacking Japs, and in full sight of them, C-47s landed with glaring headlights on the now brilliantly lit airstrip to offload their men and supplies and swiftly carry away the wounded. But the Japanese never attempted to destroy the airfield – which puzzled everyone, although it seemed like a miracle.

On the fourth night, mortar fire set the tinder-dry jungle scrub alight on a ridge to the west, and almost immediately smoke was seen rising to the east of the block under a barrage of Allied mortar fire and shells. Jim and his men scuttled back as the flames took hold of the dry lantana scrub to the front of their position. Fire was as much an enemy as any bullet, and everyone feared it, for if you were surrounded by it, you, could kiss goodbye to going home.

The order came to begin firing incendiary smoke bombs into the area to set the lantana blazing to the rear of the Japanese front line. Jim and the other men in his brigade held ready to counter-attack as the field guns, already half-hidden in drifting smoke, swung round to fire muzzle-bursts to try and turn the encroaching fire back on itself.

Jim's eyes were stinging with sweat and smoke, for the dryness in the air and in the jungle grasses had reached its peak, the heat stifling and now unbearable. He watched the flames take hold and ravenously devour the undergrowth, and wondered what would happen if they couldn't put it out and the entire surrounding jungle went up.

Just when it seemed impossible that they could hold out against the Japanese firepower, eight Allied fighter-bombers came racing out of the sky. One behind the other, they made successive runs across the outer limit of the block's wire. Their huge bombs whistled down as the orders came for rapid fire from all the mortars and machine guns.

Jim could feel the ground quake and heave beneath him as the noise came in deafening waves to beat in his head and thrum right through him. Trees were uprooted and the jungle vanished in a boiling cauldron of smoke, earth and dust as shrapnel flew in lethal shards, and the fighter-bombers came in lower to rake the enemy position with their powerful machine guns. Jim's body vibrated with the monstrous, seemingly endless roar that filled the world around him, and all he could do was hug the ground, cover his head and pray.

When the fighter-bombers flew away no one moved in the sudden, deafening silence that fell on the block, and Jim found that his trembling legs could barely support him when he finally dared to get to his feet. And yet, as he took stock of his surroundings, it seemed the Japanese had at last been pushed back and the combined brigades had miraculously come through the bombardment with no casualties. It was a measure of the brilliance and accuracy of those American pilots, and Jim vowed that once this war was over he'd buy the first American pilot he met a very large drink.

And then he felt something cold and wet on his face. He looked up through the clearing smoke and dust, noticing that the sky had darkened further, and with it had come the gloriously cool downpour that fell in great, heavy drops on his burning face and arms like a gift from God. The monsoon had finally broken in earnest.

The celebration was short-lived, for the Japanese might have retreated, but they were now using their mortars, which were six times heavier than anything the British Army had. When one of them hit an ammunition pit, there was no need for a burial party; but the padre said a few words anyway as he sprinkled a handful of yellow earth in the general vicinity of the men's pulverised remains.

The Japanese were still targeting Blighty, and as the rain fell hard and steadily over the next few days, the block began to resemble the battlefields of the Somme.

Jim's experiences of that previous war still lived with him, even though he'd only fought in it for less than a year. As he sat in a dugout up to his waist in muddy water, trying to keep his carbine dry in the incessant downpour, the scene before him brought the memories of 1918 flooding back in all their stark horror.

Trenches and bomb craters were filled with stinking water; blasted trees lay lifeless; feet and clawed hands stuck up out of the cloying yellow mud where bloody shirts, ammunition clips, boots and entrails lay scattered. Jap corpses were caught in the perimeter wires or stuck in surviving trees, their bodies rotting and fly-infested – and over it all hung the heavy, sickly sweet stench of death.

Jim gloomily regarded the flooded runway as the rain beat a steady tattoo on his hat, dripped in icy trickles down his neck and raised the level of the water he sat in. The monsoon had done the work the Japanese hadn't got around to, for nothing could land there now, which meant the injured could no longer be airlifted out. And that wasn't good for anyone's morale.

Jim huddled beneath his hat, cradling his carbine as the shelling continued hour upon hour on Blighty, and the patrol of Lightning P-38s began to search for the enemy guns that were doing so much damage. He looked across at Ernie, who was huddled beside him, the picture of misery, his eyes huge with the horror of it all. Nudging him gently with his elbow, Jim leaned towards him. 'We'll be all right, Ernie, you'll see. The CO will get reinforcements any minute now.'

Ernie just stared at him with eyes lacking any hope and then dropped his chin to his chest as if afraid Jim would see how defeated he was.

Jim realised his friend was at the very end of his endurance, and if he didn't do something quickly, Ernie could get careless and catch a bullet. As the bombardment finally petered out, and all went still, he grabbed Ernie's arm and pulled him forcibly out of the muddy trench. 'Time for a wash and brush-up,' he said with forced cheerfulness. 'To be sure, Ernie wee man, you stink.'

'Not as bad as you do,' he retorted sourly.

Jim was soaked to the skin and shivering with the cold of the mud that clung to every part of his body, but he forced himself to urge Ernie on as they scrambled down the hill past the batteries of guns guarding the ridge and towards the fast-flowing river.

He trusted the gunners on the ridge to keep a lookout, but it all seemed quiet, so he took Ernie's carbine and set it down with his own on a nearby flat rock and dragged Ernie into the shallows where, for once, there didn't appear to be any leeches.

Jim slid, fully dressed, down into the water as far as he dared to wash off the mud and muck that had accumulated over the past few days. The rain beat down on his head, hammered against the stony outcrops and dripped from the few trees along the bank. The water was clear and cold, making them both gasp, but as the filth was washed away they both felt a lightening of spirits.

Scrambling back out, they picked up their carbines and Jim glanced across the river to the far ridge, saw movement there and just managed to fling them both to the ground as the enemy mortars opened up. It was a continuous drumbeat which grew more urgent by the second and pinned them down against the unyielding rocks, caught between the mortars and their own answering Brens.

'We've got to get out of here,' he yelled.

A shell exploded within yards of them, blasting a great hole in the ridge and taking a Bren gun position with it. Bits of bodies and machinery flew everywhere and Jim started to crawl as bullets zinged and whizzed around him and more shells exploded. He looked back to make sure Ernie was keeping up. 'Come on!' he urged.

Ernie didn't move. With growing horror, Jim wondered if he'd simply frozen in fear or if he'd been injured. He scrambled back down to him, cursing his stupidity for bringing him here in the first place. When he saw the blood blossoming on Ernie's shirt he felt sick at heart. This was all his fault, and now it was up to him to get Ernie to the dressing station without delay.

'It's all right, wee man, I've got you,' he murmured, gathering Ernie into his arms and flinching as a mortar exploded within yards of them.

He felt something punch him in his side, but he was concentrating too hard on getting them both out of there to take much notice. He hooked an arm around Ernie, thanking God he was small and light, and held him to his chest as inch by inch he crawled from defile to defile, and as the mortars burst and the machine guns rattled alongside the Brens, he finally managed to get on the other side of the ridge.

It wasn't any better there, for the Japs' mortars were targeting Blighty again. Ernie groaned in protest as Jim hoisted him onto his back. 'Hold on, wee man,' Jim muttered. 'Not far to go now.'

The dressing station was a tent which had been

erected in a fork of rock to the east of Blighty. Tucked away from the main block, and deep inside that broad crevasse of rock, it was about the safest place to be – but to a rapidly tiring Jim it seemed hopelessly beyond reach.

He could feel Ernie's blood seeping into his own shirt as he carried him on his back and carefully picked his way down the slippery rocks and deep fissures of the ridge. Whatever it was in his side was beginning to make itself felt, and he blinked away the sweat from his eyes and tried to clear his head of the swirling darkness that threatened to send him tumbling.

'Are you still with me, Ernie?' he yelled as the mortars continued to boom and crash all around him and the Brens roared back.

'Aye,' Ernie managed weakly before his arms slipped from Jim's shoulders.

'Good man.' Jim stumbled and almost fell the last few feet, but suddenly hands were lifting Ernie from his back and carrying him away into the shelter of the large tent.

Jim swayed on his feet, his vision blurring as he took in the row upon row of injured men; the bloody bandages and buckets; the grey-faced, exhausted medics and orderlies splattered with gore. He saw the padre approaching with a concerned expression. 'To be sure, Father, I'm fine,' he managed before darkness eclipsed him and he knew no more.

11

The past two weeks had brought sadness and joy for Peggy. Sadness because Danuta had suffered a relapse and couldn't come home to Beach View just yet, and joy because Doris was blossoming now she had a real interest in her life and felt useful. The change had been quite astonishing since that first day she'd started work in the administrator's office. Suddenly she was animated and friendly, her head full of plans for her future once she'd earned enough to put down a deposit on a place of her own. It also seemed that she and the Colonel were getting on splendidly, which was an added bonus.

Sarah appeared to be doing very well at her new secretarial job, even though her mother's letters were stretching her patience to breaking point, and Rita had assured Peggy that work was going well at the fire station on her stairlift contraption, and would increase in leaps and bounds once she was free of the hampering plaster on her leg. She was due to go in today to get it taken off, and as Peter Ryan thought he might be able to get over from Cliffe aerodrome for a couple of hours, he'd be going with her and then treating her to lunch at the British Restaurant.

Ivy was her usual scatty, mouthy self, unable to resist tweaking Doris's tail at every opportunity, which was met with a cool response that, strangely, held a hint of what Peggy suspected was a growing tolerance – if not affection – although neither of them would ever admit this development in their relationship. Their interaction rather reminded Peggy of Cordelia and Ron, who relished their sniping banter, and almost treated it as a game.

Cordelia was back to full health, enjoying being whisked off for lunch or drinks with Bertie in between his numerous rounds of golf. And Ron had a definite spring in his step since he and Rosie had started acting like a proper courting couple. As for poor Fran, she was still waiting on tenterhooks to hear what her parents had to say about her wedding plans to Robert.

The weather had finally improved, much to everyone's relief, and July was proving to be warm and sunny. Poor old London was still being bombarded by V-1s, which had become known as doodlebugs because of the noise the engines made, but there had been few air-raid warnings in Cliffehaven and only the distant buzz of the V-1s as they made their way inland. The news on the wireless and the daily papers held even more promise, for it seemed that the Allies were advancing ever deeper into Europe, and Paris was expected to be liberated very soon.

The Russians had begun their summer offensive and captured Minsk, which had been in German hands since the start of the war. The Americans had liberated Cherbourg; the British and Canadians had liberated Caen, and the American troops were advancing fast on Saint-Lo as the Allied troops advanced from the south. In Burma and the Far East, the British and Americans were beating back the Japanese, and it seemed as if there was now real hope that the war was drawing closer to a total Allied victory.

Peggy snapped out of her thoughts and finished laying the table for breakfast. As it was Saturday, and she didn't have to go to work, she planned to pop in to see Rosie, and then spend an hour at the playground with Daisy before she met up with Kitty and Charlotte at the Red Cross distribution centre for their two hours of voluntary work. After that, she would take the bus up to the Memorial to visit Danuta. Her busy days had meant she hadn't had the chance to catch up with anyone just lately, and Peggy was looking forward to having a good gossip.

She glanced out of the window to the lines of washing she'd hung out earlier which were now drifting in the light, warm breeze of another beautiful summer day. She was hoping there would be a letter from Jim in the post, which was unusually rather late this morning. She hadn't heard from him for two weeks now, but going by his last letter, it sounded as if he was having a high old time out there, what with seeing Vera Lynn and enjoying concert parties.

Her attention was drawn back to Daisy as she charged about after Queenie, who was clearly in no mood to be caught. To Daisy's frustration, the cat scooted up onto the draining board and sought refuge on one of the shelves beside the kitchener range, where she was out of reach.

'Come on, Daisy,' Peggy said briskly to ward off a tantrum. 'Let's feed the hens and see if there are any eggs this morning.' She gathered up the small basket and bowl of feed from the scullery shelf and slipped on their wellingtons, and they went out into the back garden, Queenie scooting between their legs in a bid to escape.

The early morning sun had yet to breach the rooftops and warm the garden, so the shadows lay long across Ron's burgeoning vegetable patch, but the air was soft and the sky a perfect, cloudless blue as the chickens pecked and burbled contentedly in their run.

The hens had arrived courtesy of a bunch of Australian soldiers who'd come for Christmas dinner at the beginning of the war with them hidden in their overcoat pockets. She hadn't asked where they'd come from, suspecting they weren't exactly theirs to give – but they'd proved a godsend. Eggs were rationed to one a week per person, but at Beach View everyone could enjoy a real treat most mornings.

Peggy thought about those lovely boys with their sunny, open smiles, loud voices and cheerful manner as she opened the gate in the chicken coop and then closed it firmly behind Daisy. She'd had letters from them at first, but they'd fizzled out as the fighting had increased in intensity, and she could only hope that wherever they were, they'd come through, and would see the shores of home again.

As the hens came bustling round them, Peggy showed Daisy how to scoop up handfuls of feed and scatter it on the ground. She smiled as the little girl clapped her hands and laughed at the hens' antics as they squabbled over every grain and tried to peck at the few that had landed on her wellington boots. The simplest things delighted Daisy.

Peggy would never have dared come in here, let alone with Daisy, when Adolf the vicious rooster had been alive, but since his demise, the hens seemed far happier, and to Peggy's delight she found half a dozen lovely brown eggs hidden amongst the straw in the coop. Having gathered them up and placed them carefully in the basket, she cleaned out the coop, laid fresh straw and barrowed the mess to Ron's compost heap, for according to him, chicken poo was an excellent fertiliser.

Daisy trotted back and forth with an old dust-pan and brush, scolding the hens if they got in her way, and laughing as they scuttled and flapped around her feet.

'I think that's clean enough,' said Peggy, retrieving brush and pan. 'Come on. Let's see if the postman has been and if there's anything from Daddy.'

Daisy looked up at her, her face streaked with dirt. 'Dada come home?' she asked.

'Not yet, darling. But soon – and when he does he'll make such a fuss of you and spoil you rotten with lots and lots of cuddles. You'll see.'

She gave her a hug and together they went back into the house. Peggy placed the precious egg basket on the drainer out of harm's way, and set about washing Daisy's hands and face, her gaze frequently flitting to Jim's photo on the mantel-piece.

It was a constant worry that Daisy knew nothing

about her father other than the stories she and Ron had told her and the photographs she had of him placed around the house. Daisy had only just been born when Jim was called up, and had been too young to know who he was when he'd come home on that final leave before going off to India. Now Daisy would be three at the end of the year, and if Jim did by some miracle come home, they would be strangers.

Peggy brushed the thought aside and went to see if any post had arrived. As if he'd known she'd be anxious to hear from him, there was a letter from Jim, and she tucked it into her apron pocket to read when she had a minute to herself. There were others from Anne and the boys, and several for the girls, including one from Ireland for Fran. Peggy recognised Fran's mother's writing and fervently hoped the letter contained some sort of peace offering and a way out of the dilemma the young couple had found themselves in.

She turned at the sound of light footsteps on the stairs and smiled. Doris was looking refreshingly cool and attractive in a sprigged cotton dress and white sandals, her hair brushed to a gleam, and with only a hint of powder and lipstick on her radiant face. 'My goodness, you're up early,' Peggy said. 'Are you off somewhere nice?'

'Colonel White asked me to go in this morning for a couple of hours,' Doris replied. 'I thought I might treat myself afterwards to a cup of tea at the Officers' Club.'

'I've never been,' Peggy confessed, 'but Rosie says it's really very smart, and Bertie is always taking Cordelia there for lunch or drinks.'

'I hardly think Rosie Braithwaite is an arbiter of what is smart,' said Doris with a touch of asperity. 'I prefer to draw my own conclusions.'

'Rosie might own the Anchor, but she had a good upbringing, Doris,' said Peggy flatly. 'Better than ours, in fact, so I wouldn't be so hasty to pass judgement if I were you.'

Doris hitched the white cardigan over her shoulders, her expression obdurate. 'I speak as I find, Peggy, you know that, but to give Rosie her due, she's certainly done wonders with Ronan. His sense of humour might still be questionable, but at least he's begun to look presentable.'

'Doris, you're in danger of getting catty again,' Peggy warned. 'Please try and think before you pass judgement on everyone. Rosie's my friend, and if it wasn't for Ron being such a rock over the past few years, I would have given up long ago.'

Doris smiled. 'I doubt that, Peggy. You're as tough as old boots and nothing ever gets you down.' She went into the kitchen and made a fuss of Daisy. 'There has been many a time I've wished I had your strength,' she continued over Daisy's head. 'And I'm sorry if sometimes I speak without thinking. But I am trying, Peggy, really I am.'

'I know, and we're all delighted you've turned the corner and made a new life for yourself. You're stronger than you think, Doris, believe me.'

Doris kissed Daisy's cheek and carefully set her back on her feet. 'I do feel more able to cope with things,' she admitted, 'and that's mostly down to you giving me such loving support. I've been quite moved by the way everyone at Beach View has rallied round in my time of need.'

'They're good people,' said Peggy, 'and always willing to step up to the mark in times of trouble.'

'I've come to realise that,' said Doris. 'And I feel rather ashamed that I denigrated them in the past when I didn't really know them.' She looked at Peggy with a rueful smile. 'I still have a great deal to learn, haven't I?'

'You're doing just fine,' soothed Peggy, giving her hand a gentle squeeze. 'I'm sure your work up at the estate is helping you to see that life amongst us mere mortals isn't all that bad,' she teased.

Doris chuckled. 'Some of it has come as a bit of an eye-opener, but on the whole I feel very at ease with it all. It's lovely to be appreciated, and to know I'm doing something really useful for a change. The Colonel has so many responsibilities running that estate, and it's such a pleasure to know I can ease his way through it all.'

'I'm sure he'd be lost without you,' murmured Peggy, turning away so Doris couldn't see the soft smile creeping into the corners of her mouth. It seemed Doris and the Colonel were getting along famously, and there was a light in Doris's eyes every time she spoke of him. Could it mean...?

Peggy pulled herself together and put the kettle on the hob. 'Do you want a cuppa and some breakfast before you go?'

'I'll have some tea when I get there,' said Doris, pulling on a pair of short white cotton gloves. 'The Colonel likes to start early on a Saturday, so I don't want to keep him waiting.'

Peggy wished her good luck and Doris ran down the cellar steps and hurried across the garden to the back gate. Peggy watched until she'd turned into the twitten and was out of sight. 'Well, well, well,' she murmured. 'Who'd have thought it? Doris in a cheap dress and shoes bought from a market stall – and with a twinkle in her eye.' Whatever she was doing up there in the Colonel's office had certainly worked a miracle – and long may it last.

She'd boiled the kettle and poached an egg for Daisy, and was just slicing up the toast for her when Ron came stomping up the cellar steps with Harvey.

As usual, Harvey was delighted to see them both and tried to filch Daisy's egg as well as wash her face.

'Down, ye heathen beast, and eat your own food,' roared Ron, pulling him away by the collar and setting his bowl on the floor. 'Ach, to be sure, Peggy, the old rogue is always trying to pull a fast one.'

'Why, what's he been up to now?' she asked, hurrying to poach him an egg and make more toast.

'I finally had the time to take Doris's fancy car up to Chalky White's place to store it with yours in his big barn. Me back was turned for no more than a minute, and this divil found his way into Chalky's kitchen and ate the poor wee man's breakfast kippers.'

'Oh, no,' gasped Peggy, trying not to laugh. 'And after he's been so kind to keep the cars for the duration.'

'Aye. He didn't see the funny side of it at all, and I had to promise to buy him some more kippers. Though where I'm supposed to get them, I've no idea. Fred the Fish says he hasn't seen a kipper outside a tin for weeks.'

'Well, Chalky must have got them from somewhere. You'll just have to widen your search, Ron.' She placed his breakfast in front of him, sat down and pulled the letter from Jim out of her apron pocket. 'I got this today, so if you could keep an eye on Daisy whilst I read it, I'd be grateful.'

'Nothing for me?' he asked, digging into his breakfast.

She shook her head and tore open the brown envelope, desperate to know how Jim was faring. Like all his letters, it had been written in pencil on a page torn from a notebook, and there were smears of what looked like mud all over it, making it very difficult to decipher. However, as she digested what he'd written she felt as if an icy hand was clutching at her heart.

'Peggy? Peggy, what's the matter?' asked Ron, immediately concerned.

'He's frightened he isn't going to make it,' she managed. 'And although it's the most loving, sweet letter, it's as if he's trying to say goodbye to us.'

Ron took the letter from her trembling hand and scanned it quickly. 'Aye, the wee boy is at the end of his tether to be sure,' he muttered. 'But this is no goodbye, Peggy. He simply wants you to know how much he loves you – loves all of us.'

'But it's as if...'

'Now don't be making things of it that aren't there,' he interrupted, putting his arm about her shoulders. 'The fighting is probably bad out

221

there, and the monsoon can't be helping either. I expect he's tired, and simply felt the need to say all the things he needed to say before he's back on duty again.'

Peggy held onto her tears, not wanting to upset Daisy, but she was crying inside, the anguish and fear for her Jim building by the second. 'How can you be so sure?' she stammered.

Ron pointed to the last paragraph of Jim's letter and read it out. 'Amid the sounds of battle and in the darkest hours of the night, the love and warmth of home keeps me going, Peggy, and I pray that I will soon know it again, for I'm sick of war, and noise; of death and destruction and the endless struggle to remain strong and brave and not let my comrades down.'

'There's weariness there, Peggy girl, but he's keeping strong and looking towards coming home. My Jim is not a man to have flights of fancy; he simply wanted us to know he holds us in his heart, and that his love for us is keeping him going.'

Peggy regarded him through her unshed tears. 'Do you really think so?' she breathed.

'Aye, I do,' he said firmly, and returned to his cooling poached egg.

Peggy retrieved the letter and read through it again. 'What did he mean about you being honoured for your bravery in the last shout?' she asked with a frown.

'I have no idea,' he said abruptly.

'He must have meant something by it,' she persisted.

Ron clattered his cutlery on the empty plate and began to spread margarine on a second slice of toast. 'Sentimental talk, that's all it was,' he muttered. 'There's no honour in war, Peggy – as I'm sure Jim will tell you when he comes home.'

Peggy watched him as he began to load the toast with the last of the home-made blackberry jam, and was not convinced by his dismissal of what Jim had written. However, past experience had taught her she was wasting her time trying to fathom her father-in-law's mind. Ron being Ron, he would never tell her what Jim had meant and she'd have to wait until the end of this blasted war to find out – unless she pumped Frank for some answers. Yet Frank was like his father, and she doubted he'd tell her anything either, which was most frustrating.

With a sigh she returned Jim's letter to the envelope, praying that Ron knew his son well enough to be able to interpret his words correctly, but she couldn't shift the thought that something awful must have happened to make Jim write such an extraordinarily tender and honest letter.

She had no more time to think about it, for Rita, Fran and Sarah came into the kitchen, having helped Cordelia down the stairs. They were swiftly followed by Ivy dashing in and grabbing the slice of toast from Ron's plate. 'Can't stop,' she said, halfway out of the door again. 'I'm already late for me shift.'

'To be sure, with girls pinching me toast and dogs pinching Chalky's kippers, the world is going to hell in a handcart,' Ron muttered without rancour.

'That girl will get indigestion,' said Cordelia, settling into a chair. 'It's no wonder she's so skinny; anything she eats doesn't have time to stick to her bones the way she charges about.'

Rita poured out tea for them all and counted the eggs. 'There's only three left,' she said. 'Is Doris still upstairs?'

'She's gone to work,' said Peggy, 'I suggest you scramble them, dear. They'll go further that way.'

'I really don't want brambles and beer for breakfast,' said Cordelia, 'and as for fur and hay...' She shuddered. 'Surely the rationing hasn't got to the stage where we're expected to eat like animals?'

Everyone laughed and Peggy made winding signals to encourage Cordelia to turn up her hearing aid. 'We're having scrambled eggs,' she said loudly.

'Well, there's no need to shout,' said Cordelia with a huff. 'And where's my newspaper? I can't possibly start the day without it.'

'The news will be on the wireless in a minute,' said Sarah. 'The paper always comes a bit later on a Saturday.'

'I don't like the news on the wireless,' Cordelia said grumpily. 'It's too depressing.'

'If you turn off your hearing aid, you'll not be hearing it,' said Ron.

'Don't be ridiculous,' snapped Cordelia. 'That would defeat the object entirely.' She regarded him sharply. 'And why aren't you dressed properly in all that new finery Rosie made you buy? You look more disreputable than ever this morning.'

'This is the real me, Cordelia,' he said with a smile. 'If you want fancy then you've got Bertie Double-Barrelled. He's the fanciest man I've had the pleasure of knowing.'

'I do wish you wouldn't call him that,' retorted Cordelia with a humorous glint in her eyes. 'Bertram Grantley-Adams is a true gentleman, unlike some I could mention,' she added with a sniff.

Peggy tuned out of the conversation, for the pair of them liked nothing better than an exchange of frank views first thing in the morning, and as it seemed to enliven them both and set them up for the day, there was little harm in it.

She noticed that Fran had yet to open her letter from Ireland, and guessed she was reluctant to see what her family had made of her engagement, but her own thoughts were on Jim's letter.

Despite all of Ron's assurances, she still couldn't get the thought out of her head that Jim had had a premonition of some sort and become convinced he wouldn't make it through. The thought of him being in such a terrible situation that it had spurred him into writing that emotional letter was a knife in her heart – and there was absolutely nothing she could do about it. She couldn't telephone him, a letter could take weeks to reach him, and a telegram couldn't convey all her fears in just a few words and would only upset him. To cap it all, there wasn't the remotest possibility of him getting a long enough leave to come home – unless he was wounded badly enough to be discharged from the army. 'God forbid,' she breathed.

Ron's warm, rough hand covered hers. 'Stop it, Peggy,' he said quietly beneath the girls' chatter. 'He'll be coming home safe and sound, you'll see.'

'Oh, Ron,' she sighed. 'If only I could really believe that.'

'Fran, whatever's wrong?' Sarah's voice, filled with alarm, caught Peggy's attention.

She took one look at Fran's ashen face and haunted eyes, and rushed to the other end of the table to take her hand. 'What is it, love? Not bad news from home, I hope?'

Fran gazed up at Peggy, her green eyes swimming with tears. 'It's this letter from Mam,' she said brokenly. 'It's what I feared, Aunty Peg, but it doesn't make it any easier to see it written down so coldly like that.'

Peggy took the proffered letter and with a heavy heart began to read.

My dearest Frances,

I've taken this long to reply to your letter because your news has caused terrible trouble here. Your da will not hear of any marriage to a Protestant, and there have been times over the past two weeks when I've been truly afraid he will die from apoplexy, his raging has been so great. It reached the point where I had to send your younger sisters to your aunts so they couldn't witness their da's fury, or hear the terrible things he was saying about you.

He will not be mollified, even though I agree with him and do my best to assure him you'll be bound to come to your senses once you realise what this will do to all of us. It feels as if our family has already been torn apart. How much worse it will be if you defy him and go ahead with this wedding that none of us can recognise.

In the eyes of a true Catholic you would be living in sin, Frances, your babies tainted by illegitimacy, denied not only the sacrament of the one true church,

226

but also of a place in Heaven – forever condemned to purgatory. You would be excommunicated, and shunned by the church which has guided you since you were a wee wain, and by everyone in our village. Is that what you really want? Is this Protestant worth such sacrifice?

Your da arranged a family conference at the week-end, which I'm sad to say ended in a huge row. Some of the younger ones held some sympathy for you, but your uncles and aunts and the grandparents were as much against it as me and your da.

Have no doubts about it, Frances, if you go ahead then you will be lost to this family and never be welcomed into our homes or our lives again. You will have turned your back on all those who've loved and nurtured you from the day you were born, divided the loyalties that are generations old and defied the teachings of our church.

I blame myself for encouraging you to leave Ireland for what I hoped would be a better life in England. Your da warned me you'd be led astray being so far from home and forget who and what you are – and it seems he's been proved right. I beg you to change your mind, acushla, for you are my heart and I do not wish to see you ruined, or live the rest of my life never to see you again.

Mother

Peggy folded the letter with trembling fingers. 'That was harsh,' she managed through her anger. 'I can't believe any mother could write such a cruel letter knowing how much it would hurt you.'

'I thought she might be softer-hearted,' said

227

Fran through her tears. 'But she's turned out to be as staunch a Catholic as Da. And although I know they both love me, it's clear they'll never change their minds.'

Peggy drew her close and held her to her heart as she waited for the tears to subside. 'So what will you do, Fran?'

'I don't know,' she said sadly. 'I love Robert, and I love Mammy and Da. I don't want to lose any of them.'

Peggy held her close, her emotions in turmoil. She was angry with Fran's family for being so cold-hearted and blinkered; sad for Fran and Robert; and fretful over her inability to find a solution to it all. Poor, sweet little Fran had the hardest of decisions to make and, like Sarah, would be forced to choose between two impossible options which, in the end, could only bring heartache.

Daisy came trotting up to Fran, her face wreathed in worry as she leaned against her knee and kissed her hand. 'Not cry, Fran. Daisy kiss all betta.'

Fran reached down and drew her onto her lap, burying her tear-streaked face in her dark curls. 'Sweet Daisy,' she murmured. 'Aunty Fran's all better now she's got you to cuddle.'

Daisy looked up at her with big brown eyes full of concern. 'My daddy gone long, long away too,' she said, resting the palm of her small hand on Fran's cheek. 'He be home soon and he come with your daddy and we have lots of cuddles.' She nestled within Fran's embrace and stuck her thumb in her mouth.

'Oh, bless her,' whispered Peggy, her own eyes

pricking with tears as Fran rocked Daisy back and forth, and the others suddenly became busy at stove and sink. This war was hard enough to struggle through without old prejudices rearing their ugly heads, and if only they could all see the world through the eyes of a child like Daisy who thought all problems could be solved by a cuddle, it would certainly be a much better and happier place.

Ron left the kitchen with a heavy heart and went down the steps to the basement. He walked past the bedroom where he'd slept for many years, and opened the next door along. The room was bright with the sunlight pouring in through the narrow window that looked out from beneath the front steps.

He stood for a long moment, regarding the bunk beds where Bob and Charlie had slept before they'd been evacuated to the farm in Somerset. The mattresses had been rolled up, the blankets and pillows in a neat pile at the end of each bed, their toys and clothes packed away, the train set stowed in a large box on top of the wardrobe. The absence of these small things made him feel sadder than ever, for he loved the bones of those boys, and the house seemed emptier without them and their lively noise and mischief.

He sat on the bottom bunk and stared out of the narrow window. Fran's mother had talked about tearing families apart in her letter, but the war had already done that by sending children away, enlisting men and boys and young women into the forces and scattering them to all four corners of the earth.

He'd been raised as a Catholic, but after the trenches of the Somme, Ypres and Passchendaele, he'd barely set foot in a church, for he'd seen and heard nothing to convince him that religion was the answer to the world's ills. In fact it was often used as a weapon – an excuse to start trouble – and people like Fran's parents were part of the problem with their mulish adherence to old prejudices.

Ron sighed and scrubbed his face with his hands. He felt so sorry for Fran and Robert, but there was nothing he, or anyone else, could say or do to help them, for it would be up to what was in their hearts that would decide their fate.

As for his grandsons ... Bob could be called up within months, and Charlie was no longer the cheeky little rapscallion who'd fought so hard to hold back his tears on the day he'd left for Somerset, but a sturdy, growing boy of thirteen with a mind of his own. They would have both left these childish toys far behind them, and Ron wondered how they'd feel about coming home at the end of the war. The farmhouse was large and rambling, the acres of open space around it a paradise for boys with a sense of adventure and too much energy. It would feel strange to come back here to their cramped basement room, and all the restrictions that would entail after having so much freedom. He got to his feet, took one last look at those empty beds and discarded toys and closed the door.

Making his way back to his room, he stood for a moment deep in thought. That letter from Jim had shaken him to the core, although he'd been very careful not to let Peggy see his distress. The fighting in Burma was quite brutal if all the reports were to be believed, and now the monsoon had really taken hold, the conditions out there must be horrendous. It was no wonder his son had been brought so low as to write such a letter, and he could only pray that any premonition he had would prove to be an aberration, brought on by the gut-wrenching exhaustion, the mud and rain, and the constant, mind-numbing noise of warfare.

Ron understood all too well what that was like, had lived through it, cowering from it even though it reverberated into every atom of his being until he thought he would go mad.

He moved towards the wardrobe, dragged over a stool and climbed up to reach the shoe box he'd kept hidden away from prying eyes since 1919. He stepped back down and sank onto the neatly made bed, the box on his lap. He'd made Jim and Frank promise never to reveal what was in this box, and Jim had clearly been at the end of his tether to hint about it in his letter to Peggy.

Ron's sigh was tremulous. He hadn't looked inside this box since he'd first put it up there, and he didn't really know why he felt the urge to look today, and could only assume it was some kind of morbid need to replay his own war. His rough hands caressed the box, and before he could change his mind, he lifted the lid and drew out the four small velvet cases that had nestled in the yellowing tissue paper for twenty-five years alongside his pay-book and the jumble of loose campaign medals.

He moved his fingers amongst the 1914–15 Star, the British War Medal and the Victory Medal. His smile was sad, for the grouping of those medals had become better known to the men who'd fought alongside him as Pip, Squeak and Wilfred.

Opening the fancy velvet cases one by one, he stared down at the medals which had been given to him with little ceremony in the midst of the carnage of war all those years before. The Distinguished Service Order medal, with its red and blue ribbon, entitled him to put DSO after his name, but he'd never bothered with such ostentation. The Military Cross had a ribbon of dark and light blue, and the Legion of Honour's green and white star gleamed on its red ribbon.

Ron's gaze drifted to the Croix de Guerre bronze star with its crossed swords, green silk ribbon striped with red and bedecked with two bronze palms and a silver gilt star to denote the times he'd been honoured. He'd received that after the armistice in a ceremony in some grand Parisian mansion with all the fanfare and hullabaloo the French so enjoyed – but he'd barely taken in any of it, he'd been so exhausted.

He sighed, closed the cases and put them back in the box to return to the top of the wardrobe. They were symbols of his war, and a stark reminder of all those pals he'd lost. He had been thankful to be alive and honoured to receive them at the time, but as the years had passed he'd come to regard them as just fancy bits of metal on smart ribbons that served no real purpose. They would probably stay there now until they carried him out feet first and someone cleared the room. If nothing else, they would make fine playthings for the next generation of grandsons.

12

The washing was mostly dry, so Peggy brought it in and folded it ready for ironing before she left Beach View, consoled by the fact that Robert had arrived to be with Fran. As Sarah had decided to go into town with Cordelia, the three of them made their way along Camden Road at a snail's pace, with Daisy in the pushchair.

'It's a great shame some people refuse to see the damage they're doing to others by being so obstinate,' said Cordelia. 'If Fran's family had been forced to live through air raids and doodlebug attacks, they might be a bit more forgiving. But I suppose they're smug and safe over in Ireland and have absolutely no idea of what the rest of us are going through.'

As if on cue they heard the distant whine of an engine, and stopped walking to look up at the sky. Everyone in Camden Road came to a halt, tense and ready to run as they watched the pilotless doodlebug drone over the rooftops. The noise of it grew louder, as it kept on coming, and to their horror they saw it was not alone.

'Move,' snapped Peggy, snatching Daisy out of her pushchair and simultaneously grabbing hold of Cordelia's arm. With Cordelia between them, and the sound of those deadly weapons coming ever closer, Peggy and Sarah thrust their way through the side door of the Anchor. The motors were still running, but they could stop at any minute and blow them all to smithereens.

'Rosie, get in the cellar,' yelled Peggy, hauling Daisy onto her hip.

'What is it?' asked a breathless Rosie, running down the stairs with Monty.

Peggy didn't have to answer her, for the sirens were now screaming all over town and the menacing sound of the doodlebugs was right overhead.

Monty shot straight down the steps into the makeshift air-raid shelter beneath the Anchor, and Peggy swiftly followed Sarah and Rosie, who were all but carrying Cordelia between them. Slamming the door behind her as Rosie lit some of the lanterns and Sarah eased Cordelia into one of the over-stuffed couches, she heard the motors stop.

Peggy's heart stopped too, and it was all she could do to get to the couch and wedge herself and Daisy in before the explosion rocked the ground beneath their feet and made the sixteenth-century walls shudder, bringing down a shower of plaster and dust from the beamed ceiling. Peggy's heart was now hammering, the terror of their situation making her hold onto Daisy so tightly the child squirmed and cried out in protest.

Rosie handed out helmets to all of them. 'Ron said they were surplus to Home Guard requirements,' she shouted above the noise of the sirens.

Peggy fastened one under Daisy's chin before plonking her own on her head just as the second explosion made the beer bottles in the crates rattle and the lanterns swing from the beams, casting eerie shadows against the old walls. The women clung to each other in their tin hats as more debris rained down on them and something crashed to the floor overhead, accompanied by the sound of breaking glass.

They remained huddled together as Monty began to howl and Daisy started sobbing and clinging to her mother. 'It's all right,' soothed Peggy. 'The nasty bangs will stop in a minute.'

Rosie gathered a trembling Monty into her arms as the third and fourth explosions came – but they were further away this time and the tremor beneath their feet was lessened by the distance. 'Let's sing a song, Daisy,' she said, her trembling voice revealing her fear despite her bright, encouraging smile. 'How about, "Run Rabbit Run"? Do you know that?'

Rosie began to sing, and by the end of the first line Daisy and the others joined in, their voices faltering as yet another distant explosion echoed through the town and into the cellar.

As the song came to an end, and it seemed the last of the doodlebugs had gone over, Rosie fetched Daisy a bottle of lemonade, and beers for herself and the other women. They sat in silence, each with their own thoughts on what they might find once the all-clear sounded and they could return to the street.

Peggy could hear fire engine and ambulance bells and fretfully wondered if her house was still standing, and if Doris and Ivy were all right up on the factory estate, and if Kitty and Charlotte's cottage in Briar Lane had been spared. And then there was the fire station, the railway and hospital, the shops crowded with people on this Saturday morning. Some of those explosions sounded much too close, and the distant ones could very well have come down on the factories despite the vast numbers of barrage balloons protecting them. And where was Ron?

Daisy complained and she realised she was again gripping her too tightly and tried to relax. But it was impossible.

Doris held onto Ivy as the explosions rocked the underground shelter and the lights flickered. She could feel the girl trembling in her arms, and was shocked by how small and slight she was. 'It'll be over soon,' she murmured, silently praying she was right.

'Let's just 'ope it's third time lucky,' Ivy shivered, her brown eyes huge in her elfin face. 'I been 'ere before, remember, and it were my Andy what 'ad to pull me out when the fire come – and then Havelock Road went up too. I must be jinxed.'

'Then we're all jinxed,' said Doris firmly. 'This isn't the first time Cliffehaven's come under attack – and I doubt it'll be the last.' She reached into her cardigan pocket and passed over the clean handkerchief. 'Do stop sniffing, dear. It's most unpleasant,' she admonished gently.

Ivy used the handkerchief and then nestled back into Doris's embrace. 'You ain't such a bad old stick, are yer?' she murmured.

Doris hid a smile. 'I try not to be,' she replied. She looked around the vast shelter at the men and women who sat in clusters, some talking, others sitting huddled together for comfort. It was a gloomy, foul-smelling place with its lavatory buckets behind screens and the damp in its walls, but much sturdier than any Anderson shelter, and she could only hope it was built to withstand anything that might come down on it. She'd known about Ivy's narrow escape, for they'd both been living in Havelock Road at the time, and although she'd shown little sympathy then, the thought that the girl had virtually been buried alive in the old shelter made her shudder. It was no wonder Ivy needed someone's arm about her – she'd have felt the same. Indeed it was a comfort to her to hold her close, for the claustrophobia was starting to make her feel very edgy.

The raid had come without warning, but a keen-eyed security guard had seen the doodle-bugs approaching and raised the alarm. Colonel White ordered the men to raise the height of the barrage balloons immediately, and within seconds there was the sound of whistles and shouts as everyone poured out of the factories, canteen and workshops. Doris had had just enough time to grab her handbag and cardigan before the Colonel had hustled her down the stairs and across the estate to the underground shelter.

She glanced across at him now, admiring how calm he appeared to be as he went around the shelter to talk to some of the women who were on the verge of hysteria, or simply sobbing quietly into their hands. It came as no surprise to her that he'd risen so high within the army ranks, for he was a man who could take charge in a dangerous situation, thereby instilling a sense of security in even the most fearful.

Doris wondered what his wife was like. He never mentioned her, but as he was so beautifully turned out every day, she must work hard to make sure he always looked smart. They rarely spoke of personal things, there was too much paperwork to get through, but he had told her his son was a POW somewhere in Germany, and that although the boy would be champing at the bit to get back into the fighting, Colonel White was relieved he was out of it now.

'Are they ever going to give the all-clear?' moaned Ivy. 'I 'ate it down 'ere.'

Doris gave her a reassuring hug. 'We all hate it, dear, but better to stay until we're absolutely sure it's safe to go back up.'

'I 'ope Mum and Dad are all right,' she said. 'These doodlebugs 'ave 'it London something rotten – especially the East End – and 'aving come through the Blitz in one piece...'

'Are all your family in the East End, Ivy?'

'Just me mum, dad and sister. Me two big brothers are in the Navy and the younger ones were evacuated, but Mum's been talking about bringing 'em 'ome again when it looked like the bombing 'ad stopped.'

'I'm sure she's realised it's safer to leave them where they are,' Doris said soothingly.

'Yer right there,' said Ivy. 'Mum and Dad've been bombed out three times already, and from what it says on the wireless, it looks like Jerry's determined to wipe out what's left of poor old Bow.'

'Surely they'd be safer to leave that part of

London and find somewhere else to live?'

Ivy shook her head. 'They won't 'ear of it. Dad works for the Gas Board, Mum's got a good job in a canning factory, and they're Cockneys through and through and proud of it. They'll stick with it.'

Doris was saved from replying by the welcome sound of the all-clear wailing throughout the estate. 'Come on, Ivy,' she said, pulling the girl to her feet. 'I've got tea and biscuits in the office. I don't know about you, but I could do with a strong cuppa after that.'

'Well, if yer sure,' she said hesitantly.

'I wouldn't have offered otherwise,' Doris said briskly. She turned to the Colonel as he approached. 'I've asked Ivy here to tea and biscuits before we get back to work, Colonel. I hope that's all right?'

'Jolly good idea, Mrs Williams,' he said and shot her and Ivy a beaming smile.

They slowly emerged into the bright sunlight and a cloud of dust. It seemed the factories, warehouses and workshops had escaped, but the dairy that had stood nearby for almost a hundred years had been reduced to a flattened pile of burning debris.

'Oh, them poor horses and cows,' cried Ivy, the tears once more streaming down her face.

The Colonel pointed beyond the shattered walls of the dairy to the field beyond where four Shires stood trembling beneath a tree and the small herd of cows continued to graze in a nearby field as if nothing had happened. 'There's no need for tears, Ivy,' he said gently. 'It seems they've escaped. Let's hope the dairyman and his workers have too.'

'Shouldn't we go and see if we can 'elp?' asked Ivy, still in some distress.

'The firemen are already there along with the wardens and Home Guard,' said Doris. 'They'll make sure everyone gets out.'

She cast a quick glance over the town at the bottom of the hill, saw smoke rising in several places and could only pray no one from Beach View had been caught up in the raid. She exchanged a fearful glance with the Colonel and then purposefully steered Ivy towards the office and a welcome pot of tea.

Monty had refused to leave the cellar and was curled tightly in the corner of a chair. The women went up the steps, cautiously, wondering what they would find, for the very foundations of the old pub had been shaken, and it had sounded as if the damage could be serious.

To their immense relief, they discovered that it wasn't as bad as they'd feared. The thud they'd heard was the old grandfather clock in the hall falling down, but as it had never worked properly anyway, Rosie wasn't too upset.

What did concern her was the state of the bar, and the fact that nearly every bottle and glass on the ornate shelves behind it had been smashed, and that the big mirror in its Victorian oak surround had a crack in it like a lightning strike right across the middle.

'Well,' she sighed mournfully. 'That's seven years' bad luck for a start – and it will cost me an arm and a leg to replace those bottles and glasses – if I can get replacements at all.' She looked around the room, noting the soot which had come down the large chimney to cover everything in sticky black, and the way the old piano had been rocked across the floor in the blasts to end up leaning against the front wall.

'I don't fancy having to clean all that soot up,' she muttered, 'but I suppose I should be grateful the old place is still standing.'

'We'll help you, Rosie,' said Peggy immediately. 'I'm sure we'll have it shipshape before you have to open.'

'I don't think I'll bother this lunchtime,' she replied. 'There aren't enough glasses to go round, and we'll never get the place clean in time. Let's go and see what's happened outside.'

Peggy held Daisy's hand as she stepped out of the Anchor and into Camden Road with Sarah, Cordelia and Rosie crowding behind her. They stood in dumb shock as the clouds of dust and the stench of burning stung their eyes and throats whilst smuts of oily soot settled in their hair and on their clothes.

The house three doors down from the Anchor had taken a direct hit along with its neighbour, and was now a pile of burning rubble. The block of flats at the other end of the road had been scythed in half, the debris flung into the street and across the hospital forecourt. The flats in the half that was still standing were open to the elements, curtains flapping, furniture hanging precariously over the crumbling edges of what had once been dividing walls and floors.

And as they looked from one end of the street to the other, they could see that every window had been shattered, chimneys had been made unstable, doors had been blown off, and the pavement was littered with the tragic remnants of people's lives and homes.

Peggy covered her mouth to stifle a sob. It was a miracle the hospital hadn't been hit being so close to those flats – a miracle too that Solly's factory hadn't been touched, for when she thought of all those women working inside it, she felt quite sick.

The firemen were already tackling the blaze at the end of the road. Men from the Water Board and gas company were busy at both ends of the street, whilst the police, wardens and members of the Home Guard searched through the rubble for survivors. Ambulances were waiting to take away the injured, and Peggy could see Ron amidst it all, working furiously to help dig someone out, Harvey trawling the wreckage of the flats for the scent of anyone still buried.

As she watched, a child was pulled to safety, swiftly followed by a woman holding a baby, and an elderly man who was covered in blood. 'I've got to go home,' she said, and without waiting for a reply, she scooped Daisy onto her hip and began to run.

Dodging piles of rubble and snaking electric wires that hissed at her like multi-headed serpents, she spotted Rita minus her plaster, fighting to hold the heavy hose as it sent a vast jet of water over the remnants of the two houses. She ran faster as she saw the plume of smoke rising above the roofs on the other side of the main road. 'Oh, God,' she begged. 'Please, please don't let it be Beach View.'

She skidded to a halt at the end of Camden Road and only just avoided being run over by a racing fire truck. Grasping Daisy to her side she waited impatiently for it to pass and then fled across the road. The cul-de-sac was quiet and unharmed, Beach View looking almost serene in the sun. She pounded up the hill and stopped dead at the end of the twitten. The house that had stood directly behind Beach View was gone.

Her legs suddenly gave way and she sank to the pavement, holding Daisy to her heart, the tears of relief streaming down her face.

'Mumma cuddle,' said Daisy, winding her arms about Peggy's neck. 'All betta now,' she added, kissing her cheek.

'Yes, darling, all better now I've had a kiss and a cuddle,' she managed distractedly. Her gaze drifted to the vacant plot where the house had once stood. It was as if it had been plucked whole from existence by an unseen hand, for by some miracle the houses on either side looked as if they hadn't been touched. Thick smoke rose in a pall into the clear blue sky as firemen doused the last of the flames, and other people had come out to stand and watch, no doubt as guiltily relieved as she that it hadn't been their home that had been laid to waste. She could only pray that the elderly couple who lived there had been elsewhere and survived.

Eventually Peggy managed to get to her feet, but her legs were still shaking as she went into Beach View and climbed the steps to the kitchen.

'Thank goodness you're all right,' said Fran, throwing her arms about her. 'Where are the

243

others? Are they safe?'

'I don't know about Doris and Ivy, but the rest of us are fine, if a little shaken up.' As she told them what had happened at the Anchor, Peggy noted that Fran had changed into her nurse's uniform and then regarded the cups that had been laid out on two trays and the boiling kettle. 'You must have read my mind,' she said affectionately. 'I was going to make tea and take it back to Camden Road.'

'Why don't you sit down and have a cigarette first?' said Robert, relieving her of Daisy, and eyeing her with some concern. 'We'll see to the tea whilst you get over the shock.'

'Do you know if the Watsons at number eighty got out?' she asked once she'd lit a cigarette and eased off her cardigan, which she discovered was grimy with soot smuts and stank of smoke.

'Robert dashed out as soon as the all-clear went and found them coming back from the shelter beneath the Town Hall,' said Fran. 'They're safe, but of course devastated to have lost their home.'

'They told me they'd go down to Devon where their daughter lives,' said Robert, filling a jug with watered-down milk. 'I felt so sorry for them. They've lost a lifetime of memories and everything they possessed. I left them waiting for the firemen to finish so they could sift through the rubble, but it's doubtful they'll find anything in one piece.'

Fran finished stirring the tea in the three large teapots and placed them on another tray. 'I'll help hand out this lot and then I have to go to the hospital. There are bound to be lots of casualties, and it will be all hands on deck.'

'I'll come with you both, drop Daisy off at the factory crèche and then help Rosie clear up the mess at the Anchor. I saw Rita working the fire hose earlier, by the way. She's had her plaster off and got stuck straight in. I'll ask her if she knows where the other doodlebugs hit. They can't all have come down on Camden Road, and I'm worried about Doris and Ivy up on that factory estate – and Kitty and Charlotte in Briar Lane.'

'The telephone lines are all down, so why don't I go up there and find out?' offered Robert. 'With Fran at the hospital, I'll have nothing else better to do.'

'Bless you, dear, that would be kind,' said Peggy gratefully as she cleaned Daisy's face and hands and swiftly collected her apron and cleaning materials. There was little point in getting changed, and by the end of the day there would be another great stack of washing to do, she thought dolefully, which meant her Sunday would be very busy.

They carried the trays of tea back into Camden Road to find others had had the same idea. Peggy saw Fred the Fish and his wife Lil emerge from their shop and hurried over to them. 'Are you and the boys all right?' she asked anxiously.

'It's a right two an' eight, ain't it?' said Lil cheerfully. 'I got me boys making tea and 'elping to fetch and carry for them what's been bombed out. Lawks almighty, I thought our number were up, didn't I, Fred?'

Fred nodded and hurried off with the tray of tea, and Peggy gave Lil a hug before trying to find

Rita in the melee of people surrounding the two bomb sites. She bumped into Alf the butcher and his wife, exchanged a few words with them, checked on Cordelia and Sarah who were handing out teacups and blankets, and eventually, found Rita in the cab of the largest fire engine, chattering away to Peter Ryan. Both of them had been soaked by the water from the hoses, and their faces were smeared with soot to the point they resembled pandas.

'Do you know if the factory estate and Briar Lane were hit?' she asked urgently.

'No, neither of them were,' Rita said quickly, 'but it was a close thing. The dairy took a direct hit, but, by all reports it seems everyone got out in time and managed to chase the horses out into the back field with the cows.'

'Thank goodness for that,' breathed Peggy, with huge relief. 'Young Jane would have been devastated if anything had happened to those horses.'

Rita grinned. 'I remember how delighted she was when she got the job at the dairy and spent hours grooming and fussing over them. I wonder if she even thinks about them now she's got her important job in London.'

'Oh, I suspect she does,' Peggy murmured. 'Are you staying for tea, Peter? Only you'll have to take pot luck, I'm afraid.'

'No worries, Mrs Reilly,' he drawled. 'I have to get back on duty soon. There's an op on tonight.'

'Another time then,' said Peggy. She left them to their chatter and hurried to the other end of the street, where she could see Ron and Rosie still at the site of the bombed-out flats. Her plans for the day had been changed drastically, but as long as everyone from Beach View had come through safely, it didn't matter a jot.

Once she'd persuaded the nanny in charge of the crèche to take in Daisy for a couple of hours, Peggy hurried back to help her friend. As she neared the remains of the flats, she was concerned to see Rosie sobbing in Ron's arms.

His face was smeared with grime and sweat as he held Rosie close to his grubby chest. 'It's Eileen Harris,' he said, over her head. 'She didn't make it.'

Peggy's spirits sank as she thought about the young woman who'd been duped by Rosie's brother into giving away her baby instead of allowing Rosie to adopt her. That baby – Mary Jones – was a young woman now and had come to Cliffehaven in search of the truth surrounding her adoption, which had ultimately brought Rosie and Eileen to a tenuous armistice after what had been years of mutual dislike and mistrust.

'Come on, Rosie,' Peggy murmured. 'Let's get you home. There's nothing we can do here.'

Rosie sniffed back her tears, kissed Ron's grimy cheek and allowed Peggy to steer her back to the Anchor. 'I'm surprised at how hard her death has hit me,' she managed as they went through the side door. 'We were never that close, even after Mary brought us all together.' She came to a stumbling halt in the gloomy hallway. 'Oh, Lord, Peggy, I'm going to have to tell Mary. The authorities won't know of her relationship to Eileen so they won't contact her – and now she's married to Jack and expecting her first, it will come as a terrible blow.'

'Best you leave it for a while until you're feeling a bit steadier and the phone lines are repaired,' Peggy advised. 'Eileen's sister Julie will be notified, but I'll write to her tonight with my condolences. She was such a dear girl, and although she and Eileen had their differences, she'll be devastated to hear she's gone.'

Rosie nodded and tried to clean her face with her handkerchief, but merely smeared the soot and tears about. 'Of course, I forgot Julie was one of your chicks.' She gave a deep, tremulous sigh. 'So much has happened, and it all seems so very long ago, doesn't it?'

'It certainly does,' agreed Peggy, leading the way up the stairs to the sitting room where Monty was stretched out across the couch. 'Let's have a cuppa, and then make a start on the clear-up. A bit of scrubbing and cleaning will take our mind off things.'

Half an hour later Sarah and Cordelia had joined them and they went back down to the bar, armed with buckets, mops and brooms, swathed in aprons, headscarves and rubber gloves. They eyed the thick layer of soot which covered everything and the shattered glass, and stood in helpless silence wondering where on earth they should start.

The front door opened with a crash and Gloria Stevens swept in, similarly armed and dressed, and with a determined expression. She was closely followed by four sturdy men carrying brooms and two crates of bottled beer. 'Right,' she said in a tone that brooked no argument. 'We're 'ere to help clean up. Where do you want us to start?'

Rosie stared at her in disbelief, unable to find the words to reply.

'Look, Rosie, I knows we don't get on, but life's 'ard enough being a woman what runs a pub, so we gotta pull together in times like this. What you want doin' first?'

'I don't know,' Rosie replied, the tears once more coursing down her dirty face as she looked helplessly at the terrible mess.

Gloria immediately took charge by barking orders at everyone, and within minutes the windows and door had been opened, glass was being cleared, furniture stacked outside on the pavement, and the soot carefully brushed into pans and buckets.

Peggy started working with a will, thankful that Cliffehaven had a woman like Gloria. Loud and brassy she might be, but nothing ever got her down, and in times of trouble she was always there to lend a hand and dole out rough advice. And although the two landladies were frequently at odds – mostly over Ron – they recognised in each other the strength of character which had seen them both through the trials and tribulations of being a woman alone and in charge of a pub. Gloria was right: working together would make them even stronger.

Doris had just cleared the tea things and sent Ivy back to work, when Robert turned up to say that Beach View and Briar Lane had come to no harm and was just checking that she and Ivy were all right.

She assured him they were fine, and listened in horror to what had happened down in Camden Road. She was so shaken up at the news of the doodlebugs dropping that close to Peggy and Beach View that after Robert had left, she had to sit down and have a cigarette to calm her nerves and decide whether or not she should go down into the town and help.

Colonel White ran his fingers through his thick hair, his expression concerned. 'I think we should call it a day,' he said. 'Everything is under control, and there really isn't anything to be done that can't be left until Monday.'

'Well, if you're sure,' said Doris, still in a dither. 'But we've hardly achieved much this morning.'

'We've survived to fight another day,' he said with a soft smile. 'And I think that calls for some sort of recognition, don't you?'

Doris frowned up at him. 'What do you mean?'

He adjusted his tie and cleared his throat, the colour in his cheeks rising a little. 'I was wondering if you'd care to join me for luncheon at the Officers' Club,' he said hesitantly.

'Well, I don't know,' Doris replied, not quite sure how to handle this surprising invitation. 'I'm your secretary, and people might get the wrong idea.'

'I don't mind if you don't,' he said. 'There's been enough going on today to fuel the gossips for a week. I hardly think us sharing a table for luncheon will set the tongues wagging.'

Doris smiled at this. 'Then you don't know Cliffehaven. Besides, I should really go and help the WVS, even though I've resigned, and I'm sure your wife would appreciate being taken out.'

His eyes dulled and the smile faded. 'My wife was killed at the beginning of the war, Mrs Williams.'

'Oh, I'm so sorry,' she gasped. 'I didn't realise.'

He plucked his hat from the coat-stand. 'There's no reason why you should,' he said gruffly before turning back to her. 'The offer of luncheon still stands, Mrs Williams.'

Doris hesitated for only a second before coming to a decision. 'Then I'll be delighted to accept it, Colonel White,' she replied, reaching for her handbag.

13

Ron got his pipe going satisfactorily and gratefully accepted his third mug of tea from the WVS lady in charge of the motorised waggon which had been donated by the Queen. He was soaked to the skin from the fire hoses, weary to the bone, and covered in filth from where he'd searched through the still smouldering rubble for anyone who might have survived – and there had been survivors, despite the devastation, each one greeted with cries of thankfulness and willing hands to bring them to safety.

It had been three hours since the doodlebug strike and those who were able to do so had gone home, thankful they still had one to return to. The dead had been taken to the hospital mortuary, the injured to the emergency ward; the street and hospital forecourt had been cleared of debris, unstable walls knocked down, the gas and water mains repaired, the fires put out. Windows were even now being boarded up with plywood, chimneys made safe and doors replaced.

Thirty people had died today and twice that number were injured; the total of those made homeless was over a hundred, and some of the survivors were still wandering about, huddled in blankets, their faces blank with shock, unable to absorb what had happened or think what to do or where to go. The large band of women volunteers had been wonderful, gathering up the lost and bewildered and taking them to the Town Hall, to provide tea and consolation whilst new accommodation was desperately sought in an already overcrowded town.

Ron slurped the hot and very strong tea as Harvey gobbled down a Spam sandwich and lapped water from the bowl the kind WVS lady had found for him. The old boy had lost none of his ability to sniff out the living from beneath the rubble, but his brindled coat was matted, dirty and damp, his paws bloodied by all that digging, and he looked to be drooping with weariness.

'Come on, ye heathen beast,' Ron rumbled, putting his hand gently on Harvey's head. 'Let's see how Rosie is, then we'll go home for a wash and see to those paws.'

He tramped along the road, aching to rest and feel clean again, but Rosie had been surprisingly upset to hear about Eileen's death, coming so soon after the shock of the strike, and he wanted to make sure she was coping. He frowned as he saw the sign on the Anchor door saying it was closed until six o'clock. Rosie never shut the pub, so something must be badly wrong.

He was about to push the door open when he heard a gale of raucous laughter coming from the bar, and with a deep frown he went inside. The scene that met him was beyond his comprehension, and it took a moment to absorb it. Rosie, Gloria, Peggy, Sarah and Cordelia were sitting at a table laden with empty bottles of beer, and laughing uproariously, their faces and clothes blackened with soot.

'Well, don't stand there gawping,' shouted Gloria. 'Come in and 'ave a beer. Looks like you've earned it.'

Ron stepped down into the room, looking at Rosie in bewilderment. 'What's going on here? Why's the pub shut?'

'I had a soot fall from the chimney I asked you to sweep before I went away,' said Rosie cheerfully. 'Gloria and the others have been helping me to clear up.'

'You should have said,' he replied, easing his way carefully past Gloria to the other side of the table. 'I'd have come to help.' He eyed them thoughtfully and smiled as he realised that all five women were tipsy. 'Just how much beer have you lot got through?'

'Not enough,' said Rosie with a glint of defiance in her eye as she plucked a fresh bottle from the crate by her feet. 'It's thirsty work cleaning up a year's worth of soot – which you'd know if you'd sorted out that chimney when I asked.' She twisted off the cap expertly and took a swig. 'If you want to help, you could try and find me some more glasses. Gloria's chaps have gone back to the Crown to fetch a case she's been storing in her cellar, but they won't be enough.'

Ron frowned, 'Gloria's chaps?'

Gloria grinned lopsidedly. 'Yeah, four regulars who had nothing better to do, so I rounded 'em up and put them to work in 'ere. We was glad of it and all, for it were a right mess, I'm telling you.' She eyed him up and down. 'If you don't mind me saying, Ron, you could do with a clean-up too.'

He took a bottle from the crate, poured some for Harvey into the bowl Rosie always kept by the hearth and then glugged the rest down. 'I shouldn't cast aspersions on my appearance, Gloria – not until you've looked in the mirror,' he replied dryly.

The five women looked at one another, burst out laughing again and clashed the bottles together in a toast. 'Here's to us,' shouted Gloria. 'I hear tell a bit of soot is good for the complexion.'

Ron rolled his eyes and decided to leave them to it. There'd be no sense out of any of them for a while, and if the Anchor was to open at six, then he'd better get washed and changed and be ready to take charge. He leaned over Rosie and kissed her dirty face, delighted that she was feeling more cheerful. 'I'll see you later,' he murmured.

Ron arrived at Beach View to find it deserted, and stood for a moment at the kitchen window trying to come to terms with the gaping hole that had been left in the terrace on the other side of the twitten. The vagaries of fate never ceased to

254

amaze him, for the bomb had wiped out that house so cleanly, it was as if it had never been there. 'It just goes to show, Harvey, that if your number's on it, there's no escape,' he muttered.

He checked on his ferrets, who appeared to be undisturbed by the events of the morning, and found Queenie asleep under his bed. The next hour was spent washing himself and Harvey in the bath upstairs. It took another half-hour and most of a tub of Vim to get the stubborn black scum off the white enamel and mop up dog hairs and splatters from the walls and floor where Harvey had shaken himself vigorously. Peggy would blow a fuse if she knew what he'd done, but using the bath had saved water in the long run, and as long as he cleaned up properly, she'd never need to know.

Having tended to Harvey's paws, he fed him and Queenie and then left him to dry out in a patch of sunlight in the garden whilst he stoked the range fire to reheat the water. Everyone would need a bath when they got home, and the laundry would soon be piling up.

He got dressed in his smart clothes so he'd be ready to run the bar if Rosie was under the weather – which was quite likely – but he didn't begrudge her, and actually felt a twinge of remorse at having forgotten to sweep that chimney. It had been merely one item on a long list of things she and Peggy had wanted him to do, and what with one thing and another it had slipped his mind.

Returning upstairs, his thoughts centred on how he could possibly find more glasses for Rosie. The telephone line was still out, so he couldn't call his usual pal who could be relied upon for most things that no one else could get; Gloria had already offered a carton of hers, and he had no idea of where else to try. He began to search through Peggy's cupboards to see if she had any spare, but soon realised he'd be in real trouble if he dared take even one from the precious collection her mother had left her. Shelving the matter for now, he made a tomato sandwich and a pot of tea, and went to sit in the garden to eat his delayed lunch.

The dark palls of smoke had cleared to reveal a lovely blue sky and bright sun. Unfortunately the acrid stench of burning still remained, and he could see smuts of soot darkening his tomato plants and lettuces. He chose to ignore it all, and once he'd eaten, he closed his eyes, lifted his face to the sun and at last began to relax. There were five hours until opening time, so once he'd had a bit of a kip, he'd walk over to see his eldest son Frank at Tamarisk Bay and then drop in to visit Danuta at the hospital.

He gave a deep sigh. There were so many people relying on him, so many responsibilities and worries, that there were times when he wished he could just hide away from it all. But Peggy's shoulders were far too narrow to carry such a burden alone, and although she hid it well, she was constantly tortured by Jim's precarious situation in Burma, and the fact that her older children were so far away.

Frank and Pauline were sick with worry over their surviving boy, Brendon, who was at sea with the Royal Naval Reserve taking part in the invasion; Danuta had no other family to turn to whilst she recovered; and both Sarah and Fran were looking to him and Peggy for advice and support as they struggled to decide between two impossibly difficult choices regarding the rest of their lives.

And then there was little Rita who was putting on a brave face and trying not to show how terrified she was that her father might not make it through from the Normandy beaches – and Ivy, whose family had miraculously survived the Blitz only to be faced with this new and terrifying enemy bombardment on London. He had few answers for any of them, and although he was more than willing to support and console them and make sure they were as safe as they could be, he knew he couldn't work miracles.

Unable to rest, he dragged himself out of the deckchair, returned the teapot and plate to the kitchen and then set off for Tamarisk Bay, leaving an exhausted Harvey snoring in his patch of sunlight.

Peggy realised she was in no fit state to face Nanny Pringle and fetch Daisy from the crèche, and was much relieved when Sarah – who was slightly less tipsy – offered to do it for her. She retrieved the abandoned pushchair from the side alley at the Anchor and used it to keep herself and Cordelia steady as they waited for Sarah to return. Peggy knew she'd drunk too much on an empty stomach, and combined with the fear and anxiety the day had wrought, she was feeling decidedly the worse for wear – as was Cordelia, who was very unsteady on her feet and suffering from hiccups as well as the giggles.

On Sarah's return with Daisy, they slowly weaved their way towards home, studiously avoiding Daisy's puzzled looks and probing questions about why they were walking so strangely and what was so funny.

It was a welcome relief to finally reach the harbour of home, but rather galling to be met by disapproving looks from Doris and knowing giggles from Rita and Ivy.

Peggy returned her sister's glare. 'We've earned every drop of that beer today,' she said defiantly, 'so I'll thank you to keep your opinion to yourself.' She looked at Rita and Ivy, who'd clearly already bathed and were now in their nightclothes. 'I hope you've left us some hot water, because as you can see, we're all filthy.'

'That's not all you are,' said Doris with a sniff. 'Really, Peggy, I can smell the beer on you from here.'

Peggy shrugged and flopped down into a kitchen chair. 'You're only jealous,' she giggled.

Doris rolled her eyes and managed to hold her tongue, but her expression said enough.

Ron took charge. 'Sarah, take Cordelia upstairs so she can have her bath, and when you're both done, bring your dirty laundry down. Rita and Ivy have made a start on the washing, but they'll need to soak first.' He turned to Peggy as Sarah helped Cordelia stagger out of the room. 'I'll pour you a cup of very strong tea and sort out Daisy before I have to get to the Anchor. Is Rosie in the same state?'

Peggy slumped in the chair, still giggling. 'I expect so,' she managed. 'She and Gloria got into a drinking competition and were starting on the gin when we left.'

'Ach, to be sure that was foolish,' he sighed. 'Gloria can drink any man under the table – as I know to my cost.'

Peggy's eyelids drooped and she found it hard to focus on the cup of tea Ron placed on the table. 'It was fun, though,' she mumbled. 'I haven't laughed so much in ages.'

'I'm glad to hear it,' he replied, his blue eyes twinkling as he regarded her. 'And I have some good news to keep you cheerful. I managed to persuade my mate Fred up at the Memorial to sell me a box of glasses, so Rosie should have enough now to keep her going.'

Peggy eyed him over the teacup. She'd wondered what the big box on the table was.

Ron waited until she'd managed to take a sip of the tea. 'Frank and Pauline have had a long letter from Brendon. He's well and looking forward to getting some leave in Dartmouth before he has to go back to sea again and, though he won't be able to come home, he's hoping to spend some time with his Betty.' He paused for effect. 'And Danuta is coming home tomorrow.'

Peggy snapped out of her stupor. 'Tomorrow? But her room's not ready, I haven't been shopping and there are a hundred and one things to do before she gets here.'

'Ivy did the shopping, I finished waxing the floor last night and Doris helped me get the room sorted, so you're to stop worrying. The hospital has arranged for a volunteer to drive her home in time for lunch, and as luck would have it, Frank had a couple of brace of nice fat pheasants hanging in his shed, so we'll be eating like kings.'

'Pheasants?' She eyed him suspiciously.

'Aye,' he replied, his expression bland.

'Even I know the shooting season's well and truly over,' she hiccupped. 'Has he been poaching on Lord Cliffe's land again?'

'I couldn't possibly say,' he replied airily. 'All I know is there are two in the larder, plucked, gutted and ready for roasting tomorrow.'

Peggy giggled. 'Like father, like son – you're both very, very naughty.'

'And you're very, very tipsy, wee girl,' he replied with a loving smile. 'Drink that tea before it gets cold.'

Peggy woke the next morning with a pounding headache, which was not eased by a squadron of American planes going overhead or Daisy banging about with her wooden horse with its squeaking wheels. She had little recollection of what had happened after she'd left the Anchor, but at some point she'd clearly managed to bath and change and get into bed.

She all but fell out of bed in her haste to retrieve the horse and persuade Daisy she really did want to play somewhere else whilst she got dressed and hunted out a couple of aspirin. Having achieved both these tasks, she opened the curtains to discover that three lines of washing had been pegged out across the back garden, and belatedly noticed that there was a tantalising aroma of roasting pheasant permeating the house – and remembered that Danuta was coming home today.

Eyeing the bedside clock in horror, she realised the girl would be here within a couple of hours, and although she had a vague recollection of Ron telling her the room was ready, his idea of ready was far removed from her own, and she'd have to check it just to make sure.

'Why didn't you wake me?' she asked as she went into the kitchen to discover a hive of activity.

Doris turned from the oven where she was basting the birds and looked at her reproachfully. 'You were dead to the world,' she replied. 'None of us could shift you.'

'Snoring fit to bust, you was,' teased Ivy, who was peeling potatoes. 'You could have given me dad a run for 'is money, and that's a fact.'

'Oh, dear,' Peggy sighed. 'Was I really that bad?'

Doris grinned. 'Not so bad really,' she conceded. 'It was good to see you larking about for a change, but I wouldn't recommend doing it too often. Drink plays havoc with the complexion, you know.'

'I'll try and remember that,' Peggy said dryly.

She left the busy kitchen and plodded upstairs to the single room that had been Cissy's before she'd left to join the WAAFs. Opening the door, she stood in the shaft of bright sunlight pouring through the window and knew instantly that it would provide a perfect haven for Danuta in which she could settle into her new life and grow strong.

The old linoleum had been taken up and the

floorboards freshly waxed; there was a rag rug on either side of the neatly made bed with its temptingly plumped pillows, and a jug of beautiful roses had been placed on the chest of drawers. Much-thumbed paperback books and a small clock had been placed on the bedside table, and little gifts of cheap bracelets, earrings and brooches lay next to a small bar of soap, a tube of hand cream, half a bottle of shampoo and a bowl of talc which had been placed beside the pretty brush and comb set on the dressing table.

Peggy felt her heart swell with love and pride as she took in Sarah's faded cotton dressing gown hanging on the back of the door, and Cordelia's two nightdresses which had been folded at the end of the bed. A new pair of slippers sat on the rug, and there was one of Ivy's cotton dresses hanging in the cupboard alongside a skirt from Rita and a blouse from Fran.

Peggy had to blink back her tears, for the thought and care that had gone into all this just proved that the residents of Beach View were the sweetest, kindest people on earth, and she felt quite humbled by it. They had so little themselves, and yet they hadn't stinted in their willingness to show Danuta that she was welcome and already part of the family.

Peggy slowly returned to the kitchen where she found Ivy still peeling potatoes, Rita shucking beans, Sarah laying the table, and Fran putting together an apple cobbler under the watchful eye of Cordelia as Doris prepared some stuffing and Ron stood on a ladder outside washing the window.

'Thank you – all of you,' Peggy managed. 'Danuta's room is perfect and she'll love it.' She had to swallow her tears before she could carry on. 'And I love you for being so generous and sweet to a girl some of you have never even met.'

The girls swamped her in a hug. 'We love you too, Aunt Peg,' said Sarah, 'and it only seemed right to welcome her properly after all she's been through. You were so kind and loving to me and Jane when we came to England, and we'll never forget that.'

'Yeah,' said Rita gruffly, 'same goes for me. You took me in when I had nowhere to live after Dad was enlisted, and gave me a loving home. We just wanted to show Danuta we care about her and want her to be as happy here as we are.'

'The roses came from Stan's allotment,' said Fran. 'I called in to see him at the station this morning and he's promised to drop in to say hello sometime later.'

'Them slippers come from Doris,' said Ivy. 'She wouldn't let on, but I thought you should know she done her bit an' all.'

Peggy shot her sister a smile. 'Thanks, Doris. They're lovely.'

Doris blushed and turned away to clatter dishes in the sink. 'I know what it's like to have nothing,' she muttered. 'I just hope they fit her.'

Danuta had lain awake for most of the night, too excited to sleep. She was going home to Beach View at last, into the warmth and love of Peggy's kitchen – the memory of which had sustained her throughout the years she'd been away and kept her strong during those endless days of terror and pain. She would once again be able to listen to Ron's wildly exaggerated war stories and help Cordelia with her tangled knitting as Harvey snored by the fire and Peggy darned socks – and chat to Fran about her nursing and the plans she had for the future now she and Robert were engaged. The house would enfold her, comfort her and make her feel safe – which was something she hadn't felt since leaving Poland in 1940.

Sweet little Nurse Brown had come in after breakfast to find her hampered by her bandaged hands and struggling to get dressed, and had gently but firmly helped her into the clothes that had been donated to the hospital by the Red Cross for just such a cause. The sprigged cotton dress was faded and thin from too many washes, but felt soft against her skin and fitted her perfectly. The underwear was new, and although less than flattering and rather too large, the brassiere, pants and vest were infinitely more respectable than the rags she'd worn during her final days on the run.

The Red Cross parcel had also contained a pair of socks and some white sandals. The socks proved impossible to pull on over the bandages which also made the sandals a bit tight. She stuffed the socks into her dress pocket, and with a bit of judicious pushing and shoving she got her feet into the sandals, determined to arrive at Beach View looking as normal as possible, even if she did hobble.

Once Nurse Brown had wished her luck and left the room, Danuta regarded her reflection in the small mirror above the washbasin in the hope that the clothes and the prospect of going home to Beach View might have brought colour and life to her face. She turned away in disgust, for although her hair had grown, there were still tufts missing and her complexion was sallow after so many weeks of being indoors. With her hollow cheeks, haunted eyes and bony frame, she looked like some pre-pubescent waif rather than a mature woman of twenty-seven – and the knowledge depressed her.

Danuta sank into a chair by the open window and breathed in the scents of the early summer flowers that drifted on the warm air from the garden. She could see men and women sitting on the broad terrace, chatting in groups, playing board games, or simply enjoying the freedom of the outdoors as their injuries healed and they prepared to return to ordinary life again.

She experienced a sudden surge of anxiety at the thought of living a quiet, ordinary existence after all that she'd experienced since the Germans had invaded Poland and torn her family apart, shattering everything she knew and loved and believed in. The life she'd led before then felt so distant, so remote from the reality she'd been forced to face since, that when she looked back on it, it felt almost dreamlike – a fantasy experienced by another, blissfully innocent Danuta who bore little resemblance to the one who sat here today.

She closed her eyes, willing this momentary panic to subside, but the questions continued going round and round in her head. What if Beach View had changed and didn't feel the same? What if the memories of her time spent there had been falsely coloured by wishful thinking? What if the other girls she'd yet to meet didn't take to her, or started asking awkward questions? What if she couldn't settle after being in constant danger and having to live on her wits alone for so long? And how on earth could she return to nursing when her hands were in such a mess?

She gave a tremulous sigh as she regarded the bandages which hid the raw nail-beds and newly healed broken fingers. Fran had been encouraging on her irregular visits, urging her not to give up hope but to be patient; yet it would be a long time before she could work in a hospital theatre – even if the authorities allowed it. At least her injuries would save her from working in the laundry as she'd been forced to do by Matron Billings when she'd first arrived in Cliffehaven.

Danuta's smile was wry as she turned back to watch the activity on the terrace. Matron Billings had been in charge at the Cliffehaven General then, and was now here at the Memorial. She'd never attempted to pronounce Danuta's surname properly and had resorted to avoiding it, making it clear she would never approve of her simply because she was foreign. But Danuta had high hopes that one day she'd prove to the old witch that she was capable of far more than manning the industrial-sized washing machines in the hospital basement.

As if summoned by her thoughts, Matron appeared in the doorway and bustled over to collect her washbag and cardigan. 'Your driver is here,' she said briskly. 'Come along, you mustn't keep him waiting.'

Danuta grabbed the hated walking stick she still had to use because of her crippled feet and slowly shuffled across the room. They didn't speak as they continued at a snail's pace down the long corridors to the reception hall, and Danuta was glad of it, for she had to use all her concentration to put one painful foot in front of the other.

They reached the door, and Matron handed over the cardigan and washbag with a nod. 'Good luck,' she said stiffly.

'Thank you, Matron,' she returned with a soft smile. 'I have had the best care these past months, and I'm most grateful to everyone who has worked so hard to get me to this day. I will never forget them.'

Matron nodded again and then opened the heavy front door. 'Your driver will see to you from here,' she said before turning to bustle quickly away like a galleon in full sail.

Danuta put the washbag under one arm and the cardigan over her shoulders so she could concentrate on getting over the slight hump of the doorstep. Having achieved that, she wondered how on earth she'd navigate the few steps down to the gravel driveway where a shining black car was waiting. She took a tentative step forward, thinking rather crossly that it would have been helpful if the driver was here to give a hand down these steps, but he was nowhere to be seen.

'To be sure, wee girl, you're a sight for sore eyes, so ye are.'

Startled, Danuta almost lost her footing, but a strong pair of arms encircled her and she leaned gratefully against him. 'Oh, Ron,' she laughed. 'You did give me a fright. But why you hide from me?'

'I wanted to surprise you,' he said with a beaming smile, holding her now at arm's length and studying her keenly.

'Well, you certainly did that,' she said fondly. 'But how you get car?'

'I know a man who knows a man with a car who volunteers up here, and I thought I'd give him Sunday morning off and drive you meself.'

Danuta kissed his freshly shaven chin. 'I'm so glad,' she murmured. 'It is a big day that I once feared would never come, and I am feeling better now you are with me.'

Ron said nothing until he'd helped her down the steps and got her settled into the car. Sliding in behind the wheel, he regarded her thoughtfully. 'There's no need to feel anxious, wee girl,' he said. 'Everyone is looking forward to welcoming you home, and I've even given Harvey an extra good brush for the occasion, warning him to be on his best behaviour.'

'It will be lovely to see him again,' she said wistfully, 'but...'

Ron placed his large rough hand over hers. 'You're coming home, Danuta. Home to the love and warmth of good, kind people who want to give their help and encouragement in what they understand must be a difficult time for you. They know nothing of what you've been through, and Peggy and I have stuck firmly to the story that you were caught in a London raid – so there will be no awkward questions.'

His blue eyes twinkled as he smiled at her. 'I can't guarantee you'll always be safe now Hitler's sending over his blasted doodlebugs, but that's up to fate – and so far it's been kind to us.'

A warm glow filled her and she returned his smile, for although they lived in precarious times, this man's presence could always calm her and restore her faith in fate. 'Thank you, Ron. You have made me feel better.'

'Are you ready to go home, Danuta?' he asked, switching on the engine.

'I am ready,' she replied firmly.

14

The stately old car moved majestically away from the Memorial Hospital and out into the narrow road which meandered through the hills and gently dipped towards the town. Danuta wound down the window to let the salty air and bright sunshine touch her face as she drank in the view she remembered so well despite the passing of time.

There were inevitable changes, with a forest of barrage balloons over what looked like an industrial estate, big gun emplacements lining the clifftops and the promenade of the horseshoe bay, and large empty spaces where there had once been houses and shops. Even so, the war felt distant on this lovely summer's day, though she knew it still raged on the other side of the English

Channel, and Cliffehaven had experienced the devastation of Hitler's new and deadly weapon only the day before. But the sea sparkled beyond the guns on the cliffs and gulls hovered and mewled against the clear blue of the sky, empty for once of Allied bombers. And as they began to descend towards the town she saw the delicate church spire rising above the square stone tower amid a fold in the hills. She sat forward, her hand pressed against the dashboard, her gaze fixed to the little church that overlooked the sea.

Without a word, Ron left the main road and drove the car down the even narrower lane that led to the church which had survived fire, famine and war since Saxon times. Drawing to a halt, he switched off the engine and turned to look at her.

'I thought you might like to have a few private moments with Katarzyna and Aleksy before we go home,' he murmured.

Danuta nodded, unable to express her love and gratitude to this man who always understood what was in her heart. She struggled out of the car, aware that he was watching anxiously over her as she slowly and painfully walked through the lychgate and along the cemetery path.

There were more headstones than before, she noticed sadly, but this peaceful place was still well tended, and there were fresh flowers on nearly all the memorials – especially the newer ones – and rose bushes had been planted throughout, the sweet scent of the blossoms drifting in the soft air as bees hummed, butterflies flitted back and forth and doves softly cooed from the nearby trees.

Danuta reached the spot where a stone cherub

watched over baby Katarzyna, and a beautiful white rose scattered its petals on the small mound of grass that was studded with violets, lily-of-the-valley and black-eyed pansies. Her vision blurred as she regarded the headstone next to it and read the epitaph to her brave brother Aleksy who'd come to England in 1939 to help fight the Germans and had lost his life within months when his plane had been shot down.

The rose growing at his head was the deepest red, the petals like droplets of blood amidst the pansies and violets Ron had planted. He'd written to tell her that the man tending the cemetery had decided to plant the red and white roses in honour of the Polish flag, and the kindness of strangers had touched her as deeply then as it did now.

She took a deep breath to calm the wild beating of her heart as she remembered the night when her precious baby had been born, and how she'd sat and held her as her life ebbed away. Jean-Luc would be watching over his baby girl, just as Aleksy would be if there really was a heaven – and despite all she'd witnessed to the contrary, she hoped very much that there was, for the idea of her entire family waiting for her there was a great comfort.

Danuta managed to gather a few of the petals and held them to her tear-streaked face, breathing in their lovely perfume before she scattered them into the light breeze, watching them tumble and twist before they settled once more on the neatly tended grass.

'I will come to visit you when I can,' she murmured to her loved ones. 'I will not leave you again, I promise.'

She saw that Ron's expression was anxious as he met her at the gate and helped her back to the car. 'Thank you for looking after them,' she said, to ease his concern. 'The cherub is just as you described, and the little flowers are beautiful.'

He cleared his throat and concentrated on turning the car and getting it back on the main road. 'I planted snowdrops, daffodils and tulips to give spring colour, and those pansies will last through the summer and into autumn if there's no early frost. I'm glad you like what I've done,' he added gruffly.

An easy silence fell between them as they swept down the hill, past what remained of the station, over the small bridge and down the High Street towards the sea. Danuta noted the ugly gaping holes and piles of rubble where the cinema and Woolworths had once been, but was pleased to learn that Stan was still living and working at the station and that the Anchor was still in one piece.

They turned into Camden Road and she saw people walking their dogs or gathering in clusters to gossip as doorsteps were swept and repairs were made to walls and windows. It seemed life went on regardless of the trials and tribulations of this war, and the people of England really did possess a bulldog spirit – refusing to be bullied or cowed.

Ron drew the car to a halt outside Beach View, where Peggy, Cordelia, Fran, Ivy, Rita and Sarah were restraining an over-excited Harvey by his collar as they waited on the front steps with little Daisy.

'It looks like you've got a welcoming committee,' Ron rumbled. 'Gird your loins, wee lass, and be prepared to be swamped.'

Danuta hadn't understood what he'd meant about girding her loins, but the sight of that lovely familiar house and the smiling faces of those waiting for her swept away the last vestiges of doubt, and she fumbled to open the door.

It was hurriedly opened by Peggy, who gathered her into her arms and smothered her face in kisses. 'Welcome home,' she breathed. 'Oh, my darling girl, welcome, welcome.'

'Let the dog see the rabbit,' said Cordelia, elbowing her way through the crush to take Danuta's face in her hands and kiss it tenderly. 'It's about time you came home,' she said with mock severity. 'I've missed you.'

'I've missed you, too,' managed Danuta. She was feeling quite overwhelmed by the welcome as she tried to stay on her feet and fend off Harvey, who was attempting to climb all over her. She patted and praised him, relieved to see that despite the greying whiskers, he was as eager and energetic as she remembered.

Fran was jiggling a wide-eyed Daisy on her hip. 'To be sure, Danuta, 'tis a lot of fuss, but we're so happy you're well again, and once you've settled in I'll do something about your hair.' Danuta's wary expression elicited a chuckle. 'You're not to be worrying,' Fran assured her. 'I'll not be turning you into a fright.'

Danuta ran her bandaged hand over her ragged mop and shot Fran a rueful grin. 'Anything would be an improvement, Fran.' She smiled up at Daisy and tried to coax some reaction from her but sudden shyness made the toddler bury her face into Fran's shoulder.

'To be sure, she'll be all over you once she gets to know you,' the Irish girl assured her. 'Don't take it to heart.'

'Will ye get out of the way so the wee lass can reach the house?' said Ron in exasperation. 'You're cluttering up the street and she can't be standing about for so long.'

Danuta let him take charge, and was only mildly put out when he gathered her into his arms and carried her up the steps into the hall. 'I can walk, you know,' she protested softly.

'Aye, I'm aware of that, but why walk when you can be carried?'

'Ron's always showing off,' muttered Cordelia as she stepped into the hall on Peggy's arm. 'He thinks he's half his age most of the time, but he's heading for a sharp dose of reality any day now, you mark my words.'

Danuta smiled at the knowledge that nothing had changed between the older members of this household, for she could remember how they hid their affection for one another by continually arguing and being rude.

'This is Sarah,' said Peggy, introducing the slender fair girl who was trying very hard to keep Harvey under some sort of control. 'Remember, I told you about her being Cordelia's great-niece and how she and her sister came all the way from Singapore?'

Danuta smiled and only had time to nod a hello before Rita and Ivy pushed forward to introduce themselves. 'You are sisters?' she asked, taking in their similar build and colouring.

'Blimey, chance'd be a fine thing,' scoffed Ivy. 'My sister's up in London and she ain't 'alf as nice as Rita.'

'If I had a sister, then Ivy's about perfect,' said Rita, shooting Danuta a grin. 'Pleased to meet you at last.'

'They're a couple of imps,' said Peggy fondly, 'as you will no doubt soon find out.' She looked towards the woman who'd been standing quietly off to one side, and drew her forward. 'This is my sister Doris, who's come to live with us.'

'Delighted to meet you,' said Doris with a stiff little smile. 'I believe we may have come across one another when you lived here before, but so much has happened since, I'm sorry, I can't remember.'

Danuta's memory was not so impaired, for Doris had been the bane of poor Peggy's life and not a very nice person at all, but she said nothing and smiled back at her, hoping things had improved between them now they'd been forced to live under the same roof.

'I can smell burning,' said Ron, sniffing the air.

'Oh, lawks,' screeched Peggy, rushing off into the kitchen to rescue the lunch.

The kitchen was just as Danuta remembered, warm and shabby with faded linoleum, mismatched chairs, shelves loaded with pots, pans and crockery, the dresser covered in books, papers and all manner of strange things, and the mantelpiece above the range adorned with photographs. Even the fireside chairs were the same – if now a little worse for wear – and she could see Cordelia's

275

knitting bag propped against one as it always had been.

Amid the hustle and bustle of dishing up the meal, Danuta was glad to be an island of stillness as she gazed around her and drank in the happy atmosphere she had been missing for so long. Her gaze moved along the display of photographs until she reached the one of Jim. He looked even more handsome in his uniform, that cheeky twinkle in his eye reminding her of his lilting Irish voice, and she could almost hear him saying, 'You don't have to be mad to live here, but to be sure it helps.'

Danuta smiled back at him and then felt the nudge of a cold wet nose against her arm. She sank into a chair and Harvey rested his muzzle in her lap, sniffed her bandages and with doleful eyes placed his own bandaged paw on her leg. 'It looks as if we have both been in the wars, Harvey,' she murmured, stroking his head. 'But we will soon get better and go for long walks in the hills.'

His ears pricked up momentarily at the mention of walks, but he was soon distracted by the sound and smell of food going into his bowl.

'He's like his master,' said Cordelia, 'easily distracted by life's pleasures – especially if it relates to his stomach.' She patted Danuta's cheek. 'Talking of which, lunch is on the table, and if you don't mind me saying so, you could do with feeding up.'

The food was delicious, but Danuta found there was far too much on her plate and so shared the untouched potatoes and meat with a delighted Rita and Ivy. She enjoyed sitting quietly and watching them all, listening to their chatter, enjoying their laughter and occasionally joining in when she had something to contribute.

However, it soon became clear that, apart from Sarah, none of them had any real experience of life outside England, or indeed beyond the boundaries of Cliffehaven, and although there were only a few years between her and Fran, she felt much older and time-worn in comparison. It would be strange having to learn how to live what passed for a normal life again – to go to work, make new friends, attend parties and dances, gossip and giggle over inconsequential things, and perhaps even flirt a little – but in the light of such warmth and genuine offers of friendship, she didn't think it would be too hard if she really put her mind to it.

'Are you sure you don't mind Queenie sleeping with you?' asked Peggy as the cat settled down to purr beside Danuta.

Danuta stroked the soft black fur. 'I will enjoy her company,' she replied.

Peggy smiled. 'You won't feel quite so happy at three in the morning when she starts yowling to be let out,' she warned. 'I'll leave your door ajar so she can come and go without disturbing you – although don't be surprised if Harvey comes in and makes himself at home. He likes a nice bed just as much as Queenie.'

'He would be welcome,' said Danuta with a soft chuckle. 'But I don't think there is room for all three of us.'

Peggy reached down to caress Danuta's face. 'It's so lovely to have you home, dearest girl. I hope we haven't all exhausted you today.'

'It is a good tiredness,' said Danuta, 'and everyone has been so lovely to me that my heart is full.' She put her arms round Peggy and gave her a hug and kiss. 'Thank you for everything – especially for keeping my photographs and Aleksy's medallion safe whilst I was away.'

'It was the least I could do,' replied Peggy, embracing her carefully as if afraid of hurting her. 'Goodnight, Danuta,' she murmured, switching off the central light. 'Sleep well and try to dream only of good things.'

Danuta watched her leave the door ajar and listened to her footsteps as she hurried down the stairs. Peggy, Ron and all the others here at Beach View had gone a long way to restoring her faith in the human race, for they'd shown her such love and care today, and it imbued every inch of this little room too. She had been overwhelmed by it all, especially the little gifts of jewellery, clothes and slippers, and although the day had been long and exhausting, the memories of it would stay with her forever.

She nestled back against the lovely plump pillows as Queenie purred on the eiderdown, revelling in the delicious knowledge that at last she was home and would never again have to seek shelter in shelled-out barns, stinking ditches or dank tunnels, hiding from the enemy, stealing to eat, and never sure if she'd survive to see the next dawn.

Her gaze drifted to the faded, stained and much-creased photographs she'd rescued from the rubble of her home in Warsaw and given to Peggy to keep safe. She'd carried them next to her heart on that first perilous journey across a war-torn Europe in search of her brother, determined to get to England and join him in the fight against the Nazis. Their beloved faces were still recognisable, but it was as if they belonged in an ethereal world that lived on only in her memory.

Danuta reached for the small gold medallion that their father had given Aleksy before he left to fight the Fascists in the Spanish Civil War. Her brother had come to look upon it as a talisman and never went anywhere without it; now it was a tangible reminder of a brave and much-loved man who'd never lost sight of who he was, or what he was fighting for.

As she regarded the Madonna and child etched into the gold, she once more questioned the fact that Aleksy had given it to his wing commander, Martin Black, for safe keeping before he left on that last, fatal mission. Had he foreseen his death, and in some strange way sensed she would come to take possession of it again and find some comfort in it?

She liked to believe that he'd been thinking of her on that last day, and although she would have given anything to have him still alive, this little medallion had been precious to him, and was therefore more valuable to her than the gold it was made from.

Returning the medallion to the bedside table, she switched off the lamp and snuggled down. Staring into the darkness, she remembered her first night in this house three years ago – and it was as if history was repeating itself, for she'd owned nothing but the clothes she wore, and after her perilous journey across Europe, she'd been weary beyond words. Peggy had taken her in as she had done now with unquestioning love and understanding – and had even managed to convey the news of Aleksy's death with great tenderness.

Danuta could still feel the echoes of that painful time which had drained her of energy and momentarily extinguished the spark of vengeful determination she'd kept burning so brightly since leaving Warsaw. She'd felt utterly defeated until the flutter of new life stirred inside her, and that had spurred her out of her despondency and brought hope that her baby would be born into a peaceful world.

Danuta curled beneath the bedding and closed her eyes. She had lost everyone she loved because of this war – even her precious baby – but her work with the SOE behind enemy lines had finally quenched that thirst for revenge, the death and destruction she'd caused enough to assuage the bitter rage that had once possessed her. The Germans were on the brink of defeat, their brutal rampage through Europe beaten back by the Allies and the great army of ordinary men and women who fought in the hills, mountains, villages, towns and valleys of the occupied countries with the Resistance. And she would celebrate peace alongside Peggy and Ron, and then get on with forging a new life here in Cliffehaven.

Peggy peeked into Danuta's room to make sure all was well before she turned in, and saw that Harvey had crept in unnoticed sometime during the evening and was lying on the rug beside the bed. Not wanting to wake Danuta, she hissed at him and made commanding hand gestures ordering him out.

Harvey lifted his nose from his bandaged paws, eyed her with some irritation at being disturbed, and promptly went back to sleep, his soft snores in perfect harmony with Queenie's purring.

Peggy knew when she was beaten and retreated to the bathroom with a smile – Danuta would never feel lonely at night with Harvey and Queenie making such a racket. But at least she hadn't let Harvey climb onto the bed – that would have made for a very uncomfortable arrangement.

15

Despite the dairy having been flattened, the morning milk deliveries continued, only this time when the Shire horses arrived with the churns, the housewives came out to collect their milk ration in jugs or pans because there were no surviving bottles after the blast. Like the daily newspaper which arrived on the early train, these much loved and highly prized English traditions were what kept people going, and they were determined not to lose them.

It was now Thursday afternoon and *Workers' Playtime* was blaring out from the wireless as the sewing machines hummed and the women gossiped. Peggy had left Beach View that morning happy to see that Danuta had cast off her bandages and was now wearing light cotton gloves and socks to hide her lack of nails, and was also walking without her stick.

It was lovely to see how well she'd fitted in with the others, and how she was rapidly improving by the day – which Peggy put down to her feeling at home and safe at last. Fran had cut her hair very close so it looked thicker and it now framed her little face and enhanced her strong features. It wouldn't be long, Peggy was sure, before she plucked up the courage to taste life outside Beach View – but for now she seemed content to help around the house and keep Cordelia company.

Peggy pulled her attention back to her work. She was teaching one of the new machinists how to keep the material from bunching beneath the needle, and it was slow going, for Mrs James really had no idea of how to cope with the commercial sewing machine – but as Peggy had once been in her position, she understood that only patience would save the day.

Her gaze drifted over the many women who were hard at work, then her eyes were drawn by a movement on the staircase that led to the large office and the window that gave a panoramic view of the entire factory floor. Her mouth dried and her heart missed a beat as she saw a grim-faced Sergeant Williams making his way into Solly Goldman's office.

'Oh, lawks,' sighed the middle-aged housewife next to her. 'I'm never going to get the hang of this.'

Peggy was unable to tear her eyes from the two men behind that large window. 'Cut the thread and start again,' she murmured, watching Solly read something Bert had given him, before he glanced down at the factory floor, his expressive face haggard with grief.

Her pulse was racing, the dread growing by the second as Solly rubbed a hand over his eyes. She'd witnessed this scene before and knew that Bert Williams had brought bad news for someone – but who was it for this time? 'Not Jim,' she murmured. 'Please, God, don't let it be Jim.'

The woman next to her abruptly stopped sewing and followed her gaze and soon a deathly silence fell throughout the factory as a grim-faced Solly made his way down the stairs. They all knew what this meant, and they held a collective breath as he walked purposefully through the long lines of sewing machines towards the cutting tables at the far end.

Peggy shot a glance at Gracie, who was standing by her cutting table, her face drained of colour, her eyes wide with fear as Solly maintained eye contact with her and continued to walk towards her.

Peggy shoved back her chair and rushed to Gracie's side as he came to a halt. She grasped her hand, but Gracie was transfixed and unaware of everything but her employer's mournful face.

'Gracie, my dear,' he said, 'your husband is alive, but he has been injured and is in hospital.'

Peggy saw Gracie was on the point of collapse and quickly put her arm about her waist to help her to a nearby chair. 'Which hospital?' she asked.

Solly placed a plump hand on Gracie's shoulder. 'He's in Dover,' he said quietly as the machines started up again all around them, the easing of tension becoming almost tangible in the sighs and whispers of the other women. 'Come, Gracie. We'll discuss it further in the canteen where it is quiet.' He shot a helpless look at Peggy who nodded back, understanding he needed her to keep Gracie company.

Solly helped Gracie to her feet and she walked unsteadily between them, blank-eyed and clearly still in shock. Peggy fetched cups of tea whilst Solly settled her in a chair, and then lit them both a cigarette.

'How badly hurt is he?' Gracie managed finally.

'The bones will heal in time,' said Solly carefully, 'but his other injures will take a bit longer.'

Gracie's eyes widened as tears began to roll down her white face. 'Other injuries?' She clapped a trembling hand over her mouth as awful realisation hit. 'Oh, no, no, not my Clive. Please tell me he hasn't been burned.'

Before Solly could reply Peggy and Gracie saw the truth in his eyes, and Gracie collapsed against Peggy in a storm of tears.

Peggy held her tightly and regarded Solly over Gracie's head, seeing the helplessness and sorrow in his slumped shoulders. She raised a questioning eyebrow and as their eyes met and he shook his head she understood that Clive's burns were serious.

'I must go and see him,' said Gracie, suddenly pulling from Peggy's embrace and digging about in her overall pocket for a handkerchief. 'Which hospital in Dover is he in?'

'At the Royal Victoria,' said Solly, 'but I doubt

they'll let you visit yet as he's only just been admitted.'

'That's ridiculous,' she snapped. 'He's my husband. Of course I must go to him.'

'Oy, vay, Gracie,' he sighed. 'Your husband is heavily sedated and will not know you are there.'

'That doesn't matter,' she replied. 'I don't want him coming round and thinking I've abandoned him. The poor darling will be so confused and frightened. He'll need me there.'

Solly took a deep breath. 'I understand, Gracie, really I do – but you will have to be brave, my dear. He's a very sick man.'

'Just how badly burned is he?' she asked, tears once again trembling on her eyelashes as she stubbed out the barely smoked cigarette.

As he took her hands, Peggy could tell that he was choosing his words carefully, and it made her stomach churn.

'The doctors can do the most marvellous things with skin grafts these days, so don't lose heart.'

'It was his biggest fear,' Gracie whispered. 'Mine too. So many of his friends...' She dashed away the tears and made a concerted effort to keep her emotions under control. With a nod at Solly, she withdrew her hands from his grasp and turned to Peggy. 'I have to go to him, Peggy,' she managed, 'but a hospital is no place for a child, and I have no idea of how long I'll be away. Would you look after Chloe for me?'

'Of course I will,' Peggy said immediately. 'But I don't like the thought of you facing this alone, Gracie. Is there someone who could go with you?'

Gracie shook her head. 'Clive's parents are in the

285

Hebrides and since his father has been confined to a wheelchair, they don't travel. Mother's closer, but even if she did come, I don't think I could cope with her getting upset – she's very emotional already because of Father and my brothers being away, and it will be hard enough without having to deal with her as well as everything else.'

'Oh, Gracie,' sighed Peggy. 'I wish I could do more to help you through this.'

Gracie hugged her. 'You're doing enough by caring for Chloe,' she replied.

Peggy's heart ached for her friend, knowing how very hard it would be for her to come to terms with what had happened to Clive.

Gracie mopped her tears with a handkerchief and then turned to Solly. 'How do I get a travel warrant? Will the RAF provide one, or do I have to apply?'

'Bert and I will see to that,' he soothed. 'You go home now and I'll send my Rachel over when I've got things sorted. She'll help you get organised and drive you to the station.' His smile was wan. 'It may take a while to cut through the red tape, so try to be patient, my dear.'

Gracie was icily calm as she got to her feet. 'Thank you, Mr Goldman. I know how hard it must be for you to pass on such news, and I do appreciate what you and Rachel do for us all.' She gave Peggy a hug. 'I'll ring you when I know more.'

'Would you like me to come home with you?'

Gracie smiled through her tears. 'I need to be alone with Chloe for now so I can take all this in and prepare myself for whatever I find in Dover.' Her voice broke. 'But thanks, Peggy. Thanks for being such a good friend.'

Peggy watched as she hurried off, weaving through the lines of machines, her focus on collecting Chloe from the crèche and all the things she'd have to do before she left for Dover. Peggy was reminded of how Doris had been after hearing the news about Ted, and realised that Gracie was going through the motions without realising she was in deepest shock.

'I really don't like the thought of her being alone,' she murmured, 'but I suppose she needs time to absorb it all and gather her strength to face what lies ahead.' She gave a tremulous sigh before meeting Solly's gaze. 'How bad is he really?' she asked.

Solly dug his hands in his trouser pockets and surveyed the women working on the factory floor. 'Bert spoke to the matron at the Victoria, and although she couldn't tell him much, she did say that once his broken bones are healed he'd be a perfect candidate to be transferred to East Grinstead.' He gave a deep sigh. 'Which sadly means the burns must be extensive. But Archibald McIndoe is working miracles on men like Clive – virtually rebuilding their faces, so I've heard. She'll have to be very brave, Peggy – and so will he. I've seen what's happened to other pilots.'

Peggy felt quite ill at the thought of poor Gracie having to confront what this war had done to her Clive, and could only pray that their marriage was strong enough to withstand the undoubted trauma of the coming months. She'd heard what had happened to other couples in the same situation – and not all of them had weathered the life-changing storm.

She stubbed out her cigarette and gathered up the barely touched cups of tea, still very upset for Gracie. 'I'd better get back to work,' she said. 'Mrs James is all fingers and thumbs and if I don't keep an eye on her she'll do herself a damage with that needle.'

'Before you go, there's something I'd like to discuss with you, Peggy.'

She eyed him sharply. 'Shouldn't you be sorting out Gracie's travel permit?'

'I've already got Sergeant Williams on the case. She should have it by tonight.'

Peggy realised he needed to talk to alleviate the tension of the past few minutes, so rather reluctantly sat back down. 'So what's on your mind, Solly?'

'This war is coming to an end,' he said, settling back into one of the unyielding metal chairs. 'Once Paris falls, the rest of Europe will follow and Hitler will be defeated – and once that happens, the Japanese will surrender.' He pulled a fat cigar from his breast pocket and took his time to light it. 'There will still be a need for uniforms, but in far fewer numbers, so I have begun to think about what people might want in the future.'

Peggy stared at him, confused by this change of subject whilst her mind was still struggling with Gracie's dilemma. She had known Solly since her schooldays, and even then he'd had a keen eye on business opportunities, and was selling good second-hand clothes from a market stall by the time he was fifteen. 'And what do you think that might be?' she asked.

'I have some ideas, but I'd like your opinion – as a woman.'

Peggy made a determined effort to concentrate. 'It's going to depend on whether we still have rationing,' she said a moment later. 'But like most women I'm sick of making do and mending and only having those drab utility clothes to buy, so brightly coloured, cheap and pretty dresses would be high on my list.'

His smile was beaming. 'My thoughts exactly, Peggy.'

She glanced out of the window to the busy factory floor. 'But most of these machinists will leave when their husbands come home, and where would you get the material?'

He tapped the side of his large nose. 'The women have become used to earning their own money, and I'll wager a good number of them will stay on even when their husbands come home – and men are just as good on the machines and cutting tables – they'll want their jobs back, you'll see.'

He blew smoke and regarded her with a twinkle in his eye. 'As for the material, I have a warehouse full of it, set aside when I took on the government contract for uniforms.'

Peggy chuckled. 'I might have known you had something up your sleeve.'

'The first rule of business is to always have a plan B,' he said with a wink. 'I'll continue supplying the uniforms, but at the same time get the dressmaking business up and running again.' He grinned through the cigar smoke. 'And I'll need someone I can trust to be my eyes and ears on the shop floor and to take charge of the machinists.'

She stared at him in disbelief as his meaning sank in. 'But I can't do that,' she protested. 'I've only been working here a matter of months and there are others far better qualified.'

'My niece is planning to get married and move back to London by Christmas, and I consider you to be the best person to replace her,' said Solly. He held up his hand to silence her protest. 'You've already shown you're perfectly capable of getting the best out of the women. You have a way with people, and they are drawn to you, willing to do their best for you, Peggy. I can think of no one better.'

Peggy couldn't deny that she was tempted, but there were many obstacles to be negotiated before she could take his offer seriously. 'I'm flattered you think so highly of me, Solly, but this job was only temporary whilst the war was on and I needed the money.'

She took a breath and met his gaze squarely. 'When Jim and the rest of the family come home I'll be too busy to hold down a job – particularly a managerial one that will entail more responsibility. And besides, Jim has been away for so long, he might resent me working.'

'I think six guineas a week will ease his resentment,' said Solly, watching her carefully.

'Six guineas?' breathed Peggy.

'That's just to start with. There will be a yearly increase and a bonus when sales pick up.'

Peggy stared at him, hardly daring to contemplate such a sum.

Solly seized the moment to press his case. 'If I

know Jim, he'll soon get restless and find himself work of some sort or another and you'll be left to rattle about in that house with just Cordelia, Daisy and maybe Danuta for company. Your chicks will fly the nest; Anne and her girls will be with Martin in their own home; Cissy will probably settle down somewhere with her Yank, and your two boys are of an age when they no longer need or want to be tied to your apron strings.'

Peggy's spirits ebbed at the realisation that he was probably right.

He eyed her affectionately as she stared dumbly back at him. 'I don't mean to be harsh, Peggy, but you're intelligent enough to know things will be very different once the war is over. Just give my offer some serious consideration, my dear. It will be a while before I have everything organised, so there's no rush.'

Peggy nodded, and in a daze returned to her sewing machine. Six guineas a week plus a bonus was more than she'd made running Beach View as a boarding house before the war. Six guineas a week would cover the repairs and redecoration needed, pay for a washing machine, fridge and electric iron and make her life so much easier. And six guineas a week would mean she'd never again have to take in holiday-makers or lodgers, but could use the entire house as a proper home – giving Bob, Charlie and Ron a decent bedroom each instead of the poky and rather damp basement rooms.

It was terribly tempting – so tempting she felt the urge to run after Solly and accept his offer. But the war wasn't over, she had responsibilities at home, and when her family returned she'd want to spend time with them in an effort to make up for all the years they'd been parted. As tantalising as it was, Solly's offer needed some very careful thought.

Ron was snuggled up with Rosie on the couch, enjoying a bit of canoodling after the lunchtime rush. The dogs were sprawled in a patch of sunlight that streamed in through the open window, and the silence in the room was broken only by the distant sounds coming from Camden Road.

'We ought to go out and enjoy the lovely weather,' said Rosie, her hair tousled, her face flushed and her blue eyes hazy with desire.

Ron drew her back into his arms and softly nuzzled her neck with his lips. 'We have the sun and fresh air through the window,' he breathed, his fingers brushing the erect nubs of her nipples as he searched for the buttons on her blouse. 'Are you sure you're not wearing too many clothes, Rosie?' he groaned with wanting. 'It's getting awful warm in here.'

'Just the blouse, then,' she replied breathlessly.

Ron's nimble fingers dealt with the buttons, and she tilted her head back with a little groan of pleasure as he kissed her sweet neck and ran his lips down to the twin globes of her delicious breasts. One twist had the brassiere undone and those glorious, sweetly scented orbs were free to kiss and caress.

'Oh, Ron,' gasped Rosie.

The loud banging on the side door startled them and set both dogs barking.

'Ignore them,' said Ron fiercely. 'They'll soon go away.'

But the banging persisted and the dogs were making such a fearful racket downstairs that Ron couldn't concentrate. He swore under his breath, tucked his shirt back in and leaned out of the window. 'Who the hell is that – and what do you want?' he yelled.

Danuta appeared from the side alley, her little face a picture of distress. 'I'm sorry to disturb you, but these came for Peggy.'

Ron's impatience immediately died at the sight of the telegram. Rosie regarded him with anguish as she made herself decent. 'Go, quickly,' she urged. 'Bring her in.'

Ron's heart was hammering as he ran down the stairs, buttoning his shirt and trying to bring some order to his ruffled hair. In his haste he fumbled with the key and finally managed to open the door. 'I'm sorry, wee girl,' he said, drawing her into the hallway. 'I didn't mean to shout.'

She ignored his apology and thrust the brown envelope at him. 'The man came with this,' she said, her face pale with concern.

'Have you read it?' he asked, hearing Rosie coming down the stairs to join them.

Danuta shook her head. 'It is for Peggy, but I think better you should see first in case...'

Ron tore it open and read the few stark words.

Regret to inform *Warrant Officer 11 James Michael Reilly wounded in action* *Transferred to army hospital Calcutta.*

Ron's legs gave way and he slumped down on the bottom stair, passing the telegram to Rosie. 'It tells me nothing,' he rasped brokenly. 'How badly is he wounded? Is he expected to recover? And how on earth do I tell Peggy? This will destroy her.'

'There is a letter for Peggy also,' said Danuta. 'It has come from India, so perhaps it is from Jim.'

Ron regarded the letter. 'That's not Jim's writing,' he managed through the great lump in his throat. 'And all the letters from over there have Indian stamps on them regardless of where they've come from.'

'I am so sorry, Ron,' said Danuta with tears in her eyes.

'Ach, it's not your fault, wee girl,' he replied. 'Something like this was bound to happen sooner or later.' He gave a deep, tremulous sigh and got to his feet. 'At least my boy's alive, and for that we must be thankful.'

Rosie went to Danuta and gently steered her into the bar and sat her down on the settle beneath the back window. 'Peggy has another hour before her shift's over, and it won't do her any good to hear this news in front of a factory full of gawping women. I think it'd be best if we waited until she's at home.'

'Aye,' sighed Ron. 'She'll have love and support at home but for all her courage, this will cut deep.'

As Rosie bustled about behind the counter to get them drinks, Ron turned the letter over and over in his hands before finally tearing it open. The address on the single page was an army Post Box number for the military hospital in Calcutta.

The date showed it had been written almost three weeks ago.

Dear Mrs Reilly,

My name is Sarah Fitzpatrick, and I am a staff nurse who has been caring for your husband since he arrived here. He begged me to write to you so that when you receive the telegram from HQ, you would know the facts and be assured that although he's been injured, it is not life-threatening. He has had an operation to remove shrapnel from his torso, and is expected to make a full recovery, which will see him returned to duty once he's passed fit.

He will get the best of care here in India, I promise, and when he is able, he will write to you himself.

With very best wishes,

Staff Nurse Sarah Fitzpatrick, Royal Australian Nursing Corps.

Ron passed the letter to Danuta and then buried his face in his hands as the tears of relief finally came.

Peggy had fretted over where she could find a cot for Chloe to sleep in and how on earth she'd fit it into her bedroom, but most of all she was worried about Gracie, and how she was holding up. There had been no word from Solly, who'd left the factory shortly after their talk, so she was no wiser as to when she could expect to be taking Chloe in.

With her thoughts racing over Gracie's shocking news, Solly's job offer and all the things she'd have to do to prepare for the toddler, she clocked off her shift and headed for the crèche.

Daisy rushed to her, flinging her arms around Peggy's legs and chattering about her day nineteen to the dozen. Peggy made the appropriate noises, only half listening as she pulled on her daughter's cardigan and coaxed her into the pushchair.

'I big girl. Don't need that,' Daisy said, folding her small arms and glaring at her.

'Big you might be, but I'm in a hurry, so you'll get in and behave,' Peggy said shortly.

They held one another's gaze, and as usual, it was Daisy who looked away first. She clambered grumpily into the pushchair, her expression making it clear that she wasn't happy about it.

Peggy wheeled her out of the yard and was about to head for home when a large black car purred to a halt at the kerb and Rachel Goldman wound down the window. 'Perfect timing, Peggy,' she said with a smile. 'I'll give you a lift home before I take Gracie to the station.'

Peggy glanced into the car and saw that Gracie was staring sightlessly out of the window in her own painful world.

Daisy yelped in glee as she saw Chloe. Immaculately dressed and elegant as ever, Rachel climbed out to help Peggy fold the pushchair into the already crammed boot, whilst the two little girls greeted one another and got into an excited huddle on the back seat.

'How's Gracie holding up?' Peggy asked.

'Very quiet, which is hardly surprising,' Rachel murmured. 'But I made sure they both had something to eat, and talked to her landlady, explaining the situation and making sure the rent was paid for another month to make certain she doesn't let the room whilst Gracie is away.' Rachel's dark eyes gleamed with unshed tears. 'She's so grateful to you for taking in Chloe when she has so much else to contend with.' She squeezed Peggy's shoulder. 'You're a good woman, Peggy Reilly, and if you need anything, anything at all, you only have to ask me or Solly.'

Peggy blushed and quickly got into the car next to a dull-eyed Gracie who reached for her hand, clutching it tightly as Rachel drove towards Beach View.

'Chloe knows she's staying with you for a while,' said Gracie as they pulled up by the front steps. 'I told her I had to go and visit her daddy...' her voice faltered. 'And that I'd come back very soon.'

'It's all right,' murmured Peggy, gripping her fingers. 'She'll be safe with me for however long it takes.'

Rachel got out of, the car, ran up the steps and rapped the front door knocker, the little girls following closely behind her. As Ron opened the door the children scampered inside, and Harvey bolted down the steps towards Peggy and Gracie.

Peggy watched as Doris, Cordelia and the girls gathered around Ron to hear what Rachel was saying. She was clearly explaining what had happened, and why Chloe would be staying, and in a very short while, Ron came down the steps, silently hugged Gracie and then began unloading the boot with the help of the girls.

Peggy and Gracie followed them up the steps and into the hall, where Gracie's possessions had been stacked. 'I didn't know what you might need,

so I brought everything,' she explained distractedly.

Ron eyed the suitcases, dismantled cot and
bags of toys and bedding. 'Ach, to be sure, 'tis
better that way. The wee cot will take no time at
all to put together, and I'll be finding space for
everything, never you mind.'

Cordelia came out of the kitchen, followed by
the children who had milky moustaches and were
eating biscuits – and Harvey who was trying to
snaffle them. 'Take care of yourself, Gracie dear,'
she said softly. 'We shall all be thinking of you.'

Gracie returned her hug, bravely fighting her
tears as little Chloe wrapped her arms about her
legs. She picked her up and held her close. 'Bye,
bye, darling, be a good girl for Aunty Peggy, and
I'll see you very soon,' she said, planting a kiss on
her cheek.

Rachel pointedly tapped her watch and Gracie
reluctantly set Chloe back on her feet and turned
towards the door. She hugged Peggy and then,
without a word, followed Rachel down the steps
to the car.

Chloe happily waved goodbye and rushed off
with Daisy and an over-excited Harvey to find
more biscuits.

Peggy waited until the car was out of sight and
then closed the door. 'God only knows what she'll
find in Dover,' she murmured. 'I don't know how
I'd cope if something like that had happened to
Jim.'

Ron was all too aware of the news he had yet to
impart to Peggy, and it was with a heavy heart
that he put his arm round her and gave her a hug.

'Whatever she finds, she'll cope,' he said. 'If there's one thing I've learnt in life, it's that you women are far stronger than we men give you credit for.'

'Well, at least something sensible has penetrated that dense brain of yours,' said Cordelia before she turned to Peggy. 'How long will Gracie be away?'

'I have no idea,' she replied, eyeing the luggage in the hall. 'But I know for a fact I won't be able to fit that lot in my room.'

'You won't have to,' said Doris, who was standing in the kitchen doorway. 'You can move into my room and I'll take yours.'

'But—'

'No buts about it, Peggy,' said Doris firmly. 'You can't possibly be crammed in together in that small room for goodness knows how long – and mine is big enough to take both cots as well as everything else.'

'Well, it would certainly help,' said Peggy, clearly still unable to come to terms with this new and unselfish Doris. 'Are you sure?'

'I wouldn't have offered if I wasn't,' said Doris. 'We all have to muck in together at times like these.' She turned to Ron, who was staring at her in amazement. 'Do stop gawping like that, Ronan, it's most unbecoming,' she snapped. 'The children will need to go to bed soon, so the quicker you sort out those cots and move the furniture, the sooner we'll be straight.'

Ron tugged his forelock and grinned. 'Yes, ma'am, no, ma'am, three bags full, ma'am,' he said. 'To be sure, I feel sorry for the Colonel if this is how you boss him about.'

'Colonel White doesn't need bossing,' Doris said stiffly. 'He's an efficient man with a quick mind and knows immediately what has to be done.'

'Oh aye?' he murmured slyly. 'Does that include taking his secretary to lunches at the Officers' Club?'

Doris went scarlet and turned on her heel. 'I shall be upstairs emptying my cupboards,' she retorted.

'Lunch at the club?' asked a wide-eyed Peggy. 'Goodness, she kept that quiet.' She giggled. 'You don't think...'

'I wouldn't dare think anything of the sort,' muttered Ron. 'And I'd advise you to do the same.'

'You're just an old cynic,' teased Peggy.

'Aye, well, that's what life does to a man when he's surrounded by a gaggle of bossy women,' he rumbled, reaching for the pieces of the dismantled cot.

Ron spent the next hour carting things up and down the stairs as Peggy and Doris emptied drawers and cupboards and the girls helped Cordelia watch the children and prepare the evening meal. He had to admit it was something of a respite to be keeping busy, for it delayed the moment when he'd have to sit Peggy down and tell her about Jim – a task he was dreading. He'd been quite overcome by the others' reaction to the news when he'd told them earlier, and had steeled himself to face more tears when Peggy came home. However, Chloe's arrival had drastically changed his plans and now he'd have to wait until later.

He wrestled to get the cots back together, his thoughts in a whirl. Peggy would no doubt be angry with him for keeping such a thing from her when everyone else in the house knew about it – but his shoulders were broad and he could take anything she threw at him. Jim was alive and being well looked after. That was all that really mattered.

Peggy finished reading from the story book and kissed the drowsy children goodnight. The cots had been pushed together, the sides taken down between them so they could curl up closely beneath the blankets. They looked so sweet as their eyelids drooped and sleep claimed them, but she had the feeling that come morning, they'd prove to be a real handful, and she'd have her work cut out to get them fed and dressed by the time she had to leave for work.

She left the nightlight on and surveyed the large room with its bow window and gas fire. The furniture was dark and heavy, the rug and chair by the fire beginning to show their age. She'd never slept in here before, or had so much space to move about and put things. And yet the size of the room unsettled her, and although her own mattress had been brought upstairs, it would still feel strange not to sleep in the bed she'd shared with Jim since they'd first been married. The change of room and the change of bed somehow distanced her from him and the memories they'd made together downstairs, and she wasn't at all sure she was comfortable with that.

Her thoughts turned to poor Gracie, who was either camped out in a hospital waiting room or pacing the floor, of some rented accommodation. She would be feeling very alone and vulnerable, worrying over Clive and missing Chloe, and the knowledge brought her sharply to her senses. Her cares were very minor compared to what her friend was going through, and she had no business fretting over silly things like the size of the room and the bed she'd be sleeping in tonight.

She took one last look at the sleeping children before leaving the door ajar so she could hear if they called out and then went downstairs.

'Chloe was as good as gold and they're both fast asleep,' she said, sinking into a chair and lighting a cigarette.

She frowned as there was no response and realised that, most unusually, everyone had stayed home after tea – and that there was a strange and rather tense atmosphere in the room. Noting the furtive glances directed at Ron and seeing how ill at ease he seemed, she began to feel a creeping sense of something being very wrong. 'What's going on?' she asked nervously.

'Well, now, wee girl, there is something I have to tell you,' Ron began, not quite meeting her gaze as Cordelia reached for her hand.

Peggy's sudden fear rose to almost stifle her. 'It's Jim. Something's happened to Jim, hasn't it?'

'He's alive, Peggy,' Ron said firmly, 'but he has been hurt and is now recovering in India.'

'Hurt?' she managed as her heart stuttered then began to race. 'India?'

His large hand rested on her shoulder. 'He's in hospital there being looked after by a very nice Australian nurse who assures us he'll soon be on the mend,' he said carefully.

Peggy could only stare at him as terrible images of a wounded Jim tormented her.

'He hasn't been burned like poor Clive,' said Ron hastily, 'and he's had an operation to repair the wound, which is not serious, Peggy. The nurse assures us that he'll soon be his old self again and back with his regiment before long.'

Peggy stared at him as her mind whirled and she tried to take it all in. 'How long have you known?' she demanded.

'Since this afternoon,' he admitted.

'Then why didn't you come and tell me then instead of leaving it until now?'

'We thought it best you should hear this kind of news in the privacy of your own home,' he replied. 'And then with Gracie and Chloe turning up and all the kerfuffle of sorting out the rooms...' He let the sentence hang in the air.

Peggy looked at the others, saw their sheepish expressions, and realised they'd all known. She felt a surge of anger which swiftly died away as reason took hold and she accepted that they'd kept quiet out of love. She'd have hated to hear the news coming so soon after Gracie's, and in the full glare of the women in the factory – and with all that had gone on today, this, was indeed the first and only moment they could have told her.

She slumped in the chair as the tension and fear left her. Jim was alive and would recover, and although she would have given anything to be able to rush to his side, the impossibility of doing such a thing made her thankful that he was in the best place with the best people looking after him.

'Where's that letter?' she asked. She took it from Ron and swiftly read through it, thankful that. Ron had prepared her for what it contained and that the nurse had laid out Jim's situation clearly and that he would indeed recover. She folded the letter back into the envelope and reached for the telegram. The words were stark, telling her very little, and she squeezed her eyes shut on the tears that threatened.

'Thank God for that girl's letter,' she breathed. 'If I'd only had that telegram I would have feared the worst and gone out of my mind with worry.'

'Aye, Jim understood that, which is why he was so determined the nurse wrote to you. I don't know how the letter got here at the same time as the telegram, but I'm thinking it's a wee miracle that it did.'

Peggy nodded and put both envelopes in her apron pocket. 'Thank you, all of you,' she said. 'I know how hard you must have found it to keep this to yourselves, and coming so swiftly after Gracie's awful news, it's rather knocked me for six.' She gave them a wan smile to assure them she was all right. 'It's been a traumatic day all round, and with the children likely to wake early, I think I'll turn in.'

She lay staring into the deep shadows cast by the soft nightlight long after everyone else had gone to bed. As the children snuffled in their sleep she held the photograph of Jim to her heart, hoping that her thoughts and fervent prayers would somehow wing their way to him on the other side of the world.

The nurse's letter had imbued in her an absolute faith that he would pull through – but then
he'd be sent back to his regiment to join in the
fighting again. He'd been lucky this time. Yet for
every day this war continued his chances of escaping further injury – or worse – lessened. And
that was the awful spectre that lurked in the
shadows and kept her awake.

16

Peggy managed to get through Friday, simply
because she kept busy and made sure she didn't
have time to think. Solly had been tremendously
sympathetic when she'd told him about Jim, and
even suggested she take the day off so she had a
long weekend to come to terms with what had
happened, but she'd refused his kind offer, knowing that she needed to work through this and
firmly focus on the fact that Jim was alive and
would recover.

She'd sat down that night and written Jim a long
letter, telling him how much she loved him and
how grateful she was that he'd asked the nurse to
write to her so the telegram didn't frighten her
out of her wits. Having sealed the aerogram, she
then wrote to Anne and Cissy. Ron had gone up
to Cliffe aerodrome early on Friday morning and
managed to get to see Cissy and assure her that
her father would come through and her mother
was being well looked after by everyone at Beach

View, but Peggy needed to underline the fact that she didn't want Cissy worrying about her and taking unnecessary time off by coming to visit.

Saturday morning was chaotic, with the two little girls getting under everyone's feet, and Rita arriving with Peter Ryan to begin putting Cordelia's chairlift on the stairs. Ron quickly disappeared with Harvey, Doris and Ivy went to work, and the cat decided to make herself scarce.

Much to Peggy's relief, Sarah and Fran took the children to the park so they could let off steam, and she could get on with the washing and the housework. Yet as the banging and clattering carried on in the hall, she began to wonder if the house was about to fall down around her ears.

'Danuta's helping them now, but they're making surprisingly little mess,' said Cordelia as she came into the garden to help hang out the washing. 'Although I'm not at all sure I'll feel terribly safe being carted up and down in that contraption.'

'We'll get Ron to test it out before I'll let you anywhere near it,' said Peggy, who had grave doubts over the whole enterprise. 'If it takes his weight, then I'll give it a go. I'd hate to see you getting hurt.'

Cordelia eyed her over her sunglasses. 'I still have a sense of adventure despite my age, and if he dares, then so will I,' she said stoutly.

'He has to stay at home for more than five minutes before we can get him to do anything,' said Peggy, hooking the long forked pole into the line to raise it so the washing caught the warm breeze coming off the sea. 'I honestly don't know where he gets his energy from.'

'I suspect Rosie has something to do with that,' Cordelia twittered. 'There's definitely been a silly grin on his face and a spring in his step these past couple of weeks.'

Peggy smiled. 'So I noticed. It's about time those two sorted themselves out. My best hat is gathering dust since the last wedding.' She eyed the unusually small load of laundry with satisfaction and then hitched the empty basket onto her hip. 'Let's go and see what they're all up to in the hall.'

She helped Cordelia up the concrete steps, then they crossed the kitchen and Peggy opened the door into the hall, expecting to be met by a cloud of dust and a terrible mess. 'Goodness,' she breathed at the hive of industry going on without so much as a grain of dust.

She was a bit concerned that the stair carpet hadn't been taken up and winced at the damage they must be doing to it as Rita and Danuta held the long metal runner that Peter was bolting into a second runner which followed the contours of each stair. Another ran parallel with them against the base of the bannisters, and sitting in the middle of the hall was a sturdy chair which had been bolted to a thick metal platform fixed to four heavy wheels.

'Danuta, please be careful,' she pleaded. 'You can't afford to damage your hands, and if that thing falls on your feet—'

'I am in no danger,' Danuta interrupted. 'Please, don't worry. It's good to be useful, and I'm having fun.'

'Yeah, don't fuss, Aunty Peg,' said Rita, strain-

307

ing to keep the heavy runner steady. 'We've got it all under control.'

Peter Ryan finished fixing a bolt and looked over his shoulder with a broad smile. 'Reckon she'll be right,' he drawled. 'But a cup of tea would go down well. This is thirsty work.'

Peggy took the hint and she and Cordelia went back into the kitchen. She placed the kettle on the hob, hunted out cups and regarded the old tea leaves drying out in a saucer. 'These have already been used twice,' she muttered, 'and they deserve a good strong cuppa after all their hard work.'

She fetched the almost empty packet of tea from the larder, spooned some into the warm teapot and then sat down to have a cigarette whilst the kettle boiled. 'I wish I'd remembered to put tea on the shopping list,' she said, 'but with one thing and another it slipped my mind.'

'That's hardly surprising in the circumstances,' said Cordelia. 'But maybe Doris checked the larder before she took the list into town earlier. She keeps banging on about how efficient she is, so I wouldn't put it past her.'

'I'm still finding it very hard to take in how much she's changed,' Peggy confided. 'That job was certainly the making of her. She'd never have dreamt of giving up her room before.'

'It's certainly given her something else to think about other than herself,' said Cordelia with a sniff. 'And it sounds as if she and the Colonel are getting on very well.'

Peggy grinned as she made the tea and gave it a good stir before leaving it to brew in the big brown pot. 'So I've heard, and if it's true, then I'm de-

308

lighted – but she's being very tight-lipped about it.'

'Probably doesn't want Ivy teasing her,' said Cordelia dryly. 'Now there's a friendship I didn't expect.'

Peggy poured the tea and placed three cups on a tray. 'Neither did I, but this war has changed people – made them realise that if we don't pull together, we won't win – and I'm glad the happy atmosphere in the house is restored. We couldn't have gone on the way things were.'

'Amen to that,' said Cordelia firmly.

The telephone rang just as Peggy entered the hall, so she handed over the tray to Peter and went to answer it.

'Mrs Reilly?'

Peggy didn't recognise the voice. 'Yes?' she replied warily.

'Mrs Lloyd-Hughes here,' the rather bossy upper-crust voice continued. 'I need to talk to Mrs Williams.'

Peggy had a strong suspicion that the caller was one of the women who'd snubbed Doris at the memorial service. 'Mrs Williams is unavailable at the moment,' she said crisply. 'Can I give her a message?'

'That's most inconvenient,' the other woman snapped. 'She's needed urgently to help with the children's charity Lady Chumley was setting up before the unfortunate business at Mrs Williams's house.'

Peggy was about to comment when she charged on in her hectoring tone.

'And then there is the matter of supervising Cliffehaven's branch of the WVS. I cannot possibly do it alone, and I'm most disappointed in Mrs Williams for leaving me in the lurch.'

'Mrs Williams has just been widowed,' said Peggy icily, 'and has far more pressing things to keep her occupied than running about after you. She has not left you in the lurch at all; in fact her resignation from her post with the WVS was tendered some time ago, so I would suggest it's bad management on your part that you haven't organised a replacement.'

'Well, really!' the other woman huffed. 'I've never been spoken to like that, and will not stand for it. Don't you know who I am?'

'No, and I don't care, either,' said Peggy, who was now rather enjoying herself. 'But I do know that if you're one of the snooty, self-seeking crowd who shunned my sister at the memorial luncheon, she's better off without you.'

There was a long silence at the other end before Peggy heard the clearing of a throat. 'The charity work we do is far more important than personal grudges and perceived slights,' Mrs Lloyd-Hughes said eventually.

'Charity begins at home,' said Peggy. 'And if any of you had shown the slightest kindness or thought to how my sister felt after what you term as "the unfortunate business" that saw five women killed and Doris made homeless, she might have been willing to help.'

'I apologise if Mrs Williams feels we've been neglectful,' the woman said stiffly. 'But I need her services, both with the charity and the WVS. Please see to it that you pass on my message the moment Mrs Williams *is* available.'

Peggy heard the sharp clatter of the receiver being slammed down at the other end and softly replaced her own. 'Oh, I'll pass it on all right, but I'll jolly well make sure Doris has nothing to do with any of it.' She turned to see that all work had stopped on the stairs and everyone was looking at her wide-eyed.

'Strewth, Mrs Reilly,' breathed Peter. 'I wouldn't fancy getting on the wrong side of you. You're quite the tigress when you get going, aren't you?'

'Well done, Peggy,' said Rita, shooting her a grin. 'It's about time someone told that snooty lot where to get off. I bet whoever that was had never heard the like.'

'I don't understand what that was about,' said Danuta with a twinkle in her eyes, 'but I think you enjoyed it.'

'Damn right, I did,' said Peggy, before going back into the kitchen to tell Cordelia all about it.

Peggy decided that whilst the work was going on in the hall there was no point in trying to clean. The washing was done, it was a beautiful July day, the children were out and she had a couple of hours to enjoy the sunshine in relative peace. She took off her apron and knotted headscarf, got Cordelia settled into one of the deckchairs and put up the parasol Ron had filched from one of the bombed-out hotels on the front to shade her, and then sat down. The sharp exchange with Mrs Lloyd-Hughes had in fact released some of the tension she'd been feeling since hearing about Jim, and now the sun on her face and bare limbs soothed her.

'Oh,' she sighed, closing her eyes. 'This is bliss.'

311

'Enjoy it whilst you can, dear,' said Cordelia drowsily. 'Once the children come back you won't have a minute to yourself.'

Peggy wriggled to a more comfortable position in the deckchair. 'Hopefully Fran and Sarah will have worn them out by then, so when I take them up to the Red Cross centre they'll play quietly.'

'You do too much,' murmured Cordelia, her sunglasses slipping unheeded down her nose as she nodded off.

Peggy accepted she had very little time to herself with all the dashing about she had to do, but she liked being busy – to feel useful, and part of the great army of women doing their bit to help win this war whilst the men were away.

Her thoughts, as always, turned to Jim. At least he was out of it for a while, and she could only pray that by the time he was well enough to be returned to his regiment, the war would be at an end and he could come home.

The news was becoming more hopeful by the day. The Japanese had been all but routed from Burma. They were still fighting in Siam and throughout the Pacific, but it was clear they couldn't last much longer, for their huge losses in men, ships and planes had been exacerbated by the continuing monsoon and the lack of food and supplies.

In Europe, Allied troops were making headway south from the liberated northern shores towards Paris, and slowly advancing from the south through Italy; meanwhile, the Russians were advancing through Poland and had just liberated thousands of prisoners from the German concentration camp at Majdanek. The swiftness of this coup had meant the Nazis hadn't had time to destroy the evidence of what they'd been doing at Majdanek, and this had clearly been so horrifying that Peggy suspected the newsreader had given only a heavily censored report on the previous evening's broadcast.

The indications that the situation in Europe was beginning to shift in the Allies' favour had been reinforced by the news that had come through this morning. There had been a failed assassination attempt on Hitler by some of his high-ranking Wehrmacht officers during a conference at a place called Wolf's Lair in East Prussia. The plot to kill Hitler, negotiate a peace treaty, and thus bring an end to his reign of terror, had involved thousands, which proved to Peggy that Hitler wasn't as firmly in control as he'd once been but it was a great shame he hadn't gone up with that bomb.

'Well, it's all right for some, sitting about with nothing to do.'

Peggy's eyes snapped open as a heavily pregnant Kitty limped towards her with the aid of a walking stick, and she jumped out of her chair and gave her a hug. 'Sit down,' she urged. 'You look all in.'

'I am a bit,' Kitty confessed, 'but a lovely off-duty airman gave me a lift back on his motorbike, which was great fun.' She regarded the sleeping Cordelia with great affection. 'Bless her,' she sighed. 'Grandma Cordy does love a snooze in the sun, doesn't she?'

Peggy was not about to be deflected. 'Back from where?' she demanded.

'Cliffe aerodrome.' She massaged her back as she eyed the teapot. 'Is that tea still warm? I'm as dry as a bone.'

Peggy threw the dregs from her own cup onto Ron's vegetable patch and quickly poured the tea. 'It'll be horribly stewed,' she warned, 'and what on earth were you doing up at Cliffe in the first place? Please don't tell me you walked all that way in your condition.'

Kitty eyed her over the rim of the cup as she gulped down the tea. 'Ahh, that's better.' She ignored Peggy's stem glare and brushed back her fair hair from her hot face before running her hand over her swollen stomach. 'Exercise is good for pregnant women,' she said defiantly, 'and I didn't have to walk back, so there's no good you looking at me like that.'

Peggy gave a sigh. 'It's only because I worry about you, and with the added weight on your prosthesis it can't be doing your stump any good.'

'The walking stick helps take some of the weight off,' said Kitty, pouring another cup of tea. 'But I do admit I might have overdone it a little today. My stump is throbbing a bit.'

'Fran will be home soon. I'll get her to look at it,' said Peggy, fetching another chair from the shed. 'But why did you go all the way up there?'

Kitty squirmed in the chair as if trying to find a more comfortable position. 'Charlotte got notification from the Red Cross that Freddy has been transferred to another Stalag. This is the second time he's been moved, and knowing my brother, it's because he's been making a nuisance of himself. He's always hated feeling trapped and

314

probably kept trying to escape.'

Peggy thought fondly of the dark-haired, hand-some young man who'd always had such a lust for life, women and excitement, and could well understand his frustration at being kept behind barbed wire. 'Is it the same one Cissy's Randy has been sent to? Is that why you went to Cliffe?'

Kitty shook her head. 'He's further south, but I thought she'd like to know that this shifting of prisoners seems to be random, and probably has nothing to do with nationality. I suspect Randy was proving to be a thorn in the side of the Ger-mans too – he's just as gung-ho as Freddy.' She winced and shifted again in the deckchair. 'The little blighter's lying on my bladder. I need the loo – again.'

Peggy ran up into the kitchen to freshen the tea whilst Kitty used the outside lav. She popped her head around the door to the hall. 'Kitty's here,' she said to Rita. 'Her Freddy's been moved to an-other Stalag, and would you believe it – she only walked all the way to Cliffe to tell Cissy.'

Rita shook her head. 'That girl never ceases to amaze me,' she said in awe. 'Look, we're almost done here; tell her I'll see her in a minute or two.'

Peggy noted that the metal platform and chair was in place, the wheels on the runners, and that Danuta was helping Peter connect the wires on the small engine. 'I don't expect she'll be leaving in a hurry,' she said. 'The poor girl's worn out and needs to rest. Bring your cups with you, I've freshened the pot.'

She went back into the garden to find Cordelia was awake and chatting to Kitty. She waited until there was a pause and then asked, 'How's Charlotte taken the news?'

Kitty chuckled. 'She's just relieved he's not flying any more. Of course she's very worried he might go too far and get shot trying to escape – but by all accounts this new Stalag is where the Germans send serial escape-artists, so the security is extremely tight.'

Rita came flying out of the back door and enfolded Kitty in a hug. 'It's so lovely to see you,' she said, plumping down on the ground beside her. 'You don't visit us nearly enough.' She poured the fresh tea into her cup and eyed Kitty's huge stomach. 'Goodness,' she breathed. 'How much bigger are you going to get?'

'Not very much more, I hope,' Kitty replied ruefully. 'This baby's due in ten days' time, which frankly can't come soon enough. I haven't seen my feet in months, let alone managed to touch my toes; I can't bend or sit properly and at night she keeps me awake by kicking me.' She gave a soft smile. 'Apart from all that, I feel and look like a beached whale.'

'You look radiant and very lovely,' said Peggy with an affectionate smile. 'But you seem very certain it's a girl you're carrying. I hope you won't be too disappointed if it's not.'

'I don't really mind either way as long as it's all right. Roger would love a boy, of course, but I rather like the idea of a little girl.'

'Have you thought of names yet?' asked Cordelia.

'Faith for a girl – because I have to keep faith that Roger will come home – and George for a boy, in honour of the King.'

Peggy turned as Peter and Danuta came into the garden. She made the introductions, poured more tea and settled back to listen to them chatting, enjoying the sunshine and the prospect of babies to coo over once Kitty had delivered and Charlotte had had her twins. Freddy Pargeter had better behave, she thought darkly. His wife Charlotte was relying on him to come home in one piece to help care for his babies.

She tuned back in to the conversation to find that Rita and Peter were explaining about Cordelia's chairlift.

'It's bonzer all right,' he said enthusiastically. 'Carried me up and back several times without a hitch, so I let the girls have a go as well.' He looked at Cordelia, his mesmerising eyes lit with humour. 'Reckon it's your turn now,' he said. 'Are you up to it, do you think?'

Cordelia blushed. 'I can hardly say no with you looking at me like that.'

Peter helped her out of the deckchair and Cordelia hooked her arm in his to go and see what all the fuss was about. The others trooped after her and they all stood in the hall regarding this new addition with interest.

'You go first,' Cordelia said to Peter. 'I want to make sure that contraption really does work.'

'Right oh,' he replied cheerfully. He sat down, his large feet projecting from the footrest, fastened the belt across his hips and pulled the lever on the side of the chair. With a soft wheeze it began to slowly roll upwards, and when it reached the top, Peter engaged the brake, beamed at them

317

all in triumph and then set it rolling back down again.

'It's fair dinkum, all right, isn't it?'

'If that means it works, then I suppose it is,' said Cordelia, eyeing it with some trepidation. She waved away Peggy's offer to go next and determinedly sat in the chair. Allowing Rita to fasten the safety belt, she rested her hand on the lever, and before she could change her mind, pushed it down.

'Ooh,' she twittered as she was ponderously carried up the stairs. 'Goodness me. How do I stop it?'

'Just pull the lever up,' said Rita. 'That will work the brake.'

Cordelia yanked on the lever and she came to a halt halfway up. Tentatively pushing the lever down again, she continued the slow journey to the top of the stairs where it came to a halt against the sturdy buffer of a wooden block. She engaged the brake and beamed down at them victoriously. 'I did it,' she giggled. 'Oh, what fun.'

Peggy watched at first with her heart in her mouth as Cordelia made several journeys up and down the stairs, but it seemed the contraption was working perfectly. It would bring her a new lease of life now that she would no longer have to rely on others to fetch and carry.

Peggy stepped forward after Cordelia's eighth trip. 'I think that's enough for now,' she said gently. 'You don't want to wear out that motor, do you?'

Cordelia reluctantly stepped away from her new toy and beamed. 'It's truly wonderful,' she breathed, hugging Rita before turning to Peter.

'I'd hug you too, but you're too tall.'

'Fair go, every bloke likes a hug from a pretty woman,' drawled Peter, bending to lift Cordelia off her feet and give her a hug and a smacking kiss on the cheek.

Cordelia slapped him flirtatiously on the shoulder. 'Naughty boy, taking liberties with an old woman like that!'

Peter kissed the other cheek and very gently set her back on her feet. 'Glad you like it Grandma Cordy. Now I've gotta go. I'm supposed to be back on duty in less than an hour.' He turned to Rita. 'Thanks for helping out on the project. It wouldn't have happened at all without you working all hours.'

'Well, it was my project too,' she reminded him sternly, 'so don't think you can take all the credit, Wing Commander Peter Ryan.'

He grinned and then said goodbye and hurried down to the motorbike he'd left parked outside. With a burp and a rattle the engine came to life and he roared off, leaving a trail of black exhaust fumes behind him.

'He still hasn't sorted out that bike,' sighed Rita. 'But then he hasn't had much time to do anything in between working on the chair and flying ops. If only he'd trust me with it, I could have it running like clockwork within days.'

Cordelia was still discombobulated by Peter's affectionate response, and was trying to pull her wits together. 'Men are always a bit precious about their things – especially if it has an engine,' she said distractedly. 'I wouldn't take it to heart, Rita.'

'Kitty, are you all right?' asked Danuta sharply.

'I don't know,' she replied, unsteadily making her way to the chair by the telephone. 'I've had back ache all day and it's suddenly got much worse.'

Danuta was nearest, and helped her to sit down. 'There is other pain?'

'No, no, just my back.' She looked at Danuta and gave a wan smile. 'I've overdone things, that's all. I'm sure I'll be fine if I just have a little rest.'

The gush of water soaked through her dungarees and pooled on the floor, and she looked at it aghast. 'I'm so sorry, Peggy,' she breathed in horror. 'I seem to have wet myself. I'll clear it up immediately.'

'You'll do no such thing,' said Peggy, pressing her back into the chair. 'That's your waters breaking. Baby is on its way.'

'But that can't be,' Kitty gasped. 'She's not due for ten days.'

'Well, it looks like she's decided to come early,' Peggy told her.

Kitty stared at her in disbelief and then bent over with a groan as a strong contraction gripped her like a vice. 'No, oh, no,' she gasped.

Peggy reached for the telephone. 'I'm ringing the doctor,' she said firmly. 'Danuta, help Kitty into the bedroom and make her comfortable. Rita, clean the floor before someone slips and then put the kettle on. Cordelia, could you help strip Doris's bed? She won't appreciate–' She was interrupted by the receptionist answering the telephone, and after a very short exchange she replaced the receiver.

'Both doctors are out on call, and the midwife is

delivering another baby,' she said as she hurried into the hall-floor bedroom to find the bed stripped and Kitty shuffling back and forth clutching her stomach. 'The receptionist has promised to send someone over as soon as possible, and as Kitty has only just started her labour, we've got plenty of time to get her prepared.'

'I'm supposed to go to the hospital,' groaned Kitty, reaching for the chest of drawers to lean on.

Danuta's expression was solemn as she took Kitty's pulse and placed her hand on her stomach as another contraction came. 'This baby will come fast, so there's no time for an ambulance. I shall need towels and a rubber sheet if you have one – as well as a sharp pair of scissors, disinfectant, soap and a bowl of very hot water.'

Peggy shot out of the bedroom and raced upstairs to the airing cupboard, snatching out towels, a clean sheet and a spare pillow. Running into her bedroom, she stripped the two cots of the rubber sheeting she put there in case of accidents, grabbed her sewing scissors and almost fell down the stairs when she stubbed her toe on the safety block. Cursing under her breath, she hobbled down and dumped everything on the top of the chest of drawers.

Kitty was sweating and clinging to the footboard, almost bent double as she dealt with yet another strong contraction, and Cordelia's little face was a picture of concern as she tried to soothe her by rubbing her back.

'How far apart are they?' Peggy asked as they quickly laid the rubber sheet over the mattress and covered it in towels

'Every five minutes,' Danuta replied. 'Is a long time since I deliver baby,' she muttered. 'I hope either Fran or the doctor get here soon.'

'But you do know what to do, don't you?' Peggy asked fearfully.

'Yes,' Danuta replied shortly.

Peggy glanced at her watch. It was almost midday, and the children would be on their way home for their lunch. She called out to Rita who was running a mop over the tiles in the hall. 'We need that hot water, soap and disinfectant quickly. Then you'll have to run down to the park and get hold of Fran. This baby's on its way and in a hurry.'

Rita returned within minutes with a jug and bowl brimming with hot water, and as Kitty gave a deep groan, she shot off like a startled deer to find Fran.

Kitty panted through the contractions and within half an hour, she gasped urgently, 'I need to push.'

Danuta was very calm. 'Not yet. Is too soon. You must pant like a dog until we get you undressed.' With Peggy's help she managed to get Kitty's clothes off and settle her on the bed.

Cordelia covered her in the clean sheet and then held her hand. 'What about her false leg?' she asked fretfully. 'Shouldn't we take it off?'

'There isn't time,' said Danuta.

'I'm going to push,' grunted Kitty.

'No, you're not. You keep panting,' Danuta ordered. 'I must look to see if baby has crowned. If you push too soon you will have a tear, and you won't want stitches down there.' She swiftly washed and soaped her hands in the hot water, dropped Peggy's sewing scissors in to sterilise them with disinfectant, and tied a hand towel over her hair before lifting the sheet to examine Kitty's progress.

'It's all right, Kitty,' Peggy soothed, patting her shoulder. 'Danuta was a nurse in Poland; she knows what she's doing.'

Danuta emerged from beneath the sheet with a wide grin. 'You are fully dilated and I can see your baby's head. You may push now, but very gently.'

Danuta disappeared beneath the sheet and began issuing instructions and encouragement as Kitty pushed. 'That is good. Steady and slow. Now you can push as hard and as long as you like, Kitty. Your baby's head is almost out.'

Peggy and Cordelia looked at each other across the sweating, straining girl, their emotions a mixture of hope and fear as her grip on their hands tightened and she gave a guttural groan and strained as hard as she could.

'One last push, Kitty,' urged Danuta. 'Good girl. That's the shoulders, and here comes the rest.'

Kitty slumped breathlessly back against the pillows, sweat running down her reddened face, her damp tangle of hair flopping in her eyes. 'Is it all right?' she managed.

There was a long, ominous silence before Danuta emerged with a beaming smile and a squalling bundle wrapped in a clean towel. 'She is perfect, but first I must cut and tie cord.' Moments later she placed the baby in Kitty's arms and both Cordelia and Peggy burst into tears.

17

Danuta felt like crying too, but it was more from relief that the delivery had gone without a hitch than an emotional reaction to the baby. She watched Kitty cradling her tiny daughter as Cordelia and Peggy shed tears and cooed at the same time. It had been quite a morning, but as there was still no sign of a midwife or doctor, her work wasn't over yet.

'Mamma Peggy, would you please bath the baby whilst I see to Kitty? And *Babunia* Cordy, could you bring some newspaper and make a fresh pot of tea?'

She waited until they'd left the room and then looked down at the exhausted Kitty. 'I will remove the artificial leg first, then you will be more comfortable as you deliver the afterbirth.' She saw the startled look on her face. 'It will not hurt,' she assured her quickly.

Minutes later, Danuta checked that the afterbirth was whole, and wrapped it in the newspaper. She stripped away the dirty towels, washed Kitty as well as she could using a small towel as a flannel, and then used Doris's brush to untangle her hair. Plumping the pillows and drawing a blanket over her, she watched Kitty rest back with a weary smile and knew she would soon be asleep.

'I don't know how to begin to thank you,' Kitty said. 'I'm sorry I made such a fuss, but everything happened so fast, and I was in a panic.'

'You were very calm considering,' soothed Danuta. 'I have heard much worse from other women.'

'It was you who was calm,' said Kitty solemnly, 'and that made me feel better. I dread to think how I'd've coped if you hadn't been here.'

'Between you and Mamma Peggy you would have managed,' she replied, patting her hand. 'You have a beautiful, healthy daughter; that is all that matters now.' She turned as Peggy came into the room, the baby swaddled in a clean towel, its tuft of dark hair brushed into a sweet coxcomb. 'I will leave you to enjoy her,' she murmured, heading for the door armed with dirty towels and the bowl of water.

'I'm calling her Faith Danuta Makepeace,' said Kitty, 'and when she's old enough I will tell her all about you, and how wonderful you were.'

Danuta blinked back tears, suddenly overcome by all that had happened. 'Thank you, Kitty. That is a great honour,' she managed before quietly closing the door behind her.

'It's brought it all back, hasn't it?' asked a sharp-eyed Cordelia as Danuta entered the kitchen. She put her arms around her and drew her close. 'There, there, dear.'

'I'm not crying for my Katarzyna – she is with me always – but these tears are because I am so relieved nothing went wrong.' She drew back from the embrace. 'You see, I was so frightened of that, *Babunia.* Kitty went into labour very fast, and it can be most dangerous to both mother and baby.'

'Then you cry away, Danuta,' Cordelia said with a loving smile and a soft pat on the cheek.

'Kitty and the baby are safe and well, and you've proved you're wasting your talents by hanging about here instead of going back to nursing.'

Danuta wasn't at all sure about that. She'd found the entire episode nerve-wracking to say the least, and the thought of being plunged straight back into the hectic routine of a busy hospital was a step too far.

The silence in the kitchen was broken by Rita and Fran rushing up the steps. 'Sarah's keeping the children out for lunch at the Lilac Tearooms,' said Fran. 'How's Kitty?'

'She's had a beautiful daughter,' said Cordelia proudly. 'And Danuta managed it all wonderfully well.'

'That was quick,' breathed Fran. 'Were there any complications?'

Danuta shook her head. 'We are waiting for the doctor to come to check her, but as far as I can see they are both doing very well.'

Fran cocked her head as she heard the demanding wail of a newly born. 'It certainly sounds like it,' she said, shooting her a grin. 'Well done, Danuta. You see, I told you, you are ready to go back to nursing.'

'Maybe,' Danuta hedged. 'And it would be good if you could put something on Kitty's stump. She walked too far today and it looks very sore.'

'Can we go in and see them?' asked Rita excitedly.

'For a little while. Kitty is very tired and needs to sleep.'

Danuta remained in the kitchen as they headed for the bedroom with the fresh pot of tea. She needed a moment to settle down after all the excitement, and the sight of that dark coxcomb of hair had almost been her undoing, for, despite her protestation to the contrary, it had reminded her too much of her own baby.

Peggy was in her element. Kitty had given tiny Faith her first feed and then fallen asleep, leaving Peggy to cuddle the drowsy baby. She looked up as Rita and Fran came into the room with Cordelia and put her finger to her lips. 'They're both sleeping,' she whispered.

The girl crowded in to see the baby, their faces soft with awe as she grimaced and stretched, her rosebud mouth moving at the memory of her first feed.

'Do you want to hold her?' Peggy asked.

'No fear,' whispered Rita. 'I'd be terrified of dropping her.'

Fran had no such fears and expertly took the baby from Peggy's arms just as someone knocked on the front door.

'I'll get it,' called Danuta, and after a short conversation, brought in Doctor Sayer.

The elderly medic beamed at them all before quickly examining Faith and then shooing them out of the room with instructions to call an ambulance.

'There isn't anything wrong, is there?' asked Peggy sharply.

'No, my dear. But young Kitty here needs to be in hospital after delivering so quickly so we can keep an eye on her and protect her from any infection.'

327

Peggy telephoned the hospital and then went to join the others in the kitchen, where Fran assured her it was common practice to take newly delivered mothers in when the birth had been swift.

Doctor Sayer entered the kitchen a few minutes later and dumped his medical bag on the table. Accepting a cup of tea from Peggy, he took a slurp and then regarded them all with a beaming smile before he turned to Danuta.

'I understand from Kitty that you're a trained nurse?' At her hesitant nod, he continued, 'Where did you learn, and how long has it been since you've practised?'

Danuta hid her damaged fingers in her dress pocket. 'I trained in Warsaw, and worked in the main hospital there until I came to England,' she said cautiously.

He drained his teacup. 'Well, it seems you haven't forgotten how to deliver a baby. Was that your speciality?'

Danuta shook her head, uncertain where these questions were leading. 'I was theatre nurse.'

His bushy white eyebrows shot up. 'Were you now? So why aren't you working as such when the hospitals are crying out for nurses?'

Danuta fidgeted, all too aware of being the centre of attention. 'I was injured in bomb attack in London and have only just been released from the Memorial.'

He regarded her thoughtfully. 'You certainly look as if you need a few square meals and a dose of sunshine – but the Memorial wouldn't have discharged you if you weren't fully recovered.' He

328

brushed a finger over his moustache. 'Do you have any paperwork from your time in Poland to show your qualification?'

'Everything was destroyed when the Germans came,' she said flatly.

'That's a great shame,' he muttered. 'I could have done with another district nurse and mid-wife. Poor Mrs Higgins can barely manage now, and when the men start coming home she'll be snowed under.'

Danuta felt a spark of hope that extinguished the previous doubts. 'I could perhaps get a letter from my employer in London to confirm my qualifications,' she suggested carefully.

'And who was that?'

'A military hospital for injured servicemen.' She bit her lip. 'But it may take some time to receive a reply. They are very busy.'

Doctor Sayer stroked his beard. 'If you can get that letter, come to my surgery and we'll talk some more,' he said. 'I can't offer you work in theatre, but you'd be a godsend out in the district.' He smiled at her. 'If you decide to accept my offer, I'll lend you my textbooks so you can brush up on midwifery, and Mrs Higgins will bring you up to date should you need it.'

Danuta experienced a sudden rush of nervous hope. 'I will write to them tonight.'

Peggy didn't quite know how she'd manage that as the London hospital was purely fictional, but she set that minor difficulty aside as the ambulance arrived. With little fuss, Kitty and Faith were carried out on a stretcher. Doctor Sayer climbed into his car to follow them, and with calls of good luck and promises to visit as soon as possible, they all stood on the front step to watch her being driven away.

'Right,' said Peggy. 'We'd better get Doris's room sorted before she gets back. The last thing we need today is ructions.'

'We'll do it,' said Fran and Rita in unison. 'Go and sit in the garden,' ordered Fran. 'You've done enough today.'

Peggy looked at her watch. She had another hour before she was supposed to be at the Red Cross centre – and that reminded her, she'd yet to tell Charlotte about baby Faith, and Kitty would need the layette taken into the hospital. She lit a cigarette, then dialled the number for Briar Cottage.

Having made sure Charlotte was all right and was fully informed about Kitty's baby and the heroic part Danuta had played in her arrival, Peggy consoled her over her news about Freddy, and agreed that he was better off there than taking to the skies over Europe. She ended the call and went to find Danuta.

She found her sitting at her dressing table, and softly closed the door behind her before settling on the edge of the bed. 'You did very well today, dear,' she began, 'and I'm delighted old Doctor Sayer was so impressed that he offered you a job. But we both know you weren't nursing in London, so how can you possibly obtain references?'

Danuta met her gaze in the dressing-table mirror. 'There is someone who will write it for me,' she said. She turned and reached for Peggy's hands. 'No more questions, please. I cannot answer them.'

Peggy slowly nodded 'I understand,' she murmured. 'But are you sure it isn't too soon for you to take on such a responsibility? Mrs Higgins has to work very hard with such a large community to cover now.'

'Then it will be good to help ease her work. But I have a lot of catching up to do before then. My midwifery course was long ago, and it's very important I don't make mistakes.'

'Doctor Sayer will lend you the textbooks, and I'm sure Fran will test you on things. She's very good like that, and is keen for you to go back to nursing.' Peggy grinned. 'She remembers you working with the first-aiders and ambulance crews, and knows that when you set your mind to something, you see it through.'

Danuta grinned back. 'It is a new day and a new start, Mamma Peggy, and I will do my very best to make you proud of me.'

Peggy's soft heart melted and she embraced her. 'Oh, Danuta, I'm already so proud of you. You don't have to prove anything to me.'

18

Ron was serving behind the bar when Rita dashed in to tell him breathlessly about Kitty's baby, Danuta's part in her arrival and Doctor Sayer's job offer. Before he could say anything, Rosie was pumping the girl about what the baby looked like, what it weighed and how soon could she visit.

He gave up trying to keep track of it all and carried on serving the customers with a beaming smile. He quite liked babies, even though they mostly resembled Churchill at first, but with Kitty being such a special young woman, her baby was sure to be a little beauty. He gave a happy sigh as he continued to pull pints.

It had turned out to be quite a red-letter day all round, for Rosie had become more frisky of late and was weakening to the idea of accepting his engagement ring. As a special treat, he'd managed to get tickets for the posh fundraising ball at the Town Hall tonight, and Rosie was definitely showing signs that she was impressed with his efforts. As long as he didn't blot his copybook, he might well be on a promise later.

And yet behind his rosy glow there lurked the niggling worry over Danuta. She'd shown what she was made of today, but was she ready to be thrust back into the hectic life of a nurse-midwife? The town's population had grown considerably over the past four years, and with so many servicemen having been around until recently, there were lots of young women in the family way. He knew that Florence Higgins had her work cut out, and another pair of hands would be a blessing, but was Danuta strong enough physically to take on such a task?

Ron cleared some of the dirty glasses and wiped down the polished wooden counter. Only time would tell, he supposed, and Danuta was old enough to make her own decisions.

'You're looking very thoughtful, Ron,' said Rosie cheerfully as she gave his bottom a friendly slap. 'Not having second thoughts about taking me dancing tonight, are you?'

He put his arm about her waist and gave it a squeeze. 'Definitely not,' he murmured into her ear. 'I can't wait to see you all dressed up and looking like a Hollywood glamour puss.'

She giggled. 'It'll take me a while to get ready, so once the pub's closed, you'd better go home and prepare yourself to be dazzled.'

'I'm always dazzled,' he replied truthfully. 'I'll not let you down, Rosie girl, and will be so smart you'll hardly recognise me.'

'That'd be an improvement on what you're wearing today,' she admonished gently.

He glanced down at his old shirt and baggy trousers. 'Aye, well, I left the house with the dogs and haven't been back since – which turns out to be a good thing. What with babies being born and chair-lifts fitted, it must have been chaos.'

'I'm sure it was,' she agreed with laughter in her blue eyes. 'And like the old rogue you are, you managed to avoid it all.' With a light chuckle she went to serve a waiting customer.

An hour later, Ron left the Anchor and ambled down a quiet Camden Road. It was Saturday and therefore half-day closing, so there were no queues cluttering up the pavement, and the shop-keepers had tidied away their outdoor displays.

Harvey watered the lampposts along the way and went to inspect the newest bomb site for different smells, only to startle a sleeping ginger cat which hissed at him and took flight. Harvey went in hot pursuit, charging down the hill towards the seafront.

Ron stood on the corner and watched in amusement as he filled his pipe. The cat scampered up a telegraph pole and jumped with lithe grace onto the top of a high wall, well out of the way of Harvey, who was bouncing about in fury and barking fit to burst. Ron grinned as the cat regarded the dog with disdain and settled down to lick his paws and wash his whiskers.

Ron decided he'd seen enough. The cat was an old adversary of Harvey's, wily enough to know he was safe as long as he was on that wall. In fact he had been known to sit there for hours deliberately irritating every passing dog, and Harvey had as much chance of getting to him as Ron had of flying to the moon. He puffed contentedly on his pipe and went home, knowing that Harvey would follow him once he realised he was on a fool's errand.

Much to his relief, he discovered there was no one in the kitchen or the garden, so he decided to stretch out in a deckchair and relax until he had to start getting ready for this evening. It was an expensive business, this wooing, what with new clothes, afternoon tea at the Officers' Club and tickets for do's at the Town Hall – and he suspected Rosie wouldn't let up on him after they were married, either. But the thought of making her his own at last was enough for him. She was worth every last penny.

He woke when a shadow fell over him, and he blearily looked up to find Danuta standing there. 'I hear you were the heroine of the hour,' he muttered, trying to gather himself.

Danuta shrugged and sat in the chair beside him. 'I'm guessing Rita told you about the doctor's offer.' At his nod, she bit her lip. 'I have written to Dolly, asking her advice on what to do. But I would like to nurse again – to do something healing after...'

'I'm sure Dolly will encourage you and provide any letter you might need,' he said. 'She certainly won't stand in your way of making a new life for yourself here.' He regarded her keenly. 'How do you really feel about diving in at the deep end so soon?'

'A little nervous,' she admitted, then grinned back at him. 'But I am a good swimmer. I will not sink.'

Ron had no doubt of that. He nodded and then looked at his watch. 'Holy Mary and all the saints, is that the time?' he gasped. 'Rosie will have me guts for garters if I'm late.' He scrambled out of the deckchair looking around wildly. 'Where's Harvey?'

'I haven't seen him.'

Ron swore under his breath and hurried down to the road. The cat had gone from the wall and there was no sign of his dog. 'Harvey!' he yelled. 'Harvey, come here at once!'

There was no answering bark, and Ron dithered. He had less than an hour to get bathed, shaved and dressed for tonight, and Harvey could be anywhere. 'Ach, ye heathen beast,' he growled. 'Trust you to disappear just at the wrong time.'

Setting off at a fast pace, Ron headed towards the seafront, calling repeatedly and straining to hear any answering bark. It was unusual for his dog not to come home, especially since the vet had put a stop to his pursuit of bitches in heat. He must have been distracted by something – or was in trouble.

Ron's calls became more frantic as he searched through the rubble of the seafront hotels and then headed back up the hill. He whistled down alleyways and called over walls, but was met with only silence and some startled looks from passers-by who assured him they hadn't seen a large scruffy dog on their travels.

He had searched everywhere he could think of and now stood at the end of the twitten leading to Beach View and the path to the hills. 'Harvey! Harvey!' he yelled, following it up with a series of sharp whistles. He was about to head for the hills as a last resort when he heard a faint answering bark and froze. 'Harvey? Where are you?'

The bark came again, but it was very muffled. Ron moved slowly towards it, urging his dog to keep on barking so he could find him. The sound seemed to be coming from the next street, and as he approached the bombed-out house directly behind Beach View, the barking became a little clearer. He stood where the front wall used to be and scanned the pile of rubble. 'Harvey? Where are you, boy?'

Harvey replied with a yelp and a whine, and Ron was immediately clambering through the shifting, broken mess towards it. 'It's all right, boy, I'm on me way,' he called, his heart thudding painfully as he heard his old pal's pitiful whines.

He began to move charred rafters and singed

drainpipes, tossing aside bricks and roof slates, delving into the depths of what remained of the ruined house, fearful that Harvey might have chased something into the buried cellar and become stuck as the debris shifted.

He moved a shattered door and saw Harvey's nose poking up through a hole. He moved faster, realising he'd been right about the cellar. 'Don't move,' he ordered sternly, wary now of the debris shifting and falling on the animal. 'Ach, ye've got yerself into a fine old mess, haven't ye, yer daft wee beast,' he muttered, carefully moving away the shattered tiles and broken door panels from around his dog.

He lay on his stomach as Harvey's ears and eyes appeared, and with some difficulty, managed to grab hold of his collar. 'It's all right,' he soothed as Harvey whined and looked at him piteously. 'I've got you now.'

He cleared more rubble away, and gave a tentative tug on the collar. He could feel Harvey straining to get some purchase with his paws, his muscles bunched with the effort – but he was stuck fast and now beginning to whimper in pain and panic.

'I will help,' said Danuta, lying down beside Ron.

'We'll need to clear a bigger area,' he said. 'You hold onto his collar and try to keep him calm whilst I get rid of this lot.'

As Danuta tried to soothe the dog, Ron worked with a will to free him. Slates and bits of guttering kept sliding and shifting, and he was terrified that whatever was holding Harvey in place might come loose and send him plunging into the cellar.

'I have hold on him very tight,' said Danuta, 'but he is tiring, his weight taking him down.'

Ron worked faster to clear the area around Harvey, and then began the task of trying to make the hole bigger. He kept up a continuous soothing chatter as Danuta stroked Harvey's head and kept hold of his collar.

'Let's try again,' he said, taking charge of the collar. Gently but firmly drawing it towards him, Harvey's head came through the hole, his paws scrabbling for purchase on the slippery slates and sharp bits of concrete.

Ron knew that the next few seconds were vital, for Harvey's whole weight was on that collar and it was in danger of throttling him. 'Take the collar and don't let go,' he commanded Danuta before reaching down through the hole to grasp Harvey beneath his front paws.

Harvey yelped and snapped his teeth as Ron fought to drag him out. 'I'm sorry, wee man, I know this must hurt, but you've got to be brave, Harvey.'

Harvey's eyes were beseeching, the little whines in his throat telling of his pain and fear as Ron delved deeper, managed to clutch the dog's rear end and slowly hoist him up and out of the hole. His heart was hammering, his arms trembling from the effort, and as Harvey emerged finally, he gathered him to his chest.

Harvey was exhausted, his head drooping as he panted, and when Ron ran a gentle probing hand over him to see where he was injured, he screamed in pain.

Ron gasped as he saw the bloody, jagged slash in his dog's side. 'Run home and telephone the vet,' he rasped. 'His number's by the telephone.'

As Danuta dashed off, Ron tenderly carried his injured Harvey home, his face streaked with tears, his heart heavy with dread.

Rosie had put scented salts into her bath and then rubbed in some of the expensive skin lotion she'd been keeping for a special occasion into her arms and neck. She'd been to the hairdresser's for a shampoo and set straight after closing time, and as she carefully made up her face, she felt a thrill of excitement. She'd never been to a ball before, and it was rumoured that everyone who was anyone would be there tonight, including the Mayor and his wife. A very good ten-piece band had been hired to play after dinner, and as Ron was an excellent dancer, she could hardly wait to be whisked around the floor.

She slipped on the long, pale gold dress she'd bought before the war and never had a chance to wear. The cut of the silk enhanced her curves, and at the back, the neckline dipped in a soft cowl almost to the small of her back – which was quite daring – and would no doubt get Ron all hot and bothered. But that was all right, she thought with a giggle. She had plans for Ron when they got back tonight.

She smoothed on the sheer nylon stockings which had come courtesy of one of her American customers, and slipped her feet into gold sandals. With a pretty ribbon tied in her platinum curls, she added sparkling earrings and long evening gloves. Eyeing her reflection in the pier glass, she hooked the fox fur over one shoulder and grinned. If Ron wasn't dazzled by her tonight, he never would be.

She went into the sitting room and poured out a gin and tonic, glancing at the mantel clock as she took a sip. Ron had promised to fetch her promptly at seven, so they'd have time for a quick drink before they walked to the Town Hall for dinner at eight, but he was cutting it a bit fine.

She was aware of Monty's eyes following her as she paced the room and then went to look out of the window. It was still light and people had come out of their houses to stroll in the warm evening air, meet friends and visit the pub – but there was no sign of Ron.

Rosie lit a cigarette, determined not to get het up over Ron. He'd promised to be here, and the price of those tickets surely guaranteed he'd turn up – even so, he was now ten minutes late. She tuned in to the chatter and laughter coming from the bar downstairs. It sounded as if it was getting busy, but she had no fears that things wouldn't run like clockwork in Brenda's capable hands. Brenda was her most reliable barmaid, and she'd see to it that Flo, who was a bit scatty, didn't spend too much time gossiping when she should be pulling pints.

She began to pace again as the clock ticked away the minutes. Stubbing out her cigarette, she topped up her drink and returned anxiously to the window. It was now almost half-past seven, but still there was no sign of Ron. Perhaps she should telephone Beach View and find out what he was up to?

Hitching up the hem of her long dress, she navigated the stairs carefully in her high heels and to a chorus of wolf whistles from the bar, picked up the receiver. The line was busy. She waited a couple of minutes and tried again, and Vera Gardener assured her that there was no problem with the line, but it was still engaged.

Rosie replaced the receiver and stomped back upstairs. She'd give him another five minutes to either turn up or telephone her, and then she'd go to the ball on her own. She had the tickets in her handbag, had taken too long to prepare for the evening to let it all go to waste, and if she was lucky, she might even find a single man to dance with.

The telephone remained stubbornly silent and Ron was nowhere to be seen. 'Your five minutes are up,' she muttered crossly. Snatching up her fur and evening bag, she went back downstairs and out through the side door. It would take her a good ten minutes to walk up the hilly High Street in these damned shoes, and she'd probably be late into the dining room. Her dander was well and truly up, and if it meant making an entrance on her own, she'd blooming well do it – and in style.

Everyone was gathered in the kitchen of Beach View, their focus on Harvey who was lying shivering on the rug in front of the range fire. Ron had cleaned the wound as best he could and wrapped a length of gauze bandage over it, but Harvey was clearly in great pain.

'Where's that vet got to?' Ron demanded, distraught. 'Surely it doesn't take this long to see to a cow with a damaged udder?'

'I've tried ringing again,' Peggy told him, 'but his receptionist said he's still out at Chalky's place, and as Chalky doesn't have a phone she can't get a message to him.'

'I'd walk over there myself and drag him away if it didn't mean leaving this poor old fella,' muttered Ron, gently stroking Harvey's brindled head. 'It's time that blasted man took on an assistant.'

'I know where Chalky's place is,' said Rita, pulling on her old leather flying jacket and shoving her feet into sturdy boots. 'It won't take a minute to run down to the fire station to collect my bike.'

Before anyone could reply, she was out of the door at a run. Hurdling the back gate, she shot down the twitten and then raced along Camden Road, her boots thudding on the pavement. Every minute counted now, for Harvey was in grave trouble, and if the vet didn't see to him very soon, they were in danger of losing him. The thought of Beach View without darling Harvey brought tears to her eyes as she hurtled along towards the fire station. She had to save him – simply had to.

Rita was almost blinded by her tears, so barely saw the blonde woman tottering along in high heels, evening dress and fur wrap. She tried to avoid her, but the woman stopped suddenly and Rita ran straight into her. 'Sorry,' she gasped, grabbing her before she fell.

Rosie disentangled herself, clearly about to read her the riot act until she saw who it was. 'Rita? What's happened? Why are you running like that?'

'It's Harvey. He's been injured and I have to fetch the vet,' she replied breathlessly before breaking into a sprint for the final few yards.

The old motorbike Rita and her father had brought back to life before the war started first time. She fastened the crash helmet beneath her chin, and as she shot away from the fire station forecourt, she caught a glimpse of Rosie still standing on the pavement. It was only as she opened the throttle and the bike roared up the hill, that she remembered Ron was supposed to be taking Rosie to the ball at the Town Hall.

Rita set aside all thoughts of Rosie and concentrated on where she was heading. She had two choices. She could take the quickest route straight up the hill and across country – thereby risking missing the vet who might already be on his way back – or take the main road which wound into the hills and along the ridge. With only a momentary hesitation, she decided to take the main road and, with the hooded headlight barely showing her the way through the gloom, she accelerated until the needle on the speedometer hovered just below eighty.

The bike was running sweetly as she took the meandering set of bends that ran through a tunnel of trees to the open fields and tiny hamlets that lay on the other side of the hill sheltering Cliffehaven to the west. Picking up speed again as she reached a straighter stretch, she kept her eyes peeled for a van coming the other way. But the road was deserted.

Rita's anxiety grew as she raced through the gathering gloom, and she almost missed the track

343

which led down to the farm. Skidding to a halt and battling to stay on board as the bike lurched beneath her and the engine died, she managed to turn it round. She rammed her heel on the kick-start, and the engine coughed once, but didn't catch. She tried again and again, her exasperation and frustration reaching boiling point as it refused to start.

She was on the point of giving it a good kick when she saw a beam of headlights approaching the open farm gate. Leaving the bike on the ground, she ran towards them, waving her arms and yelling to the driver to stop.

The van came to a halt within inches of her feet. 'What the dickens do you think you're doing?' shouted the middle-aged vet crossly.

'It's Harvey,' she shouted back. 'He's been badly hurt. You've got to go to him at Beach View – and hurry. Please hurry,' she finished on a sob.

'Do you want a lift?'

'No. Get to Harvey before it's too late.'

The van rattled off at speed and Rita sank sobbing onto the grassy verge beside her bike. She could only pray she'd got to the vet in time.

Rosie's fury with Ron had fled instantly as Rita told her about Harvey. Having watched the girl go haring off on that motorbike, she'd turned back for the Anchor to get changed out of her finery.

As she pulled on slacks, blouse and a light sweater, she could only imagine what sort of torture Ron must be going through. Harvey was like his beloved child, and if anything happened to him, he'd be devastated. It was no wonder he'd forgotten about the ball tonight, and she felt utterly miserable about how angry she'd been, accusing him of all sorts, when in reality he was caring for his dog. Slipping into comfortable flat shoes, she hurried downstairs, leaving a disgruntled Monty behind, and managed to avoid being seen by the people in the bar as she left by the side door.

It was dark now, but the air was still warm and fragranced by the day's heat, and she took a deep, restorative breath as she reached the corner of Camden Road. She could see the vet's ramshackle old van parked outside the front steps of Beach View, which was a huge relief, so she hurried to the back gate and quietly let herself into the scullery.

It was awfully quiet upstairs, and as she entered the kitchen it was to find the entire household gathered around the table in tense silence. Harvey was lying there on a rubber sheet, his tongue lolling between his slack jaws as Ron stroked his head and the vet carefully stitched the wound in his side.

Rosie edged further into the room and stood by a tearful Peggy. 'How's he doing?' she murmured.

'We'll know better once he comes round,' she replied, her eyes never leaving the dog on the kitchen table. 'I thought we were going to lose him,' she added, her voice unsteady, 'and we still might if the anaesthetic affects his poor old heart.' She sniffed and dabbed her eyes with a handkerchief. 'He's got a heart murmur, you see, and at his age...'

Rosie gripped her hand in sympathy and looked

over at Ron. His face was ashen beneath the streaks of dirt, and his hand wasn't quite steady as he continued to stroke the dog's head. Her heart went out to him, but there was absolutely nothing she could do but stay here and be with him.

The vet finished his stitching, and after spreading a thick daub of iodine over the wound, applied a bandage. 'That's all I can do for now,' he said wearily. 'He should really come to the surgery so I can keep an eye on him, but I don't want to move him.'

'How long before he wakes up?' asked Ron.

'Not too long. I didn't want to give him too heavy a dose of anaesthetic because of his age. I'll ring the surgery to let Maureen know where I am and then stay on for a bit, if you don't mind, until he does wake – just to make sure the dear old boy has pulled through.'

'You can stay as long as you like,' said Ron, his attention back on the comatose dog. 'Would one of you women make the poor wee man a cup of tea? To be sure, he looks parched and dead on his feet.'

'It has been a very long day,' the vet admitted with a soft smile at Rita who was filling the kettle. 'Not helped by you scaring the life out of me by running straight into my headlights,' he admonished gently.

'Sorry about that,' she replied with a cheeky grin. 'But it was the only way to stop you.'

Rosie made her way through the crush surrounding Harvey and put her hand on Ron's shoulder. 'I'm here if you need me,' she said quietly.

Ron looked up at her in confusion. 'Rosie? What are you doing here?' And then the confusion cleared to be replaced by the shock of remembrance. 'Oh, Rosie, I'm so sorry. I forgot all about…'

'It's all right, my darling man,' she soothed, nuzzling his cheek. 'Nothing matters but Harvey.'

'Ah, Rosie, girl, I don't deserve you,' he replied, the tears making his eyes very blue in his dirty face.

'We'll discuss that in more detail once Harvey's up and about again, and you've had a good wash. What on earth have you both been up to?'

Ron explained, all the while stroking Harvey. 'It wasn't his fault,' he finished. 'Chasing things is bred into a lurcher.'

Harvey grunted and his eyebrows twitched. A shiver ran through him and he slowly opened his eyes. He rubbed his nose against Ron's hand and licked his fingers, his amber eyes still hazy from the anaesthetic.

'Don't let him try and sit up,' warned the vet. He fixed the stethoscope into his ears and listened to Harvey's heartbeat, a smile slowly lightening his expression. 'Good and strong despite the murmur,' he declared. 'It looks like our boy will pull through.'

A collective sigh of relief went round the room and Ron rested his cheek against Harvey's muzzle. 'Ye heathen beast,' he murmured affectionately. 'You'll not be giving me a fright like that again.'

'I'm sorry, old chap,' said the vet, advancing on Harvey with a large cone of stiff cardboard, 'but you're going to have to wear this until those

347

stitches are healed.'

Harvey suffered the indignity of having the outsize ruff fitted around his neck and looked beseechingly at Ron in the hope he'd rescue him. When he realised he wasn't about to, and that it hurt too much to try and struggle against it, he flopped down with a martyred sigh and promptly went back to sleep.

With Harvey now sleeping on the rug, Ron and Rosie sat in the fireside chairs throughout the night to keep watch, and as dawn finally broke, Harvey lumbered to his feet to go and inspect his food bowl and have a long drink. He was on the mend.

19

Doris didn't mind the restriction of being in the hall-floor bedroom, and had settled into Beach View far better than she'd ever expected to, and yet she was still trying to come to terms with the chaos in the house. It had been so quiet and orderly in her lovely Havelock Road home, but here she was surrounded by people rushing in and out, who didn't seem to mind coping with birthing babies, small children, erecting stair contraptions and tending to sick animals, and it was all rather a shock to the system. Although she had to admit there were times she thoroughly enjoyed feeling part of a family again – and she'd come to look on all of them as such now – even young Ivy, who had the cheek of the devil, but was surprisingly, and rather endearingly, fragile under all that sparky bluff and bluster.

It was strange how you never really knew people until you lived with them and got involved in their lives, she mused, as she left Beach View that early Monday morning. Her set ideas about them all had proven to be totally unfounded, especially over this weekend.

A smile played at the corners of her mouth. She'd seen a surprising new side to Ron, for his distress over Harvey had been awful to watch, and yet the tenderness he'd shown both towards his dog and to Rosie Braithwaite was quite remarkable. It seemed Ron had hidden depths previously masked by a cheerful disregard of his responsibilities, and that intrigued and unsettled her, for she'd always thought of him as a rough, selfish man who went his own way without a thought for anyone else.

Doris crossed the street and hurried along Camden Road, her thoughts still on Ron. He was clearly trying to reform in his pursuit of Rosie, and when she'd seen how they were together, she'd realised they shared the same sort of special relationship that Peggy had with her Jim. Although she was ashamed of it, she couldn't help but feel envious.

She and Edward had never really experienced the close intimacy that came from a deep and abiding love that bound two people together and withstood the years. She'd always known that Edward loved her, and in her own way she'd loved him back, but it was a love that stemmed from friendship, companionship and the sharing of day-to-day duties around the home – not the passion her sister shared with Jim, or Rosie with Ron.

Doris sighed. Now Ted was gone, and she was over fifty, she'd more than likely missed the boat as far as passion was concerned – though it'd be nice to experience it just once. A fleeting and rather disturbing image of Colonel White's handsome face came from nowhere, and she hastily dismissed it as the wishful thinking of a frustrated and lonely woman. Handsome he might be, with lovely manners and the sort of cultured voice that could recite the telephone directory and make it sound interesting – but he was her boss, and she had no business to think of him as anything else.

She was just approaching the side alley to the Anchor when Rosie stepped out in a loosely tied, scarlet satin robe which gaped to show too much cleavage and a lot of leg.

'Good morning,' she said brightly, handing a large jug to the dairyman as his Shire waited patiently at the kerb. 'Lovely day, isn't it?'

'It certainly is,' Doris replied rather stiffly. She still wasn't really sure what to make of Rosie, for although she seemed to be educated and quite pleasant, she ran a pub, dressed outrageously and didn't think it at all inappropriate to fetch the milk wearing something that left very little to the imagination.

'Have you got a minute?' said Rosie. 'Only there's something I'd like to discuss with you.'

Rather startled by this unexpected approach, Doris looked at her wristwatch. 'I like to be in the office early to prepare everything before the Colonel arrives, but if it's important, I could spare a couple of minutes.'

Rosie clutched the full jug of milk to her bosom with one hand and her gaping wrap with the other. 'Let's go inside before that chap over there has a heart attack,' she giggled.

Doris glanced across the road at the leering man and gave him such a glare he ducked his head and scuttled off.

'Would you like a cuppa?' asked Rosie as they entered the narrow, dark hall.

'Thank you, but I've just had one,' said Doris, giving the place a quick once-over. She'd never been in the Anchor before, and was surprised by how quaint it was with its low beams, brick floor and white walls of lath and plaster. It was all spotlessly clean and there was the smell of beer permeating through from the bar she could glimpse at the end of the hall, but the overriding scent was of beeswax and Rosie's flowery perfume.

Rosie put the milk jug on the table by the telephone, tied the belt more firmly around her waist and eyed Doris with some amusement. 'Would you like me to show you round?'

'Perhaps another time,' Doris replied, only slightly fazed to be caught snooping. 'What was it you wanted to discuss with me?'

'First things first,' said Rosie. 'How's Harvey this morning?'

'He's feeling very sorry for himself, and hates wearing that ruff, but he's eating well and seems to be on the mend.'

'And Ron? How's he holding up?'

'As robust as ever now he knows Harvey will recover.'

'Good.' Rosie folded her arms beneath her generous bosom and regarded Doris with some sympathy. 'You've been through the mill lately, haven't you, and you must be finding it hard to settle at Beach View after the peace and quiet of your other place.'

Doris was surprised by her astuteness. 'I've been extremely fortunate to have a sister who's so generous,' she replied. 'Yes, it is noisy with people coming and going and what feels like a different drama being played out every day – but strangely enough I'm rather enjoying it.'

'What about after the war? Will you stay on there?'

Doris was puzzled by the questions, not at all sure she wanted this woman knowing her business. 'I hope to have my own place once Jim and the rest of the family come home.'

'That's what I thought,' said Rosie. 'And I have a proposition for you.'

Doris raised a questioning eyebrow.

'There is a property I own just off Mafeking Terrace,' Rosie informed her. 'It's a nice little bungalow, but will need some work done to it now my tenant, old Mrs Carey, has sadly passed away. I was wondering if you'd be interested in renting it?'

'I didn't know you had other property,' said Doris without thinking.

Rosie gave a soft laugh. 'Oh, Doris, there's a lot you don't know about me – and although I own a pub and play the part of the landlady to the hilt, there's more to me than meets the eye. Like you, I prefer to keep my private life private.'

'I didn't mean ... that's to say...'

Rosie waved away Doris's stuttering apology. 'So what do you say to the bungalow?'

'I think it's a very good idea,' Doris replied, trying hard not to appear too eager. 'But I'd need to see it before I make any decisions.'

Rosie unhooked a set of keys from near the telephone. 'The address is on the tag, and you might need a bit of imagination to see yourself in there. I've yet to clear the old lady's furniture and freshen the place up.'

Doris slipped the keys into her handbag. 'I'll pop in during my lunch break. Thank you for thinking of me when there are so few places to be had these days.'

Rosie giggled. 'Don't thank me yet, Doris. You haven't seen the state of it.'

'I'm still grateful,' said Doris rather humbly before shaking her hand and hurrying off to work.

Doris walked quickly towards the factory estate, her mind in a whirl. The thought of having her own space again, of quiet evenings spent listening to the wireless, or summer days pottering in the garden unmolested by over-eager dogs and raucous toddlers, was very tempting. But would Peggy be offended if she upped sticks and left? She'd been so good to her, that the last thing she wanted to do was cause a rift between them. And yet the chance to make a home for herself again had been her driving force ever since she'd moved into Beach View, and although it had come sooner than she'd expected, she'd be foolish not to grab it with both hands.

Running up the wooden steps and into the newly built porch, Doris was about to unlock the office door when she realised the Colonel was already at his desk. 'Good morning, Colonel,' she said brightly as she stepped inside. 'Isn't it a glorious day?'

He got to his feet to welcome her. 'My goodness, Mrs Williams, you look positively radiant this morning. Can I be so bold as to ask why?'

'Indeed you may, Colonel,' she replied, hanging up her cardigan and gas-mask box before patting her hair into place. 'I have been offered the rental of a bungalow off Mafeking Terrace.'

His smile lit up his handsome face. 'It must be old Mrs Carey's place in Ladysmith Close. She was over eighty and passed away a couple of weeks ago – and it's the only one empty at the moment.'

Doris paused in the act of making tea. 'How do you know that?'

The smile broadened. 'I live in the same street.'

'Oh,' said Doris and tried to concentrate on making the tea.

'That wouldn't be a problem for you, would it?' he asked with concern.

'No, of course not,' she replied, silently berating herself for even thinking how nice it would be to have him as a neighbour as well as her employer. 'Empty houses are as rare as hen's teeth, and as long as it isn't in too bad a shape, then I'll grab it.'

'Quite right,' he said, accepting the cup of tea and eyeing it dubiously.

'I thought I'd pop over during my lunch break,' she said. 'Mrs Braithwaite will need an answer by tonight.'

Colonel White cleared his throat. 'Would you like me to come with you? Just to check on damp, roof tiles and guttering and such like,' he added hastily.

Doris's heart gave a little flutter which she determinedly quelled. 'That would be most helpful,' she said and took a sip from her cup. 'Good grief,' she gasped. 'I forgot to put any tea in the pot!'

Colonel White laughed. 'Let's forget the tea and go and see that bungalow. I have a feeling your mind is elsewhere at the moment, and there's nothing urgent to deal with here.'

Doris tried to keep her expectations of the bungalow in check as they left the estate and crossed the road into Mafeking Terrace, which ran in a loop along the side of the hill. Rosie had already warned her that the place was in a rather poor state, and as she'd never been up here before, the area might not be to her liking – although if the Colonel lived here, it couldn't be all that bad.

Ladysmith Close was about halfway along Mafeking Terrace, and proved to be a pleasant, tree-lined cul-de-sac dipping down the hill with bungalows on both sides, and a panoramic view of Cliffehaven and the sea. Number 18 was set back from the pavement behind a sadly neglected garden and low brick wall.

Doris stood and regarded it with a beady eye, noting how quiet it was and how pleasantly the cool breeze came up from the coast to temper the rising heat. There was a large bay window to the left of the front door which needed a good rubbing down and a fresh coat of paint, and a smaller, frosted one to the right, which she guessed was the bathroom. The walls and roof looked to be in good condition, and so did the chimney, but as Doris had no real idea of what she should be looking for, she was glad the Colonel had come with her.

'I'll scout around out here whilst you go in,' he said, heading for the side gate.

Doris nervously slotted in the key and pushed open the front door. Stepping inside, she noted the hall carpet was worn and the walls and paint-work were yellowing from either age or tobacco – it was hard to tell. There was a vague reminder of the elderly woman lingering in the air along with hints of boiled cabbage and fish – but that could easily be dealt with by opening the windows.

Doris pushed open the door to her right to discover a lavatory, washbasin and bath which had clearly been put in fairly recently, for it was in good condition, and then went into the front room. It was flooded with light and looked over the town towards the sea – reminding her forcibly of the vista she'd had in her old home, and endearing her immediately to this shabby little bungalow.

The curtains were heavy brocade and must have once been beautiful, but the glare of the sun had faded and frayed them and as she brushed her hand over them, she discovered they were full of dust. She surveyed the room. It was cluttered with aged, but good, solid furniture that had stood the test of time and still had wear in it. Every flat surface was covered in lace doilies, on which sat vases of dried flowers, trinkets and framed photographs from an era long since passed. An ornate mirror hung above the fireplace which still retained its lovely art nouveau tiles and brass fender, and there were framed embroidered pictures around the walls. The rug in front of the fire had scorch marks all over it, the parquet flooring would need sanding and repolishing, and the walls and ceiling were the same yellow as the hall. But Doris could see that despite all the clutter, it was a good-sized room, and with that lovely window it had huge potential.

She went back into the hall and explored the two bedrooms which were quite small, but perfectly adequate, and then headed for the kitchen which was at the back of the house and overlooked the garden.

Despite her age, Mrs Carey had clearly put her energies out there, for rows of beans and peas vied for space with onions, chives, dahlias and roses, and there were pots of herbs and pansies outside the back door. A sturdy fence surrounded the garden and behind it was a line of trees which shielded the bungalow from being overlooked by those in Mafeking Terrace.

The kitchen itself was very basic, with a Belfast sink, rotting wooden drainer and a couple of cupboards that had seen better days. The floor was tiled, but it was so grubby Doris couldn't see what colour it was. A small wooden table and two chairs had been crammed in a corner, and pots and pans hung from hooks above the tiny black range which needed a good clean.

Doris gave a deep sigh of longing for her modern kitchen with all its new appliances. She was going to find it hard to adapt, but then beggars couldn't be choosers, and with a bit of thought and a lot of elbow grease, she'd soon have this place in order.

Her thoughts were broken by the Colonel tapping on the window, and she unlocked the back door to let him in.

'It all seems to be fine structurally,' he said, stepping into the kitchen. 'The guttering and drains are clear, there's a damp course of sorts, and the brickwork has been recently pointed.' He glanced around the kitchen. 'It does look rather tired and in need of some attention in here, though, doesn't it?'

'The whole place is tired,' she replied, 'and it will take a good deal of work to get it to feel like home.' She smiled at him. 'But strangely enough, I can imagine myself living here.'

He smiled back. 'Jolly good,' he murmured.

She followed him as he inspected the other rooms, and when they'd seen enough, she locked the door behind them and pocketed the key. 'We'd better get back to the office,' she said. 'Half the day's gone already.'

'Would you think it a liberty if I was to ask you to have a look around my place? Only I thought it might give you some idea of how yours might be once the work is done.'

Doris dithered, which was most unlike her – but curiosity overrode propriety. 'I should like that very much.'

'Jolly good,' he said, shooting her a hesitant smile before turning into the next-door garden.

Doris was rather startled that he actually lived next door, but she followed him up the path, noting the neatly cut lawn, the fresh paintwork and gleaming windows. Stepping into the hall, she followed him through the sparsely furnished and painfully tidy rooms until they reached the kitchen.

The brass taps gleamed above a pristine Belfast sink, the draining boards were pale and smooth from being regularly scrubbed, and burnished copper-bottomed pots and pans were lined up like soldiers on the shelf above the modern gas cooker. The cupboards had been painted white and the red and blue tiles on the floor were spotless. She admired it all, thinking privately that the Colonel might have left the army, but old army habits clearly lived on.

'I have rather a lot of time on my hands now I live alone,' he said shyly. 'But it means I can tinker about decorating and seeing to both mine and Mrs Carey's garden, which I rather enjoy.'

Doris looked from the pristine kitchen into the back garden, which had been turned into a flourishing vegetable patch with a freshly creosoted shed tucked into one corner. 'You certainly put my housekeeping and gardening skills to shame,' she replied lightly to cover her embarrassment at how easily he'd read her mind. 'If we're to be neighbours, I shall have to look to my laurels.'

'I'm sure not,' he replied, 'and if we are to be neighbours, then perhaps we can be less formal out of the office. My name's John.'

Doris felt the heat slowly rising up her neck and into her face as their eyes met. 'Mine's Doris,' she managed.

'Well, Doris, I think we have something to

celebrate, don't you? How do you feel about me taking you to the Officers' Club this evening for drinks and dinner?'

Her blush deepening, Doris didn't dare look at him. 'That sounds very pleasant,' she replied.

He tugged at his jacket, rubbed his hands together and then dug them in his trouser pockets as if he wasn't quite sure what to do with them. 'Jolly good show.'

Peggy slowly made her way home with the two little girls who were tired after their busy day in the crèche, and inclined to grizzle and whine at having to walk. Rachel Goldman had done her best to find a pushchair big enough for them both, but they were so few and far between, it had been a hopeless task.

Queenie was preening on the garden wall as they approached, and quickly dashed off at the sight of the children. One she could tolerate; two was above and beyond her patience. As Peggy reached the gate the girls spotted Ron and Harvey in the garden, and with all grizzling forgotten and a rush of energy they pelted down the path to greet them.

Peggy was about to warn them not to hug the dog, but Ron was already warding them off, quietly reminding them how to pet Harvey without hurting him.

Harvey was clearly feeling very sorry for himself and embarrassed by the cone round his neck, the tight bandage around his middle and the leash fastened to his collar. He stood there looking the picture of misery as the children fussed him and Ron kept a tight hold of the lead.

'Is that really necessary?' Peggy asked. 'The poor boy's already feeling foolish, and you know how he hates being on a lead.'

'To be sure, if I don't have it, he'll be off and busting his stitches,' Ron muttered. 'He's already tried to make a break for it today, and I'll not be risking losing him again.'

'He's probably after the rats in the bomb site,' she said.

'They'll not be there for much longer,' Ron said. 'I put poison down that hole and covered it up good and tight so no other animal can get down there.' He tugged Harvey's lead. 'That's enough petting for now,' he told the girls. 'It's teatime and Harvey's hungry.' He looked across at Peggy. 'There's a letter for you from Jim,' he said, almost as an afterthought.

'Then why didn't you say earlier?' She raced up the concrete steps into the kitchen, and with barely a nod to the others, snatched the letter from the table and dashed upstairs to read it in peace.

Sealing into the chair, she found her fingers were trembling as she tore it open. The thin pages of the air letter slid from the envelope and a small black and white photograph fell into her lap.

She gazed at it, hardly daring to believe how handsome, fit and tanned Jim looked – all bare-chested and muscled in just shorts as he stood on a sunlit veranda surrounded by palm trees. He didn't appear to be injured at all, she thought in wonder – and in fact looked supremely fit.

She kissed the photograph and eagerly began to read.

My darling Peggy,

I know how anxious you must have been, but as you can see by the photo, I'm fine. I can only hope that the nurse's letter arrived before the telegram, and that it has gone some way to easing your worry. It was only because I managed to persuade the padre to convince my commanding officer not to send anything until I was safely in hospital that the telegram was delayed by about three weeks.

You know me, Peg, the gift of the blarney rarely lets me down and gets me out of all sorts of scrapes, and it's thankful I am that the padre is an Irishman and it didn't fail either of us this time.

Now, I realise that three weeks sounds like a long time to you, but I was completely out of it and barely noticed where I was or what was going on. You see, we were having a bit of trouble with the Japs and our planes couldn't come in, so I stayed in the field hospital until I could be air lifted out which evidently took those three weeks. The surgeon in the field hospital was terrific and got me sorted very quickly because my wound wasn't that serious, but with all the muck and bullets flying about, I got an infection – which was lucky really, because it meant I was on the first plane out of there.

So here I am, back where this madness all started, and being looked after like one of those maharajahs, with hot and cold running water, gorgeous Australian nurses and lots of peace and quiet – which is a blessing after the awful racket I've had to put up with lately.

The hospital's quite big, and there's a long veranda at the back overlooking a lush tropical garden which runs down to a sandy beach and swift flowing river. It's lovely sitting out there with a cup of tea or a cold beer, enjoying the sun, dozing off, or playing a hand or two of cards. Once I'm properly up and about again, I'm going in that river, it looks very inviting – and I'll also have a go at croquet! Did you ever imagine, Peg, that I would ever write that line? Some of the chaps are awfully good at it, and I'm longing to give it a go. I'm sure I'll pick it up in no time.

The chaps here are a good bunch, and I count myself lucky that I got off so lightly, which is more than I can say for Ernie. Poor blighter got it bad, and I feel terrible because it was all my stupid fault. I can't tell you what happened, the censors would cut it out anyway, needless to say his war's over and he'll be on his way home soon. As far as I know, Big Bert is still causing the enemy mayhem and putting himself right in the middle of things. He's what the Aussies call a 'bonzer bloke', but it strikes me he's either leading a charmed life or is invincible.

I'm sorry I got wounded and caused you to fret, but please don't shed any tears for me. I'll be right as ninepence very soon, and am having a high old time here. The nurses are great fun and don't mind mucking in with a game of cards or Ludo, and they don't get all hot under the collar if a chap swears or tells a dirty joke. I've met a lot of Aussies during my time away, and now I've met some of their women I can see why they're such a cheerful, sunny bunch. Perhaps after all this is over we should go out there and see what life could be like for us? I hear it's sunny most of the time and you can grow oranges in your back garden! How about that?

I'll write again very soon. Give my love to every-

one, kiss Daisy for me and tell Da to hurry up and propose to Rosie. I just know you're itching to dust down your wedding hat – and by the sound of it from your letters, there will one or two chances to wear it before long. I just wish I could be there to share it all with you. But things are changing, and that day is coming nearer. I send you a kiss and a prayer that the sun will soon break through these dark clouds and we can very soon be together again.

Jim. x

Peggy held the letter to her heart, thankful that he was somewhere safe and getting better. She refused to let the thought of him being returned his regiment cast a shadow on her happiness, and silently vowed to remain positive from now on.

Running back downstairs, she handed the letter to Ron to read and helped supervise the children who were squabbling over a picture book. 'Where's Doris?' she asked. 'She's usually home by now.'

'She's getting changed,' said Ivy. 'The Colonel's taking her out for dinner,' she added with a knowing wink.

'Goodness,' breathed Peggy. 'Things are hotting up.'

'I'd appreciate it if you didn't jump to conclusions,' said Doris from the doorway. 'The Colonel has kindly asked me to dinner because I have something to celebrate.'

Peggy admired the neat black dress, fake pearls and dinky concoction of black net and feathers perched on Doris's carefully brushed hair. 'It must be very special for you to have made such an

effort,' she said. 'I must say, you do look marvellous,' she added, noting the heightened colour in
her sister's face and the happy gleam in her eyes.

'Thank you,' she replied. 'It's amazing what one
can find at jumble sales these days.'

'Well, don't keep us in suspense, for goodness'
sake,' said Ivy. 'What's going on?'

Doris told them about Rosie's bungalow, and
then turned to Peggy. 'I do hope you don't mind,
Peggy, but I signed the lease before coming home
this evening, and once the work has been done on
it, I shall be moving in before the end of August.'

'Oh, my dear, of course I don't mind,' said
Peggy truthfully. 'We both knew this wasn't per-
manent, and I'm delighted Rosie took my advice
and offered it to you.'

'Oh,' said Doris. 'I hadn't realised you'd discussed it with her first.'

'She simply asked me if I thought you might
want it,' said Peggy. 'We didn't discuss your business, if that's what you're worried about.'

'No, of course not,' said Doris, clearly not truly
convinced.

'It'll take a bit to get the place straight,' said
Ron, breaking the short, tense silence. 'I'm
thinking I'll be busy for the next few weeks with
painting and such-like.'

'We'll all help,' said Ivy enthusiastically.

'Of course we will,' said Peggy. 'It's what we did
with Cordelia's place in Mafeking Terrace before
Ruby and Ethel moved in, and with so many willing hands it won't take long at all.' She reached
for Doris's hand. 'That's not to say we're in a
hurry to get rid of you,' she said, 'but a chance

like this doesn't come along often, and I know you'll settle in there very happily.'

'I'll miss not 'aving you around,' said Ivy. 'But it's near enough to the factory for me to pop in for a cuppa now and again.' She looked at Doris with a sly smile. 'The Colonel lives up that way too, don't 'e? So that'll be cosy.'

Doris blushed. 'Do try to keep your mind out of the gutter, Ivy,' she said mildly.

'What about furniture?' asked Peggy. 'I can spare a bed and perhaps a couple of bits, but–'

'I'm keeping some of Mrs Carey's furniture,' said Doris, 'but I would appreciate a bed. Mrs Carey died in hers, and the thought of it would keep me awake.'

'I bet that wouldn't be the only thing keeping you awake if the Colonel's feeling frisky,' muttered Ivy, shooting her a wicked grin.

Doris glared at her and, without a word, left the house, her face burning.

Peggy gave Ivy a light tap on her hand. 'Naughty girl,' she reproached softly. 'Poor Doris deserves a bit of fun after all she's been through, and you shouldn't tease her.'

'Yeah, I know, but she don't mind a bit of leg-pulling,' replied Ivy without a glimmer of regret.

Peggy was about to say that Doris was far more fragile than she let on when the telephone rang. She went to answer it, and after a bit of static, Gracie's voice echoed down the line.

'Hello, Peggy. I can't talk for long as I don't have a lot of change, but I wanted to know how Chloe is and how you're managing.'

'Chloe is absolutely fine,' she replied firmly,

'and so am I. What about you? How are things in Dover?'

There was a short silence and then what sounded like a sob. 'He's refusing to see me,' Gracie said brokenly. 'And it's all my fault, Peg.'

'I don't see how that can be,' she replied, her heart going out to her friend.

'They warned me he wouldn't look the same – that the burns ... that it was important I didn't show any reaction.' Her voice faltered as she fought her sobs. 'I tried, Peggy, I really did, but ... but it was such a shock to see him like that, I simply couldn't hide it. His face ... his lovely face...' She broke into wracking sobs.

Peggy gripped the receiver as graphic images flashed in her mind. She'd never met Clive, but had seen his photograph and so knew he'd been a handsome man, and the horror of what had happened to him was just too awful to contemplate. She yearned to be able to console Gracie, but couldn't begin to think how that was possible.

'Oh, Gracie,' she murmured. 'I'm so, so sorry.'

'Clive has yet to see the extent of his injuries,' she managed through her tears. 'But when I failed to hide my shock, he shouted at me to go away and not come back, and I'm ashamed to say I fled. But I went back the next morning, determined to stay by his side regardless of the fact I could hardly bear to look at him.'

She took a shuddering breath. 'You see, I knew he was frightened, terribly frightened, and I wanted him to know that we would see through his recovery together.'

'That was brave,' murmured Peggy.

There was a pause as Gracie slotted some more coins into the public phone. 'Not really,' she continued, 'because I let him down so very badly. He looked straight at me with his one good eye and demanded that I kiss him – on what's left of his lips. And I couldn't, Peggy. I just couldn't,' she wailed.

Peggy closed her eyes, imagining the awful scene – understanding Clive's need to be treated as normal and poor Gracie's inability to do so. 'It will get easier in time,' she said, hearing the trite-ness of her words even as she spoke them. 'You'll both get used to what's happened and once–'

'Maybe,' Gracie replied, calmer now. 'But I'm doing no good here. Clive refuses to see me and the doctor suggested I stay away for a while until he's come to terms with things. Seeing me has upset him dreadfully, and if he's to recover, then he needs peace and quiet and to be with other men who are going through the same thing.'

She gave a tremulous sigh. 'I'll be home some-time late tomorrow. If you could keep Chloe for one more night, I would be grateful.'

'I'll keep her for as long as you like,' said Peggy as the pips went. 'You'll need a bit of time to yourself to recover from it all and–'

The line went dead. Peggy replaced the receiver and sat for a while in the hall, thinking how very lucky she was not to be walking in Gracie's shoes. She took a deep breath, offered up a silent prayer to keep Jim safe, and went back to the light and warmth of her kitchen.

Cordelia was reading the children a story before

they had the nightly treat of being carried up-stairs on the chairlift.

Ron listened as Peggy quietly summarised the call from Gracie. He shared her concern for both of them and knew Peggy would do all she could to support her friend during this terrible time, but the real battle would be going on inside Gracie's head and heart – and because she was made of strong stuff, he suspected she'd soon go back to Dover.

This war had damaged so many young lives, and he was relieved and thankful his son hadn't shared the same fate as Clive and was on the mend. However, the cheerfulness of Jim's letter didn't really ring true, and he seemed a bit too anxious to allay their fears. Ron wondered if Jim really had got off as lightly as he'd professed. He looked all right in the photograph, but the camera could lie, and no one could see what was going on in his mind.

Ron's own experience of war taught him that Ernie's injuries would be preying on Jim, especially as he blamed himself for what had happened – although how that had come about was a mystery. Ron could only hope that Jim's worry over Ernie wouldn't delay his recovery.

He returned the letter and photograph to its envelope and, although he wasn't particularly hungry, made a concerted effort to eat the tinned corned beef and garden salad, which had been served with a couple of the tiny new potatoes he'd dug up earlier.

'So, Ron, what are your plans for tonight?' asked Peggy.

'Fred the Fish finally managed to get me a

couple of kippers, so I'm taking them up to Chalky White's. If I've time, I'll pop in and see Rosie after, but I've warned her I might not make it,' he added. 'Old Chalky can talk the hind legs off a donkey, so he can, and I could be stuck there for hours.'

'The poor man probably gets lonely, with his wife going off to her sister's all the time,' Peggy commented.

'I doubt that,' muttered Ron. 'She's always at him for one thing or another, and I'm thinking he likes the peace and quiet.'

He pushed back from the table, washed his empty plate, and then regarded his sad-eyed dog with some sympathy. 'You'll be staying put, ye heathen beast,' he said, fondling the dog's ears. 'It's a long walk, and you're not ready for that yet.'

The telephone rang just as he was about to fetch the paper-wrapped kippers from the larder. 'I'll get it,' he rumbled, stomping off into the hall.

'Hello?'

'Hello, Ron,' said Rosie with a slight edge to her voice. 'I was wondering if you could pop in? Only something's cropped up and needs seeing to with some urgency.'

'It's not the plumbing again, is it?' he asked warily. He hated plumbing.

'Oh no, it's something far more important than that. And it might take some time to fix, so per-haps you should forget the kippers tonight.'

Ron had visions of a flooded cellar, burst pipe or another soot fall. 'What the devil has hap-pened, Rosie?'

'You'll find out when you get here,' she said and

disconnected the call.

Ron frowned as he replaced the receiver. Rosie certainly sounded anxious about something, and he couldn't very well ignore her plea for help – but kippers wouldn't keep either.

He went back into the kitchen and pulled on his jacket and cap. 'Rosie's got some problem at the Anchor she needs sorting, but those kippers need to get to Chalky before they go off.' He looked at Rita who was sharing a copy of the *Picture Post* with Ivy. 'I don't suppose you could take them up on your bike?'

She set the magazine aside. 'Of course I will,' she replied before turning to Ivy. 'Fancy a ride up there, and then a pint at the Woodman's Arms for a change?'

'Yeah, why not? Andy's on duty and I ain't got nothing else to do.'

Ron nodded his thanks, dragged on his jacket and cap and left the house. Less than a minute later the girls passed him on the speeding motorbike. His smile was wry as he watched them disappear around the corner. He understood Rita's youthful appetite for speed, and she could handle that bike expertly, but if Chalky offered them any of his lethal parsnip wine, they'd find the journey home an entirely different kettle of fish.

Double summer-time was still in force, which made the evenings much lighter for longer, so Rosie had yet to pull the blackout curtains. He peered in through the heavily taped windows to the bar and saw that Brenda was again in charge, with no sign of Rosie. Monty was sprawled before the empty inglenook and all seemed calm and normal enough, so why the urgent summons?

He stepped down into the bar and headed straight for Brenda. 'What's happened? Rosie said it was urgent.'

'Oh, it is,' said Brenda with what looked suspiciously like a knowing gleam in her eye. 'She's upstairs.'

Ron frowned and hurried into the hall. Taking the stairs two at a time, he found the sitting room door was closed, which was most unusual. He opened the door and found the room deserted and in darkness but for the soft glow from a table lamp. 'Rosie? Where are you? What's going on?'

'I need you in here, Ron,' she called back. 'Please hurry.'

He couldn't imagine what might be wrong as he hurried towards the sound of her voice. And then he came to an abrupt halt outside her open bedroom door.

Rosie was resting against a mass of pillows, the soft glow of many candles gleaming on her tanned shoulders and long, slender legs. She wore nothing but a very skimpy silk petticoat and a seductive smile. 'I'm in urgent need of some proper loving,' she murmured, her blue eyes hazy with lust.

Ron could barely breathe as his eyes feasted on her. 'To be sure, darling girl, I'm the man for that,' he managed.

Rosie lifted her arms to him. 'Then what are you waiting for?'

He kicked the door shut, threw off his jacket and cap and tenderly gathered her to him.

20

Calcutta

Jim kicked off the sheet that was soaked in his sweat. He was burning up despite the ceiling fans whirring above his bed, and his head felt as if it was stuffed with burning embers that might explode at any minute. The view from the window was a blur, the vivid colours swirling into one another at giddying speed as the merciless sun glared and the voices of those around him became muffled and incomprehensible. The fever was returning and would soon overwhelm him.

In the lucid moments between these bouts, he realised he was safe and far from battle, but when the fever raged the nightmares came to haunt him, and as his wasted body shook and burned he once again heard the endless booms of the guns – saw the enemy faces looming like ghouls at him from the jungle – and felt the anguish and gnawing guilt of what he'd done to Ernie.

He turned his head towards the shadow that fell across him and saw it was Staff Nurse Fitz-patrick – his very own angel of mercy who'd come to help him through. 'You sent the letter to Peg?' he managed through chattering teeth.

'It went three weeks ago,' she replied softly. 'Don't you remember?'

He did have a vague memory of being able to

write the letter full of false cheerfulness, but it had taken an age because his wound was very painful and his hand had been shaking with the onset of the returning infection. 'And the photo? You found the photo?'

She squeezed cold water out of a flannel and pressed it against his forehead. 'It was in your kitbag.' She replaced the flannel with another and began to wash his chest and arms.

Jim fought against the deep shivers that were making him shudder, determined to focus on Peggy and the subterfuge that had been so necessary. He'd had that photograph taken several months ago when he'd been sent south of here on a short leave, and because he looked fit and healthy, he'd kept meaning to send it home – but now it had become very handy because it would allay Peggy's fears and make his letter more believable.

'I'm just going to change your bed linen,' said the nurse, 'and then I'll give you your pills and something to help you sleep.'

Like a helpless child, he let her roll him back and forth, and once the fresh sheets and pillows were in place, he obediently swallowed the pills. 'To be sure,' he managed weakly, 'I'm thinking I'll never make it out of here.'

'It might feel as if you're not getting any better,' she said, filling a hypodermic, 'but the bouts of fever are lessening in power and regularity. The infection you got at the field hospital is waning – and your wound is healing well.'

Jim wasn't sure if he believed her, but the needle slipped smoothly into the scrawny flesh of his upper arm, and as the medication raced through his veins, he fell into sweet oblivion and no longer cared.

21

Peggy knew something was up when she went down to the basement in the morning to see where Ron had got to, and discovered his bed had not been slept in. She chuckled with delight at the realisation he must have stayed with Rosie – and that her urgent telephone call had had nothing to do with emergency repairs.

However, Ron's absence meant the ferrets hadn't been cleaned out, and Harvey needed his morning constitutional. With all the girls at work and only Cordelia to watch over two boisterous children, Peggy was in a bit of a bind.

She quickly shot outside to feed the chickens, and then ran up the concrete steps. 'Ron stayed out all last night,' she said excitedly to Cordelia who was calmly eating her breakfast as the little girls banged and crashed about with the wooden horse and trolley.

'Then I'd loosen them, dear,' she said. 'They'll do you no good if they're too tight.'

'What?'

'If the bones are too tight in your stays then you should undo them,' said Cordelia. 'Though why you need such a thing when you've got nothing to hold in, I don't know.'

Peggy bit down on her impatience and made winding signals to urge Cordelia to turn on her hearing aid. Time was moving on very fast and she had to be at work in less than an hour. 'I said, Ron didn't come home from Rosie's last night,' she said loudly.

Cordelia's eyebrows shot up. 'Really?'

'Yes, really,' said Peggy, grabbing hold of Daisy, who seemed determined to batter the chair legs into submission with her trolley. 'Poor Harvey must have his legs crossed, and the ferret cage stinks. Could you keep the children occupied whilst I see to them?'

'Of course, dear. But I could always take Harvey out on his lead for you.'

Peggy had visions of Harvey spying a cat, rat or rabbit and hurtling off, dragging a helpless Cordelia behind him. 'That's very kind, but I think I'd better do it.'

She turned to the girls who were now tussling over a colouring book. 'That's quite enough of that,' she said sternly. 'Sit down, the pair of you, and behave for Gan-Gan.' She slapped a second book on the table and added a handful of colouring pencils. 'Play nicely,' she ordered.

Daisy and Chloe eyed her warily before bending their heads to the task of colouring in.

Peggy snapped the lead onto Harvey's collar. 'I won't be long. If you have any trouble from either of the girls, tell them there'll be no sweeties on the way home tonight.'

With that stern threat, Peggy left the kitchen and followed Harvey as he slowly negotiated the stone steps to the basement. She breathed in the lovely fresh air of what promised to be another hot summer's day, and then strolled alongside Harvey as they went into the alleyway. It was clear the dog was still in some discomfort, but he managed to water and sniff just about every blade of grass along the way as they slowly went up the hill.

After ten minutes, Peggy decided they'd gone far enough and turned for home, only to find that Queenie had decided to follow them. 'That's all I need,' she sighed. She tugged on the lead, and Harvey sat down with a thump to wait for his feline friend.

'Come on, Harvey. I haven't got time for this,' she urged, tugging a bit harder.

It was like trying to shift a lump of concrete. Harvey was going nowhere.

Peggy's frustration was rising, but she knew it would do no good to vent it, because Queenie would only take flight and disappear, and then Harvey would try to chase after her and burst his stitches – which would mean a trip to the vet and then half the morning trying to find Queenie. So she waited and impatiently counted to twenty as the cat limped towards them, encouraged by Harvey's little whines.

Queenie flopped down between Harvey's front legs, rolled on her back and batted at the hated cone about his neck. Peggy chose her moment and grabbed her scruff. Queenie wriggled furiously, all teeth and claws, and Harvey got to his feet, his eyebrows twitching in concern.

Peggy clasped the cat to her chest, tugged on the lead and finally managed to head for home. She was not in the best of moods. When Ron did finally put in an appearance, she'd give him an earful. It was all very well for him to go courting, but he had responsibilities – as well as deep coat pockets for hissing, spitting cats, she thought crossly, flinching from a darting set of sharp claws.

The day might have started badly, but once she'd deposited the girls at the crèche and had a quick word with Solly about poor Gracie, she managed to get through the rest of it without further dramas.

On her return home she peeked through the pub windows, but there was no sign of Ron or Rosie, and all the curtains were closed upstairs. Peggy was still smiling as she followed the children up the steps into her kitchen to find there was a party going on.

It took a glance at a beaming Ron and radiant Rosie to guess what it was for – and when Rosie flashed the ruby and diamond ring on her finger, she burst into happy tears. 'Oh, Ron, Rosie,' she sobbed. 'I'm so happy for you.'

They encompassed her in an embrace. 'He actually got down on one knee,' Rosie confided in a whisper. 'And he looked so utterly adorable without any clothes on, I could hardly refuse.'

Peggy's eyes widened at the comical image this elicited and the tears turned to laughter. 'He proposed in the nude?' she spluttered.

Rosie giggled and blushed. 'You know Ron. He's never been conventional.'

'Ach, conventional is boring,' muttered Ron who'd gone rather pink around the ears. 'And I'll be asking you not to give all our secrets away,

Rosie, me darlin' girl.'

'So, when's the wedding?' breathed Peggy as the chatter gathered volume and bottles of beer were passed around.

'We thought we'd wait a bit,' said Rosie. 'Ron would like Jim to be there, and we have a lot of decisions to make about where we'll live if we decide to sell the pub.'

'Sell the Anchor?' Peggy gasped.

Rosie shrugged. 'It's given me a good living, but the hours are long, and I want to spend my time with Ron – not a bar full of strangers.' She twisted the ring on her finger, then laughed and tossed back her platinum curls. 'We're getting too serious about things, Peggy. This is supposed to be a party. Stan, Fred, Chalky and Alf will be here soon with their wives, and Frank's coming over with Pauline later.'

'Lawks,' Peggy yelped. 'I can't feed and water that lot.'

'You don't have to,' said Ron. 'The drinks are already here courtesy of Rosie, and the extra food will be coming with the others.' He waggled his eyebrows at Peggy and grinned like a small boy who'd been given free rein in a sweet shop. 'So have a beer, light up a fag and join in.'

As more and more people arrived, the party moved into the dining room, and went on until the early hours of the morning. Consequently there were a lot of sore heads the next day, but everyone agreed with Ron that he was a very lucky man – and Peggy forgot to tell him off about having to deal with his animals.

Gracie came back to Cliffehaven looking forlorn, the trauma of what she'd been through over the past few days written in her pale face and haunted eyes. Peggy offered support and solace over the next ten days as she watched her put on a smile for little Chloe and knuckle back down to work, but she knew her friend was tortured with guilt because she hadn't been able to find the courage to face Clive's devastating and life-changing injuries.

Solly knew that neither Peggy nor Gracie could afford long-distance calls to the Dover hospital, so had insisted she use the office telephone. However, Clive was still refusing to let Gracie visit him and the doctors advised her to stay away until he'd come to terms with things more. As time went on these calls upset Gracie to the point where she started making expensive mistakes on the cutting table and forgot simple things like food shopping and brushing her hair.

Peggy knew this state of affairs couldn't go on for much longer, and it was almost a relief when Gracie came to Beach View to tell her she'd handed in her notice and was moving to Dover.

'But how will you manage with Chloe on your own?' Peggy asked as they sat in the dining room away from the bustle in the kitchen.

'I had a long talk with Mother, and she'll stay with me in Dover for a while and then take Chloe back with her.' Her smile was wan. 'I totally misjudged her, Peggy. She's proved to be an absolute brick, and instead of the histrionics I was expecting, she's been calm, supportive and practical.'

'I expect she's just glad to be able to help,' said

Peggy. 'But what if Clive continues to send you away?'

'I'll go anyway,' Gracie said purposefully. 'And I'll keep on going until he realises he's stuck with me.' She twisted the handkerchief between her fingers. 'It won't be easy for either of us to come to terms with what's happened, but as long as we're both very brave, we'll get through this.'

Peggy was in awe of her determination in the light of so many and varied obstacles. She reached for her hand. 'Of course you will,' she murmured.

'We'll be leaving early tomorrow, Peggy, so I'm afraid this has to be goodbye.'

'So soon?' gasped Peggy.

'It's been two weeks since I last saw Clive, and I need to go to him.' She grasped Peggy's hand, her lovely eyes bright with tears. 'I've treasured your friendship, Peggy, and will never forget all your kindnesses. Cliffehaven became my home and I've been happy here, but my heart is with Clive and that's where I belong.'

'I shall miss you,' said Peggy as they embraced. 'Promise you'll write when you can to let me know how things are progressing.'

'Of course I will.' Gracie eased from the embrace and smiled through her tears. 'I'd better go. Rachel's minding Chloe, and I still have some packing to do.' She kissed Peggy's cheek, gave her a hug and then swiftly turned away.

Peggy followed her to the front door and watched as she ran down the steps in the dwindling light of that late July evening. Gracie turned and waved on the corner of Camden Road, but before Peggy could wave back she'd broken into a run and disappeared into the gloom.

Peggy closed the door and leaned on it, her heart heavy with sadness. She would miss Gracie terribly, and little Daisy would miss Chloe too, for they'd both become part of the family and would leave a large void in their lives.

Peggy gave a deep sigh. There had been so many goodbyes over these war years that she'd almost lost count, but as she stood there in the quiet hall, their faces paraded before her. Jim in his uniform, Anne with baby Rose Margaret, Bob and Charlie, and Cissy all excited and glamorous in her WAAF's uniform.

And then there was little Sally, her first evacuee, who'd married John Hicks the Cliffehaven fire chief and was now in Somerset with their little boy and her young brother. Polly Brown was in Scotland with her husband and the little girl they'd thought they'd lost when the evacuee ship had been sunk; and Julie Harris had returned to nurse in London and was now in Wales courting baby William's father. Mary Jones had married her childhood sweetheart and was expecting a honeymoon baby. Her other evacuees, Ruby and April, still lived in Cliffehaven, but they both had busy lives and didn't always have the time to drop in for a cuppa and a chat, but at least she could see them now and again.

Peggy took a restorative breath and went to turn off the dining room light. The dark war years had brought uncertainty and many anguished tears, but they had also brought laughter, love and life to this old house, and that was what she must hold onto now.

There was once again an expectant air in Cliffe-haven, for as the end of July saw the Americans break out to the west of Saint-Lo and take Coutances, the Russians took Brest-Litovsk in Belarus. At the beginning of August a great uprising against the German occupiers in Warsaw was initiated by the Polish Home Army; the Americans reached Avranches and were met by a strong German resistance that everyone believed would be defeated and the Allies invaded southern France.

Towards the middle of August a Russian offensive started in the Balkans with an attack on Romania – and as the Canadians, Poles and Americans encircled the Germans in the Falaise pocket and more Allied troops approached Paris, the French Resistance began an uprising in support.

'Paris will fall any minute, I'm certain of it, despite the news blackout,' said Peggy. She reached up to finish hanging the freshly washed curtains in Doris's new bedroom. 'I just wish Charlotte would hurry up and have those babies.'

Kitty grinned. 'She's very fed up and I can't say I blame her now the doctor's ordered her to stay in bed. But he has promised he'll start things off if it doesn't happen in the next twenty-four hours.' She smoothed the eiderdown over the bed and plumped the pillows.

Peggy tweaked the curtains until they fell satis-factorily into neat folds and then looked through the bungalow's window at baby Faith who was gurgling happily in her pram and waving her tiny brown arms and legs in the warm sunshine. 'That would be a relief all round,' she murmured.

They left the bedroom and went into the kitchen to make a cup of tea and listen to the lunchtime news on the small wireless Ron had managed to get from somewhere – no questions asked. There had been a news blackout for the past week as far as the American advance on Paris was concerned, and everyone was in a lather to know what was happening.

The kitchen had been transformed – mostly through the efforts of Colonel White, who'd shown a remarkable aptitude for woodwork and seeking out bargains. In fact he'd approached the project with huge enthusiasm and had built new cupboards and draining boards, brought the sink back to its previous pristine white, replaced the taps and wall tiles, and even managed to find a reasonably new electric stove which now stood in the chimney breast – the ancient range having been carted off for scrap iron.

Doris had sewn blue and white gingham curtains for the windows and over the new shelves under the sink, and had had enough material left over to make a tablecloth, a set of napkins, and even covers for the seat pads on the newly varnished chairs. The floor tiles had been scrubbed clean to reveal a pretty pattern of blue and red, and Sarah had found a lovely vase of deep red in a jumble sale which now sat on the windowsill filled with roses from the garden.

The whole bungalow looked very different to how it had been when Peggy had first been shown around, and she felt a deep sense of satisfaction that her sister would live here in comfort.

Ron had enlisted the help of his old pals, Chalky, Stan, Fred the Fish and Alf the butcher, and together they'd sanded, painted and repaired. Peggy, Kitty and everyone from Beach View had done their bit, scrubbing, dusting, washing curtains and the treasure trove of lovely linen they'd found in a cupboard.

The old carpets and rugs had been taken up and burned, the unwanted furniture had been given to the WVS, and the knick-knacks and doilies donated to a fundraising jumble sale. The parquet flooring now gleamed, the bathroom was pristine, and when Doris came from work tonight, she'd find a real home all ready for her to move into.

'It's funny,' sighed Peggy as she poured the tea and waited for the wireless to warm up, 'but I shall miss having her around.'

'I bet you never thought you'd say that,' teased Kitty.

Peggy smiled. 'It's true, but then Doris has changed so radically since she's been forced to stand on her own two feet that I can't help but admire her. She even had the nerve to tell that snooty woman from the WVS where she could stick her demands for help.'

The newscaster's voice startled them as it suddenly came through loud and clear.

'Paris is liberated as the Germans surrender,' he began. 'After four years under German occupation, Paris is now free.'

Peggy and Kitty clasped their hands in silent delight and relief.

'Last night, the French 2nd Armoured Division under General Philippe Leclerc was the first Allied force to enter the city, greeted by loud cheers from Parisians after many days of fighting between the Resistance and the German occupiers.

'The new Free French wireless station reported the German commander of the Paris region, General Dietrich von Choltitz, signed the surrender at Montparnasse station in front of General Leclerc and Colonel Rol, commander of the Forces Françaises de l'Intérieur (FFI) in the Paris region.

'Colonel Rol praised the Resistance forces that fought the occupying Germans and opened the way for the Allies to enter the capital.

'At 1900 local time, General Charles de Gaulle – leader of the Free French who has been living in exile in London since the Fall of France in 1940 – entered the city.

'In a broadcast to the nation from the Hôtel de Ville he said: "I wish simply from the bottom of my heart to say to you: Vive Paris! We are here in Paris – Paris which stood erect and rose in order to free herself. Paris oppressed, downtrodden and martyred but still Paris – free now, freed by the hands of Frenchmen, the capital of Fighting France, France the great eternal."

'He said the French could now stand up as a great world power and would not rest until the enemy had been defeated on its own territory.

'Last evening French, American and Senegalese troops marched triumphantly down the Champs Elysées to ecstatic cheers of Parisians, young and old. But celebrations were brought to a swift halt by sniper fire from German troops and French Fascists. The battle for Paris is not quite over and as the French 2nd Armoured Division reached the Porte d'Orléans district in the south of Paris, the FFI are still fighting German soldiers and taking prisoners.

'Earlier today, Canadian and British forces joined up with American troops on the left bank of the River Seine south of Rouen. And on the French coast, Honfleur has been captured by the Allies. In the south of France, Americans have taken Cannes and Grasse, the capital of the Alpes-Maritimes.

'There will be a more detailed account of the background to the liberation of Paris in our nine o'clock bulletin.'

Peggy switched off the wireless and they turned to one another with beaming smiles. 'We're finally winning,' breathed Kitty.

'We have Paris and Rome. It'll be Berlin next,' said Peggy, clapping her hands.

'I think that could take a bit longer,' Kitty warned, 'but it will happen, Peggy. We've got the Nazis on the run.' She finished her tea and looked at her watch. 'I'd better get home to Charlotte. She's probably going quite mad with boredom now our wireless is on the blink, and this news will perk her up no end.'

They went out into the back garden which had been tidied, weeded and mulched by Colonel White and Stan from the station and was now as colourful and neat as Havelock Gardens used to be. They hugged and Peggy held the side gate open so Kitty could wheel the pram through.

'I'll ring the minute I have any news on Charlotte,' Kitty promised before heading for home, which was only a few streets away.

Peggy had nipped up here whilst Sarah and Fran were looking after Daisy, and she should be getting home, but as she breathed in the warm, scented air of summer and watched the sunlight wink and blink through the leafy trees, she decided to linger just a moment more.

She gazed down on the town that had been her home all her life, and then out to sea towards the distant shores of France. The fighting was still going on across Europe, but port by port, and city by city, the Allies were on a victorious march – and with Hitler losing his grip, it could only be a matter of time before the Allies took Berlin and it would all be over.

She returned to the bungalow, washed the cups and put them away, before setting the table and checking she'd put the note on top of the Woolton pie she'd brought from home. All Doris had to do was heat it through, and Peggy had deliberately made enough so that if the Colonel popped in – which she very much hoped he would – they could share it.

With a soft smile, she left the spare key on the table and closed the front door behind her. Romance was most definitely in the air. Rosie was wearing Ron's engagement ring, the Colonel and Doris were warming up nicely, and Fran had confided in her last night that she and Robert were planning their wedding despite her parents' objections.

22

Doris dropped that morning's post in the letter box and hurried through the factory gates. John White had seemed to understand her need to be alone to enjoy those first precious moments in her new home, and had not offered to accompany her, but promised to call in later to see if she needed anything.

She smiled as she crossed the road into Mafeking Terrace. The Colonel was a dear man, so thoughtful and kind, and generous with his time too as he'd helped refurbish the kitchen. The thought of how everyone at Beach View had willingly mucked in warmed her, for she hadn't expected such genuine delight in being able to help.

The memories of Cordelia vigorously polishing the furniture whilst she sang discordantly along with *Workers' Playtime* on the wireless, and Rosie not looking at all glamorous for once in an apron, headscarf and rubber gloves scrubbing the kitchen floor broadened her smile. Peggy had been right all along – they were good people, and she felt quite overcome by shame at how she'd once looked down on them.

She stood at the turning into Ladysmith Close, and gazed at the view of Cliffehaven sprawled between the hill and the sea. The trees were in full leaf, the shadows beneath them dappled by the sun, and she could hear the distant cries of the gulls as they rode the warm air above the rooftops.

Her gaze was drawn inevitably towards the ugly void beyond Havelock Gardens where her house had once been, and she firmly looked away. This was not a day for regrets or for looking back on what might have been. It was a day to celebrate, for not only was the war one day closer to ending with the fall of Paris, but her lovely new home was awaiting her.

She walked along the quiet, somnolent street and down the path to her front door. Slotting in the key, she stepped inside, and the tiny bungalow – so very different to the grand detached house in Havelock Road – seemed to embrace and welcome her. The scent of roses, furniture polish and fresh paint greeted her, and as she regarded the gleaming parquet flooring and wandered slowly from room to lovely room, she knew how blessed she was to have this chance to begin again.

Going into the kitchen, she still found it hard to believe this had once been dark, dank, dirty and dilapidated, for now it shone and was as neat as a pin with roses in a vase and the small table set for two with glasses, a bottle of wine, a single rose in a glass tumbler, and the cloth and napkins she'd made.

She wasn't quite sure why it had been set out in such a romantic way until she spotted the enormous Woolton pie on the hob, read Peggy's note and chuckled. 'You just can't help trying to matchmake, can you?' she murmured with affection.

Having put the pie in the oven on a low heat, she opened the back door to find a table and wooden bench had been placed beneath the kitchen window, where a trellis of clambering yellow roses scented the air and pots of sweet-smelling, aromatic herbs had been gathered to make it a cosy nook. At the centre of the table was a terracotta pot brimming over with bright red and orange nasturtiums.

Doris rarely cried; in fact she was quite proud of her ability to mask her emotions – but now there were tears in her eyes as she regarded this loving addition to her garden and wondered who could have gone to so much trouble.

She left the door open so the warm, scented air could drift through the bungalow and went into the main bedroom to find that Peggy and Kitty had been busy making the bed and putting up the curtains. With a deep sigh of pleasure she began to unpack her few belongings.

The knock on the front door startled her, for she'd been lost in her thoughts as she'd settled in, and she was quite shocked to find that almost two hours had passed since she'd left the office. She opened the door to find John White standing there armed with an enormous bunch of colourful dahlias and a shy smile.

'I hope I'm not intruding,' he said, whipping off his hat. 'But I wanted to check that you're settling in all right, and give you these.'

'I'm settling in very well, thank you,' she said, equally bashful, taking the flowers. 'And these are really lovely.'

'Jolly good,' he replied, twisting his hat in his hands. 'Well, I'll leave you to it then.'

'Have you had supper yet?' she asked before she thought about it.

'Well, no,' he said hesitantly.

She was being very forward, but she'd taken things too far to back down now – besides, she enjoyed his company. 'Then why don't you join me? My sister left an enormous Woolton pie, and with so much to celebrate today, it would be a pity not to share it.'

'That would be most pleasant,' he replied, the colour rising in his face. 'I'll fetch a bottle of wine from home to go with it.'

Doris laughed. 'There's no need. My sister thought of that too.'

He stepped into the hall and closed the door behind him. 'Jolly good show,' he murmured, admiring her neat figure and very shapely legs as she led the way to the kitchen.

Danuta tucked the bulky parcel under her arm, dug her hands into the pockets of her loose cotton trousers and slowly walked home to Beach View, revelling in the warmth of the lovely day, the knowledge that the Nazis had been ousted from Paris, and the secret she could now tell everyone. She had kept it to herself for weeks, and although she hadn't liked being evasive about her frequent disappearances from home, it had been important to her to deal with it on her own until she was absolutely certain of the outcome.

She cheerfully acknowledged the greetings of the women she'd come to know during the long hours of waiting in the queues for Peggy's shopping, and stopped to chat for a moment to Mrs Goldman who'd taken a special interest in her once she'd discovered she was also from Poland.

Danuta liked and admired Rachel Goldman and her husband, for they quietly went about their tireless charity work without any fanfare, and were responsible for rescuing many Jewish children from Europe, as well as helping to provide safe homes for the local orphans – but she knew they both harboured a terrible fear over what might have happened to their family in Poland, especially after the liberation of Majdanek concentration camp.

Rachel and Danuta discussed the latest wonderful news about Paris and the progress of the uprising against the Nazis in Warsaw, then she said goodbye to Rachel and continued along Camden Road, her thoughts now troubled by memories of the things she'd seen, not only in Poland, but right across Europe.

The liberation of Majdanek had opened the world's eyes to the atrocities carried out there, and as the Allies pushed further into Europe they would uncover more such horrors. And they would find that it wasn't just the Jews who'd been persecuted. She'd seen them dragged from their homes – seen the crammed trains and cattle cars of terrified women and children; the vicious dogs and sadistic guards…

She shivered and blinked to clear the unbidden images that came to haunt her. They would stay with her for the rest of her life, and she didn't want that for Rachel, who'd begged to know what she'd witnessed on her flight from Poland; so she hadn't told her. It would have been too graphic and made her lose hope for her loved ones – and without hope, there was nothing to cling to.

Danuta strode out determinedly, eager now to be home and amongst the people she'd come to love. She couldn't change the past, and there was nothing to be gained by looking back. She was physically much stronger, and felt fully capable of taking on this new challenge. She had a great deal to be thankful for, and the future held even more promise.

Peggy had moved back into the bedroom off the hall now Doris was safely ensconced in the bungalow. She'd liked the space of the other room, but preferred the familiarity of her old one, and knew Jim would feel the same.

She'd just settled Daisy into bed and was finishing a cup of after-supper tea when Danuta entered the kitchen, all aglow and clearly bursting with good news. 'Hello, love. I was beginning to wonder where you'd got to.'

'I wouldn't mind betting she's got some bloke hidden away,' teased Ivy. 'She's been sloping off quite regular these last weeks – and staying out for hours.'

'Ivy,' warned Peggy with a frown.

'I do not have time for blokes as you call them,' said Danuta, placing the bulky parcel on the table. She shot a grin at Ivy. 'But one day it would be nice to meet someone.'

'So, where you been going, then?' Ivy persisted, getting a nudge in the ribs from Sarah and a stern look from Cordelia. 'And what's in that there parcel?'

Rita placed the plate of potato, onion and cheese pie with salad in front of Danuta and grinned. 'You'd better tell us quick before Ivy bursts her boiler. You know how nosy she is.'

An expectant silence fell and Danuta blushed at being the centre of attention. 'I have been receiving tuition and accompanying Sister Higgins on her district rounds,' she said proudly.

'You got your letter from London?' gasped Peggy. 'But why didn't you say?'

'I wanted to make sure I was good enough to be accepted for the job,' said Danuta. 'Doctor Sayer has been very kind and taken me through the course. I sat the examination today at the hospital, and because I was the only candidate, they told me the result within an hour.'

She paused and then grinned. 'I passed, and so I will begin working as a district nurse and assistant midwife from tomorrow.' She patted the parcel. 'This is my uniform.'

Peggy leapt from her chair to give Danuta a hug. 'Oh, that's wonderful, Danuta. Simply wonderful.'

'Blimey,' said Ivy, 'you don't 'ang about, do yer?' She grinned. 'Well done, Danuta.'

'Yes,' added Sarah, 'jolly well done. We'll be more than all right now we have two nurses in the house.'

'It's a shame Fran's on nights, but I reckon this calls for a drink at the Anchor,' said Rita, reaching for her cardigan.

'Not until Danuta's finished her tea,' said Peggy. She regarded Danuta thoughtfully. 'Did Fran know about all this?'

'Yes,' Danuta admitted, 'and she has been very helpful with testing me for the examination. But

I asked her not to say anything. I am very sorry, Peggy, but I didn't want to disappoint you if I failed.'

'Oh, my dear girl,' said Cordelia, reaching across the table to pat her hand, 'you'll never disappoint us.'

'Thank you, *Babunia*,' she managed. 'I will try not to.'

'Hurry up with yer tea, Danuta,' urged Ivy. 'I've got a thirst on me that only a beer will satisfy, and we've got some celebrating to do.' She turned to Peggy and Cordelia. 'Fancy joining us?'

'Well, I might be tempted,' said Cordelia. 'I haven't had a good knees-up since that rogue of ours got engaged to Rosie.' She glanced across at Peggy. 'But I think I'll stay and look after Daisy whilst you go. You deserve an evening out for a change, Peggy, and it will do you good.'

'Perhaps just for a little while,' said Peggy, whipping off her knotted headscarf and tidying her hair. 'But I want to be back for the nine o'clock news.'

'Of course you do, dear,' said Cordelia, a knowing smile touching her lips.

It was Saturday night and the Anchor was busy, so they had to push their way through the noisy crowd to the bar where Ron and Rosie were billing and cooing in between pulling pints.

'Danuta's passed an exam and is going to be our new district nurse and assistant midwife,' Peggy said excitedly. 'Isn't that marvellous?'

'Aye, 'tis a grand thing to be celebrating,' said Ron, gently patting Danuta's cheek with his rough hand. 'I'm thinking this first drink will be on me.'

It was lovely and peaceful having Beach View to herself with just the dog and cat for company, but Cordelia was finding her knitting tiresome. She gave up on what was meant to be a matinee jacket for little Faith, and stuffed it away in the bag she kept by her fireside chair. She was fed up with trying to pick up stitches and her eyesight wasn't very reliable when it came to trying to read a pattern in this dim light. Besides, the wireless was on, and she wanted to give her full attention to the concert being given by a Polish orchestra and choir.

The music was quite moving, and she was swept away in it, dabbing at her tears as the beautiful voices rang out with such passion. And then the telephone rang.

'Who the dickens is that at this hour?' she asked Harvey crossly.

Struggling out of the chair, she tipped the cat unceremoniously from her lap and almost tripped over her as she darted between her feet for the sanctuary of the other chair. Tutting with annoyance at her clumsiness and the constant racket of that telephone, Cordelia grabbed her walking stick and hurried as best she could into the hall, worried that all the noise would wake Daisy.

'Hello,' she said impatiently.

'It's Kitty, Grandma Cordy. I'm really sorry to have disturbed you so late, but Charlotte went into labour this afternoon and has just delivered her twins.'

Cordelia's bad mood melted immediately. 'Well, how wonderful,' she said. 'It's about time. What are they?'

'One of each,' said Kitty with laughter in her voice. 'And it's no wonder she was so big; the boy was almost six pounds and the girl almost five.'

'Goodness me. Poor little Charlotte, what a weight to be carrying around.' She found she was crying again. 'How is Charlotte? And have the babies got names yet? Everyone's out, you see, and we all want to know every detail.'

'Charlotte's fast asleep in the maternity ward. She's exhausted, but very happy that both babies are healthy. They're in the nursery and I've been allowed to sneak in for a quick look. They're beautiful, Grandma Cordy,' she sighed. 'Both have Freddy's thick black hair that's already long enough to put a brush through it.'

'That explains why she's suffered so much from heartburn these past few months,' said Cordelia sagely. 'A good head of hair on a baby always gives the mother heartburn.'

Kitty giggled. 'I've never heard of that one.'

'It's an old wives' tale, dear, and there's many who've rued the day by not heeding their wisdom.'

'I'm sure,' replied Kitty, clearly struggling not to laugh. 'As for names,' she continued, 'Charlotte wants David in honour of Dwight David Eisenhower and the liberation of Paris, and Hope because it really does look as if this war's coming to an end.'

'Well, I suppose it's the modern way to call your babies after virtues, but I'd advise against calling your next one Charity – that would be a step too far,' said Cordelia rather briskly.

Kitty laughed. 'I think it might be a while before there are any more babies, Grandma Cordy

– three will be more than enough to cope with in that small cottage. Tell everyone that visiting hours are from two until four at the General. Charlotte will be in for at least a week, and I know she'd love to see you all.'

'You can be sure we'll be there,' said Cordelia. 'Give our love and best wishes to Charlotte and go and get a good night's sleep. It sounds as if you've had a busy day and little Faith will no doubt have you up very early in the morning.'

'Damn,' she muttered after disconnecting the call. 'I forgot to tell her about Danuta.' She shook her head. 'Silly old woman, you're always forgetting things.' She listened at the open door of the bedroom, and hearing only Daisy's sleepy snuffling, she returned to the kitchen just in time to catch the end of the concert.

It had been a day of celebration all round, so Cordelia gave Harvey one of his biscuits, put a drop of milk out for Queenie, and poured herself a glass of sherry before sitting back down to wait for the news.

It was much the same as she'd heard at lunchtime, and although de Gaulle's speech was quite stirring, she thought he had a bit of a cheek to infer that the French had single-handedly liberated Paris when it was clear they only rose up against the Germans because the Allies were virtually banging on the gates of the city.

As the newsreader continued to report on some of the background to the liberation, Cordelia's opinion remained unchanged – she was very stuck in her ways. It seemed that when the Allies, under General Eisenhower, had landed in France in June, many groups of Parisian workers went on strike as they sensed the Allied approach. As General Patton's US Third Army approached the German garrison, an uprising by the French Resistance began on the 19th of August, and young Frenchmen began to build barricades and shoot at the German soldiers.

'See, I told you,' she said to the disinterested dog. '*And* it took the Swedish Consul General to Paris to arrange a ceasefire and persuade General Choltitz to disobey Hitler's orders to destroy the city.'

The newscaster continued. 'General Eisenhower was reluctant to march on Paris and engage his forces in running street battles which could end in long-drawn-out conflicts like those in Stalingrad or the siege of Leningrad, but he finally relented when de Gaulle threatened to ignore the rules set down by SHAEF and take on the Germans with only his 2nd Armoured Division. Subsequently, Eisenhower's force followed General Leclerc's 2nd Armoured Division into the city on the 19th of August. The German surrender came six days later.

'Today, General de Gaulle led a parade with General Leclerc down the Champs Elysées, all the way to Notre Dame Cathedral. He braved sporadic sniper fire inside the cathedral itself from pockets of German and Fascist resistance that remained, but the perpetrators were soon disarmed and taken prisoner.'

Cordelia raised her glass of sherry in a toast to both the French and the Allies as the stirring French National Anthem was played.

'Two down – only Berlin to go now,' she said victoriously. 'At least the French have a decent, rousing anthem, not like our poor dreary thing,' she added, glancing up apologetically at the framed photograph of the King and Queen above the mantelpiece before emptying her glass and reaching for the bottle of sherry.

Doris had swiftly removed the rose from the table before he saw it, and they'd eaten the delicious pie, chatting easily about the news and everyday things as they drank the wine. John White nipped next door to get another bottle and they took it out into the garden to enjoy the warm, still evening.

'This is such a lovely spot,' said Doris, feeling rather flushed from the heady wine. 'Was it you who thought of it?'

'I can't take all the credit,' he said modestly. 'Ron found me the wood and made the bench whilst I made the table, and Stan from the station planted the rose and all the pots.' He smiled at her in the dwindling light. 'I'm glad you like it.'

'I suspect I'll be spending a lot of time out here as long as this weather lasts,' she murmured. 'You've done wonders with the garden, and the kitchen. I don't know how I can possibly thank you and all the others enough.'

'There's no need,' said John gruffly. 'We did it because we wanted you to be happy here.' He turned to her, his gaze direct. 'Do you think you could be happy here, Doris?'

She felt as if she was drowning in his eyes, but she couldn't look away. 'Oh, yes,' she breathed. 'I think I'm going to be very much at home here.'

'Splendid,' he murmured, his gaze remaining a moment longer on her face before he reached for his cigarette case. 'A last cigarette before we say goodnight?'

Doris nodded, and once he'd lit the cigarettes, they sat in contented silence to watch the moon slowly rise beyond the hills.

That Sunday morning, none of them were quite as chipper as they'd been the night before when they'd returned from the Anchor to find Cordelia asleep with the cat on her lap, the dog snoring on the rug, the wireless hissing with atmospherics, and the sherry bottle suspiciously depleted.

Peggy had fretted that Cordelia was too old and inclined to hit the sherry when she was on her own and therefore not terribly reliable as a baby-sitter – but the old lady had quickly woken up and seemed to be fully in charge of her wits as she'd relayed Charlotte's news.

'That last sherry to celebrate the twins' arrival was a step too far,' Peggy groaned as she swallowed an aspirin with her morning tea. 'Thank goodness it's Sunday and I don't have to go to work.'

'I'll be on duty again tonight,' sighed Fran. 'Roll on next week when I get a whole day off.'

'Have you set a date yet?' asked 'Sarah. 'Only the churches have to call the banns and they're very busy at the moment.'

'We're having a civil wedding at the Town Hall on the twenty-second of September,' Fran replied. 'The church won't marry us because we're of mixed religions.' She grinned at Peggy's furious expression. 'There's no use you getting all hot under the collar, Aunty Peg. That's the way it is – and we'll have a wonderful day despite all that.'

'But it's all very soon,' fretted Peggy. 'What will you wear, and how on earth will we get enough coupons together to give you both a good send-off?'

'Robert's mother sent me a photograph of her utterly gorgeous wedding dress, which she's adapting to fit me, and he already applied for extra wedding rations.' She kissed Peggy's cheek. 'Stop clucking, you wee mother hen. Everything will be fine, I promise.'

'Have you thought about where you'll live after you're married?' Peggy asked.

Fran looked suddenly uneasy. 'We've talked about it, of course, but there's no married quarters at the Fort where he works, and the nearest place we can find is a bed-sit fifteen miles outside the town.'

Peggy wanted to help, but she wasn't sure if Fran was actually asking for it, so kept quiet.

Fran fiddled with the teaspoon. 'Robert shot round to Gracie's place to see if he could take it on when she left for Dover, but it was already gone.' She took a breath. 'We were wondering if perhaps–'

'Of course you can,' Peggy butted in eagerly.

Fran grinned. 'Ach, Peggy, you don't know what I was wondering.'

'That top-floor room is empty now Ivy and Rita have gone back to their old one – and it's plenty big enough for two.' She reached for Fran's hand. 'It's not much to start married life in, but it's

403

yours if you want it.'

Fran threw her arms about Peggy. 'Oh thank you, thank you. You have no idea how much this means to both of us.'

'Well, I couldn't let him carry on sleeping in the barracks at the Fort whilst you stayed here on your own, could I?' said Peggy. She chuckled. 'I'm just glad I can help. I was dreading you leaving.'

Fran's green eyes were bright with tears as she withdrew from the embrace. 'I do love you, Aunty Peg.'

'I love you too,' she replied, patting her cheek. 'Now you go and telephone Robert and then get to bed.'

Fran was about to leave when Danuta came into the room and gave them a little twirl.

The plain blue dress, with its white starched collar and cuffs, was cinched in at the waist by a broad white belt with a smart silver buckle. A red cardigan was draped over her shoulders, and a perky little white cap sat on her short dark hair. Black shoes and stockings completed the outfit. 'I look like proper nurse?' she asked.

'You most definitely do,' said Peggy, amazed at how suddenly she'd turned from a waif into a young woman. 'But where's your apron?'

'I will collect it from the surgery along with my medical bag and bicycle,' she replied. She grinned in delight. 'I am very excited,' she confessed. 'This is big day for me.'

Fran gave her a hug. 'You've earned it, Danuta. But it's all hard work from now on, believe me.'

'I know. And that's what I am looking towards.'

'Good luck, then. I'll see you later,' said Fran,

rushing off to telephone Robert.

'Will you find time to pop in to see Charlotte and the babies?' asked Peggy, pressing Danuta into a chair for some breakfast.

'I will try. But I do not know how long my list is today.'

Peggy told her about Robert and Fran taking over the top room whilst Danuta drank a cup of tea and nibbled the edge of a piece of toast. Peggy could see she was nervous, but there was excitement too, and she just knew that Danuta was more than ready to take on this new phase in her life.

Danuta hugged and kissed Peggy, and then ran down the steps into the garden. The morning was glorious, and she felt as if she had wings on her heels. It was a new day and a new start, and she would be doing what she loved best – of course she couldn't help but smile at everyone on a day like today.

23

The liberation of Paris seemed to have given hope and added determination to those who were fighting to bring an end to Hitler's tyranny. As August ended and September began with the welcome news that the blackout was now to be a dim-out, every house, office, pub and shop kept the wireless on as victories, uprisings and astounding advances by the Allies were reported.

There was an uprising in Slovakia, the Russian troops took Bucharest, and the Allies liberated Verdun, Dieppe, Artois, Rouen, Lyon, Abbeville, Antwerp and Brussels. Finland and Russia agreed to a ceasefire – the British troops took Ghent and Liege, and the Canadians finally overcame the Germans at the Ostend garrison. By the 9th of September, the Americans had liberated Luxembourg; the first Allied troops entered the German border town of Aachen, and two Allied forces met at Dijon, effectively cutting France in half.

Great expectations were roused when Operation Market Garden began with a vast Allied airborne assault on Arnhem in the Netherlands, for if successful, it would secure vital bridges and roads into the heart of Europe and bring an early end to the war. Brest fell to the Allies, Nancy was liberated by the Americans and the British troops liberated Rimini in Italy.

No one was actually taking any notice of the wireless that Thursday night, for Fran's wedding was the following day, the kitchen at Beach View was bustling, and there was a great deal still to do if things were to run smoothly. The preparations had started days before, and Peggy was very grateful to the government for the extra food stamps, but they were a meagre amount to say the least, and if it hadn't been for Doris, Rosie, Frank and Robert's mother, Delia, donating some of theirs, the table would have looked very bare.

Peggy took the last of the sausage rolls out of the oven and quickly placed them in the larder to cool well away from Queenie's inquisitive nose. There had been lots of baking in several kitchens during the past few days, with Rosie making little cheese and egg tarts, sugared buns and fruit scones – which didn't have much fruit, but looked delicious. Doris had made fruit tartlets with the apples and plums from her garden, and would put the finishing touches to her raspberry and loganberry trifle in the morning. Delia was in charge of the wedding cake.

Robert's job with the MOD had allowed him to travel with Fran up to Warwick so she could meet his mother, and by all accounts they'd got on famously. Peggy had yet to meet Delia, but they'd exchanged letters and Peggy felt she already knew and liked her.

She'd been enormously supportive when Fran's parents had turned their backs on her, and had entered into the spirit of things by offering her precious wedding dress, which had arrived in a large box the week before. No one had been allowed to see it, and Fran had confided in Peggy that she'd locked it in the top room wardrobe and hidden the key so that Ivy and Rita's dreadful curiosity didn't lead them into temptation.

'I hope Delia's train arrived on time and that she didn't have too much trouble bringing the cake and everything,' Peggy muttered, glancing at the clock.

Fran paused in the act of dying Rita's legs with cold tea. 'Robert's probably on his way with her now and I'm sure she guarded the cake with her life,' she replied. 'Now will you stop fretting and sit down, Aunty Peg. You've been on the go all day and I don't want you tired for tomorrow.'

Peggy sat down and grinned at Cordelia, who

was twittering away like an over-excited little sparrow as Danuta painted her nails bright scarlet. 'We're never too tired for a wedding, are we, Cordy?'

'Indeed not,' she chirped. 'It's no good being tired when you want a good cry. And I do so love weddings,' she added on a sigh.

Peggy lit a cigarette and regarded them all with deep contentment. The arrival of Charlotte's twins and Kitty's little Faith had already brought great joy to Peggy, but a wedding perked her up no end, and she could see from the animated faces that the girls were delighted to be a part of it all.

Fran was like a sister to them, and because her own family was being so mean, they'd pulled out all the stops and paid for her to go to the beauty parlour tomorrow morning to have her hair and nails done, and sweet Cordelia had used up all of her clothing coupons on a set of silk underwear and nightgown for the honeymoon they had yet to know about.

Peggy couldn't help but smile, for when Doris discovered they'd planned to spend a single night in a local hotel before spending the next two days at Beach View, she'd consulted with John White and they'd managed to book a whole weekend in the bridal suite of a posh hotel just outside Brighton. Now the travel restrictions along the south coast had been lifted, things were very much easier, and they'd all heaved a sigh of relief that Delia would be able to attend the wedding, and not have to risk sending the cake in the mail.

However, the generosity didn't end there, for Rosie had got together with Stan from the station, who'd raided his allotment for the finest roses to go into her bouquet, which was now keeping fresh in the scullery sink, and she would be hosting the reception in the afternoon at the Anchor. Ron had paid for a barrel of beer, and with permission from Rosie, had gone to the Crown and bought several bottles of black-market champagne from Gloria.

Kitty and Charlotte had spent many hours making the most magnificent patchwork quilt for their bed, Bertie Double-Barrelled would drive them in his car to and from the ceremony, and Fran's nursing colleagues had clubbed together to buy a dinner service for when they set up their own home. As for her gift, Peggy had discovered that lace wasn't rationed and didn't need clothing coupons, so she'd bought several yards and made a veil during her lunch break at work.

Now Peggy smoked her cigarette and waited her turn to have her legs painted, although they were already fairly well tanned from the sun. Cordelia sat waving her little hands about to dry her nails, Ivy was drawing a line up the back of Rita's leg with an eyebrow pencil, and Sarah was now painting Fran's legs. Peggy wondered how Sarah was feeling about it all, for it couldn't have been easy for her when her heart was in one place, her duty in another.

And what was going on behind Fran's lovely smile – was she thinking of how this day might have been if her parents and family were here? The girl had confided in her that the decision to defy her parents and marry Robert had been the most difficult thing she'd ever been faced with, and

Peggy knew she'd spent many a sleepless night worrying about it. But the wedding was now only hours away, and those doubts must be returning. If only Fran's parents had been less adamant. Ireland wasn't so very far, but at the moment, Peggy suspected, it must have felt to Fran that it was a world away.

The door knocker rapped and Peggy whipped off her apron and headscarf, patting her hair into place as she went to answer it. Delia stood on the doorstep armed with a large cardboard box and a broad smile. 'Hello, Peggy. We meet at last. Sorry, can't shake hands, rather taken up with other things at the moment,' she said breathlessly.

'Let me take that,' said Peggy. 'It's lovely to meet you too, although I feel I already know you through your letters and what Robert has told us.' She glanced over her shoulder at the little black Austin sitting at the kerb. 'Isn't Robert coming in?'

'He thinks it'll be unlucky to see his bride the night before, silly boy,' said Delia with a roll of her eyes. 'I won't be able to stay long, as he's pro-mised to wait and take me back to my hotel.' She stepped into the hall. 'Oh, what a lovely house,' she continued in a breathless rush. 'Now where's this famous kitchen I've heard so much about?'

Peggy giggled. 'It's far from famous and in utter chaos at the moment, as you can imagine. But come on in and meet everyone.'

'Goodness me, what fun you're all having,' said Delia, clapping her hands in delight. 'And the kitchen is exactly how I imagined it, all cosy and lovely.'

Hardly pausing to take a breath, she turned to Fran. 'Hello, darling,' she said, giving Fran a kiss on her cheek and a quick hug. 'My goodness, you're going to make a beautiful bride with that gorgeous complexion and pre-Raphaelite hair. My Robert is a very lucky man.'

'To be sure, that's what I keep telling him,' said Fran impishly before making the introductions.

Delia unbuttoned her dark blue linen suit jacket and reached for the box which Peggy had managed to find room for on the cluttered kitchen table. 'Now, I don't want you getting too excited,' she warned. 'It's not a patch on the sort of wedding cakes we had before the war, and is rather small, but I did manage to get hold of some of the most important ingredients from a local chap who always seems to have everything – but at a price.'

She finally took a breath and lifted the lid.

They all gasped in wonder. The cake was small and square, but quite exquisite. The smooth white icing had been draped over it and brought to points at the corners, each one finished off with a golden material tassel, just like a pillow. At the centre was a spray of perfect white silk roses and green ferns, and nestled amongst them were tiny figures of a bride and groom.

'It's magnificent,' breathed Peggy. 'But how on earth did you get hold of that icing?'

Delia giggled and tapped the side of her nose. 'I got mixed fruit and marzipan as well, but when you know a man who knows a man...'

They all laughed. 'That sounds like our Ron, God love him,' said Fran. 'He's definitely the man in the know around here.'

411

Delia frowned. 'Where is Ron? I was so hoping to meet him tonight.'

'He's helping Rosie at the Anchor,' said Cordelia. 'But he's on strict instructions to be home before midnight – and sober. He has an important job to do tomorrow.'

Delia nodded and squeezed Fran's hand. 'It will all be wonderful, my dear, I'm quite, quite sure. Now I must dash. Poor Robert's waiting in the car and he's supposed to be meeting some of his friends in the hotel bar for a last bachelor party.' She must have seen Fran's concern for she quickly added that the best man was a very sober sort and wouldn't let things go too far.

Peggy accompanied her to the door and waved to Robert, who was leaning against the Austin's bonnet smoking a cigarette. 'We'll see you tomorrow,' she said to Delia. 'And thanks for the wonderful cake.'

'It's me who should be thanking you for giving them a home to start out in,' said Delia solemnly. She kissed her cheek. 'Goodnight, Peggy.'

Peggy closed the door, feeling quite breathless herself after the whirlwind that was Delia. Returning to the kitchen, she put the cake away in the crammed larder and drew out a bottle of Gloria's illicit champagne that Rosie had given her earlier.

'Who's for a glass of bubbly before bed?'

Rosie had been a bit quiet all evening, which was unusual, and Ron had a suspicion he knew why. He cupped her face in his hands as they stood in the hall, and kissed her. 'All this talk of weddings

412

isn't getting to you, is it?' he asked.

'It is a bit,' she admitted. 'I wish it was us, of course I do, but I do understand why you want to have Jim and the rest of the family home to enjoy it with us.' She twisted the ring on her finger. 'It's just that we've wasted so much time already.'

He held her close. 'I know I'm not being fair, Rosie,' he admitted, 'but we've waited this long, a couple of months more will pass in a flash.'

She pulled away from him. 'It'll be longer than that, Ron,' she said solemnly. 'Hitler's not about to surrender and we've yet to take Berlin. What with this new flying gas-pipe rocket everyone's talking about, and the awful struggle our troops are having at Arnhem, the war could drag on for ages yet.'

Ron was about to speak when she hurried on. 'And even if it ends in Europe tomorrow, there's still the war in the Far East and the Pacific, and Jim could be stuck over there for months before he's demobbed – and then it will take at least six weeks for a ship to bring him home.'

Ron saw that she cared more about delaying their wedding than he'd realised. 'Let's wait and see how things go – and if it looks like it will carry on after Christmas, we'll make new plans.' He kissed the tip of her nose and smiled. 'Come on, Rosie, don't look so glum. We're together now and a piece of paper won't really make much difference.'

She looked for a moment as if she was about to argue, then, relented and gave him a hug. 'I suppose you're right,' she said on a sigh. 'We'll talk about it at Christmas.'

He gave her a lingering kiss goodnight and then strolled home with Harvey, who was feeling very much more like his old self now he'd lost the cone and his stitches had healed.

It was a lovely late September night, with a clear sky and still just enough warmth in the air to remind him of the summer. A few of the streetlights had been turned on now the threat of bombing raids was over and the blackout at an end, and he could see the glimmer of pale lights and shadows of people moving about behind the thin curtains where there had once been a blind darkness.

The dim-out meant it was much easier to get about at night without the danger of walking into a lamppost or falling off a kerb or into a pothole, and Ron ambled along, contented with life, except for the niggling worry that perhaps he really was being unfair to Rosie by putting off their wedding.

There was no doubt the Germans were getting a pasting, and now the American Marines had landed on Palau Islands in the Pacific, the Japs would soon be on the run too. But Rosie had made a fair point when she'd said the war could drag on. The Allied troops were having a terrible time trying to oust the Germans from Arnhem, and Hitler clearly wasn't yet ready to surrender, for now there were rumours of his new and deadly revenge weapon.

The government were being suspiciously evasive on the subject, telling the press that London had experienced several gas explosions – which had led the disbelieving people who'd witnessed the aftermath to call it a flying gas-pipe. However, as these unexplained explosions continued, and over a hundred people had been killed, others spoke of seeing a silent missile drop out of the sky to cause craters several feet deep and destroy everything within a mile. It was obvious to everyone that this was a different and deadlier form of the V-1 rocket. And yet the government continued to keep a press blackout on the matter – which, to Ron's mind, meant the danger was very real.

He came to the end of Camden Road and decided to walk down to the promenade where the batteries of heavy guns had been increased to deal with the rockets coming across the Channel. Their numbers had been doubled along the headlands too, and were mostly successful in shooting down the V-1s before they reached England's coast. Yet it would be impossible to hit a target they could neither see nor hear, and Ron could only hope that the advancing Allies would find the launching sites and destroy them before they did any more harm.

He breathed in the night air and watched the moon float above the water, making it shimmer and drift like golden silk. Perhaps he was being foolish to want his family around him when he married Rosie – after all, one of those new rockets could drop on Cliffehaven and they might all be dead by the end of the week.

He shook his head to dismiss the dark thought and turned for home, his mind once more on tomorrow. His best suit had been pressed, he'd let Fran cut his hair and trim his eyebrows, and Peggy had managed to get the egg stain out of his dark blue tie. He'd been honoured when Fran had asked him to escort her to the registry office at the Town Hall in place of her father, and he was determined not to let her down.

The kitchen had been in chaos when he'd left for the pub, but it was almost midnight now, so it was likely that the hullabaloo and carry-on would have died down. Everyone would be getting their beauty sleep, so it was probably safe to slip in and make a cup of tea before he went to bed.

The house was quiet, and he could see no lights at the windows except for a dim glimmer in the kitchen. He followed Harvey up the steps, his mouth watering at the thought of sneaking a couple of sausage rolls from Peggy's larder to go with a cup of tea, and then realised he didn't have the kitchen to himself at all.

Fran was in her nightclothes, curled in the fireside chair, the traces of tears on her cheeks as Harvey pawed at her lap and whined in concern. 'Oh, Ron,' she murmured. 'I didn't mean for you to catch me like this.'

'What is it, acushla?' he said, going to her and taking her hand. 'You're not having second thoughts, are you, wee girl?'

'Not really,' she said with a wan smile. 'But I so wish Mammy and Da had given me their blessing. I miss Mammy,' she managed as the tears threatened. 'She should have been with me tonight.'

Ron perched on the arm of the chair and drew her to him so her head rested on his shoulder. 'Aye, it's a sad, sad business, acushla,' he murmured, his heart heavy. 'But choices have been made on both sides, and nothing will change unless one of you backs down.' He put a finger

416

under her chin so he could look into her eyes, which were swimming with tears. 'What's in your heart, wee Fran?'

'To be sure, Ron, me heart is breaking with it all. I love Robert and want to be his wife – but I love my parents too, and if I go through with the wedding I shall lose them forever.'

'Aye, but there's still time to change your mind and put a stop to all this,' he said softly.

'I couldn't do that,' she gasped.

'If it's about dresses and cakes and presents, they can all be dealt with,' said Ron. 'But if it's because you can't bear to think of Robert standing amongst his friends and yours at the registry office, pacing the floor as he waits for you, watching the time and eventually realising that you're not coming – then...'

He let the words hang in the air as he watched her expressive face, knowing those images were flashing through her mind. 'That man has loved you from the first moment he saw you,' he continued. 'To be sure, it will break his heart – and yours too, I'm thinking.'

Fran wiped away her tears and took a shuddering breath. 'The thought of doing that to him is a knife to my very soul.'

'Then think on this, Fran. You're a young, independent woman with a good career in nursing, who's lived far from home for many years and never shown much enthusiasm for the church. This is about *your* future and what *you* want from it. Do you wish to return to Ireland after the war and spend that future without Robert, but with people who will only accept you if you toe the

Catholic line? Or do you want to be who you really are and spend that future with Robert?'

'With Robert, always,' she replied.

'There you have it then,' he said, kissing her forehead. 'Pre-wedding nerves get to us all, wee girl, and to be sure they can be awful. Now you wash your pretty face of those tears and go to bed. I shall be walking you into that registry office tomorrow afternoon, and I'll not be wanting to see tears – unless they're happy ones.'

Fran hugged him close. 'Thanks for talking sense into me, Ron.' She drew back and shot him a watery smile. 'And if I can give you a bit of advice in return, it would be to marry Rosie very soon. You two were meant to be together, and as you're not getting any younger...' The smile turned into an impish grin.

'Cheeky wee girl,' he rumbled. 'Off to bed before I set me dog on you.'

Fran laughed and patted Harvey's head. 'To be sure, that's a terrible threat, isn't it, Harvey? You're such a fierce beast, that I'm afeared for me life, so I am.'

Harvey licked her nose.

24

Peggy had been up since six making sandwiches. She'd managed to sweet-talk the smitten Horace at the bakery to provide some lovely white bread which had cost her an arm and a leg, but had been well worth it, and as she sliced tomatoes, cucumbers, lettuce and Spam, spread fish paste, potted meat and mashed egg in with salad cream, she felt a rising bubble of excitement. Fran and Robert would have the best wedding tea possible, and it looked as if the weather was going to co-operate too, for the sky was blue and the sun was shining.

Having fetched the bread, Ron left to walk the dogs at seven. Danuta hurried off on her rounds, hoping to join them later at the reception, and everyone else was down in the kitchen by eight, chattering away and gulping down their Weetabix and toast as if they were half-starved.

Peggy happily bustled to and fro, but was a bit concerned about Fran, who looked rather washed out. 'I expect all the excitement kept you awake half the night,' she probed as Fran helped clear the table.

'I slept very well,' she replied, 'but I'm terrible nervous, Aunty Peg. What if I forget me lines or mess them up? What if I trip over me dress or me knicker elastic goes in the middle of it all?'

Peggy laughed and gave her a hug. 'Oh, Fran, you are a caution. If you're so worried about the elastic, I'll give you a safety pin. Now go and get dressed or you'll be late for the hairdresser.'

An hour later, Peggy led a straggling parade down Camden Road. She was carrying the precious cake in its box, the girls each carried trays of sandwiches and sausage rolls, and Cordelia had Peggy's best white tablecloth and linen napkins in a bag. Little Daisy had been put in charge of the two silver-plated candlesticks that usually sat on the mantelpiece in the dining room, and they were nestled in a cloth bag to be put on the wedding table.

They arrived at the Anchor and trooped upstairs to Rosie's kitchen, where her own baking had been set out. Doris arrived with her tartlets and trifle, and a ceremonial sword complete with fancy scabbard.

'Goodness, where on earth did that come from?' gasped Peggy.

'John thought it might add a certain flair to the cutting of the cake,' said Doris, going a bit pink. 'It's what they do at army weddings, apparently – and I have to say that cake certainly deserves some fanfare.'

'You'd better not let Ron get anywhere near it,' said Rosie. 'He's likely to start swishing it about after a couple of pints.' She glanced at her watch. 'He should be finished changing those barrels by now, so why don't we all have a cuppa?'

'That would be lovely, Rosie,' said Doris, 'but Peggy and I have an appointment at the hairdresser.'

Peggy gaped at her. 'But I have–'

'No, you don't,' said Doris firmly. 'All the work is done bar the shouting. Ivy has already said she'd mind Daisy, and it's time you had a decent cut, shampoo and set. I've arranged for us to have manicures, too.'

'Oh, Doris, I don't know what to say – that is so lovely of you.'

'Come along then. We don't want to be late,' Doris said crisply.

The hour and a half at the hairdresser's had been

a real treat and her hair and nails looked so lovely, Peggy was feeling relaxed and very smart indeed. It had also been really nice to sit and chat to her sister whilst she was being pampered – but now she'd have to hurry to get herself and Daisy dressed so that if Fran wanted her help in getting ready for her special day – and she really hoped she would – she'd be able to do so.

'I don't know how you managed to keep that appointment a secret,' she said to Ivy.

Ivy grinned. 'It were because it were for you,' she replied. 'You done so much for us, I was glad to be a part of the surprise.'

'Bless you, dear,' Peggy murmured

The house was bustling, with the sound of chatter, laughter and hurrying footsteps on the landing as the girls and Cordelia prepared for the most important part of the day. Peggy was wearing the same lovely blue silk two-piece suit that young Sally had made her for Anne's wedding to Martin. The dark blue hat had been steamed back into shape, brushed and then freshened with a new ribbon around the crown. With shoes and handbag to match, Peggy felt confident that she couldn't look any smarter.

Daisy was in her sweetest dress with Peter Pan collar and ruched bodice, a knitted cardigan, white shoes and socks and a sunbonnet tied beneath her chin by a pink ribbon. Peggy gave her a kiss. 'Now try and keep clean,' she begged before taking her into the kitchen where Cordelia was sitting at the table in a colourful lavender and white dress, with a lilac jacket, and a dinky white hat trimmed with real lavender set at a jaunty angle over her silvery hair.

Peggy sat Daisy down with a picture book and poured a cup of tea. She listened wistfully to the happy noise upstairs, wanting desperately to join in and spend a few minutes with Fran – but it seemed she'd been forgotten, and no doubt Sarah was helping her into her dress, for they'd become firm friends over the years.

Minutes later, Rita came flying into the kitchen looking utterly adorable in a sprigged cotton dress, her dark curls held back by a blue ribbon. 'Fran's asking for you,' she said breathlessly.

Peggy was out of her chair and running up the stairs before Rita had time to catch her breath. She reached the top floor and tapped on the door. 'It's me, Fran.'

The key turned in the lock and Fran appeared, fully made up but still in her dressing gown. She grabbed Peggy's hand, pulling her inside and slamming the door behind her. 'Where have you been?' she said anxiously. 'I've been waiting for you to help me with my dress and veil.'

'I thought... I was waiting...'

'Oh, Peggy, as if I'd let anyone else help me today of all days,' said Fran, giving her a hug. 'You've been like a wee mother to me from the moment I arrived – of course I want to share this moment with you.'

Peggy's heart swelled with love for this girl and she had to fight to keep her tears at bay – and then she caught sight of the dress hanging from the wardrobe door. 'Oh,' she gasped. 'Oh, how beautiful.' She hardly dared touch the long column of creamy white silk and lace that dipped at the back to form a short train.

'Robert's parents were married in India, and Delia had this dress made especially for her. But with all the buttons down the back it's impossible to do it up on my own.' She gave a wry smile as she touched the dress. 'Delia had servants, of course.'

'I didn't realise they met in India,' Peggy murmured, sliding the dress carefully from the hanger and draping it over her arm.

'Her father was in the army, and Robert's father was a diplomat,' Fran replied, taking off her faded cotton dressing gown to reveal the silk underwear Cordelia had given her.

Peggy guided Fran's bare feet into the dress and very carefully drew it over her slender hips until she could slip her arms into the long, lacy sleeves ending in points over her hands. The neckline of the dress sat on Fran's collarbones and showed off the lovely nape of her neck. The silk-covered buttons were small and very fiddly, but Peggy eventually managed to get them fastened.

She stood back with tears blossoming as Fran regarded her reflection in the long mirror on the back of the wardrobe door. 'You look utterly lovely,' she breathed, taking in the delicate curves of her figure, the way the lace and silk enhanced the glow of her skin, and how the tumble of autumnal curls which had been artfully arranged on the top of her head by the hairdresser glinted like fire in the sunlight.

Peggy reached for the veil which she'd attached to a comb as there was no proper head-dress, and spent some time fixing it firmly into Fran's hair so that it drifted in a cloud over her shoulders. 'There,' she breathed. 'What do you think?'

'I can't believe it's me,' said Fran with a nervous laugh, turning this way and that to get the full effect. She took Peggy's hand. 'To be sure, Peggy, I'm blessed to have been shown such love today – and it's all because of you.'

'You'll have me crying in a minute,' Peggy said lightly to mask the true depth of her feelings, 'and I spent ages doing my make-up too.' She kissed Fran's cheek tenderly. 'You're a lovely young woman, and the most beautiful bride, Fran. I love you like a daughter, and always will.'

She fought her emotions and became brisk. 'Now get your shoes on, and I'll fetch Ron to bring up your bouquet and escort you out to the car.'

Ron was grinning broadly as he carried the large bouquet through the gathering in the hall and up the stairs. A wedding certainly brought out the glad rags, he noticed, seeing the pretty tea dresses on Ivy and Rita and the elegant shantung silk dress and jacket Sarah had brought with her from Singapore. Even Cordelia looked perky, the happiness of the day giving him a glimpse of the lovely young woman she must have been.

He tapped on the door and slid inside so that no one could see the bride. 'To be sure, you take me breath away,' he murmured at the sight of her. 'Young Robert is certainly a very lucky man.'

He placed the bouquet on the dressing table and took her hands. 'I don't need to ask if you're happy, Fran, it's there in your eyes and in your smile. I might not be your da, but I'm proud and honoured to take his place today, and I want you to know that Beach View will always be your family home.'

'Oh, Ron,' she managed.

'Now, now, no tears,' he chided gently. 'This is a joyful day and I wish you luck and great happiness with Robert, acushla.' He handed her the bouquet and offered her his arm. 'Are you ready for your audience?'

Fran giggled. 'Yes, I'm ready.'

As he proudly took her down the stairs to where everyone was waiting in the hall, there were oohs, and aahs and sighs of pleasure and delight. Cordelia already had tears in her eyes, little Daisy clapped her hands, Bertie Double-Barrelled doffed his trilby in admiration, and Harvey barked, sensing that something special was going on.

When everyone had admired the dress and said their piece and Cordelia had been installed in the front passenger seat of Bertie's highly polished and ribbon-bedecked car, Ron and Fran had a glass of champagne to set them up for the day and the others made a mad dash for the Town Hall. Harvey would stay at home until after the ceremony and then Ron would take him to the Anchor once the wedding party was settled in for the reception.

The car pulled up by the steps of the Town Hall and Ron felt Fran trembling. 'Are ye all right, wee girl?' he asked in alarm. 'Not having second thoughts, are ye?'

She smiled radiantly. 'Not at all. I'm just excited.'

425

Ron helped her out of the car, and they followed Cordelia and Bertie into the Town Hall and then up the grand red-carpeted staircase to the big double doors of the wedding room. He waited until Cordelia and Bertie were settled, and patted Fran's hand. 'Here we go, wee girl,' he murmured.

As they slowly entered the room the guests stood to welcome them to the accompaniment of violin music which soared and throbbed and made Ron's old heart beat that little bit faster.

Robert and his best man were waiting by the desk where the registrar stood, and as Robert turned to look at his bride, the love shone from his eyes and the relief relaxed his shoulders – he'd clearly been anxious that Fran might pull out at the last minute.

Fran was radiant as she walked towards him and took his hand, and it was clear to everyone that the pair were lost in their own world.

Ron sat down next to Rosie, who was wearing a scarlet dress and black hat, and took her hand as the young couple made their vows and signed the register, and Peggy and Cordelia mopped at their tears. Once he and Delia had signed as witnesses the violins broke into a toe-tapping Irish jig. The bride and groom were almost dancing back down the aisle as the two young violinists led the way out to the front steps for the photographs.

Ron hugged Rosie to him as they stood on the steps, the stirring sounds of Ireland resonating with distant memories of family weddings and wakes. He decided he'd find out who those young fellows were and ask them to play at his wedding if Rosie agreed.

The reception was a triumph – mostly due to Rosie and her barmaids, who'd closed promptly at two and then set about moving furniture, laying tables and hanging up streamers and bunting. There was plenty of food and drink to go round, the cake was ceremoniously cut with the sword and proved to be delicious, and as Danuta slipped in to join the party, Ron – who'd had a few too many beers – decided to make a very short speech. He came to the conclusion that an Irish blessing would fit the bill perfectly.

He stood and raised his glass to the happy couple. 'Wishing you a rainbow, for sunlight after showers, miles and miles of Irish smiles for golden, happy hours. Shamrocks at your doorway for luck and laughter too, and a host of friends that never end each day your whole life through. Slainte!'

A great roar echoed the toast as glasses were lifted and drained, and then the other members of the band that Fran and Robert played with took over the old piano, a penny whistle, accordion and drum, and chairs were pushed back for dancing.

Ron watched as the bride and groom led the way into a waltz, soon to be joined by Doris and the Colonel, Ivy and Andy, and Cordelia and Bertie. There was a lot of love and happiness in the room, and he wanted very much to be a part of it. He looked around for Rosie, saw her beautiful smile and knew this was the moment.

Moving rather unsteadily through the crush, he took Rosie's hand and drew her into the narrow hall where he could hear himself think. 'I love the bones of you, wee girl, and seeing the happiness of those two today has made me realise that I'm wasting the precious time I could be having with you. Would you agree to us getting wed before Christmas?'

Rosie regarded him with uncertainty in her eyes. 'Is this just wedding fever getting to you, Ron, or the beer, perhaps? Do you really mean that?'

'The only fever I have is for you, my sweet Rosie. I want you for my wife, to have and hold you for the rest of my life.'

'Oh, Ron,' she breathed, throwing her arms about his neck. 'Yes, yes, yes.'

He tenderly kissed her, his heart singing with the joy of it all. And as they held one another, it felt as if the sun had broken through the clouds of war and uncertainty to warm and bless them.

Dear Reader,

I do hope you've enjoyed *As the Sun Breaks Through*. As you now know, D-Day has finally come, and although it seems the war in Europe is almost over, the tension amongst those living at Beach View has not eased. There are impossible choices to be made by some, relationships to be mended by others, whilst the anxiety over their men is increased as the fighting continues in all theatres of the war. And yet, amid all this darkness lies hope, and the unbreakable bonds between people who love and trust one another.

Peggy has always been at the heart of the Cliffehaven series, and it's through her love and stalwart support that the family at Beach View can find the courage to carry on. To have had a mother like Peggy would have been a blessing – and as mine was nothing like her, I decided to create one. I shall miss her when the series comes to an end, but I have a feeling that she'll always be with me in spirit – just as Cliffehaven and the people who live there will remain in my heart.

However, this is not the final chapter in their story, for the war has to end, and the waiting will be over as the surviving men come home. In *Homecoming*, we shall discover how everyone has to cope with the radical changes that have been wrought throughout the war years – not only on the men, but the women who've waited for them.

I'd be delighted to hear your thoughts on Facebook, and you can keep up with all my news on www.ellie-dean.co.uk. Until then, I wish you well.

Ellie x

The publishers hope that this book has given you enjoyable reading. Large Print Books are especially designed to be as easy to see and hold as possible. If you wish a catalogue please ask at your local library or write directly to:

Magna Large Print Books
Cawood House,
Asquith Industrial Estate,
Gargrave,
Nr Skipton, North Yorkshire.
BD23 3SE

This Large Print Book for the partially sighted, who cannot read normal print, is published under the auspices of

THE ULVERSCROFT FOUNDATION